STRAVAGANZA

City of Ships

Books by Mary Hoffman

THE STRAVAGANZA SERIES

Stravaganza: City of Masks

Stravaganza: City of Stars

Stravaganza: City of Flowers

Stravaganza: City of Secrets

Stravaganza: City of Ships

The Falconer's Knot

Troubadour

STRAVAGANZA

City of Ships

MARY HOFFMAN

BLOOMSBURY

NEW YORK BERLIN LONDON

For Alex, who saved the day in Toronto

First published in Great Britain in March 2010 by Bloomsbury Publishing Plc
Published in the United States of America in July 2010
by Bloomsbury Books for Young Readers
www.bloomsburyteens.com

For information about permission to reproduce selections from this book, write to
Permissions, Bloomsbury BFYR, 175 Fifth Avenue, New York, New York 10010

Library of Congress Cataloging-in-Publication Data
Hoffman, Mary.
Stravaganza : city of ships / by Mary Hoffman. — 1st U.S. ed.
p.   cm.
Sequel to: Stravaganza, city of secrets.
Summary: Feeling inferior to her talented twin brother, teenaged Isabel is transported to a
parallel world that resembles the Italian Renaissance city-state of Ravenna, where she tries to
save the city from attack by the fierce Gate people.
ISBN 978-1-59990-491-7
[1. Space and time—Fiction. 2. Renaissance—Italy—Fiction. 3. Adventure and adventurers—
Fiction. 4. Twins—Fiction. 5. Brothers and sisters—Fiction. 6. Self-confidence—Fiction.]
I. Title. II. Title: City of ships.
PZ7.H67562Svv 2010   [Fic]—dc22   2009048837

Typeset by Dorchester Typesetting Group Ltd
Printed in the U.S.A. by Worldcolor Fairfield, Pennsylvania
2 4 6 8 10 9 7 5 3 1

All papers used by Bloomsbury Publishing, Inc., are natural, recyclable products
made from wood grown in well-managed forests. The manufacturing processes
conform to the environmental regulations of the country of origin.

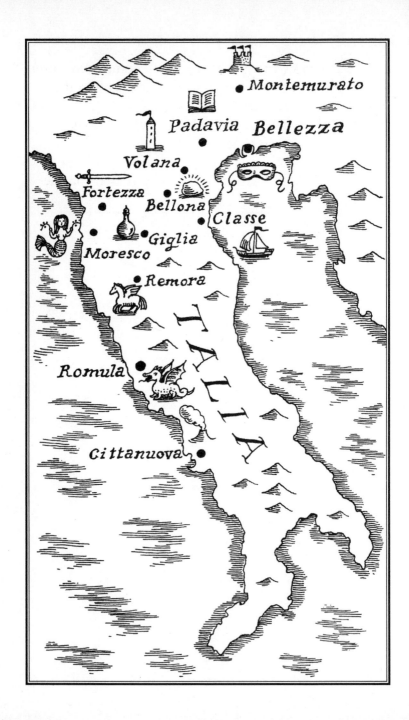

'Studies show that the first twin to come home after birth, or the first-born or healthier, is often the favorite during childhood.'
Elizabeth A. Pector, M.D., *Adolescence: 'Multiple Madness?'*

'Say in what place have you seen greater marine power?'
Gregorio Typhernas

Contents

Prologue: The Merchant of Classe   1
1. Imaginary Twin   5
2. A Diplomatic Gift   22
3. Belonging   34
4. Luciano and Arianna   48
5. Exiles   61
6. The Black Raider   75
7. Matchmaking   87
8. Defiance   101
9. Runaway   115
10. A Change of Direction   128
11. Spreading Wings   141
12. The Life Aquatic   154
13. War   168
14. The Prince of Giglia   179
15. Brothers   192
16. The Reality and the Dream   207
17. Andrea's Story   221
18. All at Sea   237
19. Out of His Depth   251
20. The World Turned Upside Down   266
21. The Gate of the Year   281
22. Death on the Water   295
23. The Battle of Classe   308
24. The Duke   324
Epilogue: A Part of the Whole   342
Historical Note   351
The Sea Battle of Classe   352
di Chimici Family Tree   354
Dramatis Personae   355
Acknowledgements   357

Prologue: *The Merchant of Classe*

If she raised herself slightly from the stool she sat on, Flavia could see the masts of ships in the harbour. And that was a bonus of her position as senior trader in the market at Classe. Presiding over her stall in the square, Flavia was in the perfect place to see if a new ship had come in.

From the goods spread in front of her, you might not realise just how rich this merchant in the russet dress was. Certainly she had unusual spices – cardamom, ginger, pepper, cloves – and bales of cloth, and dyes to colour them any shade a customer wanted. But when she wasn't trading in the market square, Flavia had more wealthy patrons who called at her house to buy much more expensive merchandise – painted pottery from Western Europa beyond the mountains, glass and marbled paper from the city of Bellezza, coral and sugar from the islands off the coast of Talia.

Some of Flavia's more exotic goods – the silks and rarer pigments, tapestries and woven carpets – came from further east, from the countries of Eastern Europa and the unexplored lands beyond the Middle Sea, including the lands of the powerful Gate people. She had a network of reliable contacts that brought goods to the eastern ports and loaded them on to her merchant ships, which called at Bellezza before sailing down the coast to Classe.

And that journey from Bellezza to Classe was the most dangerous stretch; the waters there were infested by pirates. Merchant ships offered rich pickings for those who lived beyond the law: not just the sort of goods that Flavia traded in but valuable jewels and gold coins. Every merchant ship was armed with guns and guards but it was hard to counter the recklessness and bravery of the Talian pirates.

Flavia sighed; she had her own reasons for unease when she thought of pirates and not just because they stole her goods. And now that the winter was nearly over, she had sent out her first ship of the year. She pulled her mind away from her cargo and concentrated on selling a bolt of cotton and some cinnabar to a haggling buyer.

But just then one of the ragged boys the merchants employed to watch down at the harbour came running up to the stall and tugged at Flavia's skirt. Her heart beat faster at the thought of what news he might bring but she calmly finished her business with the haggler and put the money away in the pouch at her waist before hearing what the urchin had to say.

'Pirates, Signora,' he said. 'Your ship the *Silver Lady* is back in port, but the Captain says they were boarded at sea.'

'Boarded and yet the ship came back?' asked Flavia.

'Back but lacking some of her cargo, Signora,' said the boy.

The merchant gave him a small coin. 'Tell the Captain to come to my house,' she said.

As he ran off back to the harbour, Flavia signalled to her assistant to start packing up; there would be no more trading today.

*

Arianna was obliged to hear an embassy from the Admiral of her Bellezzan fleet. His visits to her had become more frequent over recent months and his news was never good.

The Duchessa of the lagoon city sighed, and then stretched. She was in her best formal costume: stiff, light blue taffeta embroidered with butterflies and a silver butterfly mask.

There were times when she felt ready to rule the city on her own as Duchessa in her own right. But at other moments, like now, when she needed to listen gravely to the Admiral's news, she would have preferred to hand him over to the Regent, her father, Rodolfo Rossi, drag off her fine clothes and run through the piazza chasing pigeons.

Arianna was still only eighteen, and the cares of state sometimes weighed heavily on her. Her heart wasn't in them; it was in Padavia where Luciano, the man she was going to marry, was studying at the University. There was all the rest of this term and the next to live through until he came back to Bellezza and they could be together for ever.

She missed him every minute but she wasn't a lovesick island girl, mooning over her lover. She was Duchess of Bellezza and she had an admiral to receive.

Admiral Gambone was waiting in the elegant new Reception Room, which had replaced the Glass Room where the old Duchessa was believed to have been assassinated. Arianna was glad that the hateful and deceptive room with its misleading reflections had gone for good. Her ways were more direct than her mother's and she wanted to see her petitioners and ambassadors face to face.

The Admiral's face was even longer than usual and seemed to say clearly that he too would rather be having this audience with the wise and grave Regent and could not take seriously this inexperienced girl who wore the ducal regalia. But he had perfect manners and pulled himself together before launching into his news.

'Your Grace,' he said, bowing and accepting the chair she indicated to him, 'I come with grave news from the east. The Gate people are not content with blockading the Silk Road or sending their pirates to our waters. They are amassing a huge fleet of warships.'

'A bigger fleet than ours, Admiral?' asked Arianna, more calmly than she felt.

'My information is that their ships outnumber ours by maybe as much as four to one, Your Grace,' said Gambone. 'We need allies – and quickly.'

Chapter 1

Imaginary Twin

Isabel Evans was feeling sick. She always did on results day. Not because she did badly; her results were usually quite respectable. But because Charlie always did better.

It wasn't his fault that he was brilliant at school subjects any more than it was his fault that he excelled at all sports and could play any wind instrument. Or that he was attractive to girls and got on well with teachers. It wasn't even their parents' fault that Isabel felt less favoured; they had always been scrupulously fair in their treatment of the twins.

Charlie was Isabel's twin brother and she had to love him. She *did* love him. But twins were supposed to have this almost magical closeness and Isabel didn't feel that at all. How she felt was jealous.

Her brother was the older by ten minutes and had been heavier at birth by a pound, which put Isabel in an incubator for a couple of days and left Charlie to breastfeed direct, while Isabel had to drink expressed milk. What a little thing to determine the course of the next sixteen, nearly seventeen, years! But it did. That accident of birth was something Isabel felt she had never caught up with: Charlie would always be older, stronger, in some way just more satisfactory than she was.

So she had invented a different twin for herself. Charlotte was a female version of Charlie but with the crucial difference that she had been born ten minutes *after* Isabel. This gave Isabel the chance to feel just a tiny bit superior and she knew that the imaginary Charlotte was a bit jealous of her. That made her feel special. If there was any magical twin-type closeness, it was with Charlotte rather than Charlie.

'Hurry up, Bel!' called Charlie from outside the bathroom door. 'I need to brush my teeth.'

She wasn't going to be sick after all, even though she had felt too nauseated to eat any breakfast. Isabel let Charlie in and he flashed her a look of concern. 'You OK? You're looking a bit washed out.'

'Thanks for nothing,' said Isabel, then realised she was being unreasonably touchy. 'Really, I'm fine. Just a bit Monday-morningish.'

'Tell me about it!' said Charlie indistinctly through his toothpaste. 'It's the mocks results today, isn't it?'

'Yeah,' said Isabel, and ran downstairs two at a time, trying to show how little she cared.

They didn't walk to school together; that would have been taking twin-ness too far.

Isabel set off a regulation five minutes before Charlie but he always reached Barnsbury comp ahead of her, even though he picked up several mates on the way. Sometimes Isabel thought she could remember the sight of Charlie's heels as his kicked his way out of the womb before her with a cheery wave and a 'Seeya!'

Isabel's friends Laura and Ayesha usually waited for her at the school gates. They were there now, Laura looking nervous and Ayesha pretending to. Ayesha always got spectacular results.

'Hey, Bel,' they greeted her. And then Ayesha's boyfriend, Matt, came up and Isabel fell into step behind them with Laura.

Neither Isabel or Laura had a boyfriend but they didn't begrudge Ayesha hers, even though he was undeniably fit. Yesh was just so beautiful it was obvious she wouldn't be single. *Unlike us*, thought Isabel.

Laura was pretty in a thin, neurotic sort of way, with big eyes and dark brown curly hair. Isabel could have been pretty too. She had naturally blonde hair and dark brown eyes, but what was in Charlie a striking combination was in his sister easily over-looked. It had something to do with the way she did herself down, walking round with her shoulders hunched and her eyes on the ground, as if braced for bad news. She did her best not to be noticed and as a result she never was. The only person she felt more attractive than was Charlotte – and she wasn't real.

'Are you worried?' Laura asked, chewing the edge of her fingernail.

'Is the Pope a Catholic?' said Isabel. 'I can't wait for

today to be over. At least I'll know the worst.'

'You don't do so badly, do you?'

'Just not as well as Charlie,' said Isabel quietly.

Laura shot her a look. Isabel pulled herself together; she didn't talk about how she really felt about Charlie. Mostly she went along with how great it was to have a charismatic twin brother, and she knew Laura had a little bit of a thing for him.

'Take no notice of me,' Isabel said. 'It's probably just PMT.'

They walked into their first lesson and Isabel braced herself; at least she would do better than Charlotte.

The Captain of the *Silver Lady* was deeply embarrassed. Not only had he lost the most expensive silks in Flavia's cargo, but he had a horrible suspicion about the pirate who had relieved him of the goods.

'Describe him to me,' said the merchant, surprisingly calmly, pouring them two cups of Bellezzan red wine.

'Signora, he looked just like every other pirate I've had the misfortune to encounter,' said the Captain after he had drained his cup. 'Unkempt, rascally . . . but I must admit he was polite.'

'And he took just the silk?'

'He took the silk and then asked whose ship it was, Signora,' said the Captain uncomfortably.

Flavia sighed. 'And what did he say when you told him?'

'He . . . He smiled, Signora. And then he said something strange – "It's a new ship. She should have told me." Could it be . . . ?' he hesitated. 'Could it be that you know this brigand?'

Flavia did not answer. She weighed out the amount of silver due to the Captain for his entire cargo.

'But I have not brought it all safely into harbour,' he protested.

'No matter,' she said. 'I think the silk will find its way to me.'

The Captain did not wait for her to change her mind.

'Oh, well done, both of you!' said the twins' mother enthusiastically, when she got in from work.

Their father was equally encouraging and ordered an Indian takeaway to celebrate. Homework was abandoned and beer opened even though it was a school night.

Isabel painted a smile on her face and kept it from peeling off all evening, until she went to bed and let her face gratefully droop into its real expression. Their parents were always so *fair*! She couldn't blame her problems on them. Or on Charlie, who – damn him – was actually a really nice brother.

It's all my fault, she thought. *I'm rubbish. If I'd been an only child, without comparisons, my results would have been genuinely good. It's just that Charlie's are always better. Everything about him is better. And I'm a rat for even thinking what it would have been like if he hadn't been born!*

The curry and beer sat heavily on her stomach as she tried to find a comfortable position and get to sleep. She fell back into her usual habit of imagining Charlotte.

'Oh, Bel, I wish I'd got your averages! A levels will be a doddle for you.'

Then suddenly the thought of what she was doing nauseated Isabel.

Give it a rest, she told herself. *It's pathetic that you can't cope without an imaginary sister. What about your Art result?*

It was true that her Related Study work on mosaics, which had been assessed as part of the mocks, had got a stunning Charlie-type grade. Isabel was so glad that Charlie didn't do Art; it was the one area where she felt she had an edge on him and she couldn't have borne it if he had chosen it for A level.

Flavia was at the mosaic-maker's in the Via Bellezza. Fausto Ventura was the busiest mosaicist in Classe. His bottega employed a dozen people who were always busy cutting stone and coloured glass into tesserae. Others applied them to the designs and fitted them on walls and floors throughout the city. But only Fausto drew up the designs. His unique visions covered almost every important surface in modern Classe – every new church or villa.

And he was Flavia's friend. Not just because she imported most of the coloured glass and silver 'smalti' from Bellezza used in his workshop, but because she loved art and had a good eye for mosaics. She spent her considerable wealth on adorning the walls and floors of her house with his work and he often visited her there, reminding himself of the peacocks and lilies, leopards and dolphins he had created from chips of marble, glass and the silver smalti that were Classe's trademark.

But today she had come to visit him, and Fausto could see she was perturbed. He invited her into his private studio at the back of the bottega where he worked on his elaborate designs.

'What is it?' he asked.

Flavia hesitated then took the plunge. 'I have lost some of my cargo to pirates,' she said. 'The *Silver Lady* came back but lacking some of her silks.'

Fausto spread his hands in the universal gesture of pity mixed with resignation. 'It happens,' he said. 'Is the loss of money very great?'

'It is not so much that,' said Flavia. 'Although they were very fine silks. But my ships are subject to dangers on all sides now. I have heard a disturbing rumour that the Gate people have placed their own men on pirate ships along our coast.'

'So first they sell you the silk and then they rob it back off you before it even reaches Classe?' said Fausto. 'Twice the profit for them, or more, depending on how many merchants they can steal from in this way.'

'Perhaps,' said Flavia. 'Although I don't think it was the Gate people who took my silk this time. But that's not what really worries me.'

Fausto had known Flavia a long time and he was sure there was something more to the silk story than she was revealing, but he was prepared to let her tell him in her own time.

'I have heard from Rodolfo in Bellezza,' continued

Flavia. 'His daughter has been told that the Gate people are amassing a war fleet. She's coming here soon to talk to Duke Germano about an alliance between our cities.'

'Well, that's good, surely?' said Fausto. 'Germano is sure to say yes. We have always been on good terms with Bellezza.'

'Indeed,' said Flavia. 'And who are we both on bad terms with?'

'You mean besides the Gate people?'

'Someone much closer to home than them.'

'The di Chimici.'

It wasn't a question. Classe was one of the few city-states that remained independent in the north of Talia. Fabrizio di Chimici, the young Duke of Giglia, was now also Grand Duke of Tuschia, and his family ruled in half the great cities of the peninsula. But there were fierce pockets of resistance to the family's empire-building schemes, and here in the north-east Classe, Padavia and Bellezza made natural allies against the powerful di Chimici.

Two elected duchies, with Duke Germano and Duchessa Arianna at their head, plus Antonio, the elected Governor of Padavia, had held out against all attempts to compromise their independence – from threats to marriage proposals, from diplomacy to assassinations. There was a natural free spirit among the people of these three cities that resisted any attempt to bring them into the di Chimici fold.

And they were linked by more than a spirit of independence. Classe and Bellezza were both on the sea and both maintained a fleet of ships to defend their coasts; Padavia was inland and did not need ships but relied heavily on the other two cities to protect its trade routes. Antonio was willing to pay some of his city's dues to help with the upkeep of the two fleets.

'What exactly do you think they're up to?' asked Fausto, taking Flavia's silence for agreement.

'I think the di Chimici might have forged an alliance with the Gate people,' said Flavia slowly. 'Rodolfo thinks so too. He hasn't told the young Duchessa of his suspicions yet but I know he fears the worst.'

'But wouldn't it be madness to combine with Talia's fiercest enemies?' asked Fausto.

'Some say the young Grand Duke *is* mad,' said Flavia. 'Whether it's true, I don't know. But if he has really done it, then those of us living on this coast are in terrible danger.'

'It's all very well for Fabrizio di Chimici, sitting safe inland in Giglia,' said Fausto, agitated himself now. He had a vision of fierce sea-warriors from the east overrunning Classe and destroying its great buildings full of mosaics.

'Those who lie down with dogs will rise with fleas,' said Flavia bitterly. 'He will pay a heavy price, but not before we do.'

'So what can we do?' asked Fausto. 'Is there anything the Brotherhood can do to stop them?'

Fausto knew that his friend was a member of a powerful and clandestine society of people who had secret gifts. She did not talk about it much but he was aware that she had a special way of communicating with the Regent of Bellezza and others in Talia who were also members of that small band known as Stravaganti.

'We can certainly try,' said Flavia. 'And, as you know, we have allies far beyond Talia who might be able to help us. It has been done before.'

Isabel was rushing from the Art room to her next lesson when she nearly tripped over the little red pouch. She picked it up, fascinated; it looked like a prop from a school play.

It was made of soft crimson velvet, held together at the top with a drawstring – just the kind of purse full of coins that someone called Roderigo would toss across the stage to someone called Valentino or something in a Shakespeare play.

Isabel hefted it in her palm. It definitely did have something inside and she couldn't resist opening the string to see what it was. But it wasn't coins at all; it held tiny silver squares that she recognised straight away as mosaic tiles. 'Tesserae' they were called, and Isabel had thought she was the only person in the school who was interested in them. Who could it possibly belong to?

The only student who came to mind was Sky Meadows, the gorgeous butterscotch-coloured boy who sat next to her in Art and was going out with a girl called Alice. Isabel heaved a huge sigh. Sky hadn't taken any more notice of her than anyone else at Barnsbury, but she had often thought it would be nice if he did.

She dragged her mind back to the pouch of little tiles, her feet taking her in the direction of her next class without any conscious decision on her part. Sky was interested in Italian art but Renaissance sculpture was his thing; his Related Study on Donatello had been the only one with a higher mark than Isabel's. There wasn't time to take the pouch back to the Art room now – she would ask him about it at break. And if it wasn't his . . . Isabel pushed the red velvet bag deep into her pocket. She supposed she'd have to show it to the Art teacher, but she found the pouch oddly appealing. It was nice just closing her hand over it in her pocket and feeling the little tesserae through the velvet. She didn't really want to hand it over to anyone else.

Sky's reaction to the pouch at break time was a definite improvement on past contact with him. He said it wasn't his, but he was certainly taking notice of Isabel now.

'You say you just found it lying near the Art room?' he said, almost caressing the velvet, as if he knew something about it.

'That's right,' said Isabel, feeling embarrassed now that those brown eyes were at last fully focused on her own. 'It's tesserae inside,' she added. 'I looked. You know – little pieces for making mosaics.'

'You're interested in mosaics, aren't you?' he said. So he *had* paid some attention to her before.

'Yes. I love them,' said Isabel, feeling stupid and uncool even as she said it. But Sky didn't seem to mind; he just nodded.

'I'm more into sculpture myself. Don't know much about mosaics. But don't you think this bag or purse or whatever it is looks sort of Italian? It's got a kind of Renaissance feel to it.'

'Well, it made me think of the sort of Italians you

get in Shakespeare plays,' said Isabel. 'But yes, I suppose that's Renaissance in a way.'

She didn't want this conversation ever to end. Sky reluctantly handed the red bag back to her. And Isabel just as reluctantly took it to the Art teacher in her dinner hour. But Ms Hellings didn't know anything about it either. She suggested taking it to Lost Property. Isabel didn't say she would, she just nodded as if agreeing it was a good idea. But she had already decided to keep it.

'An alliance with the Gate people?' said Arianna. 'Are you sure?'

Her father shifted restlessly in his chair. 'I would not have told you if I had not been sure,' he said. 'This is the most serious news we've had about the di Chimici since they introduced their anti-magic laws.'

They were both silent for a while, remembering how close to death by burning many of the Manoush had come in Padavia only four months ago. Since then Governor Antonio had repealed the anti-magic laws that the di Chimici had persuaded him to adopt and had abandoned that method of execution completely, believing now that it was unacceptably cruel.

'Then what is Fabrizio thinking of?' asked Arianna.

'He is desperate to win over more city-states to his dead father's idea of a republic,' said Rodolfo. 'If the Gate people come in force to this coast, he thinks they could overrun at least Bellezza and Classe.'

'And then?'

'Then he thinks that the King of the Gate people

will hand them over to the di Chimici.'

'Just like that?' said Arianna. 'But what would be in it for the Gate people?'

'I imagine Fabrizio has offered him a massive sum of money,' said Rodolfo. 'That's the way these alliances usually work.'

'But why now?' asked Arianna.

'The di Chimici have tried diplomacy, offers of marriage and assassination, all to no avail. Bellezza, Classe, Padavia and Montemurato stand firm in the north, Romula and Cittanuova in the south. Talia is evenly balanced between di Chimici rule and independence. The Grand Duke desperately needs at least one city-state to go over to him and shift that balance in his favour.'

'So he will unleash the Gate people on the shores of his own country,' said Arianna, but it was not a question. She could no longer doubt that war was coming to the lagoon city from the sea.

She wished that Luciano were there. He had gone back to Padavia to spend two more terms at the University and complete his education as a Bellezzan noble worthy to be her consort. But Arianna didn't give a fig for all that. He was already worthy as far as she was concerned. She hadn't been Duchessa of this great city for long; it was only two and a half years since she had been an ordinary island girl, whose highest ambition had been to scull one of the black mandolas that glided along that city's canals.

And now she wanted his counsel as much as his company. Because he had come from another world, he often had a different viewpoint on Talian matters. Although three years earlier he had known nothing of politics and diplomacy, even Rodolfo respected his opinion.

But for now she had to decide what to do without him.

'We must speak to the Duke of Classe,' she said at last.

Rodolfo relaxed a little. He was relieved that his daughter was thinking in this way. At the beginning of her rule, she would have turned to him and asked what to do. That was why he had been appointed Regent. No one really expected a girl of sixteen, even one as gifted as Arianna, and with her lineage, to take on the full responsibility of running such an important city as Bellezza.

But he would not always be there to help her. He wanted her to be her own woman, not dependent on him or even on Luciano in future. The ruler of Bellezza must rule, just as her mother had done before her. And Rodolfo had helped Silvia too, he remembered. And as always when he thought of Silvia, his expression softened.

'Shall we involve Silvia?' Arianna asked, as if she had read his thoughts.

And as if equally telepathic, Silvia, Rodolfo's wife and Arianna's mother, was announced and entered Arianna's private room. It had been hers until the assassination attempt which most Bellezzans believed to have succeeded. Only a few people knew that it was not Silvia who had died in the explosion in the Glass Room and that she still lived, under the guise of being the Regent's second wife.

Now her gaze swept round the little parlour, resting briefly on the door to the secret passage that led to

Rodolfo's palazzo. She could have come that way herself but lately she had been seen as more of a public figure, accompanying her husband and the young Duchessa on more state occasions. Silvia wanted the people of Bellezza to get used to her presence.

'You two seem very serious,' she said.

Arianna took off the silk mask she had been wearing when the footman announced Signora Rossi. In her own family, she often abandoned the convention that all Bellezzan women over sixteen went masked until their marriage.

Silvia saw that her daughter's face was indeed drawn with worry. She glanced quickly at her husband.

'What is it?' she asked. 'Not bad news from Padavia?'

'No,' said Rodolfo. 'Luciano is well, as far as we know. The bad news comes from further afield.'

Isabel had often thought about going to Ravenna. It had played a big part in her mosaic research. Though she loved the Roman floors she had seen at Fishbourne and Verulamium, she longed to see the golden walls in the churches that she knew only from photographs. There was something about mosaic technique that spoke to her and she loved the way it could endure for thousands of years, unlike painting. Even sculpture was vulnerable, leaving statues missing noses, arms or anything else that stuck out.

Now she lay in her bed holding the mysterious little velvet bag with its silver tesserae and thought about seeing the real thing: the fishes, birds, flowers and gorgeous clothes of the wall mosaics of Ravenna. But just as she was dropping off to sleep a thought wandered across her fading consciousness. Nobody made silver tesserae; they would tarnish. To get the silver effect you had to use white gold. And then she was lost to sleep.

Isabel woke up soaking wet. At least she thought she had and then she realised she must still be asleep. She was standing up to her waist in not very warm water in some sort of, well, some sort of bath, she supposed. It was eight-sided and marble-clad. Isabel recognised where she was: it was in the Baptistery of the cathedral in Ravenna. She looked up and saw the dome above her head but there was something not quite right about it.

There were the twelve apostles, and Jesus being baptised by Saint John, just as she had often seen them in reproductions, with the tiled water rippling blue and white across the lower half of Christ's body. But instead of having a gold background there and on all the walls surrounding the bath, it was all set against silver.

What an amazing thing the human mind is, thought Isabel, even as she believed herself to be asleep and dreaming. *I was thinking of silver tesserae and here I am surrounded by them.*

But then she began to feel uncomfortably wet and hitched herself up on to the flat side of the bath. Her loose pyjama bottoms clung unpleasantly to her legs. She had never had such a realistic dream and was wondering how to get out of it when she heard a sound. Up till that moment she had believed the Baptistery to be empty apart from herself but now the wooden door swung open, letting more light into the room than the round arched windows had and illuminating the dazzling silver images.

A woman came in and stopped when she saw Isabel sitting wetly on the side of the bath. Then she said the oddest thing.

'Ah, so you've arrived. We'd better find you a towel.'

'Who are you?' asked Isabel, getting the strangest feeling that this wasn't a dream after all.

'I'm your Stravagante,' said the woman. 'And I'm glad to say that you are mine. We really need you here in Classe.'

Chapter 2

A Diplomatic Gift

Isabel squelched out into the sunlight, feeling soggy and bemused. She couldn't remember ever getting wet in a dream before. The incomprehensible woman who had seemed to be expecting her walked her briskly to a house near the Baptistery and opened the front door. Isabel noticed that she didn't use a key; wherever this was, they didn't seem to worry about crime.

And it wasn't as if there was nothing worth stealing. It was the most luxurious home Isabel had ever been in. And she saw straight away that there was an armed guard just behind the door, so perhaps the woman wasn't casual about thieves after all. She hurried Isabel up the stairs to a bedroom where a wood fire was burning in the grate and ordered her to undress.

Then she bustled around with towels and clothes

and made Isabel rub herself dry and change into a very old-fashioned dress. Her pyjamas were hung over a wooden rail in front of the fire and then the woman hurried her back down the stairs into a warm and elegant living room, summoning a servant on the way and ordering hot chocolate.

At no point did she consult Isabel about what she wanted; she just gave her instructions. But once they were sitting in front of the living-room fire and Isabel was sipping a ridiculously rich drink that was just like melted bitter chocolate with warm milk swirled in, the woman looked at her properly.

'I'm Flavia,' she said. 'What is your name?'

Isabel told her but she was beginning to feel very uneasy.

'Isabella,' said Flavia, looking satisfied. 'That is a good Talian name.'

Isabel put her cup down.

'I'm sorry but I haven't understood anything you've said to me since I got here. And where is here, anyway?'

'Classe,' said Flavia. 'The City of Ships. Though some people call it the Painted City.'

'But it's mosaic, not paint,' said Isabel, remembering the dome of the Baptistery.

'You know about our mosaics?' asked Flavia.

'Well, no, not these ones. These are silver and the ones I learned about were gold.'

'I've heard about that. They say that in your world it is silver that turns black, not gold, as it does here.'

'What do you mean, "in my world"? What world is this?' said Isabel. And felt foolish as she said it. Part of her wanted to shake herself out of this dream, and part was fascinated and wondering what Flavia would say or do next. She looked down at the green dress she was wearing and saw that it and the woman's clothing were like something from a play. And that made her think of the bag of tesserae. Where was it? Hadn't she been holding it when she went to sleep?

*

The Duke of Classe was a worried man. Germano Mariano was an elected duke and he had been ruler of his city for nearly forty years. In that time it had grown in prosperity, through its position on the coast and trading with other countries. And patrons of art came from all over Talia to see its mosaics and commission floors or walls for their own houses. Piracy had always been a problem, but that came with the territory if your city had a harbour where ships brought their luxury cargoes.

The latest news was different. A messenger had come from Bellezza with an urgent request from its young Duchessa. She wanted to visit him and that was unusual in itself. Apart from state visits, rulers did not usually meet person to person; their business was conducted through ambassadors.

He had a good idea what it was about; his own scouts had been bringing worrying news of a build-up in the fleet of the Gate people for some time. Germano sighed; he was tired. He had thought about yielding up the duchy and calling an election. Most dukes were elected for life but there was always a possibility of retirement.

But he felt that would be dishonourable if his city

was in some new danger. Germano's children were grown-up and leading busy lives and showed no interest in politics and he had no idea who might stand for election as the next duke. Perhaps a younger person would be a good idea? He simply didn't know, but the thought of retiring to a farm outside the city with his wife, Anna, was very appealing.

Germano straightened his surcoat. The Duchessa and her father, the Regent of Bellezza, would be arriving at any minute and he had ordered the finest quarters in his palazzo prepared for their visitors. His wife was still inspecting the rooms when he heard the sound of carriage wheels in the cobbled street. Interested, he stood at the window and saw descend first a tall, stooped figure in black and then a young, masked woman who could only be the Duchessa.

But what caught his breath was a large black-spotted cat that leapt down from the carriage after her and stretched its long front paws then yawned, showing its sharp white teeth.

*

A few roads away from the Ducal Palace, Flavia was trying to explain to Isabel that she was not actually dreaming but had stravagated to a parallel world.

'Other Barnsbury students?' said Isabel stupidly. 'You're kidding. Who?'

'There is one called Georgia, another called Sky and a third called Matt,' said Flavia, counting off on her fingers. 'Oh, and Luciano, who used to be called Lucien and, in a way, the one you would know as Nicholas Duke.'

How can I be making all this up in my sleep? thought Isabel. *I scarcely know those people. Apart from Sky, of course. You don't have to be a genius to guess how I came up with his name.*

'You know these other Stravaganti?' Flavia was asking.

'Well, yes,' said Isabel. 'But I don't know what you mean by "Stravaganti". You said that word before, about you and me, when you found me in the bath.'

'Travellers in time and space,' said Flavia, and Isabel suddenly noticed the woman had the little red pouch in her lap. She held it out. 'This is your talisman – the thing that enables you to travel between worlds. Every Stravagante has one. It takes him or her to the city it came from in Talia.'

'So did that come from Talia?' asked Isabel. She took the bag from Flavia and felt curiously reassured to have it back.

'Yes, it came from here, the city of Classe,' said Flavia, looking at Isabel intently. 'I took it to your world myself.'

Isabel smiled to think of this wealthy woman in her historical costume wandering through the streets of London. Then she did a double take.

'What time is it here?' she asked.

'A little before noon,' said Flavia.

'No, I mean what year is it?'

'1580.'

'No kidding,' said Isabel. So Flavia wasn't dressed up in historical costume, like someone in a play or pageant, and nor was she. It really was the sixteenth century in this place. The Renaissance. That was if Talia really existed and it wasn't a dream.

'How do I get back?' she asked.

'You have to be holding the talisman and thinking of your destination when you fall asleep,' said Flavia. 'Only I recommend you not to think of the baptismal bath when you come back next time.'

'I wasn't thinking of it last time,' said Isabel, annoyed. But then she realised what Flavia had meant: she would coming back to Classe again.

*

'He is my present to you,' said Arianna, delighted by the way that Duke Germano caressed the African cat. The animal was not yet full-grown and, as it responded enthusiastically to being stroked, she thought it looked as though man and cat would get on well.

Rodolfo smiled. He had not been at all sure about this idea of his impetuous daughter's but the present of the beast seemed to smooth their arrival at the palazzo and the Duke was clearly pleased.

The Duchessa Anna came into the reception room and gave a small shriek when she saw the cat.

'Look what the Duchessa of Bellezza has brought for us,' said Germano. 'Don't be afraid, my dear. See, he is gentle as a lamb.'

The old Duchessa came cautiously to have her hands licked and the introductions were all made in an atmosphere of laughter and friendship.

'Does he have a name?' asked Germano, now playing with the outsize kitten by dangling a tassel on his surcoat for him to catch.

'Well, I've been calling him Vitale, because he's so

lively,' said Arianna. 'But he's yours now so you can change it if you like.'

'No, no, that's perfect,' said the Duke. 'And we shouldn't confuse him – he'll be homesick at first anyway, so we should keep his name to make him feel at ease.'

Rodolfo thought that he needn't worry about Arianna's skills as a diplomat; Vitale was the patron saint of Classe.

By the time the cat had been taken to a stable and made comfortable and his diet discussed with a nervous groom, the rulers of Bellezza and Classe were chatting like old friends. They sat down to an informal dinner with Rodolfo and Duchessa Anna and no other guests. But as was customary in Talia, no diplomatic business was discussed until the servants had withdrawn and they were sitting with glasses of digestivo in a small parlour.

'These are dangerous times for our shores,' began Rodolfo.

The Duke nodded; he approved of coming straight to the heart of the matter and he now felt at ease with his guests.

'We are both fortunate and unlucky to live in such watery cities, so close to the coast,' said Germano.

'You have suffered much from piracy?' asked Arianna.

'Probably no more than any other trading port,' admitted Germano. 'But it has been worse of late. There is one particularly audacious brigand, known as the Black Raider, who has caused our merchants heavy losses.'

'We have heard of him too,' said Arianna. 'His

ambition seems to be to harry all the trade routes from the east to Talia.'

'But we have a threat more dangerous still than Black Raiders,' said Rodolfo.

'The Gate people,' said Arianna.

Germano looked serious. 'They have always been there,' he said. 'They watch our eastern coast from their shores and take advantage of any weakness in our defences. But it's been a long time since they have taken any aggressive action.'

'That time may be coming,' said Rodolfo. 'We have heard that they have formed an unlikely alliance.'

'With the di Chimici,' added Arianna.

Germano paled, gripping the arms of his chair. It had been a major part of his rule to resist the di Chimici in their attempts to woo him into their fold. Years ago, a marriage had been suggested with his older daughter, but she had already made her choice of husband and was scathing on the subject of the offer.

But Duke Germano always felt on his guard about Talia's ruling family. The mere mention of their name was enough to conjure up the nightmare of losing his city's independence.

'To what end?' he asked.

'It is an incredibly dangerous strategy but we think the di Chimici are encouraging the Gate fleet to attack our coastline – Bellezza and probably Classe too,' said Rodolfo. 'If the attacks succeed, the di Chimici will let them pillage for a little while and then expect to have the control of the cities handed over to them.'

'But that is like training a tiger to hunt for you and expecting him to hand over most of the kill!' said Duke Germano, appalled. 'They will have invited a dangerous predator right into Talia.'

Arianna was impressed that the Duke's first thought had been of his country rather than fear of losing power in his own city.

'It may not be as bad as that,' she said, though she couldn't smooth her own worry out from behind her mask. 'My father has drawn the worst picture for you, to show how serious the threat is. All we know for certain is that the Gate fleet is massing in the east and that our spies have confirmed the Grand Duke's emissaries have been seen at the King of the Gate people's court.'

'So the rest is conjecture?' said Germano.

'Conjecture and what the Stravaganti have to able to scry,' said Rodolfo.

Isabel woke at the usual time in her own bed, still holding the red velvet pouch. She was wearing her own pyjamas and they were dry. She could remember putting them back on though, in Talia, so that didn't really prove anything. She lay there a while, her thoughts whirling with all she had seen and heard during what Flavia had called her first stravagation.

They had gone out for a walk in the streets of Classe and Isabel had seen that the city was criss-crossed by canals and little bridges. Flavia had explained that it was built on swampy land, 'like Bellezza'. That hadn't helped much, but Isabel gathered she meant a greater city, further north, that sounded like a version of Venice.

They had walked through a large oblong space,

which Flavia said was called the Piazza del Foro and which was being used for a market.

'That is my stall over there,' the woman had said, pointing to one of the biggest ones in the piazza. 'My assistant is running it today, because I was waiting for you.'

Flavia had said a lot of things like that, which all seemed to imply that Isabel had been somehow expected in Classe and her arrival looked forward to as something important. She didn't understand any of it but it made her feel good.

They were on their way down to the harbour when Flavia had suddenly stopped outside an imposing-looking building.

'So,' she said. 'She is here already.'

Isabel was so used to being puzzled and confused by then that she hadn't thought to ask who. Flavia was looking at a grand carriage bearing a crest with a silver mask on it.

'The Duchessa of Bellezza has arrived,' she said to Isabel.

'Is she a Stravagante too?' hazarded Isabel.

'No, but her father is. And so is her fiancé.'

Ah, so this Duchessa was young, even with such a grown-up title.

What Isabel had liked best was the harbour, and it had helped her to believe that her visit to Classe hadn't been a dream. She had never seen a harbour or port in real life so she didn't see how she could have invented it, even with her unconscious mind. To be honest with herself, she was afraid of the water, particularly open sea, and couldn't even swim. (Charlie of course was on the Barnsbury swimming team.)

But Classe harbour was beautiful, thronged with the bobbing masts of sailing ships of all sizes, full of the cries of gulls and the smells of just-caught fish and a salty wind off the sea. Flavia had pointed out her own ships, one just arrived and one about to set out on a voyage to the east. It was a thriving, bustling centre of activity, the waterside equivalent of the busy buying and selling they had just seen in the Piazza del Foro.

It was down at the quayside that Flavia had whispered to Isabel to notice their shadows. The merchant's stretched darkly across the wet cobbles in the afternoon sunshine. But of Isabel's there was no sign. It had made her feel weak and insignificant all over again.

'It's all right,' Flavia had said. 'No Stravagante has a shadow in the other world. I didn't have one when I came to where you live.'

But soon after that she had said it was time for Isabel to go home.

'You shouldn't be here too long on your first stravagation,' Flavia said, and had taken her back to her house and made her put her dry pyjamas back on under the green dress. Then they had walked back to the Baptistery.

'You have to fall asleep holding the tesserae, remember,' Flavia had said.

Fortunately, the Baptistery had been empty and it hadn't appeared necessary to get back in the bath to stravagate. There were wooden benches around the octagonal walls and Isabel had lain down on one of them, clutching the velvet bag, certain she wouldn't go to sleep, half believing still that she was asleep already and dreaming.

But just as she was wondering if it was possible to dream of falling asleep when you already were, she had lost consciousness and the next thing she knew, she was awake in her own bed.

Her mother's voice calling up the stairs about breakfast startled Isabel out of her reverie. Whether Talia and Classe were real or not, Barnsbury Comp certainly was and she needed to get showered and dressed or she would be late.

But when she reached the school gate with her friends, something odd happened. Matt was there and she thought he was just waiting for Ayesha. But he looked straight past his girlfriend and fixed Isabel with a penetrating stare. She felt very uncomfortable, especially since she had been talking about him in her dream.

Matt flashed Ayesha a smile and said, 'Can I borrow Isabel a moment, Yesh?'

And he took her aside to where a knot of other students stood waiting. Georgia and her boyfriend Nick, Sky and Alice. These were all people mentioned by Flavia, except for Alice.

'What's up?' asked Isabel uneasily.

'That's what we wanted to ask you,' said Sky. That was the second time he had noticed her existence, and Isabel registered that Alice didn't look too pleased about it. 'Did anything happen with the velvet bag?'

That would have been a really weird question to ask. Except that something *had* happened. Isabel suddenly had a very strong sense of their all looking at her as if they knew she had been transported to Talia.

And in that moment, she was sure that what had happened to her had been no dream.

Chapter 3

Belonging

It was an eerie feeling having five fellow students looking as if they would hang on her every word and Isabel felt very self-conscious. She didn't know how she was going to explain it to Laura, who had gone on ahead.

'There's no time to talk now,' said Georgia. 'Can you sit with us at lunch?'

'What about the people you usually sit with?' said Isabel.

'Well, Ayesha's OK,' said Matt. 'She knows.'

'But you'll have to lose Laura,' said Georgia harshly. 'She mustn't suspect anything.'

Suspect what? thought Isabel all morning. *And what did Matt mean by saying Ayesha knew?*

She couldn't concentrate on any of her lessons and

drew some unwanted attention from her teacher in History. At break, she took Laura to one side and said she couldn't have lunch with her. Laura looked hurt but didn't ask why. So Isabel blundered on.

'I've got to talk to these, er, people. Friends of Ayesha,' she said. 'See you at going home?'

Laura just nodded and Isabel felt even more of a rat. Her best friend was so fragile. She tried to forget her guilt by spending the next two periods communing with the imaginary Charlotte, telling her all about Talia. By lunch break she was a wreck, dithering over what to put on her tray and looking out nervously for the group of what she found herself thinking of as Stravaganti.

When she spotted them, she was glad to see that Alice wasn't with them. Sky indicated a place next to him and Isabel sank into it with relief. Whatever they were all going to tell her, it would soon be over.

'So. This velvet thingy – it's a talisman, isn't it?' asked Georgia, without any preliminaries.

'That's what Flavia called it,' said Isabel.

'Is she your Stravagante?' asked Sky. 'I had a woman one too, a sculptor. Is yours an artist?'

'Where did you go?' asked Nick eagerly. 'Was it near Giglia?'

'You know no one else is going to go there, Nick,' said Georgia. She seemed annoyed with her boyfriend, though Isabel couldn't see why.

'Don't crowd her,' said Matt. 'Let her take her time.' Ayesha looked at him approvingly.

'She said she was a Stravagante,' said Isabel slowly. 'And she said I was one too but I still don't understand it.'

'Matt said it takes a while to get used to,' said Ayesha.

'Have you been, you know, to Talia?' Isabel asked her.

Ayesha shook her head. 'No, not me. But the others all have.'

'And Alice went once,' said Sky. 'But she didn't like it.'

'I'm not sure if I liked it exactly,' said Isabel. 'It was weird. I mean, I arrived in this big bath of water and Flavia found me and took me to her house to dry out.'

'Bath of water?' said Nick.

'Yes, it was in the Baptistery in a place called Classe,' said Isabel.

'Ah,' said Nick. He seemed a bit disappointed. 'That's more like Bellezza than Giglia.'

'Flavia mentioned Bellezza,' said Isabel. 'The Duchess of it had just arrived in Classe.'

'Duchessa,' said Georgia. 'Was she on her own?'

'I don't know. I didn't see her,' said Isabel. 'But Flavia said something about her father – and her fiancé. She said they were both Stravaganti. Do any of you know her?'

'All of us do,' said Nick. 'In a way. And her father. But her fiancé, as you call him, is even better known here. He used to go to this school.'

Isabel felt really out of her depth.

'You mean it's possible to go to Talia and not come back?' she asked.

'Only if you die,' said Georgia.

Cardinal Rinaldo di Chimici had not told the Grand Duke about his experiments, with their cousin Filippo, in stravagation. Rinaldo was wild with frustration. He had captured and tortured a young man who he was sure was a traveller from another world, confiscated the book that he believed was the key to the youth's travel to the future, and heard Filippo's account of how he had briefly visited that world.

And then, nothing. They still had the book but it never worked again. Rinaldo had gone back to Remora but felt so restless that he had summoned Filippo to visit him there.

'We must go over again what we know about the Stravaganti,' he said, as soon as Filippo arrived.

'Not again,' said his cousin wearily. 'I'm not going to let you keep on hitting me, cardinal or no cardinal.'

Rinaldo glared at him. 'No. Obviously, that didn't work. We need to make a list or chart of what we learned about stravagation together and what I knew about it already.'

'We've been through all this before,' said Filippo. 'Why is it so important to find out more?'

'We've been through that too,' said the Cardinal. 'This brotherhood has the secret of time travel, I am sure. And possibly the secret of travel to other worlds as well. If we could only find out how they do it, it would give the family a huge advantage.'

Filippo sighed. He had hated his brief trip to the future or to another world, whichever it had been, and was in no hurry to return. It had been a nightmare place, full of flames and smoke and demons, and his own view was that he had experienced a vision of hell. Perhaps that was where the Stravaganti came from?

But some were definitely Talians, like the Regent of
Bellezza.

Rinaldo sat at his desk with parchment and quill.
He would not trust a clerk with this task. After half an
hour he put down his quill and looked over the list he
had just written:

Known Stravaganti in Talia

Rodolfo, Regent of Bellezza

Suspected Stravaganti

Luciano Crinamorte, Cavaliere of Bellezza
Dottore Guglielmo Crinamorte of Bellezza
Georgio Gredi, rider of Remora, now vanished
Brother Sulien, pharmacist-friar of Giglia
Brother Tino, friar of Giglia, now vanished
Brother ?Benvenuto, friar of Giglia, now vanished
Matteo Bosco, printer of Padavia, now vanished

Facts about Stravaganti

Some do not have shadows
Luciano Crinamorte
Matteo Bosco
Brother ?Benvenuto

Some have shadows at one time and not others
Luciano Crinamorte

They come from the future or travel to the future
Vision of the supposedly dead Falco di Chimici at

his own commemorative Star Race in Remora,
cured of his injuries
Visit of Filippo di Chimici to the other world

They use a kind of book to effect this travel
Luciano Crinamorte
Matteo Bosco
Filippo di Chimici

They need to lose consciousness in order to travel?
Filippo di Chimici

'It's not much to go on, is it?' said Filippo, looking at the parchment.

But his cousin seemed excited.

'We should have done this before,' said Rinaldo. 'It makes a lot of things clearer. For instance, we are not sure if they come from or go to the future. They might just travel to a world with a more highly developed civilisation.'

'The place I went to didn't seem very civilised,' said Filippo, shuddering.

'But they cured Cousin Falco,' said Rinaldo. 'Their doctors must be greatly superior to ours. Imagine if we could go there – wherever or whenever "there" may be – and come back with science like that.'

'But Falco didn't come back, did he?' said Filippo. 'Except that one time. He died in Remora and was buried in Giglia.'

Rinaldo paced the room.

'But before Uncle Niccolò was killed in the duel – by one of our suspected Stravaganti, remember – he told me that the dead Falco had no shadow. He said there was something unearthly about the whole thing. He didn't believe, and nor do I, that the boy killed himself.'

They were silent for a while, remembering their beautiful young cousin.

'I wonder where he is now?' said Filippo.

'You died?' said Isabel stupidly. 'And so did this Lucien?'

Nick had tried to explain it to her but her brain felt as if it was suffering from information overload. And she could see it was upsetting him and Georgia to talk about it.

'Don't worry about that now,' said Matt. 'I know it seems incredible but you'll get used to it. I'm sure you'll meet Luciano in Talia. We all have.'

'And if Arianna is in Classe, you can bet he'll turn up there too,' said Georgia. Her tone was casual but Isabel noticed that Nick gave her a swift look of concern. There was obviously a lot more that she didn't know.

'But *why* do you all go there?' she asked. 'And why did I? I mean, why me and not Ayesha, for instance?'

It was Ayesha who answered.

'We're not sure, but the talismans always seem to find their way to people who are unhappy,' she said. 'I suppose I'm just too normal.'

They were all looking at her now and Isabel realised to her horror that they wanted to know if she was unhappy and why.

Fortunately, the bell rang for afternoon classes and she was able to escape.

Fabrizio di Chimici, Grand Duke of Tuschia and Duke of Giglia, was pacing the grand salon of his palace with his little son, Falco, in his arms. It was his habit to talk aloud to the baby as he walked, which both child and father seemed to find soothing.

'When you are Grand Duke, little one,' he said, 'you will rule more than Tuschia. Who knows what your title will be by then? Our family will rule over all Talia and you will be its head. Perhaps it will happen in my lifetime but, if not, certainly in yours.'

The baby gurgled appreciatively.

'And you will be the handsomest, richest, cleverest and most gifted baby – I mean ruler – the family has ever known,' said the besotted father, stroking the boy's cheek. 'You will be a patron of the arts and your many palaces and villas will be filled with paintings and sculptures of the first order.'

The child hiccuped and looked at his father gravely.

'And you will be commander of a great army,' added Fabrizio. 'With a plumed hat and a sharp sword and a ceremonial uniform covered with silver braid and medals commemorating your great victories.'

A swishing of skirts alerted Fabrizio to the arrival of his Grand Duchess.

'Let him be a little boy first,' she said, smiling, holding out her arms for the baby. Fabrizio handed him over self-consciously. 'He's too small even to have a hobby horse yet and you would have him heading armies and winning battles.'

The Grand Duke looked on indulgently as his pretty wife crooned to their baby and nibbled his plump little fingers till he crowed with delight.

'I know I am nothing but a foolish father,' he said. 'And I have many battles of my own to fight yet. But I do want him to have all Talia for his inheritance.'

Caterina was silent; she knew how important it was for Fabrizio to avenge his father, as he saw it, by extending the di Chimici influence till there were no independent city-states left in the peninsula. She did not feel the same way and would have been content to know that her brother and cousins ruled in half the cities. But she had learned in the short time she had been married – less than a year – not to contradict her husband on this issue, which had become an obsession with him.

'You do understand, don't you, Rina?' he said, kneeling beside her as she sat on a brocade chair with their darling infant in her lap.

She turned her blue gaze from her baby to her handsome husband and felt again how lucky she was to have them both. They mattered more to her than the grandest palace and richest jewels.

'Of course I do,' she said, stroking Fabrizio's hair. 'But I'm not so sure about his being a soldier. I couldn't bear him to go into battle and be wounded.'

The mood changed and Fabrizio laughed like the young man he was.

'Listen to us both talking of battles and swords when our little angel hasn't even got any teeth yet! Forgive me, my darling, but I love him so much and I can't help thinking of how father loved his namesake, my brother Falco, and how he was snatched from us.'

'I think of that too, Rizio,' said the Grand Duchess. 'And I worry that giving him the names of his two dead uncles and his dead grandfather will be an ill omen for him.'

'Then let us call him by another name,' said Fabrizio. 'In the family let him be known as – what shall it be? – Vittorio, in honour of his future victories?'

'Nothing so warlike,' said Caterina. 'I call him Bino sometimes, you know.'

'Bino?'

'Short for bambino, because he's my baby.'

'Well, you can't call a Grand Duke and a warrior Bino, my love.'

'I know,' said Caterina. 'That's why I like it.'

And from that day Prince Falco Niccolò Carlo di Chimici, the future Duke of Giglia, Grand Duke of Tuschia and head of the greatest house in Talia, was known to all his family and friends simply as 'Bino'.

The day after Isabel's encounter with the group of Stravaganti, a Saturday, she went round to Nick's house to meet them again. 'He's got the biggest place,' Georgia had said, and that was the end of it.

Isabel's mother was delighted that she had made some new friends and even Charlie was impressed.

'Nick Duke?' he said at breakfast. 'The fencing dude?'

'Yes,' said Isabel. 'But it's Georgia I know really.

And Matt – he's Yesh's boyfriend.'

'I know,' said Charlie. 'You're a bit of a dark horse. Those guys are all pretty cool.'

I can know cool people, thought Isabel. But she just nodded and carried on munching her cornflakes.

It was so cold that it felt as if it should be snowing. Isabel hunched further into her jacket and shoved her hands deep into her pockets, wishing she had brought gloves. She hadn't 'stravagated', as she was learning to think of it, the night before. She wanted to find out a bit more about it. The more she thought about going to Talia, the more it seemed like a sort of extreme sport you ought to go into training for.

Nick's house was tall and thin and he lived in it with just his parents. His father was out and his mother, Vicky, was teaching violin in one of the ground-floor rooms.

'We're up at the top,' he told Isabel, leading the way up the stairs. 'That way we won't have to listen to that kid murdering the violin.'

There was a living room running the length of the attic, which seemed to be for Nick's exclusive use. The others were all there, lounging on beanbags and drinking coffee. Again Isabel felt a pleasurable tingle as they looked up at her with intense interest.

'Hi, Isabel,' said Georgia. She seemed to have appointed herself spokesperson for the group. 'Do we call you Izzy?'

'It's Bel usually,' she said, peeling off her thick jacket and accepting a mug of coffee. She sat on a sort of squashy cube and warmed her hands on the mug. She was waiting to hear what they were going to say and didn't volunteer anything.

'Does anyone else know what you told us?' asked Nick.

'No,' said Isabel. 'No one else would believe it.'

'You're right there,' said Matt. 'We've all stravagated – apart from Yesh – and she knows it's true. But anyone else would think it was just mad.'

Isabel had been wondering how come Ayesha had known all about this weird time travel and never said anything. Her friend saw her expression.

'I'm sorry I couldn't tell you about it,' said Ayesha. 'Matt and the others swore me to secrecy.'

'So it's sort of like a secret society, is it?' asked Isabel, suddenly feeling perhaps this wasn't such a great idea after all. Suppose it was some sort of cult? Then she looked round at the group. There was nothing sinister about any of them.

Ayesha had been her friend all through secondary school and Isabel had known Matt as long as he had been seeing Ayesha. Sky was just a big heap of gorgeousness that Isabel had fancied ever since she had laid eyes on him. But he had never seemed to have any time for girls until he started going out with Alice. But that wasn't spooky – just a pain.

Georgia and Nick were another matter. Georgia was Alice's best friend and up till now had always seemed to Isabel to be a hostile presence in school. She used to have an eyebrow ring but now sported a tattoo and multicoloured hair. Nick was two years her junior and yet they were an item and had been for some time. Still, he did look older than his age and he was pretty good-looking.

There was some mystery about Nick, though Isabel couldn't remember what exactly. He had been an asylum seeker or something. So how come he now had parents in Islington?

'I thought that Matt had got caught up in some kind of cult last term,' said Ayesha quietly. 'When some weird stuff happened with Jago. But it's nothing like that.'

'It's just that more and more of us seem to be being chosen from Barnsbury,' said Georgia. 'We've become a – well, I don't know what you'd call it. They always say "Brotherhood" in Talia but that seems a bit sexist because there are women Stravaganti there too.'

'Like Flavia,' said Isabel. 'But I'm nothing like her and she is nothing like any of you. What makes us all Stravaganti?'

'None of us know that,' said Sky. 'We just know we are somehow needed in Talia, even if what we do there seems to be a small thing. In my case it was a single word that saved Luciano, but Matt rescued him and a bunch of other people too – oh, and put out a city that was on fire.'

Isabel focused on the one bit that seemed to make sense.

'Who is this Luciano that you all keep going on about?'

She couldn't miss the ripple of tension that ran through the group.

'He used to live here,' said Nick slowly. 'In this house. He was my parents' real son.'

'And then he died,' said Georgia quite harshly. She seemed to want to get this explanation over. 'We told you. Luciano used to be Lucien Mulholland, whose mum is downstairs teaching the violin. And Nick was . . .'

'Prince Falco di Chimici,' said Nick, getting up and making a bow. 'From Talia over four hundred years ago. And then I died and came to live here.'

It all clicked into place in Isabel's mind. She hadn't known Lucien but she remembered that he had died. And this was his house! Cult or not, she had got herself mixed up with something very weird indeed.

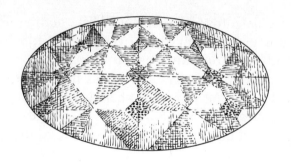

Chapter 4

Luciano and Arianna

Luciano had no idea he was being talked about four centuries in the future and in a parallel world. He was practising with Cesare in the School of Fencing in Padavia and they were both sweating profusely.

'Phew!' said Cesare, taking off his mask and shaking his damp brown hair. 'Isn't that enough for today?'

Luciano was better at this than he was and Cesare always felt at a disadvantage fencing with him. It was different in the School of Riding, where he had the upper hand.

Their tutor nodded and they put away their foils.

They walked back to Luciano's house, still breathing heavily.

'It's at times like this that I could really do with a

twenty-first-century shower,' said Luciano.

Cesare looked puzzled.

'You mean you'd like it to rain?' he asked.

Luciano threw back his head and laughed, shaking his black curls.

'No, though that might improve our scent a little. I mean hot water pouring out of a sort of nozzle above your head and standing under it with soap and shampoo and getting yourself clean and fresh after exercise.'

'Can you really do that in the other world?' asked his friend, his eyes round with wonder.

'Yes,' said Luciano. 'And even people with not much money can afford to have them in their houses. But it's no good thinking about it. I'm here for good, and showers won't be invented for hundreds of years.'

'Couldn't you invent one yourself, seeing as you know how they work?'

'No. Even if I could actually do it – which I doubt I could, since I'm not a plumber or engineer – Rodolfo wouldn't let me.'

'Why not?'

'Oh, you know what he's like. It's all about not disturbing history. Talia will get around to showers in its own sweet time. Meanwhile, we have to put up with smelling like foxes.'

'Well, we could go for a swim in the swamp,' said Cesare, grinning. 'Since you were kind enough to put it back. But I don't think it would be an improvement.'

'No,' agreed Luciano. 'I'll get Alfredo to heat us some water. We don't want to end up like Enrico.'

They were both thinking of the violent events the

previous autumn when they had rescued thirty Manoush from death by burning and Padavia caught fire. Luciano and the other Stravaganti had put the flames out by a spectacular piece of what Rodolfo called 'science' and Luciano considered magic. They had lifted the swamp from the south of the city and laid it over the fire, snuffing it out like a candle.

Enrico, the malodorous spy, had been surprisingly useful to them at that time and he was still in the city. He seemed genuinely to have transferred his allegiance from his old masters, the di Chimici, to Luciano and the Stravaganti.

In fact, he was hanging around in Alfredo's kitchen when Luciano and Cesare arrived back from their fencing. The boys exchanged guilty looks; it was true they didn't want to end up like him.

'Greetings, masters both,' he said, sweeping off his tattered blue hat. 'I bring news.'

'Oh yes?' said Luciano. 'What's that, then? Alfredo, could you heat water so we can have a wash?'

Enrico tapped the side of his nose. 'You know better than to ask so baldly,' he said. 'How about some refreshment and reward first?'

'Refreshment, yes,' said Luciano. 'Alfredo can bring us all some ale. Perhaps you'd like to talk to us while we wash? You could join us.'

Enrico looked horrified. 'Why would I want to do that? But I'll drink ale with you and welcome. And perhaps have a bite to eat?'

So shortly afterwards Luciano and Cesare were stripped to the waist and washing while Enrico lounged with a mug of ale and a plate of bread and meat, watching them.

He shook his head, uncomprehending. He would never understand the nobility and their passion for soap and water. In his view these items simply sapped a person's strength. But he kept a safe distance, remembering how these two boys had once put him under a pump and forced him to wash.

'Do you want to know my news?' he asked.

Luciano and Cesare, wrapped in towels, came and drank with him, shaking drops of water from their hair.

'Well?' said Luciano, drinking deep.

'It's about your lady,' said Enrico.

Luciano was suddenly much more alert but he kept his voice level.

'That's Her Grace, to you, Enrico. Mind your manners.'

'Sorry, master. Her Grace, the Duchessa of Bellezza, is in Classe.'

'Classe?' said Luciano. 'Whatever for? No, don't tap your nose like that – it's very annoying. You have information and I have money. Don't beat about the bush when it comes to Arianna. Tell me what's going on or we'll have you under the pump again.'

Enrico sighed. People who were in love were no fun. They took themselves too seriously and forgot all the rules of the spying game. It hurt him to come straight out with information like this, that had taken him time and care and bribes to acquire. But he wasn't going to risk an angry cavaliere, especially one with water to hand.

'Well, it's like this, master,' he said comfortably, pouring himself some more ale. 'She's on a diplomatic mission with her dad – I mean, with Senator Rodolfo

– to see the Duke of Classe. Taken him one of her cats, she has.'

'Not Flora or Lauro?' said Luciano.

'No, one of the cubs – though he's a fair size now. Present for Duke Germano.'

'We were going to keep one of the males,' said Luciano quietly to Cesare. 'I wish she'd told me.'

'Oh, it's not your one,' said Enrico hastily. 'It's the smaller male. Anyway, don't you want to know what she's – I'm mean, what Her Grace – is doing in the City of Ships?'

Of course Luciano was burning to know. It irked him that the smelly little spy knew something about Arianna that he didn't. Why hadn't she told him she was going on a diplomatic visit? He hadn't seen her for ages.

'There's a rumour,' said Enrico, 'that the Gate people are preparing for an attack on Bellezza. Or maybe Classe. I think the Regent is hoping to combine forces with the painted city.'

Now Luciano was really alarmed.

'An attack on Bellezza?' he said. 'Then why am I wasting my time here in Padavia? I'm her Cavaliere as well as her fiancé. I should be there looking after her.'

Isabel went to bed early that night, clutching the red velvet bag and trying hard to think of the Classe Baptistery without imagining the bath in the middle. This was really difficult, like being told, 'Don't think of a dog,' which of course immediately produces doggy images galore. So Isabel concentrated on the mosaics she remembered from inside the dome.

There was a baptism of Jesus she recalled; she remembered wondering at how the shimmering water up to his waist could have been made with tiny squares like those in her bag. But then, did they have Jesus in Talia? She hadn't asked the others about things like that. There had been too much else to discuss.

'You'll be tired all the time,' Georgia had said, and the others had agreed. Everyone except Nick had experienced the exhaustion of travelling to Talia by night and then having to live a full day back in their own world.

'It's day there when it's night here,' Sky had told her. She hadn't thought about that before, the first time she ended up in Talia, but it was true.

'So it's like living each day twice over,' Matt had told her. He was the most recent Stravagante to make the journey. Isabel gathered that he hadn't been back since New Year, but he could, any time he wanted, as he still had his talisman. The others had decided against going back, even though they had talismans, but Isabel didn't understand why. Still, she knew there were some tensions about it in the group.

She was just wondering about what they were when her eyes closed and . . .

. . . when she opened them, she was in the Baptistery. Not, thank goodness, soaking wet this time but that was not because she had avoided the bath. She was sitting in the middle of it, as before; only this time it was empty. It must have been bad luck the last time – just after someone had been baptised and before the bath had been drained. She could see the plughole in the middle and the way the marble sloped down to it.

As Isabel climbed out over the edge she realised she was back in the old-fashioned green dress. A quick inspection showed she had her pyjamas on underneath. She opened the wooden door quietly and saw the cobbled street outside washed in winter sunshine. It was a bit warmer in Classe than in Islington – even in February.

Cautiously she stepped out into the street. Flavia had taught her the way to her house last time and Isabel slipped quickly through the streets, very conscious of the fact that she didn't have a shadow. She was careful not to make eye contact with any of the people she met on the way, anxious not to draw attention to herself – nothing new there. She was relieved when she reached the merchant's house, but didn't know whether to knock or just open the door as Flavia had before. Then she noticed a long iron bar hanging vertically beside it.

Isabel pulled and a loud jangling reverberated through the house. Immediately the man she had taken for a guard before opened the door and peered out. He seemed to recognise her because he just nodded and opened the door wider.

'Wait here,' he said, and went off into the corridor towards Flavia's parlour.

Isabel loitered in the hall, examining the mosaic pattern on its floor, which hadn't registered last time. It was an elaborate and colourful carpet of stone tesserae in geometric patterns of mainly cream, turquoise and black, with some red and green detail. Only it wasn't old, like the ones in the Baptistery; it was as if it had been laid only a year or two before.

'I see you're admiring Fausto's work,' said Flavia, coming forward to greet her. 'He designed it specially for me.'

'You still make mosaics in the city?' asked Isabel.

'Oh yes,' said Flavia. 'There are many mosaicists working here – but my friend Fausto is the best. Now, come with me. You must change your dress. We have some important visiting to do.'

Alice in Wonderland, thought Isabel. *That's what it reminds me of. No one asks you what you'd like to do or how you are. You just get told what to do and where to go. I'm surprised the footman wasn't a fish.*

But she didn't really mind, because this was *her* adventure. OK, so some other students had done something similar but no one else had been to Classe and, most importantly, Charlie had not been found by a talisman and sent to Talia. This was the first special thing she had been chosen for on her own.

*

Arianna was down in Duke Germano's stables feeding titbits to Vitale, the spotted cat. He licked her fingers, looking for more.

'No more now, you greedy thing,' said Arianna, caressing his whiskery face. 'You'll get fat. How cross Mariotto would be to see me giving you treats when you haven't even been for a run. But he had to stay behind and look after the rest of your family. I hope you don't miss them, my handsome boy, but you are going to be very happy here, I know.'

A rustle in the straw made her turn round quickly and there was the Duke himself with a cloth package in his hand that Vitale clearly thought smelled promising. The cat turned his attention to his new master and Germano looked a bit guilty as he unwrapped his kitchen morsels.

'I wondered if he might be feeling lonely,' he told Arianna. 'But I see you had already thought of that.'

'I can see he is going to be in good hands here,' said the young Duchessa.

'He is a magnificent beast,' said Germano, stroking Vitale's head. 'Quite the nicest present you could have brought me. I was wondering about having his portrait done in mosaic on the wall of the little building I'm having cleaned and whitewashed for him. We have an excellent master of the art in the city.'

'Hear that, Vitale?' said Arianna. 'Your own house with your own picture on the wall. I doubt any other member of your family will be so honoured.'

'What are you doing with the others?' asked the Duke.

'Well, I'm keeping his brother,' said Arianna. 'And I have given one of the females to my personal maid, Barbara. She married one of my footmen just before Christmas.'

'That is a rich gift for a servant,' said Germano.

'But she is no ordinary servant,' said Arianna. 'She saved my life in Giglia on the day of the Nucci massacre.'

'We heard about that,' said Germano. 'But I thought they were trying to kill di Chimici. Do they have something against Bellezza too? You must tell me if that is the case, for the parents and their remaining children live here in Classe under my protection. Matteo Nucci is an old friend of mine.'

'I know, Your Grace,' said Arianna, touching his arm. 'I'm sorry. I make no accusation against Matteo Nucci or his family. I don't know if the man who stabbed my maid was a Nucci or a di Chimici. In the chaos and bloodshed it could have been a random attack. But Barbara was pretending to be me so I think I was the target.'

'Wasn't the attacker questioned?'

'I killed him,' said Arianna simply. 'I've never known who he was. I couldn't have identified him among the pile of bodies in the orphanage after the massacre.'

'You are very young to have experienced such things, my dear,' said the Duke.

'But the di Chimici have attacked my family before,' said Arianna. 'So it could have been one of them taking advantage of the Nucci conspiracy.'

'And now they might attack you again, through the Gate people,' said Germano.

A dark figure stooped through the stable door and Germano's hand flew to his belt. But there was no need for a dagger.

'It's all right,' said Arianna, laughing. 'It's my father. And I can guess what he's doing here.'

'Arianna?' called Rodolfo. 'And is that you, Your Grace? You have visitors, another of my calling.'

'What is that you have in your hand, Father?' asked Arianna.

'Oh, nothing,' said Rodolfo, trying to hide the bone he was holding behind his back. But Vitale gave him away, straining the length of his leash and snuffling at the Senator's clothes. 'Well, all right. I called in at the kitchen on my way. I knew you might be here and I thought you might be giving him unsuitable sweetmeats. He should be sharpening his teeth on something harder.'

He gave the bone to the big cat and, watching the way that Arianna was looking at her father, Germano hoped his own daughters were as fond of him as she was of the Regent.

They went back into the Ducal Palace and Arianna hurried to wash and change to meet the woman Rodolfo told her was another Stravagante. But when she entered the Duke's smaller reception room, hastily smoothing her silk skirt, she saw two people waiting to be presented to her.

From Isabel's point of view, a young woman as stunning as a film star had just entered the room. She was wearing a sort of lilac dress, quite simple but obviously expensive, and, surprisingly, a silver mask, so that only part of her face was visible. But she was slender and elegant and had abundant dark reddish-brown hair. More than that, she was surrounded by an aura of confidence and command, even when a little hurried as she seemed now.

Isabel thought she could never in a million years enter a room the way Arianna just had. Arianna! So this was the famous Duchessa, who was engaged to the Barnsbury student who had died in his real world. It seemed all too fantastic to be true.

'Ah, Your Grace,' said Duke Germano. 'Allow me to present a very valued member of our trading community, Signora Flavia. And her friend, Signorina Isabella.'

Arianna made a deep and graceful curtsey to them both.

'And now, if you will excuse me,' said the Duke, 'I know that you and your father have private matters to discuss with Signora Flavia. I shall have refreshments brought to you and leave you to talk in peace.'

'My dear,' said Rodolfo, 'Flavia I have told you about before. As you know, she is one of our Brotherhood. But Isabella is an unexpected bonus. She is a new Stravagante from Luciano's world.'

'Oh, you know Luciano!' said Arianna, turning a hundred-gigawatt smile on Isabel.

'Not really, Your . . . um . . . Grace,' said Isabel.

'Oh, please call me Arianna when there is no one by,' said the Duchessa, suddenly seeming much closer to Isabel in age. (Indeed she was only a year older.) 'Do you know Georgia and Tino and Matteo?'

'I know Georgia and Matt,' said Isabel. 'But no one called Tino.'

'He was called Sky in Isabella's world,' said Rodolfo.

Now it was Arianna's turn to see how Isabel's face changed when Sky was mentioned.

'Is he your boyfriend?' she asked. 'But I thought there was another girl. What was it? Aleechay.'

'We say Alice,' said Isabel. 'And I'm afraid she's still around. Sky doesn't really notice me.'

Why am I telling this stranger such a private thing? she thought. *It must be because this is another world.*

'I'm so glad to meet another girl from Luciano's world,' said Arianna. 'Especially one who "doesn't really know him". It was a bit hard to be friends with Georgia, though we were all right by the end.'

She had a twinkle in her eyes, which Isabel noticed were an unusual violet colour, like a darker version of her dress. Isabel felt Arianna would be so wonderful to have as a friend that it would be worth coming to Talia just for that. But she filed away for future attention the fact that Georgia seemed to have been the Duchessa's rival at one time.

'And if you know Georgia, you must also know . . . what is he called there? . . . Nicholas Duke?'

'Yes, he and Georgia are pretty full on,' said Isabel.

'Full on?' asked Arianna. 'I don't know what that means exactly but I like the sound of it. Are they engaged?'

'No,' said Isabel. 'Nick's only sixteen.'

Arianna shrugged. 'That would not be a barrier here. But I think we live our lives a bit faster than you do in the future. I am happy for Falco and so would his brother be. I wonder if I can get a message to Gaetano.'

Rodolfo had been talking quietly to Flavia while the young women got to know each other, but now he came to join them. He looked at Isabella with such a penetrating gaze from under his bushy eyebrows that she shrank further into the stiff brocade dress Flavia had lent her.

'Welcome,' he said at last, relaxing into a smile that transformed his stern face. Then he did the strangest thing. He put a hand on her arm and said, 'I sense a second person. Did you come on your own?'

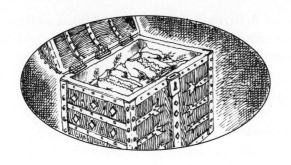

Chapter 5

Exiles

William Dethridge was in his new laboratory in his wife's house in Bellezza. He was still working on the difficult question of why talismans brought Stravaganti from the other world only to the city that the talismans came from. It would be so much more useful to the Brotherhood if their allies could arrive in whatever city they chose. Because they had to stravagate back home by nightfall, it was a real limitation that they could travel only to cities that were less than half a day's journey away.

He thought about what his foster-son, Luciano, had told him about twenty-first-century travel and sighed. It was no good wishing for metal flying-machines in Talia, when the only forms of transport were horses, sailing ships or feet. And even horses weren't an option in Bellezza, where they had been banned; that was a hardship to the old alchemist, who loved the beasts and was a fine horseman.

As if he had been conjured up by Dethridge's thoughts, Luciano burst into the laboratory.

'Sonne!' the old man cried. 'Whatte make ye here? Is some thinge amiss in Padavia?'

'No,' said Luciano, embracing his foster-father warmly. 'It is here that something is wrong – or so I am told. Enrico tells me that Bellezza faces a naval attack so I thought I should be here.'

Dethridge shook his head.

'Ah, ye are soo hotte in the hede all ways! There is no daungere yet. And Arianne and Rudolphe are in Classe.'

'I know,' said Luciano. 'Enrico told me. But aren't they coming back soon?'

'Nay, ladde, I thinke notte,' said Dethridge.

'Then I must go to them,' said Luciano. 'My horse is on the mainland – it won't take long to get to Classe.'

'Woll ye haste away so quick as ye came?' said Dethridge. 'Leonora woll notte be pleased with me if I lette ye goe.'

Luciano sighed. He had hoped that Arianna and Rodolfo would be back soon after he got to Bellezza. But now that he was here, he couldn't really leave again immediately without giving his foster-parents some time. He knew they missed him while he was away at university.

'I'll stay for one night,' he said. 'And then I really must go to Classe. I'm skiving off my lectures to be here.'

'Welle thenne,' said Dethridge. 'Lette us goe and finde Leonora and shee woll make grete plannes for dinner, I trow.'

'In a minute,' said Luciano, smiling. He was very fond of both his new parents, even though they were so different from the real ones he had left behind in his old world when he became stranded in Talia two and a half years earlier.

'What are you working on?' he asked, looking at the parchment on Dethridge's desk. It was covered in strange squiggles and symbols, some like signs of the zodiac, others unfamiliar.

'Yt is thee olde conundrum,' said Dethridge. 'How we Stravaygers mighte travell with ease between cities in Talie.'

'And how are you getting on?'

'Well, sonne, verray well,' said Dethridge. 'I thynke we woll attayne whatte we wish in the end.'

Luciano looked round the laboratory, which was different from Rodolfo's. It was fantastically untidy and he never knew how Dethridge could find anything in it.

'Is it like your old laboratory in England?' he asked.

'Some whatte,' said Dethridge. 'Yt is straunge to thynke thatte my old laboratorie is under your schole.'

'Not my school any more,' said Luciano ruefully. 'That's now the School of Rhetoric in Padavia and I suspect I'm going to be in trouble for skipping lectures when I do get back.'

He walked over to an elaborate arrangement of mirrors on the back wall.

'Can I get in touch with Rodolfo?' he asked. 'I should let them know I'm coming to Classe.'

The Nucci family were in Classe, slowly recovering from their losses. Like many bankers, Matteo Nucci had sent a large quantity of his wealth away from his native city and after his banishment from Giglia had found comfortable sanctuary in the City of Ships.

The loss of his great palace in Giglia would have irked him but he had experienced injuries worse than that. First his youngest son Davide had been killed by Carlo di Chimici and then, when his oldest boy, Camillo, had attempted to take revenge, Fabrizio di Chimici had slit his throat.

Now the only son he had left was Filippo, himself badly injured in the massacre at the Church of the Annunciation. But there were two girls too and his grief-stricken wife, Graziella, to think of. Matteo had put his shoulder to the wheel and set about rebuilding the family's fortunes.

They lived in a fair-sized house on the Piazza del Foro, which put them right in the thick of the trading heart of Classe, just where Matteo wanted to be. It was less than a year since the murder of Davide and the death of Camillo that followed a month later and Graziella Nucci and her daughters were still in black.

Graziella tried to think of the future but she couldn't see beyond the next day. She ordered food for the family, which sometimes remained uneaten. She bought rich material from Flavia in the market and commissioned seamstresses to make curtains and cushions for the house, but when they were in place she looked at them as if she couldn't remember choosing those patterns and colours.

Her greatest solace lay in looking after Filippo. He had recovered from his wounds but would always walk with one leg stiff and he had a scar that ran from his temple to his chin. Each time Graziella looked at it, she thought of how the wicked blade had missed his eye and his handsome mouth and shuddered.

'Di Chimici!' she would spit when she thought of the family that had driven hers from Giglia.

But Filippo was happy in Classe. He had never shared his older brother's hatred of the di Chimici and had fond memories of playing with the young princes and the little princess in their old palazzo on the Via Larga. Of the massacre in the church he remembered nothing. He did have vivid recall of the night his younger brother Davide was stabbed in the street and then nothing except a long period of pain before waking up one morning in Classe and hearing the gulls in the harbour.

Sometimes he had nightmares in which he cried out and said, incomprehensibly to his mother, that he was drinking silver. And sometimes he had more pleasant dreams, in which the little di Chimici princess smoothed his hair and murmured soft songs to him. But in those dreams they were both still children and the terror and fury of sharp blades was far in the future.

'I am going for a walk, Mother,' he said, a day or so after Arianna had arrived in Classe.

'A walk?' fussed Graziella. 'Wait till I get my cloak and I'll come with you.'

'No, don't trouble yourself,' said Filippo. 'I have my

stick and I'd like to get some fresh air on my own. I shan't be long.'

He waved his ebony cane at his mother, who bit her lip but smiled encouragingly at him. 'Go then and be careful. The cobbles are so very irregular.'

Filippo stepped out briskly and made an effort not to limp too obviously until he was out of sight of his house's windows and his mother's anxious gaze. Then he slowed down and walked stiffly down to the harbour.

He loved this city and felt more at home here than he ever had in Giglia. The City of Flowers was full of artistic wonders, it was true, but then Classe had its mosaics and Filippo was fascinated by them. What he really liked about his new home was that things were made and traded, bought and sold there in the open market or down here at the harbour. People caught fish and sold them the same day so that other people could cook and eat them in the evening. Traders imported silks and spices and precious jewels and other merchants came to buy them. It was all much more real and visible than lending money to foreign princes and getting it back with interest.

Filippo was proud that his father's family had made their money from rearing sheep and selling wool but, as the generations had gone by, the Nucci, like the di Chimici, had turned to banking for their wealth. He felt a little guilty about that; still, he couldn't expect his father to go back to breeding sheep in the city that had offered him sanctuary.

Filippo was tired and sat down on an empty fish barrel, not caring what it would do to his velvet breeches. He looked out further along to the deep-water mooring at what was his other favourite thing about Classe: its numerous and well-equipped warships. He wanted to travel on the sea in one of those galleys but realised that Admiral Borca of the Classe fleet would be unlikely to accept a maimed sailor. So for now, all he could do was look.

*

Isabel found Rodolfo quite terrifying. To his question about there being 'another' she did not know what to reply.

'I have a twin, sir,' she stammered eventually. 'But he is not with me.' And she hoped that he had meant Charlie and not by some sinister magic known about Charlotte.

'He has not been chosen,' said Rodolfo, smiling now. Isabel saw that he could be someone she would like but only if they were both on the same side. And she liked the idea of being chosen for something when Charlie hadn't. If only she knew what it was!

'I'm so glad you are here,' said Arianna again. 'We have a serious problem. That's why we're in Classe.'

'What sort of problem?' said Isabel, realising that she really did want to help these extraordinary people. 'I'll do what I can. But I honestly don't know what that is.'

'In Bellezza we face aggression from the sea,' said Rodolfo. 'From old enemies in the east. But now we think they are acting in cooperation with the di Chimici. Do you know about them?'

'I know that Nick was one of them,' said Isabel. 'Is he an enemy?'

'No,' said Arianna firmly. 'Some of that family are our friends, especially Falco's brother, Gaetano, and his wife Francesca. So would Falco have been, if he had not chosen to leave us. He was very attached to Luciano.'

'But the Grand Duke, Fabrizio, has an arrest warrant out for Luciano because he killed the late Grand Duke Niccolò in a duel,' said Rodolfo.

'Isn't that sort of OK?' asked Isabel. 'I mean killing someone in a duel is not the same as murder, is it?'

'Exactly!' said Arianna. 'And Niccolò was cheating anyway. He probably wouldn't have died if he hadn't put poison on one of the foils. It would have been Luciano's lifeless body on the terrace of the Nucci palace.'

She paced up and down the room and Isabel could see how devoted she was to this mysterious boy who had once been a pupil at Barnsbury Comp.

Rodolfo suddenly looked distracted.

'Speaking of Luciano,' he said, 'I think he is trying to get in touch with me.'

He picked up a hand mirror that was lying on an occasional table in Duke Germano's salon and peered into it intently.

Then he was smiling and nodding.

'Is it him?' asked Arianna, just as if Rodolfo had a phone call. 'Can I see him? Please give me the mirror.'

Rodolfo handed it over and raised one eyebrow at Isabel.

'Oh, he's not in Padavia,' said Arianna. 'It looks like Dottore Crinamorte's laboratory. What is he doing in Bellezza?'

'Concentrate, my dear,' said Rodolfo, 'and you might find out.'

Arianna frowned and then blushed and then nearly dropped the mirror.

'He says he's coming here!' she said joyfully. 'How wonderful!'

Rodolfo took the mirror from her and after a moment called Isabel over to look into it.

'I've told him you are here,' he said, though Isabel knew he had been silent. 'He'd like to see you.'

Isabel peered cautiously into the glass. What she saw was a richly dressed young man, no more than a teenager but wearing elegant clothes, smiling back at her. He had long curly black hair pulled back into a ponytail and looked a bit like an eighties glam rocker.

And yet, there was something familiar about him. He *could* have been that Lucien Mulholland who played violin in the school orchestra and who – as they had been solemnly told in assembly one day long ago – had died of cancer.

'Um, hello,' she said, 'I'm Isabel.'

'He can't hear you,' said Arianna. 'You have to concentrate really hard and you might hear him think-speak.'

Isabel concentrated and found she could sense his words: *Welcome to Talia. I hope I'll see you in Classe. I'm coming tomorrow.*

Then I shall stravagate again, Isabel thought. *I'd like to meet you. Perhaps you can tell me how I'm supposed to stop a naval invasion when I can't even swim?*

The face in the mirror laughed and held up his hands, palms out.

You wouldn't believe the things I've had to do! And I was just a Barnsbury student like you. You'll be fine.

And then Arianna took the mirror back and Isabel looked away to give them some privacy. She was a bit shaken by how dashing and gorgeous this ex-Barnsbury-sixth-former seemed now he lived in Talia.

*

On an impulse, Filippo Nucci levered himself stiffly from his barrel and walked slowly not back home but to Duke Germano's palace. Germano had been a good friend to their family and Filippo was hoping that he could do something even more for him.

When he arrived, he was shown into the Duke's salon, but after exchanging pleasantries, Germano asked if he'd like to meet the visitors from Bellezza.

Filippo was intrigued. He had seen the Duchessa and her formidable father only at a distance and, since he couldn't remember the di Chimici weddings, had only the haziest idea about them. So he agreed readily enough. If he had known or remembered about the attempt on the Duchessa's life during the massacre, he might have been less enthusiastic about meeting her.

Arianna was looking especially beautiful, flushed and happy at the prospect of seeing Luciano the next day, when Duke Germano ushered in a thin young man with a cane.

'Ah, Your Grace,' said Germano. 'I wanted you to meet Signor Filippo Nucci. We were talking about his family earlier. Filippo, may I present the Duchessa of Bellezza and her father the Regent, Senator Rodolfo Rossi?'

Filippo made the best bow he could manage. Isabel couldn't help staring at the long scar on his face, so at odds with his gentle bearing.

Any grudge Arianna and Rodolfo might have borne this young man for his part in the Nucci plot and massacre would have been dispelled by the sight of his injuries. And after a few minutes of conversation it became clear that he had no recollection of the horrors of that day.

'And this is Signora Flavia and her friend Signorina Isabella,' added the Duke.

'I think my mother knows you, Signora,' said Filippo. 'She often mentions the fine cloth you sell.'

'Well, I am overwhelmed with visits today,' said Germano, beaming. 'Will you stay to eat with us? Anna would be glad to see you all.'

'Thank you, you are most kind,' said Filippo, 'but I'm afraid my mother will have a search party out for me if I don't return soon. She . . . she is very solicitous about my health.'

'I am sorry to see you so hurt,' said Arianna quietly.

'That is kind. But I am so much better than I was,' said Filippo,

'We must go too,' said Flavia. 'We could walk with you, Signor Filippo.'

'Well, do remember to bring Isabella back tomorrow,' said Arianna significantly. 'When we have our other visitor.'

Filippo Nucci made a great show of offering his arm to Flavia but Isabel could see that by the time they had crossed the square he was leaning on the merchant for support rather than the other way round. They left him at the Nucci palazzo and went into Flavia's house.

'I wonder what that young man wanted from Germano,' said Flavia thoughtfully.

'I don't know,' said Isabel. 'But he seemed nice in spite of his poor face. I liked him.'

*

Fabrizio di Chimici was so enchanted with his son that he often rushed home in the middle of the day to see him, leaving the cares of State behind and running lightly through the special corridor that led from the Palazzo Ducale to the Nucci palace on the south side of the River Argento.

It was a very grand building and it was with great satisfaction that Grand Duke Niccolò had confiscated it from the rival family after the massacre. It couldn't bring back Carlo but it could inflict more pain on the insolent upstarts who had dared to compete with the Duke's pre-eminence in the city.

'Where is Bino?' Fabrizio asked his sister Beatrice, when he arrived out of breath in the nursery on one such day.

Beatrice was folding baby clothes and laying sprigs of lavender and rosemary between them, as she put them in a chest at the foot of the ornate ducal cradle.

'You have just missed them,' she said. 'Caterina has taken him out in the grounds in that little cart Gabassi made for him.'

'But is it not too cold?'

'He was as well wrapped up as a little tsarevich,' said Beatrice. 'You need not fear.'

Fabrizio looked at her, standing with the lacy little

garments in her arms, and felt a rush of fondness for her.

'He is a sweet baby, isn't he, sister?' he said, sitting in the low nursing chair. 'Wouldn't you like one for yourself?'

Beatrice immediately became flustered.

'I mean,' said Fabrizio, 'that it is time you were married yourself. You don't mean not to marry, I suppose?'

'I don't mean anything,' said Beatrice meekly. 'It is less than a year since Father and Carlo died. How could I think of marrying?' She gestured at her black satin gown.

'I don't intend you to do anything straight away or before it is fitting,' said Fabrizio, 'but just to turn your mind to the subject. What about our cousin Filippo? He will have Bellona before long and he is Francesca's brother. It would keep you in the family twice over.'

'Do I need keeping in the family, Fabrizio?'

'Well, there's no one else more suitable, is there?' asked Fabrizio. 'I mean, Ferrando's too old and Rinaldo's a cardinal. Who else is there?'

'I don't know,' said Beatrice bleakly. It was obviously out of the question in her brother's mind that she should find a husband outside the di Chimici family. She felt suddenly weary; maybe she should enter a convent instead.

'And Filippo's a good sort,' said Fabrizio. 'He didn't hesitate to do as I asked in Padavia – not that it did any good. But a good fellow. You have a think about him, Bice. I should like you to have a good husband and some babies of your own. You are wonderful with little Bino.'

'Thank you, brother. He is easy to love.'

'And so will Filippo be, you'll see.'

The Grand Duke got up and planted a kiss on her forehead. He had to go back to his business affairs. He hadn't managed to see his wife and baby but he was pleased with his interview with his sister. He strolled back through the corridor, humming.

Princess Beatrice flung herself into the low chair and covered her face with her hands.

'What am I to do?' she asked the empty room. 'Why can't everything just stay as it is?'

But she knew her brother better than to suppose it would.

Chapter 6

The Black Raider

Isabel had a long luxurious lie-in on Sunday. There was nothing unusual about that but there must have been something different about her because Charlie kept giving her looks.

The fact was that, now she was a new person in Talia, she was also changing in her own world. There was hardly any time to commune with Charlotte and she was also forgetting to be inconspicuous. It was only now that she realised how much effort it took not to be noticed.

The doorbell rang and her mother called up to her that she had visitors. Fortunately, she was just out of the shower and it didn't take long to fling some clothes on. It was so surprising to see Georgia and Nick in her kitchen that Isabel couldn't say anything, but her mother was chatting away to them and offering coffee and biscuits.

'Thanks, Mrs Evans,' said Georgia, 'but we were hoping to take Bel to the coffee bar. Some friends are meeting us there.'

Her mother was so obviously pleased to see Isabel making new friends it was quite embarrassing. They left as quickly as possible and went to Café@anytime, where Matt and Sky were waiting for them.

'Yesh not coming?' asked Isabel.

'No,' said Matt. 'She thought it should just be us – you know – Stravaganti.'

'And Alice doesn't want any part of it,' said Sky. 'She really hates all the Talia stuff.' He had a deep frown between his eyebrows. Could there be trouble with his love life? Isabel knew it was bad to hope so.

'Come on, then, Bel,' said Georgia. 'Tell us all about it.'

And once again her fellow students were looking at her as if she was going to give them the secret of life, the universe and everything. Isabel took her time, luxuriating in the feeling.

'So you've met Arianna but not Luciano?' said Georgia.

'He's supposed to be coming today, I mean tonight,' said Isabel. 'But I saw him in Rodolfo's mirror. He's terribly good-looking, isn't he? It's hard to believe he was once at our school.'

'You think Barnsbury students can't be good-looking?' asked Nick.

'Not in that way,' said Isabel, not looking at Sky. 'That sort of glamorous film-starry look. Are they all like that in Talia? Even Filippo was attractive, in spite of his scar.'

'Filippo di Chimici?' asked Matt, clenching his fists.

'No, Filippo Nucci,' said Isabel. 'I haven't met a di Chimici yet.'

'Huh!' said Matt. 'Wait till you see Rinaldo. You won't think all Talians are handsome then.'

'Or Enrico,' said Sky. That made Matt splutter into his cappuccino.

'Who's he?' asked Isabel. She felt she still had a lot of catching up to do.

'He's a spy and an assassin,' said Sky calmly.

'But he seems to have reformed,' said Matt. 'He certainly delivered the goods in Padavia.'

'But what's all this about the Gate people?' asked Nick. 'It sounds as if Talia is expecting rather a lot of you.'

'That's what I think,' said Isabel. 'I don't know anything about war, let alone ships and things.'

'You could read up about it here, I suppose,' said Georgia. 'I mean, on the Net or something.'

'Yes, in between working for AS exams and never having enough sleep,' said Isabel, surprising herself a bit by not just agreeing in order to be liked.

'OK, point taken,' said Georgia. 'But I had to find out about the Palio when I went to Remora.'

'And did it help?' asked Isabel.

'Not really,' admitted Georgia. 'When it comes to whatever you have to do in Talia, when it happens, you just grit your teeth and get on with it. But it might help with some of the other things that happen on the way.'

'From what I can tell, it usually seems to be about

saving this Luciano,' said Isabel. 'But I really don't know what I can do that a whole bunch of Stravaganti there can't. And why would he be involved in a naval invasion?'

'I think,' said Matt, 'that we should sort of pool resources.'

'You mean come to Talia and help me?' said Isabel hopefully.

'No, our talismans wouldn't get us to Classe,' said Georgia. 'But I think Nick's right. We could make a sort of – I don't know – dossier or something, and put in it every single thing we can remember about Talia.'

'You can't take anything from here to there,' said Sky, 'but you could study it here and it might help.'

They were excited about this idea and would have started there and then if they'd had any paper. As it was, they divided up tasks – Nick was to make a di Chimici family tree, Matt a list of Stravaganti in both worlds with all the facts he could think of about them, and Sky would draw a map of Talia and all the cities they had visited.

Isabel agreed to review her research notes on Ravenna and try to map it on to the Classe she had seen so far.

'What will you do, Georgia?' asked Sky.

'I think I'll work on stravagation itself and the talismans,' said Georgia. 'And I can draw up a list of questions for Bel to ask Luciano and Rodolfo and Flavia and any other Stravagante she comes across.'

'You'll have to memorise them,' said Sky. 'And the answers.'

Isabel realised that her new adventure had just turned into a huge subject, involving coursework, homework and four very demanding teachers. She hoped it would prove worth it.

In a tavern in the harbour at Classe sat a man being inconspicuous. This was difficult because he was a very striking figure. He was about thirty years old and only average height, but he had jet black hair to his waist and two silver teeth where his upper canines should have been. Now he had tied his hair back and was keeping his mouth closed as much as possible.

This was also difficult because normally he loved to talk. But today he was looking and listening. A hat pulled low over his brows and a dull red cloak over his black clothes completed his disguise. From the tavern window he had a good view of the entire harbour, which was organised like a smaller city in itself.

The war fleet was kept anchored in a special dock of its own at the end of the northern curve of the bay. The merchantmen lay at anchor in deep water, with smaller boats plying back and forth between them and the quays, carrying portions of cargo for delivery or sale on the spot. Then, bobbing closer to land, were all the smaller craft, the fishing boats, the pleasure ships owned by the gentry and the caravels of opportunistic sailors who would take passengers up and down the coast as far as Bellezza to the north and right down to the big island in the south – for the right fee.

Life on the quay itself was as busy and varied as life on the water. Fishermen took turns mending nets and selling their silvery cargo, bedevilled by the ever-present screaming gulls, merchants inspected goods and loaded up wagons, sightseers ambled inconveniently among them, tripping over coils of rope, and sellers of food and drink called out their wares to anyone who would buy them.

The inconspicuous man was watching a middle-aged woman in a russet dress and a young girl in a green one. This was the second time he had seen them together and what he wanted was to get the girl on her own and find out who she was; he knew the woman perfectly well.

He couldn't believe his luck when a messenger came picking his way through the detritus on the quay and engaged the older woman in earnest conversation. He had sent the messenger himself but didn't know that he would find Flavia at this moment and with her unknown new friend.

Swiftly, he left the tavern, skulking round the harbour till he was within feet of the girl, who had obligingly moved away to look at one of the caravels. It was a beauty of a ship and, as luck would have it, it belonged to the inconspicuous man. It took only seconds for him to whistle to the mariner on duty and remove his red cloak and throw it over the head of the unsuspecting girl.

She was slightly built but fought like a wildcat, clawing and kicking. But her screams were muffled by the cloth and the man had her in the ship's cabin before anyone on the quay noticed. He threw the bolts on the door and took a small dagger from his waist while the furious girl disentangled herself from the cloak. By the time she was free, he was leaning against the door flashing his silver smile at her while the ship got slowly under way.

'Scream all you like,' he said politely. 'No one will hear you above the gulls. But wouldn't it be much nicer if you sat down and had a glass of wine with me? I mean you no harm.'

*

Luciano rode into Classe with the light heart of a careless truant. He had escaped from a particularly uninspiring series of lectures on grammar and he was on his way to see the love of his life. He couldn't wait till the remaining months in Padavia were over and he could return to Bellezza and take up the life that was to be his future.

He had never been to Classe before and was charmed to find that it was like Bellezza in miniature – a much smaller city but also built on land that had once been swamp and was now threaded with canals. Unlike in the City of Masks, horses were allowed in Classe and, after stopping for directions, Luciano soon found himself in the Piazza del Foro, which seemed to be the heart of the city.

The oblong piazza was surrounded by handsome buildings of different periods, some colonnaded, some with triangular pediments, some more like the palazzos of Giglia. In the south of the square were two tall columns with decorated bases and between them and all around the piazza were stalls selling goods and traders calling their wares.

It was clearly a prosperous and well-organised city. On the far side of the square a flag bearing the image of a sailing ship told Luciano that he had found the Ducal Palace. He was able to ride right up to it and a servant took his horse while another announced 'The Cavaliere Crinamorte of Bellezza!' through the corridors of the palazzo.

He found Duke Germano in his salon and it was agonising to go through all the necessary courtesies before he was shown into a smaller room to wait for Arianna. But after an age, a flurry of skirts burst into the room, the servants were dismissed and they were together at last.

It was a long time before they could disentangle themselves and think of anyone else and by then Arianna's mask was off and her hair tumbled down round her shoulders.

'So where is this new girl from my old world?' asked Luciano at last. 'I haven't seen a twenty-first-century girl for ages.' But he was smiling.

'You're not going to make me jealous again,' said Arianna. 'I know you like sixteenth-century ones better.'

'Only one,' said Luciano, kissing her again.

There was a knock at the door. Arianna hastily tied her mask back on and did some ineffectual hair-tidying. But it was Rodolfo, who was almost as pleased to see Luciano as she had been. He clasped his old apprentice in a warm embrace.

'Well met,' he said. 'But in an ill hour, I fear.'

'I heard there was trouble brewing,' said Luciano. 'That's why I came.'

'And more than from the sea,' said Rodolfo. 'Flavia is here with bad news. The new Stravagante is already missing.'

*

'What is your name?' asked the man, who was no longer trying to be inconspicuous.

'Isabel,' said his captive. She saw no point in withholding the information. Though it should have been terrifying to be grabbed and bundled on to a ship and kidnapped, she was astonished to find that she was not scared; she was spittingly angry.

'Isabella,' said the man, savouring the four syllables. 'Bella, bella, Isabella. That is a Talian song, you know. Well, of course you do. That is if you are Talian, beautiful Isabella.'

He was looking pointedly at the cabin floor, where Isabel was clearly not casting any shadow.

She stayed quiet. No one had ever called her beautiful before but she couldn't trust this man, who had behaved so badly to her. Still, she filed it in her mind for future reference. 'Bella Isabella' did have a nice ring to it.

'Let me introduce myself,' said the man, pouring two goblets of red wine and smiling. Isabel saw to her alarm that he had two silver teeth. He looked like a pirate. 'I am Andrea.'

He said it with the stress on the 'e' so that it didn't sound like a girl's name. And he flashed his silver teeth at Isabel.

I can't stand men who think they are God's gift to women, thought Isabel. *Perhaps that's why I like Sky. He's so gorgeous but he doesn't seem to know it.*

Andrea looked a bit disappointed by her obvious immunity to his charms. Women were usually a bit more impressed by him. He gave her a goblet of wine and Isabel drank. It was rich and warming and gave her even more confidence.

'Why have you kidnapped me?' she asked. 'I demand you let me go immediately.'

Andrea shrugged. 'We are in deep water already but only a few hundred yards from the coast. There is nothing to stop you swimming back if you wish.'

Something in her expression showed him the truth.

'Unless of course you can't swim?'

'Why should I swim?' said Isabel bravely. 'You have no right to take me away from land on this boat, which I expect you have stolen.'

Andrea looked injured. 'This is my own ship. I just wanted to talk to you. I'll take you back to the harbour very soon.'

'You wanted to talk to me?' said Isabel. 'What's wrong with "Hello, can I have a word?" I'd like to know?'

'You certainly have a lot of spirit,' said Andrea. 'All right, I apologise for my unorthodox methods but I know no better. I'm a pirate.'

Did he really just say that? thought Isabel.

'Why don't you tell me who you are and what you are doing here in Classe with Flavia?' said Andrea. 'And then I'll take you safely back to land.'

'You know Flavia?' asked Isabel.

'I should think so,' said the pirate. 'She is my mother.'

*

'One minute we were walking on the quayside,' said Flavia, 'and then she was gone.'

'But who would have taken her?' asked Luciano. 'Stravaganti from my world have been captured before

– including me – but it's usually the di Chimici. How could they know about Isabel already? There aren't any in the city, are there?'

'I don't think it's the di Chimici this time,' said Rodolfo. 'Does Isabella know about stravagating home before dark?'

'Yes,' said Flavia. 'I did at least teach her that on her first visit.'

'What happened just before she disappeared?' asked Rodolfo.

'A messenger came to tell me I could buy back my stolen silks for a small sum,' said Flavia.

'Your silks?' asked Arianna.

'I lost some of my most recent cargo to pirates,' said Flavia.

'There is something you are not telling us,' said Rodolfo, looking at her intently.

Flavia sighed. 'I should have known I could not keep anything from a fellow Stravagante,' she said, 'but it was never relevant before. I don't know if it is now.'

Duke Germano passed her a glass of wine and she took a sip.

'My son, Andrea, is a pirate,' she said, 'to my shame. I think it was his ship that boarded the *Silver Lady* and took my silks. My own son stole my goods and will now sell them back to me at a bargain price. I am supposed to be grateful he didn't take the whole cargo,' she said bitterly.

'You are estranged from him?' asked the Duke sympathetically.

'How can I not be?' asked Flavia. 'I am a respectable trader and he is outside the law. If he doesn't steal from me, he is stealing from someone like me. That's *his* trade, if you can call it that.' She looked serious and sad, as if she was not telling them the whole story.

'I am very sorry for you,' said Rodolfo. 'But you are right – it doesn't seem to help us with what has happened to Isabella.'

'Could she just have got lost?' asked Arianna. 'I mean, she hasn't had time to get to know the city very well. Maybe she just missed you in the crowds down at the docks and then went to find you?'

'She knows the route between the harbour and my house,' said Flavia quietly. 'And I have had people searching the streets and buildings of Classe for hours. No, I am sure she has been abducted. I just hope that whoever has taken her has not robbed her of her talisman. I could not forgive myself if she failed to return home.'

Arianna flashed an anxious glance at Luciano, but his face was impassive.

'Rodolfo,' he said, 'she is a Stravagante and we have three more here including ourselves. Can't we combine our powers to locate her? I haven't met her but I saw her through your glass. Perhaps if we all linked minds and concentrated on her image, we could at least see where she is.'

Rodolfo, Flavia and Luciano moved close to one another, but before it could be discovered whether Luciano's plan would work, a servant entered and announced that 'Signorina Isabella' was outside and wished to be admitted.

So the first sight of the new Stravagante that Luciano had was of an excited and dishevelled girl rushing into the room and coming to a halt when she saw him.

Chapter 7

Matchmaking

'Isabella!' exclaimed Flavia. 'Where have you been? We've been so worried.'

Isabel noted that Talian adults were exactly like their other-world counterparts in one respect: when they were relieved, they sounded cross.

'I was kidnapped,' she said, relishing the drama. 'But it was OK. It was your son who did it.'

Luciano stopped Flavia's protests by coming forward to introduce himself.

'Isabella,' he said, 'I'm Luciano who used to be Lucien. I suppose it's Isabel really?'

'Yes, Isabel Evans,' she said. 'But everyone here has decided I'm Isabella.'

'Something similar happened to me,' said Luciano. 'I'm sorry but I don't remember you from school.'

'No one ever does,' said Isabel. 'But you probably know my brother, Charlie.'

'Charlie Evans?' said Luciano. 'Wasn't he on the swimming team?'

'Excuse me, Cavaliere,' said Flavia, 'I need to know what my son has done to Isabella and why.'

'Do they all know about Andrea?' asked Isabel slowly, looking round at the company.

Flavia bowed her head. 'They do now,' she said. 'You can say what happened.'

'Well, he captured me and took me out to sea on his boat,' said Isabel. 'But he wasn't unkind. He . . . he said he was a pirate.'

Rodolfo stepped forward and held up one hand. 'This is obviously a personal matter. Let us leave it for private discussion. What matters is what happened to Isabella and what relevance it has to her mission as a Stravagante.'

'But that's just it,' said Isabel. 'Andrea knows something that might be useful to us. He knows about the Gate fleet.'

*

Filippo of Bellona would have been annoyed to receive another summons from the Grand Duke so soon after getting back from Remora, but in fact he had nothing better to do and he was anxious to keep on good terms with his illustrious cousin. So he ordered up the royal carriage again and headed for his sister's palazzo in Giglia.

Francesca di Chimici had been married to her cousin Gaetano for less than a year but she already thought of Giglia as home. The palazzo in the Via Larga was where Gaetano had grown up with his sister and brothers and he still talked fondly of those days. His parents and two brothers were now buried in the family chapel but both Francesca and Gaetano knew that one of them was alive in another world.

Filippo was Francesca's only brother and he was causing her some worry. He had turned up last October and just as suddenly disappeared. Now there was a message to say that he was visiting them again. And she knew that he had been involved in a murderous plot in Padavia.

'What do you suppose it is this time?' asked Gaetano.

'He says that Fabrizio wants to see him,' said Francesca. 'That's what he said last time and we know what that led to. Your brother wanted mine to kill Luciano.'

'Fabrizio's like a dog with a bone,' said Gaetano. 'I don't think he will ever get over his hatred for Luciano.'

'He seems to have inherited it from your father,' said Francesca. 'But it isn't reasonable to pursue this vendetta after death in a duel, particularly when your father had tried to rig the outcome.'

'I know, my love, but Fabrizio is obsessed.'

'I thought he had been less vengeful since Bino was born,' said Francesca. 'Thinking more of the future and less of the past. I know that's what Caterina wants.'

'The trouble is,' said Gaetano, 'the future and the past are all bound up for him. He feels he has to take on Father's plans for the family and bring other cities in Talia under our family's rule.'

'But why do you suppose he wants Filippo to help him?' asked Francesca.

'That I don't know, but perhaps he will stay longer this time and we can find out.'

They didn't have long to wait. Filippo's carriage arrived soon afterwards and a liveried servant from the Grand Duke invited them all to dinner at the great residence south of the river that was still known as the Nucci palace. Matteo Nucci and his family had never lived in it and it had been confiscated when he was sent into exile, but the design and conception was his and Gaetano always thought it ill-omened. It was where he and Fabrizio had recovered from their wounds after the massacre and their father had died on the terrace outside, choking on his own poison.

But Fabrizio and Caterina seemed happy enough there, thought Gaetano. He wasn't so sure about Beatrice though. She seemed very quiet that evening.

'You are all very welcome at my table,' said Fabrizio, raising his glass in a toast, 'and especially Cousin Filippo. We don't see you in Giglia often enough.'

There was a murmur of agreement but Beatrice said nothing and remained looking at her plate. Fabrizio seemed determined to bring her into the conversation.

'Doesn't he look well, sister?' he asked, drawing everyone's attention to the reluctant young woman.

She glanced up briefly at Filippo and smiled wanly. 'Yes indeed, brother,' she said.

Francesca shot Gaetano a worried glance and then engaged Filippo in conversation about what was happening in Bellona.

It wasn't possible to speak openly in the carriage on the way home but, as soon as they were alone in their room, Francesca burst out, 'He's decided to marry your sister to my brother!'

'Really?' said Gaetano. 'Are you sure?'

'You'd have to be a block of wood not to see it,' said Francesca impatiently. 'And not to see that Beatrice doesn't want the match at all.'

'I thought she was looking a bit unhappy,' said Gaetano. 'But Fabrizio can't make her marry anyone she doesn't want to.'

'No, but he can make her life miserable if she refuses,' said Francesca. 'Think of it – she has no home other than the one he offers her, no fortune of her own, no future outside the will of the Grand Duke. What is she supposed to do but yield to Fabrizio's wishes?'

'Would it be such a terrible idea?' said Gaetano. 'I mean, Filippo's not a bad sort. Wouldn't you like Beatrice to marry your brother? I suppose she should marry someone.'

'But not someone she doesn't love!' said Francesca. 'Surely you understand that? Remember how nearly you married Arianna and that I actually *was* married off to someone I hated? And both of those terrible ideas came from within the family.'

'You're right, my darling,' said Gaetano, taking her hand and kissing it. 'Except that Arianna would never have had me. And Filippo is at least young and good-looking, unlike that ancient councillor Rinaldo bullied you into marrying. But I'm sorry to have awoken such painful memories. If Beatrice wants to defy Fabrizio, she can always have a home with us, can't she?'

Francesca put her arms round his neck. 'I knew you would understand,' she said. 'You are a dear and I should like to visit Beatrice tomorrow and tell her what you said. If she knows that even his sister wouldn't press Filippo on her if she doesn't want him, she might feel braver about standing up to your brother.'

The Barnsbury Stravaganti had become almost like an after-school club. They met regularly either in Nick's attic or in their favourite coffee bar and compared notes. Ayesha sometimes joined them but she was working very hard for her AS level exams and as long as she got a couple of evenings alone with Matt each week she didn't mind.

Alice was another matter. She complained bitterly to Georgia about it.

'I'm sorry, Alice,' said Georgia firmly. 'This stuff is important to Sky. You know there's a new Stravagante and we have to support her.'

'I know that Bel Evans has got her eye on my boyfriend,' said Alice. 'And all these cosy get-togethers of yours just give her the opportunity to make a move on him.'

'Don't you trust him?' asked Georgia. Alice had been her best friend for ages but they had never seen eye to eye about stravagation. 'You remember that you thought I was making a play for him when all we were doing was talking about Talia.'

'I know,' said Alice, 'but this is different. She is obviously keen on him.'

'Look, we're not a dating club! We really don't talk about anything except stravagation. I'm sure Sky is just being kind to Bel. But if you get jealous, that could change.'

Alice looked at her with icy fury. 'Don't make it my fault – you with your . . . your wizards and sword-fights and magical objects. It's pathetic! Like those people who dress up for *Star Trek* conventions.'

'But you know it's real – you've been there,' protested Georgia. But Alice had stormed off.

Another person who wasn't happy with Isabel's new social life was Laura but, being Laura, she didn't make scenes about it like Alice; she just withdrew further into herself.

And Isabel's latest news gave the others little time to worry about people outside their group.

'A pirate?' said Matt. 'What, with a gold earring and seashells in his hair?'

'This is Flavia's son,' said Isabel. 'Not a Hollywood actor. He does have silver teeth though – just a couple. And he dresses all in black.'

'He's the Black Raider?' asked Sky.

'Yes, and supposed to be very dangerous, though he was perfectly polite to me – except when he offered to throw me overboard.'

'What?' said Georgia.

'But not in a bad way. He said it would teach me to swim, but I bottled out.'

'Never mind all that,' said Nick. 'What about the Gate people?'

'He's had some dealings with them – no, I didn't ask – and has decided he's against them,' said Isabel. 'But more important, because he's always on the sea and has contacts everywhere, he knows all sorts of stuff like how big the fleet is, what kind of ships they have and all kinds of useful information I could pass on to Rodolfo and the Duke.'

'But how come Flavia, who's a Stravagante and a respectable merchant, from what you've told us, has a son who's a pirate?' asked Matt. 'It seems so unlikely.'

'I don't know,' said Isabel. 'I didn't ask that either. Can't you just accept that he is?'

'But does that make him a good guy or not?' said Matt. 'I mean, you say he's against the Gate people but does that make him an ally of the Stravaganti?'

'People don't come with T-shirts saying "villain" or "hero" in Talia,' said Nick. 'It's not like a Hollywood film. You just have to see how things pan out.'

'I remember that we thought the Nucci must be on our side in Giglia,' said Sky, 'because they were against the di Chimici. But Arianna could have been killed in the massacre they plotted.'

'And not all the di Chimici are enemies, remember,' said Georgia.

'I know Luciano thought Filippo was OK in Padavia,' said Matt. 'And then Filippo tried to kill him – as well as helping to torture me.'

'It's very complicated,' said Isabel. She had decided that she rather liked Andrea, once he had stopped trying to charm her.

'Well, let's look at what we've got,' said Georgia. They were in Nick's attic, spreading out sheets of notes, maps and family trees. 'Let's start with the di Chimici,' she continued, looking sternly at Nick. 'Here's the family tree. Now, we should divide them into allies, enemies and unknowns. Yes, Nick, I know it's not as clear as that but we can make a start. Bel needs to know who can be trusted in Talia.'

Nick looked a bit mutinous but didn't protest.

'And now that Nick's here, the only one we can really be sure of is Gaetano,' said Georgia.

'And Francesca,' said Nick.

'OK, so that's Gaetano and Francesca we can rely on,' said Georgia, writing their names in one column. 'Anything else we know for sure?'

'Rinaldo and Filippo are definitely not on our side,' said Matt, rubbing his face as if he could still feel the bruises he had got when in their custody.

'And my brother Fabrizio,' said Nick. 'He hates the Stravaganti as much as our father did.'

It was weird for Isabel to hear him talking about a 'brother' living in another world and time but she supposed the others were used to it.

'I think Alfonso of Volana is OK,' said Sky, poring over the family tree. 'Even though he is Rinaldo's brother. He was great during the massacre and afterwards he looked after all the brides.'

'So there's a pattern?' said Isabel. 'The siblings aren't the same. Fabrizio's an enemy but Gaetano's a friend, Francesca's a friend but her brother Filippo's an enemy. And this Alfonso's OK even though Rinaldo is against us?'

'You're right,' said Georgia. 'I'd never thought of it like that.'

'What about, what's-her-name . . . Caterina?' said Isabel, consulting the tree. 'She got one good brother and one bad one and she's married to Fabrizio. What does that make her?'

'I don't think any of my female relations are

enemies,' said Nick. 'Caterina, Bianca, Lucia, my sister Beatrice – I can't see any of them waging a vendetta.'

'So let's put all of them and Alfonso with a question mark,' said Georgia. 'That makes two we are sure are friends, three enemies and five possible sympathisers – four of them women.'

'What about the Pope?' asked Sky, making Isabel jump.

'The Pope?' she asked. 'Is he a di Chimici too?'

'Yes,' said Nick wearily. 'He's my uncle Ferdinando.'

'He was impressive after the massacre,' said Sky. 'He stopped Niccolò from executing all the Nucci.'

Isabel wondered if she'd ever catch up with the others. They had often mentioned this Niccolò, who had been Nick's father in Giglia; he sounded terrifying and she was glad that Luciano had dispatched him.

'I think he's OK,' said Nick. 'Basically a good man, but weak. And there's my other uncle, Jacopo, Prince of Bellona, who's Francesca and Filippo's father. And there's another Jacopo too, a sort of cousin. He's Lucia and Bianca's father. He's known as Jacopo the Elder and is Prince of Fortezza.'

'So the di Chimici are in charge of lots of cities in Talia?' asked Isabel.

'Not as many as they'd like,' said Georgia. 'But yes, the two Nick mentioned plus Giglia – obviously – and Remora, Moresco and Volana.'

Isabel counted on her fingers. 'That's six. How many others are there?'

'Well, there are lots of cities,' said Nick, 'but they all come under the rule of one or other of the city-states and there are six that are independent of my family.'

'Of the di Chimici, Nick,' said Georgia, softening towards him and putting her arm round him. 'You must stop thinking of them as your family.'

'And Classe's one of those,' said Isabel, to cover up the awkwardness. 'Is there a pattern to the cities we go to?'

Four pairs of eyes gave her the same surprised look. This was a new way of thinking about stravagation; they'd never tackled it as a group before.

'The first city was Bellezza,' said Georgia. 'Where Luciano went and still lives.' She was scribbling furiously a new list of their names and the cities they had stravagated to. 'And that's independent, obviously.'

'Then I went to Remora – that's under the di Chimici, because the Pope's the Prince of Remora too,' continued Georgia.

'And I went to Giglia,' said Sky. 'Di Chimici again.'

'Mine was independent,' said Matt. 'Padavia is governed by Antonio.'

'And now Classe,' said Isabel. 'I can't see any pattern.'

'It was a good idea, though, Bel,' said Sky. 'Keep them coming.'

Fausto Ventura was surprised by the knock on his workshop door. A thin young man with a scarred face peered round it.

'I am sorry to disturb you, Maestro,' he said, 'but I

wondered if I might talk to you. I am Filippo Nucci, son of Matteo, formerly of Giglia.'

'Why yes,' said Fausto, wiping his hands on his apron before offering one to Filippo. 'I have heard of you. You are welcome. What can I do for you?'

A commission for a mosaic from the Nucci, he was thinking.

But Filippo had something quite other in mind.

'I have been looking at the mosaics in Classe, ever since I have been well enough to leave the house,' said Filippo. 'And I have seen some of your own work – in the Palazzo of Duke Germano and elsewhere. You are a very great artist.'

'Thank you,' said Fausto. He had no false modesty.

'And I wondered if you would ever consider taking an apprentice from someone of my . . . class? Well, me actually.'

Fausto was nonplussed. Well-dressed young men from wealthy families did not beat a path to his door asking to be apprentices. But there was something about this one, with his large dark eyes and yearning expression, that made him reluctant to say no straight away.

'It is sometimes quite taxing work, physically,' he said hesitantly. 'I have no wish to insult you, Signore, but are you quite fit and strong enough to crawl around floors or climb tall ladders to put the tesserae in place?'

Filippo looked alarmed and disappointed.

'You don't assemble them in the workshop?' he asked, looking around at all the activity going on.

'Yes, sometimes and for some parts of major mosaics, we do,' said Fausto. 'But there is still a lot of hard physical work involved in putting them in place.'

He took pity on Filippo's woebegone face.

'But perhaps, Signor Filippo, you are more interested in the design aspects of my work?'

Filippo's eyes lit up. 'Is that something I could learn?' he asked eagerly.

'May I suggest something?' said Fausto, wondering why on earth he was even contemplating taking the young man on. 'Rather than indenturing yourself to me as an apprentice, which I think Signor Matteo would not like, why don't you come in and watch while I am working on a design? You can ask questions and after a period of study, which will also involve visiting the great churches in the city, you can try your hand at a mosaic design of your own.'

Filippo was delighted with this suggestion. He wouldn't even need to tell his father.

'I am so grateful to you, Maestro,' he said. 'My father is a banker and would like me to follow in his footsteps. But our business is greatly reduced since we . . . we had to leave Giglia.' He unconsciously touched his scar. 'He doesn't need me yet and I really want to do something with my life. To make something beautiful, preferably. And my hands are uninjured, see?'

He tucked his cane awkwardly under one arm and spread his long white hands, which had never done any work, for Fausto to inspect.

The mosaicist managed to stop himself from shaking his head.

'So I see,' he said kindly. 'And do you have any artistic gift?'

'I've never tried,' admitted Filippo. 'But I do love beautiful things.'

'Well, that's a good place to start,' said Fausto.

In Giglia, Beatrice was finding her cousin's visit very difficult to cope with.

Fabrizio must have said something to him, she thought, because Filippo was constantly seeking her out, presenting her with nosegays, reading her poems he had written and generally behaving like a lovesick swain.

Beatrice was a very practical young woman. She accepted that she would have to marry one day; the only alternative was to enter a convent and that did not appeal to her. But she hadn't really believed that Fabrizio would insist on a dynastic marriage for her – and so soon after their father's death.

Now she tried to see her cousin Filippo, someone she had known all her life and played with as a child, in the light of a possible husband. He was handsome enough – most of the di Chimici family were good-looking – but she felt there was something lacking in his character. He was too easily led.

Take this visit of his to Giglia. It wasn't his idea, Beatrice was sure. Fabrizio had sent for him and told him to court her so that was what he was doing. But Beatrice felt guilty because she knew how powerful her brother's role was within the family and how difficult it would be to disobey him. And yet that was what she was planning.

She just prayed that she would have the strength to do it.

Chapter 8

Defiance

Vicky Mulholland had an unusual relationship with her children. Her first son had died more than three years ago and yet she had seen him several times since. At first it had been hard but she had accepted that this was how it was and she could talk about it to no one except her husband, David. And then, a few months ago, Lucien had come into their house and they had held him and hugged him and she still couldn't speak of it with anyone.

Her second boy, first a foster-child but since the summer her officially adopted son, Nicholas, had almost as great a mystery attached to him. He had materialised out of nowhere, his memory gone and his body shattered but with a luminously beautiful face, which showed his loving and trusting nature.

Over the past two years she had watched him grow strong and tall and seen him learn to walk without assistance. He was now the captain of the Barnsbury fencing team and as apparently normal as any other teenager in Islington.

But Vicky and David knew that the amnesia had just been a cover story. On Lucien's last visit, during that terrible time when another boy had nearly died, he had told them that Nick and Georgia knew all about the mysterious world where he lived now and that Nick had come from the same place.

When Lucien had gone, after eating a pizza and taking a shower like any normal living boy, Vicky had collapsed into misery. She knew that things were happening that were beyond her control or comprehension and she couldn't deal with it straight away. Her mind just closed down.

David and Nicholas were both anxious for her but equally unable to talk about what had happened. So it remained a big unspoken topic in the family. Vicky wanted to know where Nick had come from and what Georgia had to do with it but she simply couldn't bear to talk or think about Lucien.

And then one day she walked into the dining room and found Nick and Georgia poring over what looked like a family tree. They both started guiltily and covered up what they were doing. Then Nick saw how drawn Vicky's face looked and he sat back and slid the paper back out into the open. He looked at his adopted mother and suddenly she knew the moment had come. She sat down opposite them and prepared herself to hear what she needed to know.

'Tell me about it,' she said quietly.

'It is the lineage of my first family,' said Nick. 'The di Chimici.'

'And you know about them too?' Vicky asked Georgia.

'I do,' she admitted.

'Then who are they?' asked Vicky. 'Are they even . . . human?'

'Very human,' said Nick wryly. 'But they live in another world.'

'That's what you said about Lucien when you first came here and saw his photo,' said Vicky. 'And that man at his funeral said the same.'

'That was Rodolfo,' said Nick. 'He looks out for Luciano, I mean, Lucien, in this other world.'

'He's a wonderful person, with great powers,' said Georgia, 'only a bit scary till you get to know him. And even then he's scary if you do something he doesn't approve of.'

'Like a strict parent?' asked Vicky.

'More like a teacher,' said Georgia. 'But Lucien does have foster-parents.'

'Are they Nick's original parents? Can it really be that neat?' said Vicky.

'No, nothing like that,' said Nick. 'My first mother died years ago and my father . . . my father died in a duel nearly a year ago.'

'Lucien's foster-parents are much older than you and David,' said Georgia hurriedly, feeling they were in dangerous waters. 'They're called . . . William and Eleanor,' she said, rapidly translating in her head the names of Guglielmo and Leonora Crinamorte. 'They're really nice.'

'And where exactly is this?' asked Vicky at last.

The 64,000-dollar question.

'It's a parallel world,' said Nick matter-of-factly. 'In a country called Talia, which is like your Italy.'

'You might as well ask *when* it is,' said Georgia, who had noticed that 'your'.

'When?' asked Vicky.

'Over four hundred years ago,' said Nick.

'So that's why he wears those clothes,' said Vicky, almost to herself. 'So he's not really dead?'

'I'm afraid he is,' said Georgia. 'In this world anyway. It's just that he has this other life in Talia. It's really difficult to explain.'

'Try,' said Vicky. 'Tell me everything.'

Georgia swallowed. 'You need to know about Arianna,' she said.

When Isabel next stravagated, Flavia took her straight to the Ducal Palace. To her alarm, Arianna and Luciano were playing with a huge cat, maybe a cheetah. But he turned out to be very gentle.

'This is Vitale,' said the young Duchessa. 'I have his parents and three other kittens, but I brought this one for the Duke.'

'Kitten?' said Isabel. 'But he's enormous.'

'He'll be bigger,' said Luciano, 'and his brother already is. That's the one we're keeping.'

'I'm glad you came today,' said Arianna. 'I am going back to Bellezza soon.'

'And I must leave today,' said Luciano. 'I'm going to be in so much trouble for cutting classes at the University.'

'Does this mean there's no more danger?' asked Isabel.

Arianna laughed. 'I don't think that will ever be true in my lifetime. But I'm used to it. No, it's just that the Duke has agreed to join fleets with us. I must go back and commission more ships to be built before the spring really starts.'

'We are safe for a couple of months,' said Rodolfo, entering the room. Isabel saw that he bent to greet Vitale as if they were old friends.

'The Gate people won't attack in this weather,' he said. 'And if I have your permission to take up your son's offer to bring us information, Flavia, we will have the edge on them. We will at least know whether their attack will come here or in Bellezza first and then the other city's fleet can take to the sea straight away.'

'Of course,' said Flavia. 'It is a strange thing to say about someone with my son's reputation – and goodness knows we have had our quarrels in the past – but you can trust him. Once he has made his mind up about which side he is on, he will not turn traitor.'

Isabel wondered again how the respectable merchant could have a son who was so outside the law.

'We will grant him safe conduct and immunity from prosecution in Bellezza, since he will help us against the Gate people,' said Arianna, glancing at her father. Rodolfo nodded.

'I will get a message to him to find you in Bellezza,' said Flavia. 'Thank you, Isabella – you have already helped with the invasion and the threat to Talia. And maybe done something to bring my son back to me.'

Beatrice knew what it meant when Fabrizio called her to his private office in the Palazzo Ducale. She realised as soon as the servant came what the summons signified; if it had been anything about household matters, her brother would have come to see her in her own little room in the Palazzo Nucci.

She walked slowly through the corridor across the river, the liveried servant following behind, putting off the moment that was to come. But when she entered the room overlooking the River Argento, which had once been her own parlour, she was relieved to see that Fabrizio was alone. The servant was soon dismissed and the Grand Duke himself settled her into a visitor's chair.

'You are well, Bice?' he began, although they had breakfasted together not more than two hours earlier.

'Very well, brother,' she said.

'Good, good,' said Fabrizio. He seemed nervous, as if he were about to propose himself.

Which in a sense he was.

'Our cousin Filippo has asked me to speak to you on his behalf,' he said. 'I'm sure you will guess why.'

Beatrice did not trust herself to speak. She inclined her head slightly, which encouraged her brother to go on.

'He has quite rightly come to me first with his proposal, since I am not only your older brother but head of our family.'

The princess wondered when Fabrizio had become so pompous. And she would have smiled at the notion that Filippo had put the request for her hand to her brother, rather than the other way round, if her situation hadn't been so serious.

'It is a good match and I was happy to tell him that it would have my blessing,' said Fabrizio quickly, noting that the princess had still not said anything. 'You do like him, don't you, Bice?'

There was a pleading tone in his voice. And Beatrice really wanted to please her brother. It would make her life so easy to marry Filippo, to remain a di Chimici princess and live in Bellona, the City of Dreams. But it was not her dream. Still, her brother did have authority as head of the family and it was unbearably hard to stand up to him.

'I do like him,' she said softly. 'He is my cousin and I have known him all my life. Of course I like him but, as a husband . . . ?'

'I understand,' said Fabrizio eagerly. 'It is a big step. But look how well it has worked for me and Caterina, and for Francesca and Gaetano. And remember Alfonso is happy with Bianca too. It is best for us to marry within the family. No one outside can possibly understand what it means to be a di Chimici in Talia. And you would continue to be loved and cherished in the kind of style you are used to.'

'But you and Caterina love each other,' said Beatrice. 'As do the others. I do not love Filippo and I don't think I ever will.'

'But love will come,' said her brother, getting up and taking both her hands in his. 'I promise it will. Once you have his children you will feel differently.'

He dropped her hands and looked serious. 'And there is more to be considered here than girlish fancy. Filippo will be Prince of Bellona and need heirs to that title. Who better to give them to him than a di Chimici princess? *The* di Chimici princess, I may say, since you are the only daughter of the family's leading branch. He is very well aware of the honour you would do him by accepting.'

Beatrice had gone to this meeting braced to refuse the offer and secure in the knowledge that Gaetano and Francesca would give her a home if Fabrizio cast her out. But she felt her resolve was like a castle under siege and that her brother was bombarding her with engines she could not resist for ever. Its walls were weakening and beginning to crumble.

'We must have more di Chimici children,' said Fabrizio. 'It's what Father wanted when he arranged last year's marriages. It was the only thing that would console him for Falco's death. And then we lost Father too – and Carlo. Our family was shrinking. But now we have Bino, and I'm sure Gaetano and Francesca will have their own children soon. You could join us in filling Talia with babies that will carry the di Chimici name and the di Chimici blood.'

He had tears in his eyes and Beatrice was not unmoved. An appeal to the names of both her adored younger brother and little nephew in the same speech was having a powerful effect. It was as if the siege-engines had been removed and an ambassador in silks and satins had been sent through the breach in the wall with a basket of delicacies to negotiate terms for surrender.

'Promise me you will marry Filippo,' said Fabrizio, putting all the emotion he felt into one last plea.

Beatrice closed her eyes. 'I will marry Filippo,' she said. 'Or I will marry no one.'

The next day Isabel got a text from Nick saying 'Vicky on way. Knows everything.' But before she'd had time to work out what that could possibly mean there was a ring at the doorbell and her puzzled brother let Vicky Mulholland in. He'd assumed she was here to see their mother, who was out at the supermarket. But she'd asked for Isabel, and Charlie couldn't understand why.

He knew who she was; lots of students in the school orchestra had been taught by her. But Bel had never shown the slightest interest in the violin. Then he heard Vicky say something about Nick and it all clicked. She was the fencing guy's mother. Or adoptive mother or something. She must have come round with a message from Nick. Though as Charlie went back to his room and left them to it, he puzzled over why Nick hadn't just rung.

Isabel had never been alone with Vicky before and couldn't imagine what the woman wanted. She looked dreadful – tired and drawn.

'I've been talking to Nick and Georgia,' she said. 'They've told me about Talia.'

Light began to dawn.

'You go there, don't you?' said Vicky. 'They told me you are the current – what was it? – Stravagante. Do you see Lucien when you go there?'

'I have met him,' said Isabel. 'But I didn't know him before, you know . . .'

'Before he died? No, I didn't think so. But you've seen him in this other world. How is he?'

'He . . . He seemed fine,' said Isabel, realising how inadequate that sounded. 'He's at university in Pad—. . . somewhere.'

'Padavia,' said Vicky. 'It's like our Padua. I've looked it up.'

Another person doing homework, thought Isabel.

'That's right. Only I saw him in Classe – that's like Ravenna.' Isabel thought she had better not tell Vicky that Luciano had been skiving off his studies: she was a parent, after all.

'And did you see this Arianna person?' asked Vicky. 'Georgia told me he was engaged to her.'

'She's really lovely,' said Isabel. 'Really good-looking but warm and friendly too. Only, she's this sort of duchess.'

'I heard that,' said Vicky. 'And if my son marries her, he will be a duke.'

She ran her hands through her thick curly black hair, which was now streaked with silver.

'Lucien a duke?' she said. 'I can hardly believe I'm saying it. And to be married? He's only nineteen – I mean, eighteen. He told me there'd been a time-shift of a year here, so to him it feels a year less that he's been away.'

She made it sound as if she still thought he might come back.

'I think things are a bit different in Talia,' said Isabel cautiously. She didn't want to get into the whole shorter life-expectancy thing the others had told her about. 'They seem to get married much younger. Arianna's the same age.'

'But what would a duchess see in my son?' said Vicky.

'They're definitely in love,' said Isabel. 'I've seen them together.'

'Will you do me a favour?' asked Vicky. 'Will you take him a message from me?'

'Oh, Mrs Mulholland,' said Isabel, 'I would but I'm afraid he's left Classe and gone back to Padavia.'

*

After Vicky left, Isabel went to the café, where she was pretty sure she would find at least Nick and Georgia.

'I'm sorry,' said Nick straight away. 'I tried to stop her and then I tried to warn you.'

'It's OK,' said Isabel. 'I got your text. But you can buy me a coffee. It was quite hard core.'

She was telling them about it when a distraught-looking Sky joined them.

'What's up?' asked Georgia. 'You look awful.'

'It's Alice,' said Sky. 'She's dumped me.'

Isabel's heart leapt and then she felt ashamed; Sky seemed really upset.

'No! She didn't say anything to me,' said Georgia. 'But I know she was a bit fed up with all the time you've been spending with us.' Her eyes swivelled to Isabel, who was concentrating on not blushing by stirring her cappuccino vigorously.

'Yeah, that's what she said,' said Sky. 'It was a sort of me or them ultimatum.' He sank despondently into a chair. Alice had been his first girlfriend.

'And you chose us?' asked Nick quietly.

'Looks like it,' said Sky. He tried to smile. 'Better get me a double-strength latte.'

Nick went back to the counter; he seemed to be

buying for everyone today. So he got a plate of blueberry muffins too.

'Here,' he said. 'We all need sugar. Bel's had a shock too.'

He told Sky about Vicky.

'That's a complication,' said Sky, frowning. 'Is she going to be on our backs all the time?'

'She's not like that,' said Nick defensively. 'But you can't blame her for wanting to know about her son.'

'She wanted me to take him a message,' said Isabel. 'She was really upset when I told her he'd gone back to Padavia. She didn't really understand why I couldn't just go there from Classe.'

'But doesn't it make her the only person in our world who knows about Talia without being a Stravagante?' asked Sky. 'Is that safe?'

'Well, Ayesha knows,' said Isabel, 'and she's never been there. And didn't you say Alice had only gone once? That hardly makes her a Stravagante.'

'David knows too, don't forget,' said Nick. 'And I'm sure Vicky will tell him everything she's found out from us.'

'Alice is the one I'm worried about,' said Sky, moodily tearing up his muffin. 'She's so negative about the whole business. Supposing she tells Ros?'

'Who's Ros?' asked Isabel.

'My mum,' said Sky gloomily. 'She's in a relationship with Alice's dad.'

Isabel thought this sounded extremely weird but didn't say anything.

'She wouldn't believe her,' said Nick. 'Vicky and David only believe it because they've seen Lucien since he died – and Rodolfo.'

'And Ayesha saw Filippo, though only for a moment,' said Georgia.

'Ros met Sulien and Giuditta,' said Sky.

'Yes, but she doesn't remember it, does she?' said Georgia. 'Sulien did something to her mind. It was like what Rodolfo did to Niccolò when Falco died.'

There was an awkward silence while everyone looked at Nick and Georgia put her hand over her mouth.

'Shall I get some more coffees?' said Isabel.

'I'll come with you,' said Sky, jumping up quickly so that they could leave the other two together.

'It must be really awkward having a boyfriend who's sort of dead,' whispered Isabel while they waited at the counter.

'I wonder if Arianna thinks so,' said Sky.

Grand Duke Fabrizio was pleased with his morning's work. He hummed as he walked back through the corridor to his home. He had spent a profitable hour with the Ambassador from the Gate people, signed off some further details on the anti-magic laws and had a very satisfactory meeting with his younger sister. It would soon be spring and then the fleet from the east would attack one or both of the independent coastal cities; everything was going his way.

He arrived to find the palace in confusion, with servants hurrying back and forth and his wife in tears.

'Whatever has happened, my love?' he asked.

'It's Bice,' sobbed Caterina.

'What about her? I saw her only this morning in my

office and she seemed perfectly all right.'

'Oh, what did you say to her, Rizio?' wailed Caterina. 'She's gone.'

'Gone where?' said Fabrizio stupidly.

'Away,' said Caterina. 'No one knows where. She has taken her things and disappeared!'

Chapter 9

Runaway

Filippo Nucci was designing a mosaic – his first. It was supposed to be a portrait of the goddess, the ancient deity worshipped throughout the Middle Sea centuries earlier. She was still actively prayed to by many people in Eastern Talia, particularly in the Bellezzan lagoon, and was the deity of the nomadic people known as the Manoush.

He was trying to depict her as the moon, but the face was turning out to have a strong resemblance to Princess Beatrice di Chimici. And work as he might, the mouth had a sad expression. Filippo sighed.

'What is it, Lippo?' asked his mother.

He was drawing in the salon of their palazzo, where the light was good in the mornings.

'I am having difficulty with my design,' he said.

'And until I get it right on paper, Fausto says I can't move on to placing the tesserae in a frame.'

Graziella came to look. And looked closer. She gave a sniff. 'It's the di Chimici girl, isn't it?'

'It is the goddess of the lagoon, Mother,' said Filippo. 'But yes, it does look a bit like Princess Beatrice.' And he sighed again.

'Why do you think of her?' said Graziella. 'Her family are our worst enemies.'

'I know that,' said Filippo, fingering his scar. 'None better. But not Beatrice. She saved my life.'

'Well, it was probably that monk who did that,' said Graziella. 'But I agree she's different from the rest of them.'

'I wish I could remember Brother Sulien,' said Filippo. 'I owe him a lot. But I do remember Beatrice, and I could never think of her as an enemy.'

*

When Isabel came out of the Baptistery next day, she found the Piazza del Foro full of brightly dressed musicians. She stopped to look at them before going to find Flavia. They were playing flutes and tambourines and lutes and wore coloured ribbons in their long hair – even the men – and clothes with bright embroidery and mirrorwork. Isabel thought they were some of the most glamorous people she had ever seen.

In the corner of the square, one of the newcomers sat on a stool playing a harp. Gradually, all the other musicians fell silent as the liquid peal of the harp's notes dominated their sounds. Isabel stood enchanted, caught up in the music, which was both sweet and sad. At the end, many people threw coins into a velvet hat carried by a tall young woman who seemed to be the harpist's companion.

Isabel suddenly spotted that Flavia was working at her stall so wove her way across the market to her.

'Who are they?' she asked. 'Do you know the one with the harp? He's brilliant.'

'They are the Manoush,' said Flavia. 'Wanderers from country to country and city to city. Most Stravaganti are drawn to them. And that is Aurelio – would you like to meet him?'

Isabel felt a bit shy when Flavia left her stall to her assistant and took her over to the harpist, stopping on the way to buy two cups of ale. As they got close, Isabel realised that the man was blind, and his companion seemed to act as his eyes.

'Greetings, Aurelio, Raffaella,' said Flavia, giving the woman the drinks. 'It is good to have you in Classe again.'

'I thank you, Signora Flavia,' said the harpist before drinking deep, even though the merchant had not said her name. 'And who is this with you?'

Flavia introduced Isabel and she felt in the strangest way that Aurelio was scrutinising her even though he couldn't see her. He seemed satisfied. 'You are not from Talia,' he said quietly.

'No,' said Isabel, wondering how he knew when she hadn't even spoken. And she knew he didn't mean that she was just from another country.

Before she could say more they were joined by another Manoush, a rusty-haired man with a most attractive smile.

'Hello,' he said, flashing his very white and pointed teeth at both Flavia and Isabel. 'I'm Ludo, their cousin.'

'This is Signora Flavia and her friend Isabella,' said Raffaella, who was strikingly good-looking herself.

Isabel found herself falling under the spell of these exotic Manoush. She noticed that Ludo was definitely giving her the once-over but his expression suddenly changed and she realised he was no longer estimating her attractiveness but appearing to recognise her in some way. Then she realised that he had looked down at her feet and seen she had no shadow.

'You are one like Matteo,' he whispered to her.

Isabel nodded and then thought, *But Aurelio can't have seen that. So how did he know?*

*

Beatrice had gone first to her old home on the Via Larga where Gaetano and Francesca now lived but it took only minutes for her to realise she had made a terrible mistake.

'How could I have forgotten Filippo was staying with you?' she moaned to Gaetano. 'Where can I go now?'

'Don't be afraid,' he said. 'Filippo is out. I believe he has gone to the silversmith to order some jewellery. He will be some time.'

Beatrice put her face in her hands.

'I expect he is commissioning wedding finery for me,' she said.

'You are safe here with us,' said Francesca. 'You can't be made to marry against your will. It happened to me and I am determined no relative of mine will ever be made to do it again.'

'But I can't stay in the same house as Filippo,' said Beatrice, restlessly pacing the room.

'Then let us send you somewhere else safe till he goes,' said Gaetano. 'You can have a carriage. It will take you wherever you want to go.'

'Where is that though?' said Beatrice. She felt utterly lost, her only refuge closed to her.

'What about Bellezza?' said Gaetano suddenly. 'Fabrizio is not likely to follow you there.'

'That's perfect!' said Francesca. 'Arianna will welcome you. She is a really good friend.'

'A friend to the di Chimici?' said Beatrice doubtfully.

'To us,' said Gaetano firmly. 'She does not hate all our family. And she will understand very well why you would not want to marry where you did not love.' He looked fondly at Francesca.

'But surely I would need to leave today?' said the distracted princess. 'How can we get a message to her?'

'Leave that to me,' said Gaetano, full of energy now that something had been decided. 'Francesca will conceal you in her apartments and I will be back with an answer within the hour.

*

Flavia invited the Manoush back to her house for some refreshment and a handful of them came, including Aurelio, Raffaella and Ludo. Isabel had worked out that Ludo must be one of the Manoush who had been rescued by Matt in Padavia.

They were soon chatting away like old friends.

'How is Matteo?' asked Ludo. 'Does he come to Talia any more?'

'No,' said Isabel. 'None of them do. There seems to be a sort of one Stravagante at a time rule. At least now.' She realised as she said it that her time in Talia would come to an end too and it made her feel unbearably sad.

Ludo picked up her mood immediately. He took her hand.

'You have only just got here,' he said gently. 'Your adventure is at its beginning.'

'You're right,' said Isabel. 'But why are the Manoush here at this time? Do you think my adventure, as you call it, will involve your people?'

'I don't know,' admitted Ludo. 'We are just passing through. We never stay anywhere for long, unless there is one of our festivals to celebrate. But I'll ask Aurelio. He sees more than the rest of us in spite of being blind.'

'I'm really not sure what I'm here to do,' said Isabel. 'I mean Matt was quite heroic but I can't see myself saving Classe or Bellezza from a fleet of Gate people.'

'The Gate people?' said Ludo, surprised.

'Perhaps I shouldn't have told you,' said Isabel, suddenly wary.

But Ludo laughed heartily, showing his pointed teeth again. He reminded her of Andrea when he did that.

'It's all right, Isabella,' he said. 'We are on the same side. I shan't betray you. And don't worry about your role as a Stravagante. I'm sure that when the time comes, you will be able to do whatever is required of you.'

Isabel knew he was just being nice but it made her feel better.

*

Arianna was travelling with her father to Bellezza in the ducal carriage, Luciano riding alongside, when Rodolfo told her that a Stravagante was trying to get in touch with him. He had to rummage in his valise for the hand mirror but he was right: there was the face of Brother Sulien. Neither of them had seen him since the aftermath of the massacre and Rodolfo's second 'wedding' to Silvia and they were delighted, if surprised, to hear from him now.

Rodolfo ordered the carriage to halt and Arianna waved to Luciano out of the window to get him to stop and pay attention.

I have Gaetano here with me, thought-spoke Sulien. *And he has an urgent message for Arianna.*

Rodolfo passed the message to Arianna out loud and Luciano thought how jealous it would have made him in the past. Now he was pleased to have any news of their old friend Gaetano.

He is not adept at using the mirrors, said the black friar, *so when you have seen him I shall convey his meaning to you.*

Gaetano's ugly face replaced Sulien's in the mirror. His mouth was moving but neither Rodolfo or Arianna could make anything of what he wanted to say. But his smile was as wide as ever and he looked well, if a bit agitated.

He would like Arianna to give hospitality to his sister Princess Beatrice, said Sulien, taking over. *She is* running away from a marriage their older brother would force on her.

When Arianna passed this on to Luciano, he leaned into the carriage and asked Rodolfo if he might borrow the mirror.

Who to? he asked Sulien.

And got the reply he expected: *Filippo di Chimici.*

It is good to see you, said Sulien. *And to see you safe in Bellezza.*

Ah, said Luciano, *we are not there. Arianna and Rodolfo are driving back from Classe and I'm accompanying them as far as Padavia. But it's good to see you too, Sulien. And how are Sandro and Brother Dog?*

Both are well and enjoying life in the friary, especially in the kitchen, said Sulien. *I think Gaetano would like to see you.*

Gaetano's face came back and he looked pleased to find Luciano, his old fencing student.

He says to send his love to you both. And Francesca's, said Sulien. *But he is anxious to know if he may safely send his sister to Bellezza.*

'We must have her,' said Arianna impulsively. 'Gaetano would never ask if it were not important. And we have nothing against her, do we, Father? She was wonderful after the massacre, helping all the injured.'

'Indeed,' said Rodolfo, taking the hand mirror back.

We shall be back in time to prepare a room for her before she can reach Bellezza, he said. *But I think it will annoy the Grand Duke very much.*

I think so too, said Sulien. *I'll tell Gaetano she can come then?*

And tell her she will be very welcome in my palazzo, thought-spoke Arianna, taking the mirror from her father's hand. She had learned how to do it from Luciano, even though she was not a Stravagante herself.

Gaetano's face swam back into view and there was no mistaking the universal gesture of thanks he made to them.

Then the mirror clouded over – like a phone going dead.

*

Filippo di Chimici returned from the jeweller humming. He hadn't exactly placed an order but he had looked at lots of designs for rings and necklaces and coronets and felt well pleased with his afternoon's work. Beatrice was not the most beautiful of all the di Chimici cousins but she was perfectly presentable and had a very sweet nature; Filippo could imagine being happy to be her husband. He fully expected to hear from Fabrizio today that he was to be welcomed into the senior branch of the family.

So he was not surprised when a servant announced to Gaetano and Francesca that His Grace the Grand Duke of Tuschia was below in the great salon and waiting upon their pleasure. It didn't occur to Filippo not to go down with them and he completely missed the looks they exchanged.

So it was a shock to see that Fabrizio's face was dark with anger and he was barely containing his temper.

Fabrizio was equally disconcerted to see Filippo,

who he had forgotten was staying with them in the Via Larga. The Grand Duke would rather have said what he had come for without Filippo standing by, but it couldn't be helped.

'Brother,' he began, 'I come with alarming news. And I fear it will affect you too, cousin. My sister has vanished.'

'Beatrice? Vanished?' said Filippo. He immediately felt relieved that he hadn't actually ordered the jewels. 'Do you mean she has been kidnapped?'

Fabrizio didn't entertain that suggestion for a moment. 'It might be better if she had been,' he said bitterly. 'No, I fear she has run away.'

Filippo was so shocked that he made up for the lack of reaction from Gaetano and Francesca.

'Run away, but why? And where?'

'I am sorry to say this so publicly,' said Fabrizio uncomfortably, 'but I fear it was a result of my putting your proposal to her this morning.'

Filippo looked mortified. 'She . . . She refused me?'

'On the contrary,' said Fabrizio, anxious to mollify him. 'She very clearly promised to marry you – or no one.'

'Then perhaps she has entered a convent?' said Filippo, still stung but feeling it was better for Beatrice to be a nun than to refuse him in favour of another suitor.

'Perhaps,' said Fabrizio doubtfully. 'But it is inexcusable. You have my deepest apology that any sister of mine should so forget her position as to leave her home, without any message about where she was going and none for you either. It is not the behaviour of a princess.'

Filippo bowed his head. He was beginning to think that this was a lucky escape.

'Of course,' he said. 'There is no question now of repeating my offer, if it is so distasteful to my cousin.'

'You are very quiet, Gaetano,' said Fabrizio. 'What do you think about this?'

'I think that Beatrice has the right to decide whom she will marry,' said Gaetano.

'Well, of course she does!' exclaimed Fabrizio. 'Did I ever suggest anything else? But why should she refuse Filippo? Look at him! Where could she find a better husband?'

Filippo felt rather self-conscious but tried to look like the model of an ideal husband. Francesca felt sorry for him.

'I'm sure my brother did not wish to force himself on Beatrice if she didn't care for him,' she said. 'There must have been an unfortunate misunderstanding. I'm sure Beatrice will return when everything has calmed down.'

'But where is she?' said Fabrizio. 'Poor Caterina is wild with worry and so am I. How could she disappear without leaving a note? And where could she go?'

'Might she have gone to another branch of the family?' suggested Filippo. 'Perhaps to Cousin Lucia in Fortezza? She has often invited her, I believe.'

'That is a good thought,' said Fabrizio. 'I shall send messages to all the family asking for news – but discreetly of course,' he added, nodding to Filippo.

Gaetano was relieved that the suggestion had come from Filippo; he and Francesca had not needed to tell any lies. And now Fabrizio had something to do, he was eager to leave.

Francesca ordered the best wine from their cellar and poured Filippo a goblet herself. He was looking white but whether with shock or anger it was hard to tell.

'I shall go back to Bellona in the morning,' he said after two goblets of wine. 'I've wasted enough time here. It was a fool's errand.'

'I'm so sorry, Lippo,' said his sister. She knew just how humiliated and hurt he must feel.

Gaetano was sorry for his brother-in-law too and throughout dinner kept him engaged in conversation about affairs in Bellona, deferring to Filippo's opinions on all sorts of matters until the prince, flattered and under the influence of their good red wine, felt a bit better.

'It would never have worked,' he said, slightly slurring his words. 'She didn't love me, you know. Don't know why. But you need a wife that loves you, don't you? I mean you love Gaetano here, don't you, 'Cesca?'

'I do, dear,' said Francesca. 'And I agree with you. A marriage should come only with love. And you will find a wife to love you, I'm sure.'

'Maybe Lucia would have me?' said Filippo.

'I think you should forget all about marrying for a while,' said Gaetano. 'You've had a bad experience and you need to get over it. How about another glass of wine?'

*

It was only an hour or so after the Duchessa returned to her palazzo that the State mandola she had sent to collect her guest moored at the piazzetta. It was very late at night by then. Arianna herself went down to the courtyard to meet the little party of arrivals. Her heart went out to the slight figure in the green velvet cloak, whose pitifully small luggage was carried by the mandolier.

'Princess!' she said, going forward to embrace the sister of her enemy.

And Beatrice, who once feared she might have this warm young woman as a stepmother, now fell gratefully into the arms of her rescuer.

'Welcome to Bellezza,' said Arianna. 'Please stay as long as you would like. We are honoured by your visit.'

'Thank you, Your Grace. You are so kind,' said Beatrice. Now that she felt safe at last, she feared she might cry.

'Then you must repay my kindness by calling me Arianna,' said the Duchessa. 'We shall be like sisters. Can I offer you something to eat or drink?'

'No, thank you,' said Beatrice, exhausted. 'But I should be so grateful if you could just have me shown to my room. I feel I should like to sleep for a long time.'

Chapter 10

A Change of Direction

Isabel's life had changed out of all recognition. She was so busy and so tired leading two lives in parallel that she almost always forgot to be unnoticeable. Even though she often had dark circles under her eyes, at least two boys had started chatting her up since she'd been stravagating and she hardly ever thought about Charlotte these days.

Laura had noticed the difference in her. 'What's been going on?' she asked one day on the way to school when Ayesha wasn't with them. 'Are you seeing Sky now?'

'I wish,' said Isabel.

'He doesn't seem to be with Alice any more.'

'I know,' said Isabel, who hugged this thought to herself daily.

'Do you know why they broke up?' asked Laura.

'Not a clue,' said Isabel. She was discovering it was easier to lie, even to a good friend, than risk talking about Talia to non-Stravaganti. 'He's still really cut up about it,' she added quickly, to distract Laura. 'I don't think he'll be dating again any time soon. More's the pity.'

'But you do spend a lot of time with him and his friends,' said Laura wistfully.

It was true. The coordinated approach to stravagation had become a sort of obsession with the group. After every trip to Talia Isabel felt like a soldier or spy reporting for debriefing. If it was a school day, they'd try to grill her during lunch, but if they couldn't get her on her own they expected to meet up at the café or at Nick's house after school.

Isabel had drunk more coffee since she started stravagating than ever before in her life. And the caffeine was really useful now that she wasn't getting much sleep.

In Talia, she spent time with Flavia, Fausto and Duke Germano. She was now quite used to Vitale, the spotted cat, who seemed bigger each time she saw him. She was also getting used to Andrea the pirate, who was a much more dangerous domestic presence.

He had come to visit Flavia once or twice and an uneasy truce had been struck between them. Isabel knew there was a lot of family history she had not been told, but didn't dare ask who Andrea's father was or if he had any brothers and sisters.

And he had produced one positive effect on her: she was learning to swim. Not by being thrown overboard by a pirate, but by having private lessons at the local swimming pool. It was a deadly secret between her and her mother and Isabel was paying for her own lessons out of unspent Christmas money.

She could now put her face underwater without freaking out and could do a width of breaststroke. She was never going to rival Charlie but at least if she fell off a pirate ship she would not sink straight away.

William Dethridge was relieved to have Rodolfo and Arianna back in Bellezza but was quite confused to find them entertaining a di Chimici princess.

'This is our dear friend Dottore Crinamorte,' said Arianna, introducing the old Elizabethan to Beatrice. 'Dottore, the Principessa Beatrice is staying with me for a while. She is in need of a holiday.'

Dethridge's manners were far too good to query this explanation and he kissed the princess's hand with great courtesy but soon found an excuse to visit Rodolfo in his laboratory; there was nothing he could safely ask or tell Arianna in front of a di Chimici, even an apparently well-disposed one.

'I wolde tell thee summe thynge,' he said to the Regent as soon as he had found him. 'I have resolved the probleme of the talismannes! At the leaste, I thynke so. We moste try yt oute.'

'But that is wonderful!' said Rodolfo. 'It means that any Stravagante will be able to go to any of our cities. How did you do it?'

'Ye moste allowe mee summe mysteries,' said the Doctor, smiling. 'I have a reputatioune to holde up as the source and origine of oure brethren, do I notte?'

'True,' said Rodolfo. 'But what must the Stravaganti do?'

'Wolle, atte this tyme they moste fall asleep thynking of their citie. Botte if they wishe to go to anothire, they moste thynke of yt.'

'It can't be as simple as that, surely?' said Rodolfo.

'Noe, yt is notte,' said Dethridge. 'Firste, they moste already be Stravaygers, who have travelled to their proper citie bifore. Thenne I thynke they moste speake out the name of the citie they want to visit – notte just thynke yt. Bot I cannot bee certaine until a Stravayger has made assaye.'

'What a pity we don't have a Stravagante from the other world in Bellezza just now,' said Rodolfo. 'But perhaps I could get a message to Isabella and see if she can try coming here?'

'Thatte wolde be beste,' said Dethridge. 'Now, telle mee how ye fared in the Citie of Shyppes.'

'Well, very well,' said Rodolfo. 'Duke Germano has agreed to join forces with us and I have found a spy who will give us the word when the attack is to be launched.'

'A bettire espial thanne thatte Henry, I hope,' said the doctor.

'Enrico?' said Rodolfo. 'Well, I'm not sure you'd think so. He is a pirate known as the Black Raider, but in fact he is called Andrea and is the son of our sister Flavia in Classe.'

Dethridge's bushy eyebrows shot up. 'A brigand? Are ye certaine hee is trusteworthy?'

'We have Flavia's word,' said Rodolfo. 'Not as a mother but as a Stravagante.'

'And whatte of those Chymists?' asked Dethridge.

'The di Chimici are indeed in league with the Gate people,' said Rodolfo.

'Thenne wherefore do ye have one of these Chymists here in the palace?' asked the Elizabethan. 'Is shee a hostage?'

'No,' said Rodolfo. 'Princess Beatrice is a runaway. She has defied her brother the Grand Duke, who wanted her to marry Filippo di Chimici.'

'Thenne shee is a yonge mayde of goode sense!' said Dethridge, 'and worthy to be protected.'

*

Isabel had not long arrived at Flavia's house when her Stravagante took her to her inner chamber where she had an elaborate set of mirrors. At first, Isabel thought it was the dressing table arrangement of a vain woman but then she saw that each mirror already had an image in it, though these were not reflections of anything in the room. Isabel peered closer and saw that each glass seemed to show a room or outdoor scene in what she guessed were other Talian cities. And then she spotted Rodolfo's face in one of them.

'He is trying to tell me something,' said Flavia. 'Wait – he says he wants to speak to you.'

Isabel sat in front of the mirror and tried to concentrate on the Bellezzan Stravagante.

Greetings, Isabella, he thought-spoke. *I have a commission for you.*

Isabel was thrilled.

But Doctor Dethridge is going to explain what we want you to do, Rodolfo continued. *And I should warn you that you might find him difficult to understand. Luciano says that all Stravaganti from your world hear him talking in old-fashioned language, because he is an English speaker from your world hundreds of years ago.*

The others had told Isabel about William Dethridge, the man who had started the whole business of stravagation – by accident.

Another face replaced Rodolfo's in the same glass; it was a man in his sixties with white hair. He seemed very hale and had twinkly eyes.

Signorina Ysabel, he thought-spoke, *how wolde ye lyke to visite us hire in Bellezza?*

Very much, replied Isabel. *But how can I do that? My talisman takes me only to Classe.*

Ah, I have bene laboring on thatte probleme. The nexte tyme ye stravayge, as wol as thynkinge about Bellezza in stede of Classe, ye moste say the name out loude bifore ye slepe. Do ye ondirstonde?

I think so, said Isabel. *I must think about Bellezza and say the city's name out loud before I go to sleep?*

Yt wolde holpe if ye canne thynke about the palace of the Dutchesse, said Dethridge.

How will I do that? said Isabel. *I have never seen it.*

I wolle aske Maistre Rudolphe to describe yt to ye, said Dethridge. *Fare ye woll, Ysabel.*

Rodolfo came and drew a thought-picture for Isabel of the Ducal Palace in Bellezza. In particular he described Arianna's private sitting room. And Isabel agreed to give the new method a try that very night.

*

Cardinal Rinaldo received a summons from his uncle

the Pope in Remora. This was not unusual. Less than a year ago, when the Cardinal had first taken orders, he had been his uncle's chaplain. And the Pope sometimes forgot that his nephew had been elevated to the scarlet hat, Rinaldo's rise in the church had been so sudden and dazzling.

Pope Lenient VI was also Ferdinando di Chimici, the Prince of Remora, and it was a family matter he wanted to discuss with Rinaldo on this occasion.

'Ah, nephew,' he said when Rinaldo was shown in. 'How are you? You are looking rather thin.'

Rinaldo could not say the same of his uncle. Ferdinando, always corpulent, was now so fat he could hardly get out of his chair.

'I am well, thank you, Holiness. Just preoccupied with our continued struggle with the Stravaganti.'

'No progress then?' asked Ferdinando.

'No. We had a good lead in Padavia but it has all gone quiet again,' said Rinaldo regretfully.

'Well, enough of them,' said Ferdinando. 'I have had an urgent message from your cousin Fabrizio.'

'From the Grand Duke? How is His Grace?'

'Most perturbed. His sister has run away from home.'

'Cousin Beatrice?' said Rinaldo. 'Whatever for?'

'Apparently she did not want to marry Cousin Filippo.'

Rinaldo closed his eyes. That dolt Filippo again! He could quite imagine his botching the business of proposing marriage as he had done the capture of the Stravagante.

'I'm sorry to hear that, Holiness. But where is she now?'

134

'That is what Fabrizio is trying to find out. He writes to ask if she has sought the sanctuary of the Church in Remora.'

'And she has not?'

The Pope raised an eyebrow. 'Certainly not. I would have informed her brother straight away. Not that I approve of forced marriage, as I think you know.'

He frowned at Rinaldo, who had forced his cousin Francesca to marry an old man and then had to come and beg the Pope to dissolve the marriage.

Rinaldo pretended not to understand him.

'I don't suppose you have any news of Beatrice,' said Ferdinando. 'But what about that spy fellow you used to employ? Could he be used to search for the princess?'

'As far as I know, Enrico is still in Padavia,' said Rinaldo. 'He is not working for the di Chimici any more. You can't have forgotten that he helped to kill your brother in the duel.'

'Ah yes,' said the Pope vaguely, who had forgotten that. 'Pity. Well, can you find another spy? I'm worried about little Beatrice. Such a quiet and innocent girl. I don't like to think of her wandering in the world without the protection of a husband or brother.'

In one respect, Rinaldo and Enrico were very alike: they had a good nose for opportunity. Rinaldo gladly accepted the commission to search out Beatrice. If he could find her, it would put him in Fabrizio's good books.

He stepped out into the circular campo and looked with distaste at all the astrological signs inset in its twelve panels. The anti-magic laws had been introduced in Remora, as in all the cities controlled by the di Chimici, but the Pope was doing nothing to enforce them.

He is too old and too tired for the job, thought Rinaldo. *Now, if I were in control here I'd have all this superstition uprooted in no time.*

*

Arianna spent the morning in her private room but she had to make her excuses to Beatrice; she sent Barbara to tell the princess that the Duchessa had a bad headache. Arianna did not feel ready to trust Beatrice with the secrets of the Stravaganti yet.

Besides, she did not know if this new scheme of Dottore Crinamorte's to bring Isabella to Bellezza would work. Rodolfo came to wait with her for some of the morning but still the time dragged. Arianna was not the sort of young woman who had embroidery to occupy her. She sent for Mariotto and asked him to bring the remaining male African kitten so that she could begin to socialise him.

Rigello, which was what he had been named, was fascinated to be in his mistress's chamber and sniffed everything in it. He was extremely puzzled by the full-length mirror and advanced cautiously on his own reflection, a ridge of fur rising along his back as he confronted this other cat.

Arianna was so entertained that she didn't notice Isabel's arrival in the room. But Rigello did and with one leap pinned the startled girl to the floor.

'Oh no, Gello, let her go – she's a friend!'

But the half-grown cat growled. He knew there was something unnatural about the way this person had appeared in the room. The cat in the mirror had been bad enough – another male as big as him but without any smell. But this was worse: a human being where there had been empty space before. He took a lot of coaxing to release his grip on Isabel's dress.

He went off to sit in the corner and wash his ruffled fur but every now and again uttered another rumble from his deep chest.

'I'm so sorry,' said Arianna, helping the flustered girl up.

'He's much bigger than Vitale, isn't he?' said Isabel, shaken. 'And much fiercer.'

'He's not usually bad,' said Arianna, 'but he's never seen anyone stravagate before. He's a dear really. Just as gentle as his brother.'

She fetched the cat a strictly forbidden sweetmeat and he took it daintily between his big white teeth.

'What about me?' said Isabel, grinning. 'I've had a shock too.'

Arianna held out the silver dish and Isabel took a couple of sugared almonds.

'You did it,' said Arianna. 'You stravagated to a different city!'

Isabel was looking round the room, comparing it with Rodolfo's description and committing it to memory in case she needed to get here again. It was a room with two doors, one of them bolted. That must be the one to the secret passage that led to Rodolfo's old palazzo with his laboratory in it.

A knock on the other door preceded the entrance of a very good-looking middle-aged woman, who could only be Arianna's mother, Silvia.

'Good heavens,' she said, looking at Isabel. 'You

must be the new Stravagante. And Guglielmo's trick has worked.'

Silvia came forward, her grey taffeta dress rustling over the floor, and made a close inspection of Isabel. Rigello whined from his corner and the former Duchessa laughed.

'Remarkable,' she said. 'We live in remarkable times.'

But she caressed the cat. 'What is wrong, Rigello? Has Arianna put you in the corner because you have been bad?'

'He put himself there,' said Arianna, 'because he pounced on Isabella as soon as she arrived.'

The spotted cat came cautiously forward to sniff at Isabel, letting Arianna and Silvia stroke him. Isabel held out her hand to his furry muzzle.

'You are not afraid?' asked Silvia approvingly.

'I have met his brother in Classe, ma'am,' said Isabel.

'Oh, call me Silvia,' said Arianna's mother. 'All the Stravaganti from your world do. How is young Tino? What is his name in your world?'

'Sky,' said Arianna.

'He is well,' said Isabel. 'But a bit sad,' she added impulsively.

'Why sad?' asked Silvia.

'Well, it's his story, I suppose,' said Isabel. 'But he has broken up with his girlfriend.'

'Broken up?' said Silvia. 'How vivid your modern language is. But I understand. Poor Tino, poor Sky. Still, she never did like Talia.'

Isabel was impressed by the older woman's immediate grasp of Sky's situation.

'Well, we must take you to Rodolfo,' said Silvia briskly. 'Though I think you have met him before. But Arianna, you must give her a mask. She is over sixteen, I'm sure.'

And Isabel had to accept a green silk mask, which Arianna tied over her eyes.

'I think we should take the secret passage, don't you?' asked Silvia. 'Come, Rigello, this will be an adventure for you.'

*

Grand Duke Fabrizio was beside himself with worry and anger. No messenger had brought back any news of Beatrice from any of the di Chimici cities of the north and now he was reduced to sending to the independent city-states. It would soon be public knowledge that the di Chimici princess was missing and had run away from her brother.

In this state he went to see Gaetano. Filippo had left the palazzo on the Via Larga and gone back to Bellona, feeing humiliated that his marriage proposal had been so badly received.

'There is still no news,' said Fabrizio, pacing the salon. 'Suppose something terrible has happened to her?'

'You mean something more terrible than a forced marriage?' asked Gaetano quietly.

His brother rounded on him. 'Of course I would not have *made* her marry Filippo against her will,' he said. 'Not if she really hated the idea.'

'But perhaps she *thought* you would,' said Gaetano. 'You must admit you are a forceful character.'

Fabrizio stared him in the eyes. 'You know where she is, don't you? You've known all along!' He took Gaetano by the collar as if he would hoist him up and choke him, but something in his younger brother's unwavering gaze made him stop.

He slumped into a chair and covered his face with his hands. 'What has happened to me?' he muttered. 'My sister fled from me and my only remaining brother a conspirator.'

'We were going to tell you when you had calmed down,' said Gaetano, putting his hand on his brother's shoulder. 'She is safe, I promise you.'

'Where is she?' asked Fabrizio, raising his face from his hands. Gaetano was moved to see it was streaked with tears. He didn't doubt that his brother was really worried about Beatrice.

'Well, I will tell you,' said Gaetano. 'But you must promise not to fly into a rage.'

Fabrizio nodded.

'She is with the Duchessa of Bellezza.'

Chapter 11

Spreading Wings

'It was fantastic!' said Isabel when she met the others after school next day.

She had been bursting to tell them about going to Bellezza but had decided she really must spend some time with Laura and they had lunched together in the cafeteria. Her friend had looked at her with envy; Isabel seemed so much more confident these days, with a wider group of friends, but Laura was still the same – a mass of neuroses and phobias.

Isabel was sorry for Laura but she knew she couldn't explain to her why she herself felt so much more full of life and energy.

It all burst out as soon as they were in Nick's attic though.

'Bellezza is amazing,' she said. 'Have you all been there?'

'I went to Luciano and Arianna's engagement party,' said Matt. 'But I didn't see much – just the palazzo.'

It made Isabel feel special to have wandered the streets of Bellezza in daylight. Each city seemed to have had its own Stravagante from her world but Bellezza's had been Lucien and he was no longer here.

'So, it really works then – you really can go to different cities with the talismans?' asked Georgia.

'It would be very useful if we were going back to Talia,' said Nick, a bit wistfully.

'You'd better tell us how to do it, in case we need to come and rescue you in Classe,' said Sky, smiling.

It was the first time Isabel had seen him smile for ages. The split with Alice seemed to have been final and she was even being cold to Georgia. Isabel was beginning to see how it could be problematic in both worlds, being a Stravagante. But she told them Dethridge's simple formula.

'I met him, you know,' she said. 'Arianna took me round to his house and I met him and his wife.'

'We've all met him, I think,' said Matt. 'Did he sound funny to you?'

'It was really weird,' said Isabel. 'But I found I could understand him OK. He was so happy about the talisman bringing me to Bellezza. And his wife was really kind. She insisted on feeding me up. Arianna said she was her aunt or something.'

'Did you meet anyone else new?' asked Georgia.

'Only Silvia. Oh, and the other spotted cat, the one Arianna's keeping,' said Isabel. 'He attacked me when I arrived but it was all right after a while.'

'Did you stay all day?' asked Sky.

'Yes. After we'd visited Doctor Dethridge, Arianna took me to see the ships being built in the Arsenale.'

'Warships?' asked Nick.

Isabel nodded. 'It was fantastic. The whole place was swarming with people. Of course they were all in a panic because their Duchessa had come on an unexpected visit.'

'Were you on your own?' asked Matt. 'She always had a sort of bodyguard when she came to Padavia, though she was in disguise then.'

Isabel laughed. 'You bet we weren't alone! There were these sort of soldier guys with metal helmets and big pikes. It was quite embarrassing but I suppose she's used to it. There were about half a dozen of them around us wherever we went. Oh, and Arianna's maid, who was carrying spare cloaks with hoods in case it rained on us.'

'Tell us about the ships,' said Nick.

'It wasn't just ships,' said Isabel, remembering that extraordinary day. 'There were people making huge guns and cannonballs and nails and sails and rope and all sorts of things. And everything smelled of tar and salt water and the noise must be deafening on a day when the city's ruler isn't visiting!'

'It sounds as if you enjoyed it,' said Georgia. 'Will you go back?'

'I hope so,' said Isabel. 'I'd like to see all the cities.'

'So would I,' said Nick quietly.

Fabrizio's messengers had been recalled from the independent city-states but were sent out again immediately back to the di Chimici ones to say that Princess Beatrice had been found and was well and happy. The letter he had hand-delivered to Filippo di Chimici in Bellona said a little more than that. After the formalities, the Grand Duke had written:

> *I cannot believe that my sister is now in the heart of our enemies at Bellezza! And that my brother should have conspired with her to this end. I shall not forget the insult to you and to myself. And I shall try to find you a more grateful bride.*

Filippo smiled when he read the letter. He had not come out of this too badly. He had still been smarting from having failed in the mission his cousin had given him in Padavia and having let Luciano escape. But over this business of marrying Beatrice, he could not be faulted. And now Fabrizio felt indebted to him and would seek to do him favours.

It wasn't as if he had felt any particular love for the princess, in spite of the verses he had written her and the posies he had given her. That was all just what he thought a suitor should do, but his heart was whole. And he was sure he would find another bride one day. After all, wasn't he a di Chimici prince? And a handsome one at that, as his looking-glass told him daily.

'There *was* someone else, though,' said Isabel, once she had told the others all she could remember about the ship-building in the Arsenale. 'When we got back to the palazzo, Arianna introduced me to some di Chimici princess who was staying there. I was a bit surprised but I had to leave soon after that.'

'Which one?' asked Nick.

'Her name was Beatrice,' said Isabel, stumbling over the Italian way of pronouncing all the syllables: Bay-ah-tree-chay. 'She seemed nice but very sad.'

'That was my sister,' said Nick flatly.

Isabel was horrified. She hadn't studied her family tree carefully enough and she'd just assumed that Beatrice was one of the distant cousins – not someone so close to Nick.

'I'm sorry,' she said. But Nick wasn't taking any notice of her. He was fiercely whispering to Georgia.

'Don't worry,' said Sky. 'They have issues about Talia. You were bound to meet one of Nick's family one day. Shall we leave them to it?'

So Isabel, Matt and Sky made their excuses and left, while Georgia and Nick seemed to have got into a full-scale row.

On the way back home, they ran into Isabel's brother, Charlie. His expression at seeing her with two of the school's most sought-after males was pure delight to his sister.

'Hey, Bel,' he said, clearly impressed. 'What's up?'

She introduced him to the boys, but they said they had to head off and Isabel and Charlie ended up walking home together.

'You OK?' asked Charlie.

'Fine,' said Isabel. 'You?'

'Yeah. But that's not what I'm asking. I mean, what's going on with those guys?'

'Matt and Sky?' said Isabel. 'Nothing. Why?'

'I mean why are you always out nowadays? You're never at home except for dinner and homework. We haven't hung out together for ages.'

Isabel shrugged. 'I suppose I'm growing up. At last,' she added.

She couldn't tell Charlie the truth about Talia so it was easier, as with Laura, to tell lies. But then she felt sorry for him. He was her only brother and she really did love him.

'Why don't we catch a movie on Saturday?' she said. 'If you aren't doing anything.'

She had got into the habit of not stravagating on Saturdays, just to catch up on sleep. Sunday was the only day when she could lie in without feeling guilty.

'OK,' said Charlie. But he was still looking at her strangely.

Beatrice was getting used to being in Bellezza. She had even agreed to wear a mask when she appeared in public and rather liked the feeling of anonymity it gave her. In Giglia everyone knew the di Chimici princess; here she was just another young noblewoman with a hidden face.

And she found she really did like Arianna and admired her. Although the Duchessa was so much younger than the princess, she had been through a lot in her life, not knowing her true parentage till she was nearly sixteen and then being on trial for her life till she was revealed to be the daughter of the previous Duchessa.

And then that Duchessa had been assassinated,

horribly, blown up in her glass-panelled audience room. Arianna had glossed over that part of her story but Beatrice had heard rumours that the killing had been authorised by her own father, though carried out by a hireling.

And yet here was Arianna treating her as kindly as any host could and listening to her troubles. It was hard to believe that this was the young woman Beatrice's father had wanted to marry and who had refused him in favour of the young Cavaliere who later killed him in a duel.

Beatrice hadn't met Luciano since arriving in Bellezza but she remembered him from a dinner her father had given in Giglia after he had been poisoned, and she saw how Arianna looked whenever she mentioned him.

'You are happy in your engagement,' she said. 'And I am glad for you. That's all I wanted for myself – to be happy at the thought of the man I should marry. Not full of dread.'

'And why did you dread Filippo?' asked Arianna.

'There is nothing wrong with him – except that he is a bit weak,' said Beatrice. 'But he was not my choice and I do not love him.'

'That is a good enough reason for anyone,' said Arianna.

'I hope my brother will think so,' said Beatrice. 'If not, I don't know if I can ever go back to Giglia.'

'Don't think about it now,' said Arianna. 'You are safe here with me. Would you like to speak to Gaetano now?' she added impulsively.

Beatrice looked at her as if she had gone mad. 'How could I do that when he is in Giglia?'

'You know my father has . . . certain powers?' said Arianna.

Beatrice found Rodolfo quite terrifying and would have believed anything of him but it was one thing to have suspicions and quite another to hear his daughter offer her his magic. She remembered how adamant Fabrizio had been about the anti-magic laws in Giglia. But then she thought, *I am not under Fabrizio's control any more.*

'But can he really communicate with people who are not in the same place?'

'Did you not wonder how Gaetano was able to tell me you needed a place of sanctuary?' asked Arianna. 'We have a friend in Giglia who is of the same Order as Rodolfo. He is able to get in touch with my father and Gaetano went to him. I think it would be a good idea for you to speak to your brother yourself and I shall ask Rodolfo to show you how. Though you might find it difficult. It is not exactly "speaking". But you would see his face and be able to send your thoughts to him.'

'I should like that very much,' said Beatrice.

Over the next few weeks, Isabel had her wish and travelled to all the cities the other Stravaganti had visited. She had become quite adept at making the transition. But she still visited Classe more often and limited her other trips to once a week, on a Friday night.

Her first choice after Bellezza had been Remora. She wasn't horsey like Georgia and Nick but she loved the idea of the City of Stars. Georgia had described very carefully the stables in the contrada of the Ram.

'But Cesare won't be there,' she said. 'He's still in Padavia with Luciano. Perhaps you can meet him when you go there. Oh, I wish I was coming with you!'

'Why don't you?' said Isabel. 'I mean, you wouldn't even have to use the new method. You'd stravagate to Remora anyway.'

Georgia stared at her and then started to laugh.

'You know that Nick and I have been arguing nonstop ever since you went to Bellezza? He wants to go there too and see his sister. I've been telling him for days that it's madness and he must forget all about his Talian life. And now you say "Come with me" – simple as that – and I'm suddenly thinking "Why not?" I must be mad myself.'

'But why?' said Isabel. 'I can see the point about Nick – he might be recognised. But what's to stop you?'

Georgia sighed. Isabel hadn't been part of that whole terrible time when Nick had wanted to die again in this world and go back to Talia. He had even wanted Luciano to swap places with him and be Vicky and David's son again. It was so complicated and difficult to explain to anyone who hadn't lived through it.

'I agreed to make a choice with him nearly a year ago,' she told Isabel, aware that the other girl didn't know about the whole state of affairs with Luciano. 'I said he needed to live his life here and forget about the past. And I said I would too.'

'Did that have something to do with Luciano?'

asked Isabel, startling Georgia.

'Well, I don't know how you know that,' said Georgia slowly. 'But yes, it did. Nick and I both made our choices.'

'But there's no chance of seeing Luciano in Remora, is there?' said Isabel. 'Wouldn't you just like to see it again? I mean the flying horse and everything?'

A wave of nostalgia swept over Georgia. To see her Stravagante Paolo again and his family, and all the horses, including Merla, the miraculous black mare with wings! What harm could it do? She had suppressed her memories for so long out of love and loyalty to Nick and now they came flooding back, threatening to overwhelm her. She longed to see the red and yellow flags of the Ram again and teach someone else about the complex feuds and loyalties of the City of Stars.

She looked at Isabel and took a deep breath.

'OK,' she said. 'But just once – and don't say anything to Nick.'

So the next Friday the two girls, sleeping in their separate houses, clutched their talismans and thought of Remora. Georgia arrived first and just sat in the straw inhaling the smell of the stables that was familiar to her in both worlds. A soft whickering from one of the stalls took her to Arcangelo and that was where Isabel found her, her arms round the big chestnut horse's neck.

'Wow!' said Isabel. 'It worked. I still can't get used to it.'

She looked round at the quiet, dusty stable; it was still quite early in the morning in Talia. They had both managed to stravagate as soon as they went to bed.

There was a sound of buckets clanking and then a burly grey-haired man came into the stable. His eyes lit up when he saw Isabel, who was wearing her green dress, just as she had in Bellezza.

'Isabella?' he said, putting down his buckets and coming towards her with hands outstretched in welcome. 'I am Paolo,' he said. 'Welcome to Remora.'

'Hello, Paolo,' said Georgia, coming sheepishly out of Arcangelo's stall. Unlike Isabel, she was wearing twenty-first-century nightclothes.

Paolo gasped. 'Georgio! I mean Georgia. I wasn't expecting you.' He gripped her in a bear hug. Isabel found herself thinking that Georgia was never so emotional in their own world as she seemed to be in Talia.

'It was a spur of the moment decision,' said Georgia, not entirely truthfully. She had wondered about consulting Rodolfo and then decided against it. Once she'd made up her mind to return to Remora, she couldn't have borne it if he had forbidden her.

'Can I borrow Teresa's red dress again?' she asked.

'Of course, I'm sure you can,' said Paolo, grinning broadly. 'Come into the house and meet her. Welcome to both of you. What a pity Cesare isn't here.'

'I'm hoping to meet him in Padavia,' said Isabel.

'It is a wonder what the Dottore has accomplished with the talismans,' said Paolo.

They went into the warm kitchen that Georgia remembered so well and Paolo's wife, Teresa, gave a little scream when she saw them both. Georgia let herself be kissed and fussed over and asked after the little children she had last seen a year and a half ago.

'There's no Stellata to prepare for at the moment, is there?' Isabel was asking Paolo.

'It doesn't happen till August,' he said. 'But we say in Remora that the Stellata is run all year round. We are always preparing for the next one, from the minute the last one is over.'

The girls stayed long enough to share the family breakfast but then Georgia wanted to show Isabel the city. Paolo had many jobs to do in the stables, with Cesare away at university, but he promised to take them to visit Merla in Santa Fina later in the afternoon. The winged horse lived in the stables there now, with her mother, to protect her from the overwhelming attentions of the Remorans.

Isabel was as enchanted by the city as Georgia had hoped. They were in the circular campo, where Georgia was explaining again the astrological symbols and the complex web of alliances and rivalries between contrade that dominated the city. Suddenly Georgia grabbed her arm and hissed, 'That's Rinaldo di Chimici!'

Isabel saw a thin, bony-faced man with a scarlet hat and soutane striding across the campo. The girls were completely exposed, with nothing to hide behind in the open campo. Georgia spun Isabel to face her and pretended to engage her in deep conversation while the Cardinal passed by. She was shaking.

'What's the matter?' asked Isabel. 'Is he very dangerous?'

'Oh, he wouldn't stab you in public,' said Georgia. 'But he's captured Luciano twice and Matt once and was behind Cesare being kidnapped. And he gave the orders for the assassination of the last Duchessa – twice!'

Isabel caught Georgia's mood. Up till then being in Talia had felt a bit like a role-playing game, even in Classe, even when being kidnapped by a pirate. But now she was looking at the retreating back of a genuinely ruthless man and she felt in real danger for the first time.

'What if he had looked at us and seen we didn't have shadows?' she whispered to Georgia.

'We've got to be more careful,' said Georgia. 'Let's go and visit the Lioness's stables. It won't matter not having shadows when we're indoors.'

The rest of their stravagation passed without incident. And Isabel saw the flying horse, something she thought she would never forget. As it began to get dark, the two girls climbed into Paolo's hayloft and settled down holding their talismans. Isabel admired the little model that looked so like Merla.

'It's been great,' she said. 'I'm so glad you came with me. I wouldn't have known that was Rinaldo in the campo and he might have spotted I was a Stravagante.'

'You haven't been doing your homework,' said Georgia. But she was smiling. And Isabel felt at last that Georgia was her friend.

Chapter 12

The Life Aquatic

Isabel got out of meeting the other Stravaganti the next day, on the grounds that she was going out in the evening with Charlie and needed to do her homework. She knew she wouldn't be able to look Nick in the eye if he asked her about Remora and she was amazed that Georgia thought she could get away with it. But Isabel would have to meet them on Sunday; she hoped Georgia would have got used to lying to Nick by then.

All day, while she wrestled with her English essay on *The Woman in Black*, Isabel couldn't help remembering Remora and the stables where she had seen the flying horse. There hadn't been time to ride Merla, and she wouldn't have dared to get up on her if there had been, but just seeing her, with her glossy black wings folded down on her back, had been enough. Merla had even spread them out when she realised that Georgia was in her stable.

Isabel knew that Georgia had ridden Merla once. It had been a gift to her from Paolo after Rodolfo had been angry with her. It had been something to do with Nick and smuggling him away from Talia to their world. The more time Isabel spent stravagating, the more she realised what a huge step that had been – for Nicholas and the people who helped him.

She might have problems with her family from time to time but to leave them all and go and live with strangers in a world hundreds of years in the future! That took guts. But she remembered that Nick had needed medical help to lead a normal life, help that hadn't been available in his world. And she wondered if Luciano would have done such a brave thing in search of a cure for his cancer.

'How's the essay going?' asked her mother, popping her head round the door.

She was carrying a tray of juice and biscuits. Isabel noted one glass; she had been to Charlie's room first.

'You're being a storybook mother,' she said.

Sarah Evans laughed. 'No. If I was, the biscuits would have been rustled up in our kitchen this morning instead of being Sainsbury's finest. What are you writing about?'

'What is the ghost's motivation in *The Woman in Black*?' Isabel read from her homework sheet.

Sarah grimaced. She had been with the school party to see the play in the West End and they had both been terrified.

'Rather you than me,' she said. 'Only . . . you don't seem to have got very far.'

They both looked at the blank white screen on Isabel's computer with the essay title typed at the top.

'Yes, well, I've been thinking,' said Isabel, cramming a big bite of chocolate cookie into her mouth. 'These are better than if you'd made them,' she said.

'Cheek,' said her mother. But she got the message and left her daughter to it.

Try as she might, Isabel couldn't wrest her mind away from sunny Remora and back to the misty fens of the novel she was supposed to be writing about.

Even in early March the Reman sunshine had warmth in it and she could just imagine what it would be like in high summer when the Race of the Stars would be run. She wished she could be there to see it but her task in Talia might be over by then, one way or another.

Even if she could stravagate to only one city of her choice it would still be Classe, however much she had fallen in love with the City of Stars. It was Georgia's place, not hers.

Isabel shook herself. 'The ghost's motivation is . . .' she typed.

Rinaldo had paid spies to look for Princess Beatrice in every city in Talia. So he was not best pleased to hear that she had been in Bellezza all the time.

'Why there, of all places?' he muttered under his breath, dismissing the messenger who had brought the news. The Cardinal was going to have to give his spy network a new task and that involved sending out messengers of his own: a costly business.

But he cheered up when his local spy from Remora was shown in with a very reluctant-looking stable-boy.

'Tell His Eminence what you told me,' prompted the spy. 'He'll be very interested, I promise you.'

'I work in the stables of the Lioness, signor,' said the boy.

'Your Eminence,' corrected the spy, cuffing him round the head.

'Ouch! Sorry, Your Eminence,' said the boy. 'And yesterday we had a couple of ladies visit.'

The Cardinal couldn't think what on earth interest a 'couple of ladies' might be, but he motioned to the boy to continue.

'Very keen on the horses they were, Eminence. And one of them, the one in the red dress, she was very knowledgeable about them.'

'And?' asked Rinaldo. *When would this oaf ever get to the point?*

'It was strange,' said the boy. 'They both seemed quite ordinary and normal, but when they left the stable I noticed that, well, that they didn't have any shadows!'

And then he curled his right-hand thumb to little finger and touched it to his breast and brow, like someone trying to ward off danger or the supernatural.

'Now that is very interesting,' said the Cardinal more kindly than before. 'You are quite sure? No shadow for either of them?'

'Not a one, sir, I mean Eminence,' said the boy, relieved to have got his story out and not been told off for wasting the time of the man in red.

'Now would you describe both these ladies to me?' said the Cardinal. 'Every detail you can remember –

what they wore, what they looked like, where they were going when they left you?'

'The one in the red dress had a tattoo on her shoulder,' said the boy. 'It was of the flying horse. You know, the one that was born in the Ram.'

The Ram! Rinaldo's instincts had been right. The Horsemaster was a Stravagante; he was sure of it now. These must have been people of his.

The boy went away happy, with several of the Cardinal's silver coins in his pocket.

Isabel somehow managed to scramble through her essay and her History revision for a test on Monday and be ready in time to go to the cinema. She and Charlie had the usual wrangle over what film to see; Isabel would have quite liked *Date Movie*, but Charlie insisted they should go to Islington's little art house cinema, which was showing *The Life Aquatic*. Isabel let him have his way – after all, this was supposed to be an evening to placate him.

And he did seem mellower as they walked home, sharing chips from a paper bag. But he still kept looking at Isabel in a funny way. Finally, he stopped in the middle of the pavement.

'Are you having sex?' he asked abruptly.

'No!' said Isabel. 'Are you?' She felt completely wrong-footed. Charlie was so far off the mark.

'That's not the point,' said Charlie. 'I mean, you've changed. You're more, I don't know, attractive, I suppose. And you hang out with those guys at school . . .'

'Listen,' said Isabel. 'If I *were* having sex with Matt or Sky, or Nick Drake – or all three at once, come to that – it would still be NONE OF YOUR BUSINESS! But, as it happens, I'm not.'

They glared at each other for a bit. Then Charlie relaxed.

'I'm sorry, Bel,' he said, offering her the chip bag. 'It's just that I didn't know what to think and you don't tell me anything any more. You're right. It's none of my business what you do.'

'Too right,' said Isabel, still glowering. But she took another chip. 'Why should I tell you things if you come out with stuff like that?'

They walked the rest of the way home in silence, both wrapped up in their own thoughts.

'There *is* something that's been happening,' said Isabel as they reached their front door, 'but I can't tell you what.'

'I knew it,' said Charlie, then stopped, alarmed. 'It's not something dodgy, is it?'

Isabel sighed. 'No. At least not exactly. It's not illegal. But it's private and it's not my secret so I can't tell you.'

She didn't know she was echoing something Georgia had said nearly three years ago.

And with that Charlie had to be satisfied.

Isabel hadn't meant to stravagate that night but the conversation with her twin had unsettled her so much that she did. But she didn't get very far from the Baptistery before someone came up behind her and put his hand over her mouth.

'Don't scream,' said Andrea.

Isabel felt like biting him hard but she just nodded and he took his hand away. She spun round and glared at him.

'What is it with you?' she hissed. 'Just because you're a pirate, you can't come up and say "hello" like an ordinary person?'

Andrea put his fingers to his lips. 'There's no need to tell everyone,' he whispered. 'I thought you might like to come pirating with me.'

The idea was so outrageous that Isabel suddenly found herself thinking, *Why not?* She was a different person in Talia, much more reckless than in her everyday life. Not that anyone had ever offered her a day's pirating in Islington; her lips curved at the thought. The closest she got to piracy at home was dodgy DVDs in the local market.

Andrea was watching her and could see she wanted to go with him. He smiled back at her, showing his ridiculous silver teeth. 'Come on then,' he said, taking her arm, and walked her briskly down to the harbour.

They boarded the same light caravel on which he had kidnapped Isabel before and sailed out into deep water and round into a bay along the coast from the harbour. Then Andrea let down a small rowing boat and took her over to everyone's idea of a romantic pirate ship.

It was a galleon, a medium-sized roundship, painted regulation pirate black.

'Where's the skull and crossbones?' Isabel asked Andrea. 'It's all that's missing.'

'What's that?' he asked, surprised. He didn't seem to have heard of that basic pirate symbol.

It was all that Isabel could do not to giggle; Andrea's ship was about as piratey as you could get. If the Walt Disney Company had been able to get their hands on it, they would never have needed to build the *Black Pearl* for Johnny Depp.

She had to climb a rope ladder up the side of the *Raider's Revenge*, as the ship was called, tucking her skirts into her waistband to do it. Andrea's crew were lined up on the deck to greet them. Isabel untucked her dress quickly, embarrassed; she hadn't expected a reception committee.

She remembered that in her world there was a superstition that women were bad luck on a ship. That didn't seem to be the case in Talia.

'Anchors aweigh!' ordered Andrea, and took her to his cabin, which was much bigger than the one on his caravel.

'Where are we going?' she asked, used to his style of entertaining by now.

'Out into deeper water for a start,' said Andrea, 'so we can't be shot at from shore. And then east to see what merchant ships we can find.'

'Are you really going to board one?' asked Isabel.

'Certainly,' said Andrea. 'Not much point in pirating otherwise.'

'I thought you'd become a respectable government agent for Bellezza,' said Isabel.

'Spy, pirate – we're all outside the law,' said Andrea. 'And I don't think the authorities will arrest me while I'm doing important work for the Duchessa and Regent of Bellezza, do you?'

'You mean, you'd use your safe-conduct thingy they gave you to get away with piracy?' asked Isabel.

Andrea just shrugged.

'How did you become a pirate in the first place?' she asked, but Andrea's good-natured face closed up.

'I might tell you one day, Bella Isabella,' he said. 'I've taken quite a shine to you. But not today.'

Georgia did her best to avoid Nick on Saturday. It wasn't one of her days for going riding and she had her own English essay to write. But really she just didn't want to talk to him. Her knew her so well, especially where Talia was concerned, that she was sure he would guess she had been back there as soon as he looked at her.

But after a while, she couldn't bear being shut in her room any more and went out to the market. She'd offered to do some shopping for her mother and was looking at a big pile of oranges when someone tapped her on the shoulder. She spun round but, to her relief, it wasn't Nick. It was Matt.

'No Nick?' he asked.

'No Ayesha?' she replied.

He grinned. 'She told me to keep out of her hair till this evening. You?'

'I told Nick I wouldn't see him till tomorrow because of my English essay,' said Georgia. 'But I can't seem to concentrate so I volunteered to do the shopping.'

'Me too,' said Matt. 'I mean not shopping but not being able to concentrate. It's Maths in my case but I keep wondering if Bel got to Remora all right – and back all right too.'

'Oh, she got back all right,' said Georgia quickly. 'I spoke to her this morning. But she's working today too. We won't see her till Nick's tomorrow morning.'

'Shall we go for a coffee then?' said Matt. 'There's plenty of time to do the shopping.'

But Georgia didn't want to risk running into Nick at their café so she suggested going to see Mr Goldsmith instead.

Mortimer Goldsmith ran an antiques shop not far from the market. Georgia's and Matt's talismans had both come from there and he knew all the Barnsbury Stravaganti – even if he didn't know that's what they were. They all regarded him as a sort of honorary grandfather.

As Matt fell into step beside Georgia, she realised she had never been alone with him before. And there was something she had been dying to ask him for months.

'Will you tell me about Arianna and Luciano's engagement party?' she asked.

'I did,' said Matt. 'You remember – I went to it with Constantin just after New Year. I still had a hangover in this world from New Year's Eve but at least the party in Bellezza didn't give me another one to bring back with me.'

'I know you told us you went,' said Georgia, 'but none of the details. I mean, what everyone was wearing and how Luciano and Arianna behaved to each other.'

Matt looked at her as if she had asked him to explain the movements of stars and planets. Actually, he would have found that easier than remembering what someone had worn over two months ago.

'Erm, Arianna looked very nice,' he hazarded.

'Very nice?' said Georgia. 'Is that the best you can do?'

'Rodolfo made a sort of announcement and then he tied their right hands together with a silver ribbon.' Matt was rather pleased with himself for remembering this detail.

Georgia could see she wasn't going to get any more than that out of him.

The subject of her probing was feeling a bit disgruntled with life. Luciano had got into terrible trouble with Professor Constantin and his other teachers for taking a week off in the middle of term without leave. He had been given a hefty fine and had to find other students whose notes he could copy to make up for what he had missed.

Cesare was able to help him with some subjects and came round to his house to share notes.

'You have terrible handwriting,' said Luciano.

'That's not very grateful,' said Cesare. 'Why didn't you hire someone to take notes for you while you were malingering in Classe? All the rich students do that all the time.'

'Sorry,' said Luciano. 'I was in such a hurry to get away. I didn't think I'd miss a whole week.'

'You'll never make a nobleman,' said Cesare. 'What kind of a duke forgets to pay people to do his dirty work for him? You'd never catch a di Chimici doing that.'

'You're right,' sighed Luciano. 'I don't think I'm cut

out to be a duke. I never expected to become one.'

'Arianna didn't expect to be a duchessa, did she?' said his friend. 'But she does a good job.'

'She does indeed. But even she needs to get away sometimes and come here dressed as a boy,' said Luciano. 'It's too much of a strain for her, being genteel and fashionable all the time.'

'It must be weird having your girlfriend – I mean "betrothed" – visiting you in boy's clothes,' said Cesare.

'Not really. She was dressed as a boy the first time I met her,' said Luciano, throwing down his pen and smiling at the memory. 'I thought she *was* a boy. And she was furious with me, though I didn't understand why.'

'You two,' said Cesare, smiling himself. 'You have such a complicated story. When is she coming here again?'

Luciano's face clouded. 'I don't know. Not for ages now she has this war with the east to worry about.'

'But it isn't long since you saw her in Classe.'

'No, but we were hardly ever alone together.' Luciano fiddled with the feather on his quill. 'I can't wait till all this studying is over and we can get married. Then we'll always be together – for the rest of our lives. However long that may be,' he added.

'I can't imagine spending my whole life with anyone,' said Cesare, who had been very popular with girls in Remora ever since he had come riding through the sky over the campo on the winged horse.

'Neither could I when I came to Talia,' said Luciano. 'I hadn't even had a girlfriend before Arianna. But now I feel as if I'm just marking time till we start our life together. I mean, why wait till after the Gate people attack? Any of us might be killed. Or Arianna might lose Bellezza.'

'Then you wouldn't have to be a duke after all,' said Cesare grimly.

*

'If you're going to be a real pirate, you should have a tattoo,' said Andrea.

They were way out to sea now and up on deck, the coast of Classe faint in the distance, but Isabel didn't feel afraid.

'I'm not though, am I?' she said. 'Anyway, my mum would have a fit if I came back with a . . . I don't know, cutlass on my arm.'

'Nothing so obvious,' said Andrea, rolling up the sleeve of his black shirt. And there was a perfect little dolphin, done in tiny squares, like a mosaic. 'We all have them on this ship. She was called the *Blue Dolphin* when we took her.' He gestured to the figurehead. 'We kept her sign but changed her name and painted her black.'

'Who did it?' asked Isabel, admiring the detail.

'My first mate,' said Andrea, nodding to a burly man with arms like hams. 'Salvatore. He'd make a nice little dolphin for you.'

'But would it hurt?' asked Isabel dubiously.

'Not a bit,' said Andrea, taking a bottle from his jacket pocket. 'You drink some of this and put some on your arm, then a bit more when it's done and you won't notice a thing.'

He leaned in close to her, silver dazzling in his

mouth. 'And when you are back in your safe little world and your brother starts lording it over you, you can roll up your sleeve and remind yourself you've been on a pirate ship with the Black Raider.'

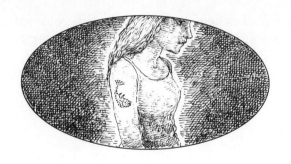

Chapter 13

War

Rodolfo was overseeing the building of warships at the Arsenale. The shipwrights and gunmakers had got used to him and no longer got self-conscious when he was around, the way they had when the Duchessa visited them. There were about a thousand people working flat out at the Arsenale and yet Rodolfo doubted they would have enough new ships ready if the attack came in April.

There was a shortage of wood in the lagoon city; it all had to be brought in from the mainland and transported down the Great Canal on barges. And the warships needed many different kinds of wood – oak, pine, larch, ash, fir, beech and walnut. The woods of the mainland were not near the coast in that part of Talia and orders had been given to transport large loads from further inland; the coffers of Bellezza would be much lighter after the war with the Gate people.

Rodolfo walked back to the palazzo, deep in thought. And went to find Arianna.

He tracked her down in the stables. She was teaching Princess Beatrice not to be afraid of the spotted cats. Mariotto was holding Rigello and the two young females on leashes until Beatrice was used to them. The parents were much calmer beasts and the princess could already stroke them without too much nervousness.

The maid Barbara was already familiar with the she-kitten, Dolcissima, who had been one of her wedding presents from the Duchessa, and stroked her confidently, which helped to reassure the timid princess.

'What a pretty sight!' said Rodolfo. He knew Arianna's face well and, even though she was wearing a mask, could see from the sparkle in her eyes how much she was enjoying being with the animals.

'You know these handsome creatures were a present from your father, Principessa?' he said, as the cats came to greet him and sniff his pockets. They knew that this tall stooped man in black often brought them nice things to eat.

'So I believe,' said Beatrice, tentatively putting out her hand to the parent cats. 'It was one good thing he did, I suppose,' she said, turning her large dark eyes towards Arianna.

'I'm sure he did more than that,' said Arianna warmly, hoping Beatrice wouldn't press her for examples. 'He was a devoted father, I know.'

'I think it destroyed his mind, losing Falco,' said Beatrice quietly. Arianna and Rodolfo exchanged looks above the princess's bowed head.

'And then Carlo,' she continued. 'When my other brothers were also injured, it was too much for him. I know he behaved badly to your betrothed,' she said to Arianna.

Perhaps the ducal stables were not the right place for it but here was a di Chimici apologising for di Chimici deceit and intended murder.

When they had gone back inside the palazzo and Beatrice had retired to wash the smell of the cats from her hands, Rodolfo followed Arianna to her parlour.

'I have been thinking,' he said. 'It was a good thing you agreed to take in the princess.'

'She's a dear, isn't she?' said Arianna.

'She is indeed a "dear", as you say, but that's not what I meant,' said Rodolfo.

'What then?'

'Think about it. The Gate people could attack us here or in Classe. And they are in an alliance with Fabrizio di Chimici. Don't you think he will suggest they pass by Bellezza while his sister is here?'

'If he doesn't hate her for disobeying him and running away,' said Arianna.

'He is not that wicked,' said Rodolfo. 'Any more than his father was. Family feeling is strong in the di Chimici. I shall send word to Classe that I think it is their city that will feel the brunt of the sea-attack.'

*

Andrea was right. The tattoo did not hurt – much –

and Isabel was delighted with it. But no sooner had Salvatore finished than a call came from the crow's nest that a merchant ship was in view. The *Raider's Revenge* put on more speed and gained on the other ship surprisingly fast.

Isabel was horrified to see men preparing to fire the cannons but in the end it was just a warning shot across the bows of the merchantman. Isabel stayed on deck but most of the crew, led by Andrea, soon swarmed on board the plump galleon and were in parley with the terrified captain.

No blood was shed. As pirating went, it was almost civilised. Andrea's men swiftly flung planks between the ships and lashed them firm so that they could roll barrels and carry bales and trunks over to the *Revenge*. Isabel kept well out of their way. When the other ship had been stripped of its cargo, the pirate bridges were just as quickly removed and the merchantman left to go on its way. Andrea even waved to them.

'Well, that was quick!' said Isabel, watching as the crew stowed their booty. 'They didn't put up any kind of fight.'

'They knew better,' said Andrea. 'It wasn't the first time they'd been boarded. And the Black Raider's reputation means they prefer cooperation to resistance.'

'What reputation?' asked Isabel.

'Merciless bloodshed,' said Andrea, grinning wolfishly.

'Do you mean you've killed people?' she asked.

But the shutters came down on his expression again and he said he had to deal with the new cargo.

'You didn't!' said Georgia when Isabel showed them her tattoo on Sunday morning. She was glad there was the pirate adventure to hear about; it might distract Nick from asking too much about Isabel's trip to Remora.

'I didn't know if it would come with me or not,' said Isabel. 'I thought you said your bruises in Talia didn't show back here,' she said to Matt.

'That's true,' he said, rubbing his jaw and remembering the beating up Rinaldo and Filippo di Chimici had organised for him in Padavia.

'But Nick and I got stabbed in Giglia,' said Sky. 'And our wounds were clearly visible when we got back – and the stitches Sulien put in them.'

'Maybe it depends if the skin has been pierced or not?' suggested Georgia.

'We should add that to our dossier,' said Nick. 'What will your parents say about you getting a tattoo, Bel?'

'I don't think they'll be too impressed,' admitted Isabel, who was beginning to wish she had asked about whether the dolphin would stravagate with her. But she wasn't sure that Andrea knew she was from a parallel world. Though he did seem to know more about her than she had suspected.

'Tell us about the pirating!' said Sky, who clearly was impressed by the tattoo.

And Isabel filled them in, making it sound rather more exciting than it had actually been.

'And you weren't scared – or seasick?' asked Nick.

'No,' said Isabel, a bit insulted. 'It wasn't actually that frightening. Andrea made me stay on his ship. And I've never been seasick.'

'Will you go again?' asked Georgia.

'Maybe. If he asks me. But I don't usually stravagate on a Saturday night so Flavia wasn't expecting me. I don't know if that will happen again.'

'What about Friday?' asked Nick. 'Did your talisman take you to Remora?'

Isabel deliberately didn't look at Georgia while she told them what had happened. She was very careful to say 'I' and not 'we' about everything. And the boys were interested that she had seen Rinaldo.

'But he didn't see you – you're sure?' asked Matt.

'He didn't,' said Isabel. And then she told them about Merla.

Nick was listening as carefully as anyone; he had ridden the winged horse on his only stravagation to Remora. But he was looking at Georgia.

Fabrizio di Chimici was closeted with an ambassador from the Gate people, though that was a grand description for the fierce-looking warrior who had come to the Ducal Palace. The Gate people didn't go in for diplomats, only soldiers off-duty.

By the time the two men came out of the Grand Duke's private room, Classe's fate was sealed. Rodolfo had been right; Fabrizio would not have Bellezza in danger as long as Beatrice was there. But he suspected that the Duchessa might have planned it all to save her city. That she had offered to give the princess sanctuary in order to deflect any attack on Bellezza from the sea. Fabrizio was becoming so devious himself that he attributed the same motives to other people.

And yet at the same time he liked to think that Bellezza knew nothing of his plans and his dangerous allies. He still hoped that any attack from the sea would come as a surprise.

But he didn't like having to deal with the Gate people and he knew that he was taking a risk in bargaining to have Classe delivered to him after they had sacked it.

On an impulse, he walked back across the private corridor from the Ducal Palace to his home on the other side of the Argento. He needed to see his son and convince himself that what he was doing was worthwhile. Classe would be another city in the di Chimici fold, maybe one that future children of his would rule. And it would shift the balance of power in Talia. Bellezza could be dealt with later, maybe when its Duke was that upstart Cavaliere. He would enjoy that.

The Nucci palace was a sadder place without Beatrice. The Grand Duke and his Grand Duchess were so rich that they could afford a host of servants to look after their every need. But it wasn't the same as the attentions of a loving sister and aunt. And Caterina missed having another woman of her own rank to talk to. More and more she sent for Francesca to keep her company and play with the baby.

It had created a small rift between Caterina and Fabrizio; she believed that her husband had driven his sister away with his insistence on her marriage to Filippo di Chimici. And he, in his heart, knew she was right. But he was too proud to admit it and Beatrice's name was not mentioned between them.

After spending time with a Gate warrior, it was like cold wine on a hot day for Fabrizio to scoop his newly bathed son into his arms and bury his nose in the crease between Bino's chin and neck, breathing in his scent.

'Is something wrong?' asked Caterina. 'You are back early.'

'Nothing wrong. I shan't be here long. I just wanted to see you and Bino,' he said. He sat in the low nursing chair, stretching his long legs in front of him, and dandled his son on his lap.

'I should be so lonely without you,' he said. 'It is a solitary business being Grand Duke. And I never thought it would happen while I was still so young. I thought Father would teach me everything I needed to know before he died, but he was snatched away before he could.'

Caterina had her own views about what Niccolò might have taught Fabrizio if he hadn't died in the duel but she kept quiet about them. She just had to hope that if she went on loving him and giving him children, that would be enough to keep Fabrizio human. She pushed to the back of her mind the thought that love of his family had not stopped Niccolò from losing his humanity. Because if she did not, then she would have to contemplate that she could lose her son as her father-in-law had lost two of his, and that was simply not to be borne.

'You've been lying to me,' said Nick.

Georgia gave a guilty start. She had been worrying all weekend about having deceived him. And now he had found her at break on Monday and confronted her.

'I'm so sorry,' she said. 'I just couldn't help myself.'

Nick's expression had changed from crossness to real alarm but Georgia didn't notice. She just ploughed on, making things worse.

'I mean, Isabel asked me to go with her and I couldn't think of a good enough reason not to.'

She looked up and saw that Nick had gone quite white.

'And when were you going to tell me?' he said.

'I don't know,' she said miserably. 'When did Bel tell you?'

'She didn't,' said Nick. 'I didn't know.'

'But you said I'd lied to you!'

'Matt told me he'd met you in the market on Saturday and you'd gone to see Mortimer,' said Nick. 'I meant you'd lied about not being able to see me because you were working.'

The bell rang for classes. Georgia reached out to Nick and he brushed her off.

'Don't touch me,' he said very quietly. And he turned and left Georgia standing alone. She hadn't felt this bad since the Nucci massacre.

*

Isabel had lunch with Laura. Her friend was looking tired, with big dark circles under her eyes.

'Are you OK, Lol?' she asked. 'Is anything wrong?'

Laura shrugged. 'Oh, you know,' she said. 'Just the usual. You know I don't cope well with pressure.'

'What pressure?' asked Isabel, and Laura looked at her as if she was mad.

'What pressure? It's only two months till the exams start!'

'Oh, I know,' said Isabel quickly. 'It's crazy. I thought you meant, you know, at home.'

'There's nothing wrong at home,' said Laura stiffly.

'I'm sorry,' said Isabel. 'I didn't mean . . . Look, would you like to come back to mine after school?'

Laura looked at her gratefully; Isabel had been very elusive lately.

'I'd like that,' she said. 'Maybe you could help me with my History notes? I can't get a grip on the difference between Dunkirk and D-Day.'

'Mmn, yes, sure,' said Isabel. She had noticed that neither Nick nor Georgia was sitting with Sky and Matt and Ayesha. In fact, they were nowhere to be seen. Her first thought was that they must be somewhere together but then she saw Nick come in by himself and take his tray over to some students in his own year. He never normally sat with them and at least two girls started to flirt with him.

But he didn't seem to notice and just sat hunched and tense, concentrating on eating his food but not looking as if he knew what was on his tray.

Isabel saw that the other Stravaganti were also looking anxiously at him. And of Georgia there was still no sign.

But she was in their English lesson that afternoon, looking as miserable as Nick.

What's the matter with everyone? thought Isabel.

These Stravaganti couples don't seem to last long. She looked at Sky, who was sitting on the opposite side of the room from Alice. *Would it be any different if he were with me?* she thought.

She stopped Georgia after the lesson and the stripey-haired girl said simply, 'Nick knows.'

'I didn't tell him,' said Isabel.

'I know,' said Georgia. 'It was me. Oh, I didn't mean to, but he knows now and he's furious with me. I don't know what to do.'

There was no question of going back to Nick's after school. The others might have met at the café but Isabel was glad she had another arrangement. It was surprisingly soothing to be in her own room with Laura, talking about the Second World War.

Then she got a call from Nick.

'We need to talk about Giglia,' he said. 'I need to describe Sulien's cell to you.'

'Well, yes,' said Isabel. 'Or Sky could, I suppose.'

'No,' said Nick. He sounded quite calm. 'I'll tell you. Let's meet after school tomorrow. I'm coming with you.'

Chapter 14

The Prince of Giglia

The phone call marked the beginning of a week in which Isabel felt like a long bungee rope, tied to Nick at one end and with the heavy plunging weight of Georgia at the other. After the call, she had been so thrown into confusion that she talked to Laura a bit about it. Not about Talia of course; that was off-limits.

'That was Nick Duke,' she told her. 'And he's got me mixed up in this massive row he's having with Georgia.'

'Can't you just tell him you don't want to get involved?' asked Laura.

'Not really,' said Isabel. 'I'm sort of involved already. And he wants to come here after school tomorrow.'

'Are you having a thing with him?' said Laura,

round-eyed. 'I thought Georgia was your friend.'

'No, nothing like that,' said Isabel. 'I'm not interested in him in that way. But I've sort of got caught up in this fight that's going on between them. I'm sorry I can't tell you the details.'

All Tuesday she worried about whether to tell Georgia what Nick had said and tried to keep out of her way until she realised that Georgia wasn't in school. Again Nick spent the lunch break with other people. And Isabel sat with Laura and Ayesha and kept the talk away from Nick, Georgia or anything that might lead back to Talia.

It was an interminable day at school even though Isabel hadn't stravagated for two nights. But it ended at last and she went back home on her own. It was a miserable grey afternoon, with a cold wind blowing. It didn't feel as if it would ever be spring.

She huddled in her room, pretending to read through more History notes, and then Charlie knocked on her door.

'OK?' he asked. 'I'm going to make tea and toast – do you want some?'

'Mm, please,' said Isabel, having visions of butter melting into hot brown toast. She was suddenly aware she had eaten hardly anything at lunch.

She came down to the kitchen with her brother and that's where they were when Nick rang the doorbell. Charlie just put more bread in the toaster but Isabel could feel the disappointment coming off him; he'd obviously been hoping for a chat. And there was something else: disapproval? But was it because Nick was two years younger, or someone else's boyfriend, or because on Saturday she had denied there was anything going on between them?

'He's all right, your brother,' said Nick when they were in Isabel's room with their stacks of toast, warming their hands on mugs of tea.

'Yeah, he's everyone's favourite person,' said Isabel.

Nick looked at her quizzically. She realised that she'd managed to avoid telling all her fellow Stravaganti what her personal unhappiness was. And now she just felt mean. She knew Charlie wanted to spend time with her the way they used to and she had made him take second place to her new friends and her new life in Talia ever since half-term.

'Forget it,' she said now. 'Are you going to tell Georgia you've decided to go to Giglia?'

She has not been here since Thursday, Flavia thought-spoke into the mirror. *I am beginning to worry about her.*

Sulien wants to speak to her about her stravagation to Giglia, she sensed Rodolfo replying. *But I suppose Sky can describe to her what she needs to know. Have you spoken to Duke Germano?*

About the Gate people? Yes, I told him what you thought. He says the ship-building is coming on well and the rest of the fleet is ready for action.

I wish I could say the same. We will not be ready if they attack in early April, but we'll send the fleet we have as soon as we get word from Andrea. Have you seen him recently?

No, said Flavia. *And that worries me too. I don't know where he is.*

When she had finished communicating with Rodolfo, Flavia took a black velvet bundle out of a drawer and spread the cloth on a table. She shuffled the Corteo cards and set out an array of thirteen.

The first card, at the top of the circle, was the Moon, which did not surprise her. Then, to the left of the Moon, the Spring Maiden, which was also not unexpected. But she drew her breath in sharply to see the King of Serpents coming next. Yet the Stravagante knew that all the cards were subject to more than one interpretation and she waited till all thirteen cards were laid out on the black velvet.

The Princess of Fishes, the Eight of Birds, then the Three, Four and Prince of Salamanders one after the other. Next to the Prince was the Princess of Serpents, followed by the Tower, the Five of Birds and the Prince of Serpents. The thirteenth card, laid face upwards in the centre, was the Ace of Birds. None of the cards had been set down the wrong way up, which would have reversed their meaning.

Flavia sat back and looked at the array, muttering under her breath.

'The Moon is a journey over water clearly enough, but whose? The Gate people? The fleets of Classe and Bellezza? Or does she refer to my son?'

She shifted in her seat, uneasy as always when thinking of Andrea.

'The Spring Maiden is Isabella, of course, but why the King of Serpents? That would have been Grand Duke Niccolò but is it now Fabrizio di Chimici? I would not like to see him so near to the young Stravagante, but she has the Moon on her other side. Perhaps it is Isabella that will travel by water?' Flavia knew nothing of Isabel's extra stravagation and voyage with Andrea.

Then she relaxed. 'Of course! The King of Serpents also stands for a merchant or rich man, so that could be me.' She felt much more hopeful to see Isabella flanked by the Moon and herself.

'The Princess of Fishes is usually the young Duchessa,' she mused. 'I wonder when she will become the Queen? The Eight of Birds is self-defence. That's all right. Arianna will act in defence of herself, her city and her allies. But the Three of Salamanders? Ah, yes, that is also good. Preparation. Both Classe and Bellezza are preparing for a war at sea.'

So far the reading seemed to be all about the coming threat from the Gate people and what the Talians could do to fight back.

'The Four of Salamanders is alliances – well, that's obvious, Classe and Bellezza. Or perhaps the di Chimici and the Gate people. But what is the Prince of Salamanders doing there? Exile. That could be Filippo Nucci. And right next to him the Princess of Serpents and then the Tower, which is exile again. Beatrice is the Princess, I'm sure, and she's in exile almost as much as the Nucci boy. Hmm, I wonder.'

She got up and walked round the room, not wanting to confront the eleventh card. The Five of Birds meant defeat.

'But,' reasoned Flavia, 'where there is defeat for one side, there must be victory for the other.'

The twelfth card was the Prince of Serpents; the court cards were well represented in this array.

'It means self-confidence,' said Flavia. 'Which is what the Gate people are probably feeling, but it could mean one of the princes of Giglia. Not Fabrizio – he would be the King now – so it must be Gaetano, since Carlo and Falco are dead or as good as dead.'

Flavia knew that Falco now lived in another world but Carlo did not. Still, she couldn't think what Gaetano di Chimici had to do with the coming attack.

'Then the last card is the Ace of Birds, which is Conquest, and the thirteenth card dominates the interpretation of the array.'

It could be viewed quite optimistically on the whole: a possible prediction of victory at sea, helped by a Stravagante from this world and one from the other, resulting in Arianna's triumph over the Gate people and the di Chimici too.

Or that conquest card could mean victory for the other side.

But Flavia could not see what Beatrice di Chimici or Filippo Nucci had to do with it, either way. And nor was she happy about the possible involvement of a di Chimici prince from Giglia.

Maybe the Prince of Serpents was Fabrizio after all, since the King was being used in its merchant meaning? Flavia sighed. She would train one of her mirrors on the Corteo cards and see what Dottore Crinamorte thought.

Once she had talked to Nick, Isabel knew she'd have to tell Georgia. He was determined to come with her to Giglia and Isabel had no idea how dangerous that might be for him. From what she remembered, he looked very different now from how he was when he was 'translated' and there was the extra year that this world had leapt forward, making Nick a year older than he would have been in Talia.

But still, he would look like a di Chimici. There was even a family resemblance to the princess she had glimpsed in Bellezza.

Nick dismissed the whole problem.

'Sulien will give me a novice robe, the way he did last time,' he said. 'And I can pull the hood over my face if I see anyone I know.'

Isabel couldn't budge him. She had stravagated to Classe that night for the first time since her pirate adventure with Andrea. But something stopped her telling Flavia about that or about Nick. Still, she had seen Brother Sulien in the mirror and spoken about her stravagation to Giglia. Again she didn't mention Nick's plan.

By Wednesday, she had to talk to Georgia, who was back in school, looking as pale as someone recovering from a tummy upset, which was what she had persuaded her mother to tell the school she had been suffering from the day before.

'He's still not talking to me,' she told Isabel. 'And I don't really blame him. What I did was wrong and it's really hurt him.'

'He still wants to come with me on Friday,' said Isabel. 'Do you think it's safe?'

'Who knows?' said Georgia wearily. 'I can't stop him if he's determined to do it, and anyway he won't listen to me, the mood he's in.'

'You could steal his talisman,' said Isabel.

'But the way things are between us, I don't think I

could even get into his house,' said Georgia. 'At least not before Friday.'

'Let's ask the others what to do,' said Isabel. 'We can meet in the coffee bar after school.'

Nick had avoided seeing the other Stravaganti too, though apparently they had been in the café the last two afternoons. It was embarrassing for Georgia to air her problems with Nick in front of them, but in the end she admitted she had gone to Remora with Isabel.

Matt and Sky were shocked but Ayesha was more sympathetic.

'I don't see why Nick should begrudge you one trip back for memory's sake,' she said. 'As I see it, you gave up Talia to make things easier for him here, to make him live in the present. That was really nice of you.'

'It was the not telling him he minds,' said Georgia. 'And he's right. I should have talked to him. Maybe he could have come too. He'd have been less likely to be recognised in Remora than in Giglia, where he's dead set on going now.'

Georgia couldn't explain how sometimes she just felt tired of Nick. Of being responsible for him all the time. She had wanted just that tiny break of a trip to Talia to see her old friends without the burden of having another person's life on her hands. And yet she loved Nick and now he wouldn't even talk to her.

She had lost her best friend, Alice, she was sure, over Talia and now she was afraid of losing Nick too. If it hadn't been for Isabel and the other Stravaganti, she would have gone mad.

'So now he's insisting on coming to Giglia with me on Friday,' said Isabel. 'And there's no way I can stop him.'

'Well,' said Sky, 'I could come with you too, if that's any help.'

A trip to Talia with Sky and definitely no chance of bumping into Alice, thought Isabel.

'That would be great,' was all she said. 'I'd be glad to have another Stravagante around in case he does something stupid. Do you think we should tell him?'

'He didn't tell us,' said Sky.

Brother Sulien was looking forward to meeting another Stravagante from the other world. His life at Saint-Mary-among-the-Vines had returned to its usual order and calm after the massacre nearly a year ago, apart from the daily disruptions caused by Brother Sandro and Brother Dog.

He had to explain to Sandro that the visitor would be a girl but not Georgia. Nevertheless, the young novice, who had been a street urchin a year ago, was eager to wait with the pharmacist and see the Stravagante arrive in his cell.

So it was a huge surprise to both of them to see materialise on the cot not a girl from the future but a honey-coloured boy with dreadlocks from their own recent past.

'Tino!' cried Sandro, hurling himself at the older boy. Brother Dog barked wildly and Sulien flung his arms round Sky, who had once been 'his' Stravagante.

Sky struggled off the bed, trying to respond to all the greetings while making room for the other Stravaganti to follow.

'Isabel's coming,' he said. 'And . . .'

But before he could finish there was Nick on the bed. No, not Nick but Falco. Seeing him in his own context, even in twenty-first-century nightwear, Sky knew that no one could mistake him for anything other than what he was: a prince of Giglia. It was extraordinary how his life in the future had kept him disguised.

'Brother Benvenuto!' cried Sandro. 'It is a reunion. Is everyone coming – Luciano and Gaetano too? Sulien said it would just be one new girl.'

And there she was, struggling out from underneath Nick, who had not managed to get fully out of the way. Isabel sat, flushed and awkward, in her green dress, looking at the scene around her.

She had been told about Sandro and had seen Sulien's face in Flavia's mirror a few days earlier. What she wasn't prepared for was the way Nick was glaring at Sky.

'What are you doing here?' he asked, ignoring the others.

'Looking out for Bel,' said Sky calmly.

'So is this a conspiracy?' said Nick. 'Was everyone going to come but me? You said you weren't coming back.'

'That was my decision,' said Sky. 'I didn't make a pact with you, like Georgia. Be angry with her if you like, but I can come and go as I please and I wanted to see Giglia again.'

'Why didn't you say?' grumbled Nick, but Isabel could see he was losing steam.

'You haven't been talking to any of us all week,' Sky reminded him.

'Why are you fighting?' said Sandro, distressed.

Brother Dog was barking furiously. Sulien put a hand on Sandro's shoulder.

'I think you should all walk my maze,' he said.

*

Half an hour later Brother Sandro was hurrying along the Via Larga to the old di Chimici palace, with his dog at his heels. He was readily admitted but left again within minutes, accompanied by Prince Gaetano di Chimici, whose step was as eager as the boy novice's own. They were soon back at Saint-Mary-among-the-Vines, where Sky and Nick were waiting for them in the cloisters, both now dressed as novices themselves.

Isabel watched the brothers' reunion, moved. She had never seen Nick like this. And Gaetano was just as he had been described: not beautiful to look at like his brother but warm and generous and good-hearted; she could feel it radiating from him as he pulled away from Nick and clasped arms with Sky and then turned a wide smile on her, asking to be introduced.

'Isabella,' he said. 'You brought my brother back to me!'

No one contradicted him, not even Isabel; it was too complicated to put him right. The early spring sunshine had some warmth in it in Giglia and Isabel felt an overwhelming urge to explore the city. But Nick just wanted to be with his brother, so Sky offered to show her around.

'Can we go and see Giuditta, do you think?' he asked Sulien.

'She will be pleased to see you,' he said. 'She was

expecting to meet Isabella, but you will be a bonus. I will stay here with the princes.'

'It's hard to think of Nick as a prince, isn't it?' said Isabel as she and Sky headed down to the great cathedral whose bulk dominated the city.

'Well, I've seen him here before, remember,' said Sky. 'Although he was always dressed as a friar. Only Georgia has seen him as a di Chimici prince.'

'Maybe she still does,' said Isabel.

Sky stopped and took in great lungfuls of air. He smiled at her. 'Let's forget them both,' he said. 'And Alice and everyone else. Let's just enjoy being in Giglia. I love this city.'

He spread his arms wide, his dreads flying. 'See it? Smell it? This is like Florence over four hundred years ago, where you might run into the equivalent of Michelangelo or Leonardo. It's a city full of art and beauty.' He lowered his arms. 'And plots and murder, of course,' he added. 'But we won't think of that today either. We'll just have a good time. Only keep out of the full sun.'

His enthusiasm was infectious. It was a huge bonus for Isabel to have this time alone with him and for him to be the one to say he didn't want to think about Alice.

'Yes,' she said, smiling back, 'let's do that.'

*

Nick wanted to talk about Beatrice. Gaetano explained the whole thing to him over a late breakfast of warm rolls and ale in the Refectory. Sandro had been sent about his business but had left Brother

Dog to keep an eye on them.

'And is she really OK?' asked Nick.

'Oh-kay?' said Gaetano. 'I don't know what that means but she is safe and happy in Bellezza, I think. Arianna will look after her. But what about you? You look wonderfully healthy and handsome. And how is Georgia?'

A cloud passed over Nick's face. 'She's fine,' he said.

'You have quarrelled?' said Gaetano immediately, sensitive as ever to his brother's mood.

Nick shrugged. 'Yes, but I think we'll get over it.'

And then he realised this was true. A warm feeling spread through him. He would forgive Georgia and she would forgive him and everything would go back to normal. And for now he was back with his favourite brother in his home city.

'I hope so,' Gaetano was saying. 'There is nothing like the love of a good woman.'

He looked so solemn that Nick couldn't help laughing. The happiness that had eluded him for days came bubbling through him and he felt invincible.

'Let's go and see Fabrizio,' he said.

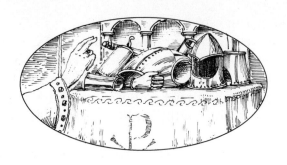

Chapter 15

Brothers

The two brothers walked through the Piazza Ducale where once they had both watched the tournament before the weddings that had ended in such terrible bloodshed. Neither of them knew what was likely to happen if they went in to see Fabrizio together. Gaetano was desperately thinking of a way to stop his younger brother from doing anything so dangerous. But Nick's blood was fizzing in his veins and he felt more alive than he had for ages in his new world.

He looked around, delighted at the statues in the loggia, the fountain with the statue of Neptune which had run with wine at the di Chimici wedding celebrations and the crowds of people meeting to chat or barter goods. This was his city in a way that London never could be.

'It's so good to be back,' he said.

'But you are only visiting, surely?' said Gaetano. 'I mean, I love having you here but you can't stay, can you?'

'No,' said his brother, 'but I don't want to think about that. We have until sunset – let's make the most of it.'

On an impulse they went into a tavern for a cup of red wine. Nick stretched his long legs out in front of him and grinned at his brother. No one looked twice at a novice drinking wine in Talia; it was safer than water.

'This would be out of the question in my new life,' he said.

'Why?' asked Gaetano. 'Do they not have wine in the future?'

'They do but you can't drink it in a public place until you are eighteen years old,' said Nick. 'But even if I could, I wouldn't. At least not in the middle of a weekday morning. It would be bad for my training.'

'Training?'

'I'm quite a sportsman now,' said Nick. 'I'm the captain of my school's fencing team. So I have to be careful about what I eat and drink and stay fit.' He sipped the wine with relish; nothing in twenty-first-century London tasted quite like it.

'How wonderful,' said Gaetano. 'I can't believe how tall and strong you are.'

'Enough about me,' said Nick. 'Tell me about everyone here. How is Fabrizio?'

Gaetano sighed. 'It has been very bad for him to become the head of the family so young,' he said. 'And to lose Carlo. He expects me to be able to fill our brother's place in our father's financial dealings and I disappoint him.'

'You were never very good with money,' said Nick, grinning. 'It was always Carlo who understood the banking business.'

'And I can't change just because he has gone,' said Gaetano. 'I wanted to resume my courses at the University here but Fabrizio says that is not fitting now I'm his only brother. I must prepare to be Prince of Remora.'

'Is Uncle Ferdinando not well?' asked Nick. He was fond of his old uncle the Pope, whose other title Gaetano would inherit on his death.

'He is in good health, as far as I know,' said Gaetano, 'though fatter than ever. And our cousin Rinaldo is a cardinal now – doubtless he would like to be Pope himself.'

'Then I hope our uncle employs a food-taster,' said Nick grimly. He knew what Rinaldo was capable of.

'But one good thing about Fabrizio,' said Gaetano, 'is that he is a very fond father. I wish you could see Bino.'

'Bino?' asked Nick.

'Yes, that's what we call the little prince now,' said Gaetano. 'You know he was born nearly three months ago?'

'So I have a nephew,' said Nick. 'What is his real name?'

'Falco,' said Gaetano softly. 'They called him Falco, after you.'

*

One of the best things for Luciano about seeing Arianna in Padavia was that she didn't have to wear a mask in public. She hadn't been able to get away from state affairs in Bellezza much this term. When after his morning classes Luciano suddenly saw 'Adamo' in the tavern of the Black Horse it was the first time he and Arianna had been together since his trip to Classe. He had to restrict himself to a delighted smile and a masculine arm-clasp while his disguised fiancée grinned back and tried to look like the boy she was dressed as.

She was still guarded by Marco, who was now married to the maid Barbara and was an old friend of the younger couple. He understood that they would want to get back quickly to Luciano's house and made himself scarce with Alfredo in the kitchen.

'It's so good to have you here again,' said Luciano when the first rapture of their reunion had run its course. 'I don't think I can wait till May to come back to you.'

'Don't be silly,' said Arianna reprovingly, propping herself on her elbow. 'We have a war to fight before then.'

'All the more reason to get married sooner and be together whatever happens,' he said.

'But the Duchessa of Bellezza can't marry her Duke in a little parish church with a few friends back for bread and cheese afterwards,' said Arianna.

'Sounds good to me,' said Luciano, brushing a loose curl back over her shoulder. 'I didn't think you cared about all that stuff anyway – clothes and jewels and pomp and ceremony.'

'I don't,' she said. 'At least the me that is Arianna

doesn't. But I'm also the ruler of my city-state and the people demand and deserve a good show. That takes time to prepare.'

'Now you sound like Silvia,' said Luciano.

Arianna laughed, 'Well, blood will out, I suppose. And I don't want Fabrizio di Chimici to think we got married in a hole and corner way – because we were afraid of his plot with the Gate people.'

'So you'd rather do it in full view in the cathedral of the Maddalena, where any of his assassins could kill me?' said Luciano. 'Or both of us.'

'Don't joke about it,' said Arianna seriously, putting her finger on his lips. 'It is my worst nightmare.'

*

Gaetano and Nick left the tavern and walked towards the Palazzo Ducale. Suddenly Gaetano clutched his brother's arm and dragged him back behind the fountain.

'It's him!' he hissed. 'Fabrizio's coming out.'

The Grand Duke of Tuschia emerged from the Ducal Palace, where he had his office, flanked by a small band of guards. There was a murmur of greeting and deference wherever he went like the sound of a wave breaking on the shore. He looked haughty but inclined his head to a favoured few.

'I wonder where he's going?' whispered Nick.

'I don't know,' Gaetano whispered back. 'Not to his home in the Nucci palace. He gets there by the corridor our father had built.'

Nick shuddered. He wouldn't have wanted to see Fabrizio in that palazzo. The last time he had been there he had watched his father die from his own poison.

Fascinated, he looked from behind the fountain as his oldest brother progressed slowly across the square, dispensing favourable looks and small waves to privileged Giglians who happened to be in his path. He was taking a route that would lead him up to the cathedral.

'Come on,' said Nick. 'Let's follow him.'

They walked up the long straight road where the shoemakers plied their trade, Nick still revelling in being back in the city that he knew so well but as a sort of invisible tourist. When they reached the Piazza della Cattedrale and saw the great cathedral of Santa Maria del Giglio, he caught his breath. This was what he missed in London more than anything: that vast beneficent presence that could be glimpsed from almost every quarter of the city, the place where his parents had been married and in whose Baptistery every Giglian prince and princess had been welcomed into the Reman church.

The brothers stopped when they saw the guard surrounding the Grand Duke in even tighter formation as he walked up the steps of the cathedral.

'Is it a public service?' asked Nick. 'Can we go in?'

There was no one to stop them and no one who would have dared deny Prince Gaetano entrance – or any companion of his. And inside the great church was full of people milling around, just as Nick remembered it. It was nothing like the churches he had occasionally visited in Islington. No one kept quiet and the service that the Grand Duke was attending was down at the main altar while tourists and pilgrims wandered around the rest of the imposing building, looking at frescoes and statues or peering up at the inside of the mighty dome.

Among them were several monks and friars and the brothers soon spotted Sky and Isabel. They moved up to join them.

'Isn't that your brother?' whispered Sky.

Nick nodded.

'That's the Grand Duke of Tuschia, Fabrizio di Chimici,' Sky told Isabel.

The name echoed round the open space as others mouthed it too. Di Chimici was a potent word in this city and many who had come to look at the cathedral were drawn instead to stare at Giglia's ruler, so young and handsome and rich.

'What's he doing?' asked Isabel.

'It seems to be some sort of service of dedication,' said Gaetano, then slapped his head. 'Of course! I remember now. He told me. He ordered some fancy new armour to wear into battle. That's it there on the altar. The Bishop of Giglia is blessing it for him.'

'Battle?' asked Nick.

'Yes. He invited me to come but I forgot,' said Gaetano. 'He has some new plan brewing about dominating other cities.'

'It's Classe,' said Isabel softly. 'He's planning to invade Classe with the Gate people.'

'Really?' asked Gaetano, appalled. 'But Classe is a Talian city and the Gate people are our enemies. Or they were.'

'Don't you see?' said Nick bitterly. 'The Gate people will invade from the sea and Fabrizio will head an army from the land. Wearing his fancy new armour.

The City of Ships will be caught like a nut in a pair of crackers.'

Isabel felt a kind of despair overwhelm her. Now that she had seen the Grand Duke with her own eyes she began to think his battle plan might work. And then what would happen to all the wonderful buildings in Classe, the churches and temples and private residences with their mosaics dating from one and a half thousand years ago to the present-day work of Fausto?

'What can we do to stop him?' she asked.

'We can give him something else to think about,' said Nick.

And as the Grand Duke made his way back to the cathedral's entrance with one of the guard carrying the burnished silver armour, Nick threw back his hood and stepped into his path.

Fabrizio stopped, clutching his chest as if his heart were trying to leap out of it.

'Falco!' he said faintly. Then, as people clustered around him and the figure he had seen slipped away behind a pillar, he cried out more strongly to the guards. 'After him! That fellow in the robes of the Black Friars. Leave me – I am fine. Just catch that man.'

Isabel called Georgia from the coffee shop next morning.

'Come and join us,' she said. 'Nick's here. He wants you to come.'

It had been a close thing in the cathedral. Nick had

slipped away and gone back to Brother Sulien's. The guards had, quite naturally, captured Sky and brought him to the Grand Duke, who had spat out his disappointment at their catching the wrong friar.

And Gaetano had appeared out of nowhere to calm his brother and say he must have been having hallucinations.

Fabrizio had given orders to release Sky, who had played dumb throughout the whole incident, and to search the cathedral for another friar in the black and white robes of the Hounds of God. Isabel and Sky had eventually left Gaetano comforting his brother and had gone back to Saint-Mary-among-the-Vines, to find that Nick had already left.

'What did you think you were doing?' Sky asked Nick now. 'You could have blown everything if he'd caught you.'

'And what would he have done to me?' demanded Nick aggressively. 'Aren't I his special little brother that he named his own kid after, miraculously back from the dead?'

'I remember when you showed yourself to your father,' said Sky.

'So do I,' said Nick. 'It helped to kill him. I'm not likely to forget that. But there was no danger of that with Fabrizio. I just wanted to distract him from attacking Classe.'

The atmosphere in the coffee bar was very tense between Sky and Nick. Matt and Isabel, who had not been in Giglia before and knew about the massacre and the duel only at second hand, couldn't imagine what it had been like and why Sky was so angry with Nick now. They were relieved when Georgia joined them.

'Hi,' she said nervously, looking at everyone but Nick.

He suddenly relaxed and put his arms out to her.

'Hi,' he said, rubbing his chin on the top of her head.

'You got back safely then?' she said, looking up at him.

'Just about,' Sky answered for him.

And then the whole story had to be told again for Georgia's benefit. She looked horrified at the risk Nick had taken but was so glad that he was speaking to her again that she didn't press the point.

'And how was it – apart from nearly getting caught?' she asked.

'It was fantastic,' said Nick, his eyes sparkling. 'Just – I don't know – being there again. And seeing Gaetano. Even seeing Fabrizio was good in a weird way.'

'And we found out something that will help in Classe,' said Isabel. 'We think Fabrizio's planning a land attack to coincide with the Gate people's sea invasion. I'll tell them in Classe tonight.'

'You're going to stravagate?' asked Matt.

'Yes,' said Isabel. 'I know I don't usually on a Saturday but I think they need to know as soon as possible. I'll go to Padavia next Friday, just to complete my talisman-testing mission.'

'Should I go with you?' asked Matt. 'Just to make the full set?'

'You can if you want,' said Isabel. 'The more the merrier.'

'I think I should spend some time with Ayesha till Friday,' said Matt. He glanced uneasily at Sky, making it clear he had been going to say something about his girlfriend getting tired of his involvement with Talia but thought better of it.

*

Charlie had started spying on Isabel, in spite of what she had told him. He was intrigued by having met her with two boys from school and then Nick's visit. His sister had never been so popular. And her whole demeanour was different; she sort of sparkled.

Isabel had had her hair cut to a shaggy collar-length bob; they were looking more like twins than ever. Charlie couldn't wait to have a growth spurt and be more than the inch taller than her that he was already. It wasn't that he wanted to leave his sister behind; he just wanted to emphasise the differences rather than the similarities.

And he had a feeling that Isabel had some sort of secret life she wasn't letting on about. He almost wondered if she was leaving the house at night to go to some private rave or house party because she always seemed elated but exhausted in the mornings. Their mother had been having to yell at her to get up for school ever since half-term and she always used to be good about waking early.

And the parents had gone ballistic when they saw the dolphin tattoo on her arm, which Charlie secretly admired. The old Bel would never have gone and got that done on her own.

So he had decided to keep tabs on her.

Isabel was blissfully unaware of this new development. On Monday, she and Matt met in the café after school to talk about what she would find in Padavia.

'I've seen your Professor Constantin in the mirror,' she said. 'But I didn't tell him you were coming. It's getting to be a habit. I've no idea what Rodolfo or Doctor Dethridge would say if they knew you were all coming back.'

'Don't you think Paolo or Sulien would have said something by now?' asked Matt. 'And no one ever said we weren't to go back. It's just that the others had reasons to decide not to.'

'What about you?' asked Isabel.

'Well, I sort of didn't want to keep doing something that Yesh wasn't a part of. I reckoned I'd done my bit – at least whatever it was Talia wanted me for – and I came so near to losing her for ever.'

'You old romantic,' said Isabel. 'But I think you're pretty safe. What did she say about you coming to Padavia with me?'

'She's cool about it – reckons you need some muscle to look after you.' He grinned at Isabel and she thought what a good mate he was. He wasn't her type and she presented no threat to Yesh, who was one of her best friends, but it was nice to think she'd have a well-built companion on her next trip to Talia. That business with the guards in the cathedral had unsettled her.

'Did you enjoy stravagating with Sky?' he asked innocently.

Isabel wondered how much Yesh had told him.

'And Nick,' she corrected him, trying not to look embarrassed. But then her own happiness spilled out.

'It was great actually, till Nick did that stupid thing in the cathedral. We went to see that sculptor

Stravagante Sky thinks so much of. And she looked me over quite carefully and then nodded to him and said, "This one isn't afraid of Talia" – which was weird.'

'She meant compared with Alice, I suppose,' said Matt.

'I suppose so,' said Isabel, who couldn't keep the smile off her face. 'He said, "Bel isn't afraid of anything," which is so not true, but still . . .'

'I think you're in with a chance there,' said Matt, smiling. 'But hadn't I better describe the Scriptorium to you?'

They were deep in conversation when Charlie walked into the coffee bar.

'Hi,' he said brightly. 'Can I join you?'

They agreed a little too enthusiastically and made worried faces at each other while Charlie was at the counter.

'I'm not interrupting anything, am I?' he asked as he sat down at their table.'

'No,' said Matt, wildly trying to think of a reason he might be talking to Isabel. 'We were just talking about . . . that guy who runs the antiques shop.'

'Oh,' said Charlie. 'Why?'

'Because he seems to be going out with my auntie Eva – my great-aunt she is actually,' said Matt.

'But aren't they, like, really old?' asked Charlie.

'Don't be ageist!' said Isabel, playing along. 'I think it's sweet.' (Though this was the first she had heard of it.)

'They're both widows or whatever you call it for a man,' said Matt. 'I introduced them before Christmas and now they seem quite full on.'

But Charlie wasn't really interested in the love life of two senior citizens and started to ask Matt about the school rugby fixtures. Isabel was churned up with frustration inside. She would just have to talk to Matt again later.

When Luciano and Arianna went into the kitchen, suddenly ravenous, they found not only Marco but Enrico. He and kitchens had an affinity; he would stuff his face whenever he could, although his frame remained scrawny. Now he scrambled off his chair and attempted a bow, with a half-eaten pasty still in his right hand.

'Your Ladyship,' he said. He had seen the Duchessa in her boy's disguise before and was not deceived.

'Signor Enrico,' acknowledged Arianna. She had come to a sort of acceptance of this man who had tried to kill her mother. He had recently shown himself to be a friend to the Stravaganti and she knew he would never return to working for the di Chimici.

'Enrico,' said Luciano, 'I have a task for you.'

'Anything, Cavaliere,' said Enrico, gobbling the last of his pasty.

'I want you to go to Classe,' said Luciano. 'You will find there a merchant called Flavia and occasionally her young friend, Isabella. They are both members of my . . . Brotherhood.'

'What do you want me to do there?' asked Enrico.

'I want you to keep your nose to the ground and find out anything you can about the di Chimici in that city. I know that the Grand Duke wants to take

Classe, by sea and by land, and I can't believe he has no spies set there. So keep your eyes open, and, if you need to, you can get a message to me through Flavia.'

'Well, that might cause a bit of expenses, Cavaliere,' said the spy.

Luciano gave him a small bag of silver, resisting the temptation to toss it to him like a character in an Elizabethan play.

'All reasonable expenses will be paid, Enrico,' he said. 'But no more than two glasses of strega a day.'

'Understood, master,' said Enrico, stashing the bag in his jerkin with one hand and tapping the side of his nose with the other. 'If there's anything to be found out in Classe, I'm your man.'

Chapter 16

The Reality and the Dream

Luciano raced towards the Scriptorium in Padavia on the Friday morning, skipping yet another class. Constantin greeted him at the door.

'Your studies are suffering, Luciano,' he said, but he was smiling.

'Shouldn't you be teaching, Professor?' asked Luciano innocently.

'No,' said Constantin. 'I think you have forgotten it's Good Friday and you don't have any lectures to skip. But come, I have visitors.' He led him into his private studio.

Luciano had expected Isabel, but Matt was a surprise. Isabel watched amused as the two young men clasped each other in their arms. *Matt would never be so emotional in Islington*, she thought. He was behaving as Georgia had in Remora.

But looking at them together, equally tall but one so slender and the other so broad-shouldered, she marvelled even more at Rodolfo's skills. Matt had told her the whole story of how the Bellezzan Stravagante had made him and Luciano resemble each other enough to fool a di Chimici. *That must have been some pretty powerful magic*, she thought.

At last Luciano turned to her.

'Isabella,' he said. 'Welcome to Padavia! You have now proved that Doctor Dethridge's method works for four cities. I'm sure that means the English Stravaganti can go anywhere.'

'What about you?' said Isabel, who had heard about Luciano's last stravagation. 'Does that mean with your talisman you could go to . . . I don't know . . . Glastonbury or Edinburgh if you wanted?'

Luciano looked at her in amazement. 'I never thought of that,' he said. 'I'll ask the Dottore as soon as I can. What a great idea!'

Isabel felt absurdly pleased that the famous Luciano had taken notice of a suggestion of hers.

'Let's show her Padavia,' said Matt, who was wearing his old printer's devil clothes. He didn't look elegant enough to be a companion of the Cavaliere or even of Isabel in her green Talian dress.

'Let's find Cesare,' said Luciano. 'Then she can meet another figure in the story.'

Constantin sighed. 'Another good student to be beguiled from his studies,' he said.

'It's the Easter holiday,' said Luciano. 'You told me so yourself.'

'Lucky you,' said Matt. 'We've still got two weeks to go.'

'Can we see Enrico too?' asked Isabel as they walked down Salt Street. 'I've been warned about the smell.'

'I'm afraid you're more likely to run into him in Classe,' said Luciano. 'I've sent him there to spy for me.'

On the Friday night that Isabel and Matt were in Padavia, Georgia and Nick were together at her house.

They had made up their differences. Stravagating to Giglia had done something positive for Nick. He had loved being in 'his' city again, but his encounter with Fabrizio had shaken him. He realised how dangerous it was to be where he might be recognised. It certainly hadn't taken his brother any time to recognise him in spite of his improved health and height and his Dominican disguise.

'I wonder how they're getting on in Padavia,' said Georgia, voicing the thought that Nick was sharing.

'Would you like to go there too?' asked Nick.

'Padavia?' said Georgia, surprised. 'Why would I? I've never been there.'

'Well, you could see Luciano,' risked Nick, giving her a wicked smile. 'But no, I meant Talia.'

Georgia punched him gently on the shoulder.

'Where exactly?'

'I was thinking Bellezza,' said Nick. 'I feel like visiting my sister.'

Isabel was beginning to realise that Matt was a bit of a hero in Padavia. He had been greeted enthusiastically by the printers in the Scriptorium and stopped in the street by several passers-by on the way to the University.

The big, shy boy she thought she knew from home was different in Talia. He walked straighter and met people's eyes like a confident person. Isabel wondered if she did that here too.

They found Cesare in the Refectory, eating crumbly sugary pastries. He spluttered crumbs all over the table when he saw Matt. But he brushed himself off to be introduced to Isabel.

'Another Stravagante?' he said, lowering his voice. 'Padavia is lucky to get a second one.'

Isabel liked him straight away, with his open honest face.

'No, she is for Classe,' Luciano put him right. 'But Doctor Dethridge has made the talismans work for any city and Isabella has been trying hers out.'

'Have you been to Remora?' asked Cesare.

'Yes, and met your family,' said Isabel. 'And the horses,' she added.

'Even Merla?' asked Cesare.

'Especially Merla,' said Isabel. 'And Georgia came with me.'

'Oh, how is she?' asked Cesare. 'I would love to see her again. She is brave as a lion and a fine horsewoman.'

'She's well,' said Isabel, thinking of Nick and

Georgia's reconciliation. 'She's very happy.'

'And she could come here now!' said Cesare, realising. 'Do ask her if she would.'

'Are you all stravagating again, then?' asked Luciano. It made him feel uneasy, a bit like a mother cat when her kittens start exploring outside the box.

'Well,' said Matt, 'it's true everyone has. It all started when Georgia went to Remora with Bel. Nick found out and when Sky went with her to Giglia, he decided to go too.'

Luciano and Cesare both looked horrified.

'Falco returned to Giglia?' said Cesare.

'The idiot,' said Luciano. 'Did anyone see him?'

'I'm afraid Fabrizio did,' said Isabel. 'Nick showed himself to him deliberately.'

'Why on earth . . . ?'

'He wanted to weaken him,' said Isabel. 'Fabrizio's planning to lead an army to Classe when the Gate people invade from the sea.'

Now Luciano looked really worried. 'You'd better all come back to my place,' he said. 'We need to contact Rodolfo by mirror and see what he says about that. And I think he should know about all you Stravaganti coming back to Talia.'

*

Georgia had never been to Bellezza and Nick had only vague childhood memories of one trip there so they didn't attempt to stravagate directly to the palazzo. Instead, Georgia thought about the front of the great cathedral, imagining San Marco in Venice but substituting rams for horses and silver for gold. She and Nick held hands as they fell asleep, thinking of the City of Masks and saying its name out loud till drowsiness overtook them.

They found themselves in the early morning light in the square outside the Maddalena. They were only feet away from the two pillars by the lagoon and Georgia shuddered to remember what Luciano had told her about that being a place of execution by fire. She turned to Nick and smiled. 'We made it,' she said.

He was looking at her, horrified.

'But we're both wearing pyjamas!' he said. 'And shouldn't you have a mask? We didn't think this through.'

Georgia started to giggle; they both looked so out of place.

'We'd better go and find Arianna, before we get into trouble,' she said. 'I hope it's not that Forbidden Day she told us about.'

'That's in May, I think,' said Nick as they walked across the square to the Palazzo Ducale, trying not to look conspicuous.

Fortunately, there were few people around and, although they picked up some curious looks, no one stopped them. By the time they arrived at the gates, they had hastily cobbled together a cover story.

'Good day, sir,' said Nick to the guard, trying to look more confident than he felt. 'We are the Anglian clowns, expected by the Duchessa.'

'Anglian clowns?' said the guard. 'I don't know anything about any clowns, Anglian or otherwise. Where are your papers? Or your gear come to that?'

'Alas, sir, my sister and I were robbed on our way here,' said Nick smoothly. 'But if you would send word to Her Grace to say that Nicholas and Georgia Mulholland are here, I'm sure she will want to see us.'

After much grumbling reluctance, which they were not able to soften by any tip, since they had only the nightclothes they stood up in, the guard agreed to summon a footman.

By great good fortune, this was Marco, whose keen eyes took in what the guard had not: that they were without shadows. He didn't understand everything about the Stravaganti but he knew enough to tell that this was an important sign. He agreed to take news of them to the Duchessa and gestured to them behind the guard's back to get out of the sun.

He was back as quickly as it took to run up the stairs to the Duchessa's private apartments and come back with a confirmation that they were expected, though Marco had noticed the widening of the violet eyes behind the silver mask when she heard the names.

Georgia looked about her as they were shown up the grand staircase, marvelling at the candelabra, the dark oil portraits on the walls and the sheer number of servants moving about the palace.

'Can you imagine living in a place like this?' she whispered to Nick.

'You forget,' he whispered back. 'I have.'

Marco ushered them into the Duchessa's private parlour as ceremoniously as if they had been the most richly dressed aristocrats.

'Ah!' said Arianna. 'My clowns,' and dismissed Marco.

As soon as they were alone, she tore off her mask and hugged them both affectionately.

'What are you both doing here?' she asked. 'And is

it safe for you, Falco? Oh, I must organise clothes for you straight away.'

She rang for her maid, not waiting for an answer. Barbara came as quickly as if she had been waiting outside the door. Georgia suspected that Marco had told her about their arrival.

Arianna had no problem ordering a dress and a mask for Georgia; that could be easily supplied from her own extensive wardrobe. But she and Barbara fussed and frowned over Nick, making him turn round and measuring him with their eyes and hands.

'Milady, I think Marco's clothes would fit him but does the Signore wish to be mistaken for a footman? We have nothing fitting for a nobleman in the palazzo except for your father's clothes.'

'What do you think, Fal— I mean, Nicholas?' asked Arianna. 'Would it help you to be dressed as a palace servant?'

Nick nodded. 'I don't really mind,' he said.

Then, as soon as Barbara had gone, he said, 'I'm here to see my sister.'

Arianna looked grave. 'I'll have to ask Rodolfo,' she said. 'He didn't tell me you were coming. Or Georgia,' she added.

'He didn't know,' said Nick. 'It was a spur of the moment decision.'

*

Luciano was in contact with Rodolfo through his hand mirror when not only his master but his fiancée came into view.

Arianna, thought-spoke Luciano, *I have something to tell you and Rodolfo.*

And we have something to tell you, she replied. She wasn't wearing her mask and her eyes were sparkling with excitement. *You first*, she said.

Well, I don't know how you are going to feel about this, Maestro. Not only Isabella but Matteo is here with me in Padavia.

Welcome to both, Rodolfo communicated. *I should like to see them.*

Matt and Isabel crowded together so that the Bellezzan Stravagante could see them and they him.

Isabella, said Arianna, *it is good to see you. We have much to talk about. And, Matteo, you are looking very well. Welcome back to Talia.*

The two newest Stravaganti were not very good at it yet and Isabel was better than Matt because she had had more practice, but they managed to understand Arianna and send their own greetings. Luciano took the mirror back.

The new stravagation is still working well on Isabella's talisman, said Rodolfo.

Yes, Maestro, but there is more, said Luciano. *When Isabella went to Remora, Georgia stravagated with her.*

There is no reason why she should not have, said Rodolfo.

And when she travelled to Giglia, not only did Sky go with her but Nick too.

Luciano braced himself for Rodolfo's displeasure and was amazed to see the Regent's rare smile.

That does not surprise me. He is here now, in the palazzo with Georgia. It seems that young man is indifferent to danger.

'Nick there!' said Luciano out loud, he was so surprised. The others were equally shocked.

Why? he thought-spoke to Rodolfo.

I am about to find out, came the reply, half amused, half exasperated as even the onlooking Stravaganti could tell.

*

Princess Beatrice was in her room at the palazzo trying to concentrate on some embroidery she had undertaken for Arianna. The Duchessa was a poor needlewoman and Beatrice was much more nimble-fingered. But she found it difficult to keep her mind on her work. Her thoughts kept wandering back to her life in Giglia and whether she would ever be reconciled to her brother. She couldn't bear the thought of never seeing little Bino again.

She had always hoped that he would grow to resemble Falco, the little brother he had been named after, and had imagined that would be a comfort to her in her later years. A tear fell on the expensive silk and she was trying to brush it away when there was a soft knock on her door.

It was the Duchessa herself.

'Beatrice,' she started, then stopped. 'Oh, you are sad?'

'It's nothing,' said the princess. 'I was just thinking about Falco – you know, my younger brother who died last year.'

'Well, that is a coincidence,' said Arianna. 'It was Falco I came to speak to you about.'

'Really?' said Beatrice, surprised. 'What can be said

of him now? He lies in his tomb with a fine statue above him.'

'Come and sit down with me,' said Arianna. 'What I have to tell you will seem very amazing to you and you might feel afraid, but I promise you it will end with a kind of happiness.'

*

Nick paced the parlour anxiously, dressed in his footman's clothes. Rodolfo watched him, marvelling at the boy's wonderful physique and steady walk.

'It is like a miracle, what they did for you in the other world of the future,' he said.

It had not taken him long to decide that Beatrice could meet this revenant from the past. He trusted the di Chimici princess not to reveal secrets of the Stravaganti.

'You can't imagine,' said Nick, stopping. 'I've got used to it now, but when I first arrived there it was quite terrifying, the speed with which everything worked. But now I see they take a lot longer over some things. They get married and have their children much later – just because they live longer. Some people even live to be over a hundred, you know.'

'Really?' said Rodolfo. 'They must be treated with much honour.'

'Well, actually, no,' said Georgia. 'They get a message from the Queen but they're usually in an old people's home and often pretty gaga by then.'

'Ga-ga?' queried Rodolfo, but he was destined not to know the answer, as the door opened and Princess Beatrice rushed in.

She had listened to Arianna's explanation of what happened to her brother, had failed to understand and had it all explained again. But nothing could have prepared her for the sight that met her eyes: Falco, upright and strong, a year older than he would have been if he had lived, tall and handsome but still recognisably her adored little brother.

The two di Chimici, one still living in the sixteenth century, the other a visitor from the twenty-first, fell into a tearful and happy embrace.

Rodolfo beckoned to Georgia. 'Let us give them half an hour,' he said.

And Georgia left with him, feeling a strange mixture of emotions. She knew this was what Nick had wanted, but seeing him with his sister made her realise all over again what an alien past her boyfriend had.

Sky had an awful lot to catch up on when they all met next day. He felt rather left out. He was the only Stravagante who hadn't been in Talia the night before and he wanted every detail of both visits.

'How was it?' he asked Nick at the end of their account.

Nick hadn't said much so far; it was Georgia who had talked about their stravagation to Bellezza. Now he ran his hands through his wayward hair.

'What can I tell you?' he said. 'When I'm here, Talia seems like a dream – and vice versa.'

Georgia was clearly worried; she had seen Nick like this once before, when he had thought up the crazy idea of changing places with Luciano again.

'Well, at least the talismans must be working, since neither of you had one for Bellezza,' said Sky.

'Hey, wasn't that your special topic, Georgia?' asked Matt. 'Can we see what you've got?'

Georgia pulled out a list and showed it to them:

Talismans

Lucien/Luciano	*marbled notebook/white rose*
Georgia	*winged horse*
Nick/Falco	*Merla's feather/black quill pen/silver earring*
Sky	*perfume bottle*
Matt	*spell-book*
Bel	*bag of silver tesserae*
William Dethridge	*copper dish*
Rodolfo	*silver ring*
Paolo	*?*
Brother Sulien	*silver cross*
Giuditta Miele	*?*
Constantin	*?*
(Filippo di Chimici	*Matt's spell-book)*
Flavia	*?*

They all pored over it.

'I don't know all of them,' said Georgia. 'I forgot to ask Bel to find out about them.'

'Why do some have two?' asked Isabel. 'Look – Nick's even got three!'

There was a babble of explanations from the other four about talismans having to come from the opposite world to your own.

'Then how come Filippo di Chimici was able to come to our world using Matt's?' asked Isabel.

There was total silence in Nick's attic, as four pairs of eyes looked at Isabel as if she had just announced she had found a cure for cancer.

'What?' she asked. 'Am I being stupid or something?'

'No,' said Matt. 'We're the ones who have been stupid. You're the clever one. How did we miss that? And how DID Filippo get here?'

Chapter 17

Andrea's Story

Filippo Nucci's mosaic was complete and so was Fausto's portrait of Vitale, the spotted cat. Duke Germano had installed the great cat in his new house with his picture inside the door and had allotted a stableman to his personal care so that the cat was regularly exercised and fed fresh meat. Vitale accompanied his master on some ceremonial occasions and was always beautifully behaved.

There was a small gathering in honour of the cat's new home.

'It's wonderful,' said Filippo when Fausto unveiled Vitale's portrait.

'A remarkable likeness,' said the Duke. 'You have so much skill, Maestro.'

He gave the mosaic-master considerably more than

the agreed fee, he was so pleased with the result. With all the worries about the Gate people hanging over him, the presence of Vitale and the beautifying of his quarters was a pleasure the Duke could indulge and enjoy.

Lurking at the back of the small crowd gathered in Duke Germano's courtyard was a disreputable-looking individual in a blue jerkin. He had insinuated himself in among the spectators and soon found out who the mosaic-maker was.

'And who's the tall thin one with the cane?' he asked his neighbour.

'That's young Filippo Nucci,' Enrico was told. 'He's been here nearly a year, since his folk were exiled from Giglia.'

Enrico looked at the young aristocrat with interest. So this was one of the people who had taken part in the massacre at the di Chimici weddings and let all hell loose in Talia. At the moment he didn't look as if he'd come off best against a glass of milk but Enrico was used to the deceptiveness of appearances. He decided to follow Filippo.

Unlike Fausto's, Filippo's mosaic did not have a patron who had commissioned it. But his parents allowed him to have it inset in the wall of his room. A portrait of the goddess was not against the law in Classe, as it would have been in a di Chimici city. Such an ornament was more likely to be seen as appropriate defiance of the repressive anti-magic laws. A defiant fist shaken in the face of Talia's dominant family.

And yet for the young man it had a private meaning that had nothing to do with hating the di Chimici – in fact, the very opposite. As he walked home, Filippo thought about Beatrice and wondered if he would ever see her again. An unpleasant smell broke into his thoughts and he was aware of a scruffy little man coming to walk beside him.

'Salutations, Signore,' said Enrico. 'You liked the cat picture?'

'The mosaic? Yes, very much,' said Filippo. 'Fausto is teaching me. But do I know you?'

'Enrico Poggi,' said the man, sticking out a grubby hand. 'Here on business for the Cavaliere Crinamorte.'

Filippo wondered what business the elegant Cavaliere of Bellezza could possibly have with this unprepossessing man. But politeness was part of his upbringing.

'I was in Giglia last year,' said Enrico chattily. 'At the Church of the Annunciation.'

'Ah,' said Filippo. A frown creased his brow. 'I'm afraid I have no memory of that.'

Enrico believed him. He did not sound like a cold-blooded murderer and Enrico had known some in his time.

'But you remember the di Chimici?' he said. Enrico had decided this scarred young man would be an ideal ally in his mission to oppose the Grand Duke's plans.

'How can I ever forget them?' asked Filippo bitterly. 'They have destroyed my family.' Then he added, 'But they are not all bad.'

'No,' said the spy. 'That Princess Beatrice now – she's a good one.'

This chimed so well with Filippo's feelings that, on

an impulse, he invited him in to see his mosaic, even though the little spy was an unlikely visitor in the Nucci's elegant palazzo.

'But that's remarkable,' said Enrico. 'It is Princess Beatrice to the life.'

'You think so?' said Filippo, pleased. 'It was supposed to be the goddess but somehow it has turned out to resemble the princess.'

'You know she's in Bellezza?' said the spy.

'No!' said Filippo, looking at Enrico as if he were the oracle. 'I imagined she was still in Giglia, from which I am exiled. But I thought Bellezza was Giglia's enemy.'

'The Grand Duke's maybe. But Beatrice and the Grand Duke have had a falling out. The princess and I used to be quite close,' said Enrico importantly. 'You could always go and visit her there at the Ducal Palace. Bellezza's not far away.'

The English Stravaganti were completely puzzled by Isabel's discovery. It made no sense. Now they came to think about it, there was no more reason why Matt's talisman would transport a Talian to this world than the fake book Rinaldo had taken from Luciano.

'Shall I fetch it?' asked Matt.

'It's getting late,' said Nick, looking at his watch. 'My parents have some people coming for dinner and I promised I'd eat with them. Let's meet tomorrow morning and bring our talismans. And we should all try to work out what happened with Filippo.'

No one was very confident of coming up with an

answer but Isabel, being the most recent Stravagante among them, was a bit fresher in the way she looked at how they made their journeys.

She thought about it all the way home.

'Where've you been?' asked Charlie when she let herself in.

'Round at Nick's,' she said.

'Again?' he said, rolling his eyes.

'What's it to you?' asked Isabel. 'You have your friends.'

'Sure,' said Charlie. 'But I don't spend every waking hour with them. You see far more of those guys than you do of your family.'

'Ah, do you miss me?' said Isabel, trying to recapture the lightness of tone that used to be part of their relationship.

'Yes, I do, actually,' said her brother. 'I don't like the way you are these days.'

That smarted; Isabel was shocked by his seriousness. Then she just felt annoyed. Charlie was jealous. Fine. Let him feel a tiny part of what she had been putting up with for seventeen years.

'You mean you don't like it when I'm not just a clone of you,' she said. 'When did you ever ask me to go out with you and your friends? All I'm doing is having a life of my own.'

'What are you two rowing about?' said their father, coming out of the living room.

'Nothing,' they both said simultaneously. This was not twin-telepathy, just teenage solidarity in the face of parental nosiness.

'Oh good,' said Tony Evans. 'Then perhaps you could go and argue about nothing further away?'

'I don't think he'll ever make a mosaicist,' Fausto told the Duke as they watched Filippo limp away from the ceremony, accompanied by a small man neither of them recognised.

'No?' said the Duke. 'That's a pity. He seems to love the work so much.'

'He has made a good piece,' said Fausto. 'But one good piece is not enough. It was a straightforward portrait, like the one I've made of your cat, Your Grace. That's just painting using tesserae. It takes more than that to design a floor or wall mosaic.'

'Poor soul,' said Flavia, who had come up beside them. 'He so wants to be useful, to find how to make his way in the world. And he doesn't care for banking.'

'He told me he really wanted to be in your fleet,' Fausto said to Duke Germano, 'but he realises that his injuries make that path impossible.'

'It's true that he can't shin up a mast or be nimble on deck,' mused Germano. 'But there are other tasks in my navy and he is an intelligent man. Let me see what I can find for him to do. If you think his father would approve.'

'I think his father would be glad to have him usefully employed,' said Flavia. 'He would prefer him to follow him into the money business. But he sees how unhappy the boy is and knows he would be better off doing something he enjoys.'

'I wonder if he has any talent for diplomacy?' mused Germano.

Isabel had missed seeing Vitale's house opened. She had her usual long sleep on Saturday night and when she did get up on Sunday she prepared to go back to Nick's. Charlie saw her just as she was stuffing the talisman into her pocket.

'What's that?' he asked.

Isabel felt very reluctant to tell him but could think of no reason not to. She drew the red velvet bag back out of her jeans pocket. It sat innocently on her palm, giving nothing of its magical properties away.

'What's in it?' asked Charlie, prodding it with his forefinger.

'Silver tesserae,' said Isabel truthfully. 'You know, the little blocks mosaics are made from?'

Charlie immediately lost interest. 'Oh, one of your Art things,' he said.

'That's right,' said Isabel, shrugging her jacket on.

'You off again?' he asked. 'Back to Nick's? As if I didn't know. Honestly, if the whole school didn't know about his thing with that girl in our year, I'd definitely think you two were an item.'

'Georgia,' said Isabel. 'She's called Georgia. And she's going to be there too. You've got a one-track mind.'

'Oh, are you going out again?' asked their mother, who was on her way in through the front door with her arms full of the Sunday papers. 'Will you be back for lunch?'

'Yes, I'm study-buddying over at the Mulhollands' place,' said Isabel.

Charlie snorted. 'And why do you need those tessy-things for that?'

Isabel was stumped for an answer. But her mother stepped in.

'Sky Meadows is going to be there, isn't he?' she said. 'I bumped into Rosalind at the newsagent's and she told me. And he's doing A level Art, like Bel.'

Isabel flashed her a grateful smile and escaped.

She was the last to arrive at the Mulhollands' and the others had already set their talismans out on the coffee table. Isabel had read Georgia's list, like the others, but it was different seeing them all there – the black flying horse like Merla, the quill pen, the blue perfume bottle and the leather-bound spell-book. Shyly, she took out the velvet pouch and laid it beside them. The only England-to-Talia talismans missing were Doctor Dethridge's copper dish and Luciano's marbled notebook.

Sky moved up to make room for her next to him on the sofa and no one but Isabel noticed. It felt so right and natural to squeeze in beside him.

'So how far have you got?' she asked.

'Nowhere,' said Sky. 'We waited for you.'

The sense of belonging was overwhelming; Isabel felt so lucky. If she hadn't found the talisman – or it hadn't found her, as Dethridge would say – she would never have found this degree of acceptance in the group. It was amazing how they had opened up and let her in.

'I wonder who will be next?' she said, without realising she was speaking out loud.

'What do you mean?' asked Georgia.

'Sorry,' said Isabel. 'I mean, who will be the next

Stravagante? It's always someone from our school, isn't it? It's probably someone we know already.'

'I can't get my head round that at the moment,' said Nick. 'It's hard enough understanding about the Stravaganti we've got already. Have you had any ideas about Filippo's stravagation?'

Isabel had to admit she hadn't.

'Can I touch the talismans?' she asked.

When they all agreed, she picked up each one in turn. There was nothing that could be concealed about them, until she reached Matt's book. Perhaps that was a clue? She unwound the leather strips carefully. And then she opened the book.

'Where's the counter-spell for the evil eye?' she said.

'There,' said Matt, leaning over and pointing. 'There's a bookmark.'

Isabel stared at him and then so did the others.

'A bookmark?' asked Georgia. 'You mean like an ordinary paper bookmark from this world?'

Matt looked quite comical, with his mouth open.

'That's it, isn't it?' he said at last. 'I did it. I opened the gate for Filippo by putting a bookmark in the spell-book. It wasn't my talisman that sent him to our world at all.'

Isabel held up the bookmark, which advertised Mortimer Goldsmith's antiques shop. Such a flimsy little thing to have brought a di Chimici prince through the portal to their world, even if only for a few seconds.

'Wow!' said Sky. 'I thought only really advanced Stravaganti could do that – could make a talisman from our world.'

'Well,' said Georgia, 'I did it when I brought Nick

here. He used my eyebrow ring.'

'I remember that ring,' said Sky. 'You haven't worn it for a while now.'

'I destroyed it,' said Georgia.

'I asked her to,' said Nick. 'I didn't want to be tempted to go back.'

'But you have a new talisman?' asked Isabel.

'I've had two,' said Nick. 'Brother Sulien gave me the quill pen to take me to Giglia, but Georgia gave me Merla's feather before, to get me to Remora. I had to swap.'

'Then it's Georgia who's the powerful Stravagante,' said Isabel. 'You've made a talisman in both directions.'

'Well, at least we've solved the mystery,' said Georgia, embarrassed.

'I'll tell Flavia tonight,' said Isabel. 'And I'll ask her what hers is – maybe she can tell me about the others' talismans too?'

But when Isabel arrived in Classe there was no time to ask Flavia anything. Andrea was at her palazzo, burning with news.

'It's only three weeks till the attack,' he said. 'I'm just off to tell them in Bellezza.'

'How do you know?' asked Isabel. But even as she asked she knew Andrea would not let them in on everything he knew and how; it was part of his image to be mysterious.

Three weeks! Her first thought, incongruously, was that it would at least be happening in the Easter holidays in her world. If she had to take part in a sea battle, it would be pretty hard to go to school the next day. The very thought was absurd; what could she do in a battle of any kind? But perhaps that wasn't what her task would be. Isabel had thought about this for so long that her mind was weary.

'Come with me,' said Andrea impulsively. 'Come to Bellezza.'

'Me?' said Isabel, startled.

'Why not?' asked Andrea. 'Flavia tells me you can come and go as you please now.'

He never says 'my mother', thought Isabel. *And he knows I'm a Stravagante.*

'Do you think I should go?' she asked Flavia.

The merchant shrugged. 'You might as well. There is nothing more to be done here. And it isn't as if you need to come back here by nightfall any more – you can stravagate home from Bellezza. I'll tell Rodolfo you're both coming and then go and talk to the Duke.'

Andrea walked Isabel briskly down to the harbour and on to his caravel. They could easily make the whole journey to the lagoon city that way, he said.

As she looked over the side at the rushing waves, Isabel realised that she was no longer afraid of the water. She wondered if it had anything to do with her swimming lessons at home.

'What are you thinking?' asked Andrea.

'I can swim now,' she said, turning to him with a smile. 'Oh, not far and I'm not a very strong swimmer. But I wouldn't sink if you chucked me over the side now.'

'You know I would never do that,' he said reproachfully, then grinned, flashing his silver canines.

'It wouldn't be any fun if you can swim.'

'Do you really think the Gate people will attack Classe in three weeks?' she asked, looking back at the familiar shape of the city's harbour as the caravel rapidly left it behind.

'I know they will,' he said calmly. 'They think I will help them lead the attack.'

'What?' said Isabel.

'I offered them my services,' he said.

'So you're a . . . double agent?' said Isabel. 'Isn't that incredibly dangerous?'

Andrea laughed. 'I'm a pirate, Isabella. It's what I do.'

There was such a contrast between being alone with him on deck in the middle of the water, quietly contemplating Classe receding behind them, and this fantastic revelation of Andrea's dangerous double life. It gave her the courage to ask again what she had always wanted to know.

'Why do you do it?'

Andrea looked at her for a long time and then clearly made a decision to tell her.

'When I was young,' he said, 'I killed a man.'

Isabel was shocked but she didn't interrupt. She knew if he didn't tell her everything now, when they were away from everyone else they knew, he never would.

'It wasn't an accident,' he said, looking out to sea. 'I planned it. He was my father.'

Isabel was glad he was looking away from her. She didn't think she could have kept her expression neutral. But still she kept quiet.

'He was a villain,' Andrea went on. 'He led my

mother a terrible life – drinking, womanising. Always had. He took any money she made out of the business and gambled it away. And then he started beating her. Even that he got away with, until I was old enough and big enough to defend her.'

He clenched his fists on the ship's rail.

'And then she took on an assistant, Anna Maria. She was seventeen and very beautiful. How old are you, Isabella?' He didn't turn round.

'Seventeen,' she said.

'I thought so. You remind me of her, you know. I don't know why Flavia didn't realise the danger. She thought she was doing the girl a favour. I was eighteen and supposed to be going to the University in Bellezza. I fell in love with Anna Maria. She felt the same way about me and I didn't want to leave her. But she insisted I should go and get an education. I was going to be a teacher. Can you believe it?'

It was a question that didn't need an answer. Isabel realised she was holding her breath.

'The first time I came back from Bellezza, everything was different. Anna Maria was very quiet, couldn't look me in the eye. It was Flavia who told me. I don't know to this day if she knew what I'd do. She was just anxious to get Anna Maria away. When my father got back from his drinking bout that evening, I was waiting for him.'

The silence on the deck lengthened.

'I didn't take any chances,' Andrea continued at last. 'I told him what I thought of him and then I cut his throat.'

Isabel put her hands over her mouth to stop herself from crying out.

'Both the women went mad. They said I'd be put away for ever. But I didn't care. Then, when my blood cooled, I regretted what I'd done. Oh, not to him, before you ask. I'd do it again in the blink of an eye for what he did to Anna Maria. But to them.' He sighed deeply.

'Flavia managed it all. No one knew I was back – I hadn't told them I was coming. She smuggled me out, told me to run and keep running. Then she would raise the alarm and tell the city watch when they came that an intruder had killed her husband for his money. She would break into the money-chest and hide the contents. It was all her money anyway.'

Isabel had to speak. 'But why did you have to stay away if no one knew it was you? Couldn't you have just come back from university and pretended you didn't know?'

Andrea turned round and looked at her.

'I didn't go,' he said. 'It was a good plan but I couldn't leave Anna Maria. She was pregnant.'

'With your child?' whispered Isabel.

The hatred on his face was terrifying. 'No. I had treated her with respect. I wanted to marry her. The child was the result of rape.'

He turned back to sea.

'Flavia never managed to tell the guards anything. They caught me with blood on my clothes still loitering outside the house, unable to go away. They dragged me in while she was still screaming. One look at me and she knew it was useless to pretend.'

'What happened to Anna Maria?' asked Isabel.

'She killed herself,' said Andrea quietly. 'She filled her pockets with loose cobbles in the harbour and jumped off the pier as soon as she heard I'd been arrested. So I killed her too, in a way. When I heard about it, I wanted to die too. But I was in the Classe jail with no means at hand.'

'So how come you got away?' asked Isabel.

'My mother,' he said simply. 'You know she has powers. You and she belong to the same Order. Somehow, and don't ask me how – I've never understood what you do – she put some sort of glamour on the guards, took their keys away and let me out.'

He started pacing up and down the deck.

'I think she felt responsible, too, for what had happened. She should never have brought Anna Maria anywhere near that monster.'

'So what did people think had happened?'

'She locked the cell once she'd let me out and put the keys back on the guard's belt. They didn't even remember she'd been there. A rumour sprang up that I'd been spirited away by magic but no one ever associated it with her. Very few people in Classe know she's a Stravagante.'

'And what did you do?'

'I think I went a bit mad for a while,' said Andrea, 'because I don't remember much about the first few months. I knew I could never go back to Classe. At least not to live as my mother's son. I can get away with the odd day there, especially now I've changed my appearance. But my old life was over. Patricide is a terrible crime anywhere but especially in Talia.'

'But how did you become a pirate?' asked Isabel.

'I am a person outside the law,' said Andrea. 'Someone who belongs nowhere. Drifting in and out of ports scratching a living, it wasn't hard to fall in with brigands. And then I found I took to the life.'

'But why do you steal your mother's goods?'

'It would look suspicious if I did her any favours,' said Andrea. 'And I always sell them back.'

'Sell, not give?' risked Isabel.

'Yes, well. I know she saved my life but perhaps she was guilty too.'

'Guilty?'

'She was right. She was responsible. She was the one who put the only woman I've ever loved into the clutches of the man I killed.'

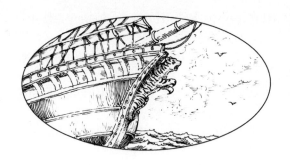

Chapter 18

All at Sea

There was quite a reception committee waiting for Andrea and Isabel at the Ducal Palace in Bellezza. Rodolfo and Dethridge took the pirate away to hear his news while Arianna led Isabel off to meet Princess Beatrice.

'Don't you want to know what Andrea has to say too?' asked Isabel on their way.

'I know already,' said Arianna. 'Flavia has been in touch through her mirrors. We shall be at war within weeks.'

'But do you know how he knows it?' asked Isabel.

'He's a spy and a pirate,' said Arianna, surprised. 'I assume he has his methods.'

'He is working with the Gate people,' said Isabel.

'He's pretending to help them and then telling us their plans.'

'So he is risking his life – even more than we thought.'

'I don't think he cares what happens to him,' said Isabel.

She was remembering how Andrea had talked with disgust of having his father's tainted blood in his veins. He always seemed to act without care for his safety, as if it didn't matter to him whether he lived or died.

'You know more than you are saying,' said Arianna. 'But I shan't press you.'

They had arrived at her private apartments by then. She stopped as she reached the door. 'You know that Georgia came here with the person who used to be Falco?'

'Yes,' said Isabel. She couldn't believe it had been only two nights ago. 'How is Beatrice? I mean, how did she take seeing him?'

'She doesn't understand it, of course. Which of us really does? But she knows that her brother is happy and healthy in another world and that is enough for her.'

It isn't enough for Vicky Mulholland, thought Isabel, but knew better than to say it.

And then they were in the Duchessa's parlour and there was a pale-faced young woman who bore a strong family resemblance to Nicholas Duke. The big cat, Rigello, sat at her side, leaning into her silk skirts.

'This is my friend Isabella,' said Arianna to the princess. 'You met her once before. She is another of the same Order as Georgia and your . . . and the young man Nicholas, who came here on Friday.'

Beatrice got up, the colour rushing to her face.

'Oh, I am most glad to see you,' she said. 'Anything you can tell me will be welcome.'

Isabella bent down to pat Rigello, who was sniffing her hands. She wished she had brought a message from Nick but when she stravagated she hadn't known she was going to end up in Bellezza.

'I know that Nick was very pleased to have seen you,' she said. 'He and Georgia told us about it.'

'It was a miracle to see him so healed in body,' said Beatrice. 'Tell me something about this other world you live in. Arianna has tried but she has never been there and I cannot understand what Senator Rodolfo has tried to explain to me.'

'Well,' Isabel began, wondering how best to explain life in a comprehensive school in twenty-first-century London to an Italian Renaissance princess who had never known anything but luxury and being waited on. 'You know it is in the future compared with Talia?'

'So Falco told me,' said Beatrice. 'He said hundreds of years have passed.'

'That is true,' said Isabel. 'And the modern world has all sorts of . . . machines and . . . science that it is hard to describe to you. But some things are still the same. Families live together and the children must go to school from the age of five to sixteen.'

'And how old are you?' the princess asked.

'I'm seventeen, but I'm staying on at school another two years and so will Nick, I'm sure. You do that if you want to go to university in our world, or just to get more qualifications.'

'He told me that he is sixteen now,' said Beatrice, 'and yet he was only thirteen when he died a year and a half ago. It is another miracle.'

'I don't really understand that bit myself,' said Isabel truthfully. 'But I do know that when he came to our world he couldn't walk without crutches and now he's a fencing champion.'

Beatrice sighed. 'He told me that. And I could see with my own eyes how tall and strong he has become.'

'What else would you like to know?' asked Isabel.

'Tell me more about Georgia,' said Beatrice.

*

Luciano had made up his mind that he would take part in the sea battle whatever Constantin or Rodolfo – or even Arianna – had to say. In the Easter break from university, he went back to Bellezza and straight to the Arsenale to find the Admiral.

Admiral Gambone had his offices overlooking the shipyard, where he could keep an eye on the building of new ships for the fleet. The work was going well but he knew that once April began the invasion would be imminent. It was a relief to be distracted from his calculations by the announcement of a visitor.

'Good afternoon, Admiral,' said Luciano, making a bow.

'Cavaliere,' said Gambone, putting out a hand to him. 'It is good to see you. How are the studies going in Padavia?'

Luciano smiled ruefully. 'I am not the best of students, I'm afraid. At a time like this, I feel too restless to concentrate.'

'Ah, you are a man of action,' said the Admiral approvingly. 'Like myself. All this paperwork . . .' He gestured at the maps and plans on his desk. 'It is not my favourite part of the job.'

'I wanted to ask if you could find room for me on one of your ships,' said Luciano. 'I should like to take part in the defence of Classe.'

The Admiral looked thoughtful. He was in a delicate position with regard to the defence of Classe; he must defer to the Admiral of their fleet. But he could take on mariners at his own discretion.

'You are interested in a career in the navy?' he stalled.

'Not really, sir,' admitted Luciano. 'But you know that I shall be this city's Duke in May. And I want to learn all I can about defending it. Your fleet is the most important protection we have in the lagoon.'

It was the right thing to say. It didn't occur to the Admiral to consult the Duchessa or the Regent; he assumed they knew.

'What experience of ships do you have?' he asked.

'None at all of warships,' said Luciano. 'I am a strong swimmer and have spent time aboard fishing boats. And of course I scull my own mandola on the canals. But I realise that is very different.'

'No matter,' said Gambone. 'You have your sea legs, which is a good thing. If you are serious about this, you can join the fleet straight away on their manoeuvres. Every ship will have trained fighters as well as the regular sailors who man the ships. The mariners are used to the landsmen. They'll soon get you into shape.'

Isabel stravagated back without knowing that Luciano had returned to Bellezza. She was still full of Andrea's terrible story and had decided not to tell the others about it. It was his secret. But she resolved she would speak to Flavia about it when she could.

The last two weeks of term yawned ahead of her and she wondered how she could wait for the Easter break. If Andrea was right, the attack from the Gate people would come right in the middle of the holiday, around Easter itself. It wasn't that she was exactly looking forward to it, more that she wanted to get it over with.

The one thing that might distract her from the coming battle was that Sky really did seem to be showing an interest in her. They now always sat next to each other in Art and the camaraderie that had come from being fellow Stravaganti seemed to be changing into something more personal. That Monday they walked back together from the Art room and Isabel told him about meeting Beatrice.

'What were you doing in Bellezza again?' asked Sky.

Damn, thought Isabel. 'I went there with Andrea, to tell them about the Gate people's plans,' she said quickly.

She had meant to keep the information about the attack until they were all together. She also didn't want Sky asking more about the pirate, but the mention of the Gate people had worked; he was now talking excitedly about whether they would all be in Classe for the attack, the way that the Stravaganti had been called to Giglia.

'They don't even need to get us new talismans now,' he said. 'We can all just get there with our own.'

'And you want to?' asked Isabel. 'Even after getting wounded at the weddings?'

'Well, you're going to be there, aren't you?' said Sky. 'Isn't that likely to be when you do whatever it is you're supposed to do?'

'I guess,' said Isabel. *Was he offering to protect her?*

'I'd like to be there when it happens,' said Sky seriously. 'I might not be able to do anything to help – what do I know about ships? But it would be better than being here wondering what was happening to you.'

Duke Germano sent for Filippo Nucci and asked him to accept a diplomatic commission.

'I am sorry to take you from your artistic studies,' he said, 'but Fausto assures me he will be able to manage without you and I need your help.'

Filippo was flattered and honoured to be asked to do anything for the Duke of Classe. As Flavia had guessed, all he wanted was to be useful.

'Anything you command, Your Grace,' he said. 'Just tell me what I can do.'

'I need someone to act as a go-between for the navies of Classe and Bellezza,' said Germano. 'Your first task is to meet my admiral and talk to him about the fleet. Learn everything you can about every nail and plank in every ship, the ordnance on board, the crew, the fighting men – everything. And then go to his opposite number in Bellezza, Admiral Gambone, and talk to him about the proposed tactics. Can you do this?'

'I can,' said Filippo. 'When shall I start?'

'Today if possible,' said the Duke. 'Time is short. We are expecting to be attacked in less than three weeks. The sooner you get on with it the better.'

*

When Isabel next got back to Classe, she was sent off to the harbour too.

'You're going to need to find out something about fighting at sea,' said Flavia.

'Am I really going to be on one of the ships?' asked Isabel.

'I took the talisman to your world because we needed help,' said Flavia. 'It chose you. So you must be the one who can save us.'

'I'm your secret weapon,' said Isabel wonderingly. 'But what do you think I'll have to do?'

'Our secret weapon,' said Flavia thoughtfully. 'That is a good description. Like you, I don't know what will be required of you. It seems that no Stravagante from your world knows that until the moment it is called for. But don't worry – we shall not rely on you alone. We have a good fleet of ships and a good force of men, led by an experienced admiral. You must meet him. And you will also meet Filippo Nucci there. He is going to be our link officer between the two navies.'

'Really?' said Isabel. 'Good. He's a good man.'

'And he'll be going to Bellezza,' said Flavia. 'Which is what I think he really wants.'

They had walked to the far end of the harbour, where the war fleet was moored. Isabel could see men swarming over the rigging and bustling about the decks of the ships. But they turned away from the water and into the Duke's Arsenale. It was very like the one in Bellezza, with its dry docks, sailmakers and cannon foundries. Just as bustling, with people shouting orders and going about their business. Isabel found it thrilling even though she was not looking forward to taking part in any kind of battle.

Admiral Borca was in his office talking to Filippo. The young Nucci still had a cane to walk with but he looked much more alert and alive than the last time Isabel had seen him. He looked up and greeted her with a very sweet smile.

He's still good-looking, thought Isabel, *in spite of the scar*.

After the introductions, during which the Admiral completely accepted that Isabel would be needed on board one of his ships, Filippo took her back down to the war fleet.

'The lead ship, which the Admiral will be on, is that one,' he said, pointing. 'The *Tiger*. He will direct operations from there.'

'But how?' asked Isabel, realising suddenly how hard it must be to coordinate a battle at sea without radio or mobile phones or any modern technology.

'He'll have meetings with all the ships' captains and pilots before the Gate people get here,' said Filippo. 'They'll have a battle plan that they think will take care of anything the Gate people throw at us. If there is any change of plan while we're at sea, the ships always stay within sight of the lead ship and there's a flagman on board who will run up a new standard. It's a sort of code.'

It was the longest speech Isabel had ever heard Filippo make; she could see that he was enjoying his new role.

'And where shall I be?' she asked, feeling worried that she would be in the way on board a ship where everyone knew what they were supposed to be doing.

'I think you'll be on the *Tiger*,' said Filippo thoughtfully.

'And you?'

'Either with you or perhaps with the Bellezzan fleet,' said Filippo, 'depending on whether there's time to get back here before the fighting begins.'

It's really going to happen, thought Isabel. *Those cannons in the foundry are going to fire real iron balls into the Gate people's ships. Wood and people are going to be shattered.*

And then she remembered that Andrea's ship would be right in the front of the attack.

The next two weeks passed in a blur for Isabel. The weight of accumulated sleep loss kept her walking through the school like a zombie. Only Sky could get her attention and he was clearly worried about her. All the Barnsbury Stravaganti knew how tiring it was to live two days for every one and Isabel had told them how busy she had become in Talia.

Every day she went out with one of the warships, being shown where everything went and meeting more sailors, gunners and halberdiers than she could remember. She had really got her sea legs now and could keep her footing on deck even when a galley was running at full speed.

But when she was back on land, even in her own world, the ground often seemed to tilt and sway underneath her. She was lucky enough not to suffer from seasickness but she felt permanently just slightly nauseated as well as tired.

And she was keeping up her swimming lessons, going after school every day. Charlie just thought she was seeing Nick and the gang but in fact Isabel hardly had time to talk to them at all. Only on Sundays, after a good night's sleep, did she feel awake enough to go round to the Mulholland house and meet her friends, who were also supporting her through homework and coursework so that she didn't get behind at school.

Towards the end of the second week, when they had reached the Thursday before the Easter holiday began, Isabel felt herself beginning to relax. Once she didn't have to go to school, she could sleep most of the day and just put up with some flak from her parents.

And that night her talisman disappeared.

While Isabel had been sleepwalking through the end of term, she had neglected her twin even more. Charlie had been carrying out his own investigations into what had happened to his sister.

He had talked to Laura, who had been thrilled by his attention, though Charlie didn't notice. And he had talked to Alice Greaves, who had been quite forceful on the subject of Isabel.

'So she hasn't told you?' Alice had said. 'I'm not surprised. She and the others are all living in la-la land.'

'What do you mean?' Charlie asked.

'I can't explain it to you,' said Alice. 'All I understand is that they mean more to each other than anyone outside the group does. Sky was quite willing to give me up rather than leave them. And now I know he prefers your sister to me.'

'So I was right,' said Charlie softly.

'I can't tell you any more,' said Alice, 'because you wouldn't believe me. But if you want to find out where she goes and what she does, you must take her talisman.'

'What's that?'

'It's different for each of them. Mine was a chalk drawing.'

'So you used to be part of this . . . cult, or club, whatever it is?'

'Only once,' said Alice, which didn't make sense to him. 'Look for her talisman. It will look sort of Italian and old and she'll always have it with her.'

It did not take Charlie long to identify what Isabel's talisman must be. She had shown him the red pouch with the tesserae, after all. He hadn't been interested in it at the time. And he had to wait a long time before he got his hands on it.

But Charlie was not like Georgia's stepbrother, Russell, who had stolen her winged horse talisman and wilfully broken it. He was really worried about his twin and, though he didn't understand what the talisman could do, he knew it was the key to the mystery.

On Thursday, Isabel was very tired and went to run herself a bath. Instead of undressing in the bathroom, she had changed into her night things in her bedroom and left her clothes on the floor where they dropped. Charlie passed her on the landing and grinned; this was his chance. He couldn't help feeling a bit mean as Isabel smiled back.

As soon as she had locked the bathroom door, Charlie was in her room rummaging through her things.

'Bingo!' he said, drawing the red velvet pouch out of her jeans pocket.

He took it back to his room and tipped the silver tesserae out into a glittering pool on his bed. There was nothing else in the bag. Charlie felt like a Neanderthal confronted with a BlackBerry; he just didn't have a manual to help him understand how to get the talisman to work.

In the end, he scooped the tesserae back into the bag and lay back on his pillows, still holding it. He closed his eyes and thought about Isabel and what could have changed her so much since half-term.

When he opened his eyes again, Charlie was in the Baptistery in Classe, surrounded by colourful mosaics. He blinked but they didn't go away.

Funny dream, thought Charlie, noticing he still had the red pouch in his hand. Then he saw he was sitting in a sort of huge bath. *That's it*, he thought. *I was thinking about Isabel and tesserae and mosaics and she had a bath and that's all got mixed up in my brain to produce this weird dream.*

But after a while he felt a bit stupid just sitting in the bath with nothing happening and no one else in the room. He cautiously climbed out over the side and went towards the only door in the room. When he opened it, bright sunlight streamed into the small round building and his curiosity took him outside.

It seemed to be somewhere Mediterranean, probably Italy. There were cobbled streets and horses everywhere and it was gloriously warm. Charlie didn't feel at all cold even though he was only in a baggy T-shirt and tracky bottoms. But he did feel a bit conspicuous; no one else was dressed like him. They all seemed to be in costume like characters from an old play, the women in long dresses, the men in ruffled shirts and velvet trousers with buckled shoes.

Now that is weird, thought Charlie. *I wasn't thinking about pantomimes at all.*

Stranger still, a tall thin young man with a cane and a scarred face stopped him in the street.

'Isabella!' said the young man. 'Why are you dressed like that? Is it so you can be more comfortable on board ship? Only, I have to say, I think the crew of the *Tiger* will find it a bit distracting.'

Charlie had no idea what was going on, but at the mention of a ship he noticed that there was a salty smell in the air and he heard the cry of gulls. And an unsettling feeling crept over him that perhaps he was not in a dream at all.

Chapter 19

Out of His Depth

Isabel was frantic when she couldn't find the talisman. She had planned to have a couple of hours' sleep before stravagating and had set her alarm to wake her at midnight. But when it went off she took a few minutes to remember where she was and what she was supposed to be doing, her sleep had been so deep. Groggily, she got out of bed and picked up her jeans. The velvet pouch wasn't in the pocket.

Fully alert now, she put the main light on and hunted through the mess on her floor and then in every other place she could think of. Nothing.

Then she remembered Georgia's stories about Russell and decided she was going to have to wake Charlie and confront him.

Quietly, she opened the door and crept to his room.

There was no point in knocking; Charlie was a deep sleeper. So she turned the handle and slipped into her brother's bedroom. He was lying on his back, snoring lightly, an angelic expression on his face. Isabel thought for a moment that he really was very nice-looking.

Then she saw what he was holding.

A jolt went through her body like the ones you have in your sleep when you think you have fallen into an abyss. Charlie had stravagated!

Two emotions wrestled in her mind. Firstly, that her brother would find himself in Classe – at least she hoped it would be Classe – almost undressed by Talian standards, alone and without any idea of what was going on. And secondly, that as long as he was there with the talisman, there was no way she could get there herself. She knew from Matt's story that she couldn't just take the talisman out of his hand and use it herself.

Panic overwhelmed her. But then she started to think straight. It was all right – at least that second worry. If one of the other Barnsbury Stravaganti would lend her their talisman, she could get to Classe by saying the city's name out loud. She knew what the place looked like and would surely get there. Then all she had to do was find Charlie and show him how to get back.

But time was of the essence. Who was the best person to try?

Sky, she thought. *He stays up late. I can ring him and he'll come round with his perfume bottle; I could meet him at the front door.*

And then she saw it. Just one silver tessera winking

in the light from the street lamp shining through Charlie's window. It was lying on the duvet a good foot away from where Charlie lay. He must have emptied the bag out to investigate it and then not put them all back in. Gingerly Isabel picked up the little shining square. Would it, could it, work on its own?

There was only one way to find out.

Charlie was completely at a loss in Classe. As soon as he spoke, Filippo realised he wasn't Isabel.

'Do you know Isabella?' he asked. 'She looks very like you.'

'I have a twin called Isabel, if that's who you mean,' said Charlie cautiously.

'And I can't help noticing you have no shadow,' whispered Filippo.

Charlie looked down; this weird bloke was right. He had no shadow. 'What does that mean?' he asked.

'Isabella is without a shadow here too. Look, we should not stand talking in the square. Come into my house and I'll lend you something to wear. You are attracting attention and we don't want anyone else to notice you have no shadow.'

Charlie let the man lead him across the market square to a handsome building, making introductions on the way. So this was Filippo and he seemed to have decided that Charlie was to be called Carlo.

Footmen eyed them curiously as Filippo led Charlie across the grand hall and up a marble staircase. His chamber was much grander than any room Charlie had ever been in but it seemed to lack a few basic essentials, like a wardrobe. There was a large wooden chest, through which Filippo was now rummaging for clothes that would fit Charlie.

It wasn't easy: Filippo was much taller than him. But Charlie was eventually dressed in one of the ridiculous ruffled shirts and a spare pair of black velvet trousers that Filippo commandeered from one of his footmen. White silk stockings and black shoes with silver buckles completed his outlandish outfit; at least Filippo didn't have big feet.

Charlie looked at himself in a long glass. The surface was greenish and uneven, with a few bubbles in it, but he could see that he would now pass for a local.

'That's better,' said Filippo. 'Now tell me why you are here. And where is Isabella? Is something wrong?'

'You're not going to believe this,' said Charlie. 'but I really have no idea who you are or where I am. I'm sort of . . . er . . . here by accident. I didn't mean to come.'

Filippo looked at him.

'This is beyond me,' he said. 'We must go to Flavia.'

'Whatever you say,' said Charlie.

*

Isabel had never been so pleased to see the inside of the Baptistery; she would even have accepted another wet bath if that was the price of being there. She took the little silver tessera and kissed it before carefully putting it in the pocket of her green dress. It was her tiny passport home.

In the end she hadn't dared to make the experiment

without telling someone and had rung Sky after all. He had answered straight away and, as soon as he understood what had happened, had volunteered to come over and sit with her while she tried to stravagate.

But the thought of what Charlie and her parents would say if they found Sky in her room made her reluctantly turn him down.

'Let me call Georgia then,' he said.

'No, it's all right,' said Isabel. 'I feel better now you know.'

'Well, text me when you're back,' said Sky.

It had taken ages to get off to sleep even though she'd been so tired before; all the adrenalin that had flooded her system when she realised what Charlie had done kept her wired for at least another hour.

So it was a huge relief to be back in Classe. She ran out of the Baptistery and into the street before realising that she had no idea what to do next; where could Charlie be? Normally she would have gone straight down to the harbour and met Filippo there. They were supposed to be studying the code of the Admiral's flags today. But how likely was it that her brother would be there?

She tried hard to think what he would do in this unfamiliar city, and the thought of him standing about barefoot and in his night things made her grind her teeth in frustration.

She found herself automatically walking towards Flavia's house, crossing the square and looking at all the market stalls. There was no shaggy blond boy in twenty-first-century nightclothes. She reached Flavia's and pulled on the iron bell.

A familiar footman showed her straight to Flavia's parlour, where, to her surprise, she found Filippo. On the settle lay a young man she had never seen before. He was dressed as a Talian but there was something familiar about him; he appeared to be asleep.

Then light dawned.

'Charlie!' she cried, flooded with relief.

'It is all right, Isabella,' said Flavia, holding up a hand. 'He is falling asleep and should be back in his own body soon.

Before Isabel could reach her brother, the figure on the settle started to waver and turn transparent. Then he was gone.

'What happened?' asked Flavia. 'How did he get your talisman and how did you get here without it?'

Isabel took out the shining little tessera. 'He'd dropped one of these,' she said. 'I didn't know if it would be enough to bring me here but it did.'

'Well, you'd better go straight back,' said Flavia. 'I've spoken to Rodolfo and he thinks you need to go home and check that your brother is safe and then take the talisman from him. Come back again today if you can but don't take any risks.'

'I don't think I'll be able to sleep,' said Isabel. 'It was so strange seeing him in this room.'

'It was strange for him too,' said Filippo.

'It was Filippo who dressed him in Talian clothes,' said Flavia. 'Thank the goddess he was the one who found him. Now, let me give you a light sleeping draught. I gave some to Carlo and told him to think of home. He should be safely back in his body in your world by now but none of us will feel certain of that till you come back and tell us.'

Charlie had accepted the drink and the explanation from the friendly middle-aged woman. And he had fallen asleep really quite easily, worn out by his adventures.

But when he woke, he was not in his familiar bed. He was in a hayloft over a stable, with dry stalks tickling his face. He gave a great sneeze and then groaned.

I must be in some other part of that crazy world, he thought. All he wanted was for the adventure to be over and to be back in his own home in Islington. But it was nowhere near as warm as in Classe, so maybe he was somewhere else in London?

Cautiously he descended the ladder. He didn't think there were any stables in Barnsbury, and once he stepped out into the light, he could see straight away that it was nothing like his street outside.

The road was roughly cobbled at the sides with a channel of filth running down the middle. The houses were so close together at the tops that people could talk to one another leaning out of their top-floor windows; he saw some women doing this. But it didn't look Italian any more and he noticed with a jolt that he *did* have a shadow.

Does this mean I'm back in my own world? he wondered. *But where? Or do I mean when?*

It was horrible, literally not knowing where in the world he was. And he suddenly felt very hungry. He was still in the clothes that Filippo had given him but had no money, and no pockets, come to that. All he had was the red velvet bag, which he now stashed up one of his full sleeves, making sure it was tightly tied at the wrist. He was going to have to forage.

He stepped out into the street, noticing that the houses had pigs and chickens in the yards beside them. It looked as if he was in a village in the country but one that had been dressed up for a BBC costume drama. Not cleaned up though; the smell of animals and manure was terrible. But there was no other kind of pollution in the air. No smoke or petrol fumes.

He looked back at the house whose stable he had woken up in. And went up to its front door and knocked.

If this is where I'm supposed to be, I'd better get it over with, he thought.

A woman in an apron answered his knock.

'Ah, hello,' said Charlie. 'I was wondering if you could give me something to eat.'

The woman looked at him uncomprehendingly. Perhaps this was Italy after all? Charlie mimed putting food into his mouth and drinking something.

Understanding dawned but the woman was still looking at him dubiously. At least he was wearing the right sort of clothes; Charlie wondered what she would have made of him if he'd been barefoot and in pyjamas.

While she was weighing up whether to let him in, a man came up behind her.

'Whatte doth the varlet wante?' he said.

'Vittels and ale,' said the woman.

Charlie could just about understand them but they had broad country accents.

And while he was wondering what to say to them, a

familiar presence suddenly appeared at his side.

'What's up, Charlie?' said Isabel as casually as she could manage.

He had never been so glad to see her in his life.

'Bel!' he said, grabbing her arms. 'Thank God! What's going on?'

'You tell me,' said Isabel. 'Why did you steal my talisman?'

'I didn't,' said Charlie. 'At least I didn't mean to. I was just sort of looking at it and then I fell asleep. Here, you can have it back.' He started to fish in his sleeve.

'No,' said Isabel, stopping him. 'You'll need it if you're ever to get home. Where are we, anyway?'

The two people in the doorway were watching and listening, fascinated.

'Mayhap we sholde summone the watch?' said the woman.

Isabel froze. This woman sounded just like Doctor Dethridge. It was clear that Charlie didn't understand what she meant by 'the watch', but his sister did.

'No neede for thatte,' said Isabel, trying to speak in the same way. 'We . . . meane no harme. We are just lost.'

'Lost?' said the man. 'Why, ye are in the village of Bernersbury. Where wolde ye bee?'

'Barnsbury?' said Isabel. A suspicion was dawning on her that made her feel sick to her stomach. 'Can you, I mean, canne ye telle mee whose house this be?'

'Yt bilonged to my olde mastire,' said the woman. 'Doctor Dethridge. Bot he has been gonne these five yeares.'

'No more of thatte,' said the man, rather angrily.

'Thoughe yore mastire is dede, yore mistresse liveth.'

'And as fore ye,' he said, looking at the twins curiously, 'mayhap ye are of good faithe and are gode servauntes of the Queen, or mayhap ye are scoundrels.'

All Isabel could think was, *This is William Dethridge's house!*

And then, *We're in Elizabethan England!*

She pulled Charlie away from the house, nodding and smiling like a mad thing to the couple in the doorway.

'Wow!' he said. 'You speak the local lingo.'

'Don't be an idiot,' said Isabel. 'I'm just winging it. But I think we've ended up in Barnsbury in 1580.'

In Classe, Flavia was sitting anxiously by her mirrors in constant contact with Rodolfo and Dethridge and waiting for Isabel's return. She had sent Filippo off to wait in the Baptistery.

Still no sign, she told the Bellezzan Stravaganti. *I thought she would be back by now.*

Yt likes me notte, said Dethridge. *There is somme thynge about this day thatte is notte ryghte.*

Another face joined them in the mirror. It was Luciano. In her head Flavia heard him responding to the old Elizabethan: *What do you think could have happened?*

The talismanne was notte for hym, said Dethridge. *Sich a chaunge of ownire myghte make a bygge difference in the gatewaye bitwene oure worldes. Who knowes where those twain have stravayged to?*

Sky had hardly slept. There had been no text message from Isabel. As soon as it was light, before six, he was on the phone to the other Stravaganti. It took a while to make them understand, especially Matt, who was a heavy sleeper. But they were all outside Isabel's house by six thirty, dressed and looking more or less awake.

'We've got to have a reason to get in there and cover for them till Bel gets them both back from Talia,' said Sky.

The others nodded and mumbled but it was difficult to think of anything convincing.

Luckily for them, Tony Evans had an early meeting out of town and, while they were all still arguing outside, he came out of the door, briefcase in hand. It was a quarter to seven.

'Oh, hello,' he said. 'What are you all doing up so early? Are you waiting for Bel? She's still asleep.'

'If only,' muttered Sky under his breath.

But Georgia had an inspiration.

'She'll be down in a minute, Mr Evans. And Charlie. We're all going on a run before school.'

'Really?' he said. 'She never mentioned it.'

He wasn't sure if they were dressed properly for running but he could never really tell with young people's clothes; there didn't seem much difference between sports gear and fashion any more.

'Well, why don't you go and wait inside?' he said, obligingly holding the door open. 'Help yourself if you want anything in the kitchen, but don't wake their mum if you can help it. She'd like another half-hour.'

Four relieved teenagers trooped gratefully in, staying as quiet as they could. After a whispered conference in the kitchen, they wrote notes to leave by the stravagating twins and then Georgia crept up the stairs to their rooms. It was a relief to see that neither door was locked. Quickly, she left the notes beside them on their beds, then left, locking their doors behind her.

She pocketed the keys as she hurried down the stairs. Sky was writing a third note, in what he hoped was a good enough imitation of Isabel's handwriting.

Gone for an early run with Charlie and friends from school, it said. *See you later. Bel.*

'Do you think she'd put kisses?' he asked doubtfully.

'Does it matter?' asked Nick.

'Yes,' said Georgia.

'Girls!' said Matt.

Sky added *xxx*. He propped the note against the kettle.

'If Sarah Evans is anything like my mum,' he said, 'it's the first place she'll go to in the kitchen.'

They let themselves out but, before they shut the door, Matt stopped them.

'Hold on – one of us will have to stay,' he said. 'Suppose they get back from Talia? They won't be able to get out of their rooms.'

Georgia groaned. 'It's got to be me, hasn't it? Just in case one of the parents spots me. They'd be less alarmed than by one of you.'

'We'll cover for you at school,' said Nick.

'And for Bel and Charlie,' said Sky. 'It'd better be a stomach bug.'

262

'They'll think there's an epidemic,' said Matt.

Georgia closed the front door quietly behind her and crept back up to Isabel's room. She was just in time. As she locked the door, she heard the parents' bedroom door open and someone cross the landing to the bathroom. A few minutes later Sarah Evans headed down the stairs as predicted and straight for the kettle.

Georgia realised she had been holding her breath. She tiptoed over to Isabel's bed and sat on the end. Her friend was apparently in a deep sleep, breathing evenly. The hand that was outside the duvet was clenched into a fist; Georgia guessed the single silver tessera was held tight inside.

The note seemed to have worked. Isabel's mother came back upstairs and turned on the shower, without knocking on her children's bedroom doors. But Georgia couldn't really relax until Mrs Evans was out of the house at eight o'clock.

She left it another ten minutes before creeping down to the kitchen to make tea and toast; there had been no time for breakfast at her house. She phoned Nick and found that the three boys were stuffing themselves with coffee and bacon rolls in the café. There was still plenty of time before school.

Then she wondered how on earth to fill her day. She could only pray the twins would be back soon.

*

Four centuries earlier Isabel and Charlie were lying low in Barnsbury. She had tried to fill him in on the situation and, though he didn't want to believe it, he sort of semi-understood about Talia and the talismans.

'But why didn't I just go back to our time the way you always do?' he asked. 'If you're right, we're in the right place but the wrong time by hundreds of years.'

'I don't know,' said Isabel, tugging her hair. 'It's never happened before. No one in our time has ever taken someone else's talisman and stravagated, even by accident.'

'So what do we do next?' he asked.

'No idea,' said Isabel. She suddenly felt overwhelmed with tiredness.

'I'd settle for somewhere I could get my head down,' she said. 'I'm knackered. I've been up all night and so have you.' Then she realised what that meant.

'Oh no! What will Mum and Dad think when they can't wake us?'

'I don't know,' said Charlie. 'I don't understand any of this. All I know is I'm really hungry.'

Isabel realised she wasn't going to get any sense out of him till he'd eaten.

'Well, we haven't got any money so we'll either have to work for some or we'll have to steal some food.'

'No one's going to give us a job,' said Charlie. 'Those two back there looked at us as if we were Martians.'

The door to William Dethridge's old house was shut now but Isabel still felt drawn to it as the only halfway familiar thing in this strange situation; she knew that Barnsbury Comprehensive was built partly on the ruins of this house and the old alchemist's laboratory.

'Let's go round the back,' she said.

They turned up an alley and walked round to the

back of the row of houses. Doctor Dethridge's was a little apart from the rest in the row and looked prosperous compared with the others. It had several outbuildings, as well as the stable.

The woman who had opened the front door was feeding the pig with apple peelings and other kitchen waste. Charlie's stomach rumbled. The woman went back into the house and he vaulted over the fence.

'Charlie, you can't!' hissed Isabel, trying to scramble after him. But she was too late.

He was bending over to see what was in the trough when the pig started squealing. The man came rushing out through the back door and grabbed Charlie by the ruffles on his shirt.

'Robbers, raiders!' he cried. 'Raise the alarum, Martha. Fetch the constable.'

Isabel didn't hesitate; she ducked back down behind the wall and ran as fast as she could back along the houses. There was only one way to help her brother and it wasn't by getting caught.

Chapter 20

The World Turned Upside Down

Isabel kept her head down and ran without looking back. She stopped, out of breath, and looked for some sort of landmark so that she could find her way back to Doctor Dethridge's house. At the end of the road was a church with a square stone tower. It looked vaguely familiar.

St Edward's, thought Isabel, distracted for a moment from her situation. It was a church she passed every day on the way to school but she had never wondered before about how old it might be. Now it looked newly built and unstained by time. There was something else different about it but she couldn't think what.

She carried on until she found another stable with a hayloft she could climb into without being seen. She had decided that the only way to help Charlie was to see if she could get back to Talia and talk to Doctor Dethridge, even if only through the mirrors.

She lay back on the straw, clutching the single tessera that was her lifeline, and toyed with the idea of going straight to Bellezza. But she simply didn't dare believe that this frail object could take her not only to Talia but to any city in it. So she concentrated on Classe and on the Baptistery, imagining the mosaic in the ceiling with its depiction of flowing water made only out of tiny squares like the one in her hand.

But it was a long time before she could calm down enough to relax into sleep. Although she was quite exhausted, she had already stravagated twice, had found herself back in Elizabethan England and seen her brother captured. What did they do to thieves four hundred years ago? Might they cut his hand off? She didn't even know if *she* could get back home, let alone Charlie, and she was desperately worried about what might be happening at home anyway. Had Sky got it all sorted? Or were her parents standing over two apparently comatose teenagers?

And what about Classe? Had Filippo gone back to the fleet to get on with the urgent business of the day? Isabel felt like a mosaic herself, fractured into thousands of tiny pieces and about to become unstuck from the wall.

She took deep breaths of haydust-filled air and tried to let her mind float free of the chaos.

Filippo was startled from his long watch by a loud

sneeze coming from the baptismal bath.

'Isabella!' he cried, jumping into the bath himself. He was very pleased to see her. 'Is everything all right? Has Carlo returned safely home?'

Isabel was shaking, she was so relieved to be back somewhere familiar that she could understand. But she shocked herself by bursting into tears.

'Oh, Filippo,' she sobbed. 'No. We both ended up in Doctor Dethridge's time, right near his old house. And now my brother's probably under arrest for trying to steal pigswill. It's all such a mess.'

Filippo offered her a large lace-edged handkerchief. 'Come with me to Flavia's,' he said hurriedly. He felt it would take a Stravagante's skills to unravel this problem.

They walked quickly, with Isabel mopping her eyes and genuinely leaning on Filippo's arm.

They went straight up to Flavia's room, where she sat by the mirrors. But the merchant saw straight away from Isabel's face that nothing had gone to plan.

Back in Barnsbury, Georgia was bored out of her skull. She had mooched around Isabel's room, flicking through her books and CDs. She had even been in to peek at Charlie. But basically there was nothing she could do for either twin and she couldn't focus on anything else. She texted the boys to find out what had happened at school and discovered that there had been a few raised eyebrows at three students being off sick at the same time with a tummy bug. Especially since Georgia had already had time off with the same illness.

Apparently their form tutor had asked if they'd all been eating out at the same place. That would be another complication, if they got their favourite café closed down.

She was just beginning to wonder whether she could bear to read *Twilight* again when the figure on the bed suddenly sat up.

Georgia gave a little scream.

'Bel!' she said. 'You scared me half to death! What's going on?'

'George,' gasped Isabel, 'am I glad to see you! Is everything OK here? What happened with my parents?'

Georgia filled her in as quickly as she could.

'What about your end?' she asked. 'Is Charlie back too? I've locked his door.'

'I wish,' said Isabel. 'You wouldn't believe how complicated it all is.'

'Try me,' said Georgia. 'I've been going mad with boredom here. You owe me.'

'I'd settle for some boredom,' said Isabel. 'Somehow Charlie stravagated back to Barnsbury but in Doctor Dethridge's time. And I think I followed him there because I was focusing on him rather than on home.'

'No way!' said Georgia.

'Yeah, but it gets worse. I think he's possibly been arrested – four hundred years ago.'

'So you just left him?' asked Georgia.

'What do you take me for?' said Isabel. 'I stravagated back to Classe to ask Flavia and Doctor Dethridge what to do.'

'And what did they think?'

'I've got to go back to him with a talisman from this

world. That's why I'm back. What do you think I should take?'

Georgia thought furiously; she knew she was supposed to be the expert on talismans but her mind was a blank. Then she remembered.

'Matt's bookmark,' she said. 'That's what you need. Remember it's already done one stravagation – and that was from Talia to here too. Do you think it'll work?'

'I don't know,' said Isabel. 'But I've got to try. Let's ring Matt. We need his talisman.'

It was nearly lunchtime, so Georgia texted him; Isabel's hands were shaking too much. And he phoned back within minutes. He had the talisman and the bookmark with him and he was soon ringing the doorbell at the Evanses' house.

'God, you look ghastly,' he told Isabel.

'Thanks,' she said.

'No, I mean, sorry. What's been going on?'

'Let Georgia fill you in,' said Isabel. 'I've got to get back to Talia with this.'

'Talia? I thought you were going back in time to rescue Charlie?' said Georgia.

'Doctor Dethridge says I've got to go back to Classe first before I can stravagate back to his time.'

'I don't understand any of that,' said Matt.

'I don't have time to explain,' said Isabel. 'Look, would you and Georgia mind going to the kitchen or something? I have to try to get back to sleep.'

She lay back, exhausted and very nervous as she heard them going downstairs. What she had to do seemed so huge and unmanageable.

Charlie hadn't understood anything that had happened to him since he had woken up in the Baptistery of Classe. But he knew that what was going on now was definitely the worst thing so far.

He had been taken to a local lock-up and questioned by people he could barely understand. They had pushed him roughly into a barred room with three other men, who smelled really bad, and locked the door. There were two benches alongside the side walls and a reeking bucket in one corner, which Charlie decided he would rather burst than use.

Several hours passed while the other occupants dozed or argued but he dared not lose consciousness. After what had happened the last two times he had no idea where he might end up. Charlie remembered when he was a kid watching a TV series called *Quantum Leap*. The main character hopped back and forth through time becoming other people and never got back home. Now it was haunting him. What if *he* never got back home?

He wasn't too keen on the look of the other men either. What had they been arrested for? Charlie wondered if they had been frisked for knives before being locked up. He certainly hadn't. So he could not relax. He wondered what had happened to his sister. He knew her too well to believe she had abandoned him but what could she do?

After what seemed like an eternity, he heard a voice he recognised.

She was talking in that funny old-fashioned way but it was Bel.

'I am seeking a youthe taken in charge for stealing,' she said. 'He is yclept Charles.'

'Wee have one Carolus, son of Antonius,' said the clerk. 'Wherefore do ye seeke hym?'

'Hee is my brothire,' said Isabel. 'Maie I see him?'

There was some more low-level muttering and then footsteps outside the door and a clanking of keys. Charlie felt torn between fear and a sense of incongruity – was he in an episode of *Blackadder* or something?

But the jailer didn't unlock the door; he just gestured towards Charlie.

'Thanke ye,' said Isabel politely and he left her there.

The other men in the cell became alert in the presence of what Charlie heard them call a 'comely mayde' and 'fayre wench' when they spotted Isabel. It took a while for them to calm down.

'How are you?' she asked when she could speak to him.

'Still hungry,' he said, trying not to sound too bothered about being a prisoner in a place over four hundred years behind his own time.

'Well, I can't help you with that,' said Isabel. 'But I do know how to get us home, which is more important.'

'Good for you,' said Charlie, touching her arm through the bars. 'I knew you hadn't just deserted me.'

'Well, the good news is that all you have to do is fall asleep holding the red velvet pouch and thinking of the place you found yourself in last time,' said Isabel. 'You know, the place with the bath and the mosaics? You have still got the pouch, haven't you?'

Charlie nodded. 'What's the bad news?' he asked.

'We've still got two more journeys to make,' she said.

'So?'

'It's getting late,' said Isabel. 'Both here and in our time. I'm not sure we'll make it back before Mum and Dad get in. Georgia and the others are still covering for us but there are going to be some awkward questions to answer.'

'If we get back,' said Charlie, 'I don't think I'll ever care about anything else again.'

'Me either,' said Isabel. And realised it was true. If she could only get her brother back where he belonged, she didn't think she would ever be jealous of him again.

They were grinning at each other through the bars when, without warning, the ground started to shake.

'What's that?' asked Charlie but Isabel couldn't come up with any explanation.

There were cries from the street and sounds like tons of bricks falling. Charlie's fellow prisoners were shaking the bars and shouting for help. Charlie was pushed away from the door.

'Bel!' he cried. 'Help me!'

She had been standing paralysed with fear but now ran to the outer room and saw it empty of people, with the outer door wide open. The man with the keys had gone but she saw a spare set hanging on a hook on the wall. With fumbling fingers, she took it and ran back to the cell, the floor rippling and buckling underneath her.

The men shouted encouragement while she tried all the keys till she found the right one. Praying that she wasn't releasing dangerous murderers and robbers,

Isabel opened the door and the criminals barged out. One stopped and gave her a smacking kiss, which she wiped from her face with disgust.

'Come on, Charlie,' she said, half dragging him out of the cell.

Soon they were out in the street, which was full of frightened people milling around. Instinctively, Isabel led Charlie away in the direction of the church that looked like St Edward's. As they ran towards it, the building seemed to shudder and, with a deafening crack, the stonework of the tower split open. They stopped in their tracks.

That's it, thought Isabel. *Our St Edward's has an old crack in the tower. I'm watching how it happened in the past.*

'What is it, Bel?' said Charlie. He was like a small child seeking reassurance from an adult.

'It's an earthquake,' said Isabel. *How are we supposed to fall asleep during an earthquake?* she thought. 'Keep hold of your talisman and maybe we'll still get out alive.'

She clutched the little tessera in her pocket. Bricks and tiles were falling all around them, dropping from roofs as the powerful tremor heaved the buildings up as if a subterranean giant were turning over in his sleep and shrugging the ground with his shoulders.

Suddenly realising what could happen to them, Isabel yelled, 'Think of Classe!'

Then the chimney of the house nearest to them collapsed and she was knocked unconscious by a flying brick.

*

Nick, Matt and Sky raced round to Isabel's house straight after school and rescued Georgia, who had watched a stack of DVDs and eaten a whole bar of cooking chocolate she found in the kitchen.

Luckily neither Evans parent had got home and they remembered that Isabel's father had been going out of town for a meeting, so might be back late.

'What does her mum do?' asked Sky.

'She works in the City, that's all I know,' said Georgia.

'So she could be anything from a secretary to Governor of the Bank of England?' said Nick. 'It doesn't help us know when she'll be back.'

'I reckon we've got till seven, seven thirty,' said Matt. 'After that, our parents are going to expect us back to eat.'

'Do you really think they'll be back by dinner?' said Georgia, who was feeling a bit sick.

'The twins or the parents?' asked Nick.

He was wandering restlessly round the room, picking up objects and putting them down.

'Sit down, Nick,' said Georgia. 'You're driving me mad. And I meant Bel and Charlie. Parents like ours are always home in time for dinner, even if it's frozen pizza.'

'Well, we can't just sit here for the next three hours,' said Matt.

'I could stravagate,' said Sky quietly. 'I've got my talisman.'

'To Classe?' asked Nick.

Sky nodded. 'I could find out if Bel ever got back there at least and come straight back,' he said.

'Let's think this through,' said Matt.

He made them all strong mugs of tea and they pieced together everything Isabel had told Sky and Georgia.

'So there's a chance the gateway between our worlds has been permanently damaged?' said Nick.

No one wanted to accept that this might be true. They all knew what that would mean for the twins, none better than Nick.

'It could be dangerous trying to stravagate while the gateway's unstable,' said Georgia.

'But Bel didn't think twice about it, did she?' said Sky. 'She just did what she had to, to get Charlie back.'

'But hang on,' said Matt. 'Even if you do stravagate all right, if you just turn up in this Baptistery place she goes to, wearing what you are, you'll stand out like a sore thumb. Is that safe?'

'Maybe we could find you something less conspicuous here?' said Georgia.

They went up to Charlie's room and Georgia unlocked it. It was uncanny to be rummaging through his cupboards while he lay there on the bed, apparently just asleep.

'I wonder what he's doing now?' said Nick.

'What about this?' said Georgia, pulling out a black velvet cloak from the wardrobe. 'He must have had this for a Hallowe'en party.'

'I remember,' said Sky. 'He came to Chrissie's as Dracula.'

'If you put it on over your clothes before you stravagate, you won't attract so much attention,' said Georgia. 'I can't do anything about your trainers, though. Charlie doesn't have any other kind of shoe.'

'Are you sure you want to do this?' asked Matt when they were back downstairs.

'Quite sure,' said Sky. 'Though I don't know how I'm going to get to sleep.'

Isabel opened her eyes just long enough to register that she was in the Baptistery and stuff the tessera in her pocket – and then she lost consciousness again. She didn't even see that her brother had followed her into the bath. Charlie opened his eyes to find the limp and almost lifeless body of his twin.

In the end he lifted her up and carried her to Flavia's house, because he couldn't think of anything else to do. It was such a relief to hand Isabel over to her calm presence and let himself and his twin be fussed over by servants.

As he sat in Flavia's parlour, drinking a glass of strong red wine, even though Bel was still unconscious and they were both in Talia, he was shaking with relief at having escaped from Elizabethan England. Being arrested had been horrible and the earthquake terrifying but nothing had been as bad as that feeling of not knowing where he was or how to get back to his own world and time.

Talia was just as much in the sixteenth century and he was even less in his world here than he had just been. But here there was a vital difference: there were people who knew and cared about his sister and, by extension, him. This handsome middle-aged woman and the man with the scarred face and a whole bunch of other people who could be seen in a set of mirrors that Flavia was constantly looking into – these were the cast of whatever drama Bel had been living in for the past few weeks, he could tell that.

'She is coming round,' said Flavia, who had been burning feathers under Isabel's nose. The smell was so horrible that Charlie could see why his sister had sat up spluttering.

'OK, Bel?' he said. 'How's your head?'

There was a big purple bruise spreading across her forehead and a lump swelling underneath it. Isabel put her hand to her head. 'Ouch!' she said.

'It was a brick,' said Charlie to Flavia. 'There was an earthquake and a chimney fell on us.'

'Did you get hit too?' asked Isabel.

Charlie nodded but in fact nothing hurt and he was pretty sure he had just fainted. Still, he wasn't going to admit that.

Flavia bathed and dried Isabel's forehead and gently smeared an ointment on her bruise.

'You're going to have quite a shiner to explain to the parents,' said Charlie.

'It won't show back home,' said Isabel, wincing. 'Matt got beaten up really badly in Talia and there was nothing to be seen in our world. It's only bad sword wounds and things that travel back with you.'

Charlie kept quiet; there was so much going on here that he didn't understand. Who would have beaten Matt Wood up in Talia and why?

'Can we go home?' he asked, aware that he sounded like a petulant child.

'We can try,' said Isabel. 'Flavia, do you think we could have some of your sleeping draught?'

There was a knock on the door and the footman

showed in a tall figure in a long black robe. The newcomer looked round the room hesitantly, smiling to see Isabel, then moving to her side with concern at the sight of her injury.

'It's all right, Flavia,' said Isabel. 'He's one of us. I think he's come to rescue me.'

'This is going to be dead awkward if the parents get back before he does,' said Matt, looking down at the apparently sleeping figure of Sky, wrapped in the velvet cloak, on the Evanses' sofa in their living room.

'We'll think of something,' said Georgia. 'We keep having to.'

It was quarter past seven. Sky had been gone for hours.

They heard the unmistakable sound of a key in the front door.

At the same moment Sky yawned, stretched and sat up. Georgia immediately stripped the cloak off him and bundled it under the sofa.

'Parents!' she hissed. 'Are the others back?'

'They should be,' said Sky.

'Damn!' said Georgia. 'Did I lock Charlie's door again?'

'Hello!' called Sarah Evans. 'Is anyone going to give me a hand unpacking this shopping?'

The three Stravaganti went out into the hall.

'Gracious!' said Isabel's mother. 'Is this a homework club or something? Where are the twins?'

'That's why we stayed,' said Matt, improvising wildly. He and Sky picked up shopping bags and went into the kitchen, sure that Sarah Evans would follow. Georgia could hear them explaining as she raced up the stairs to the bedrooms.

'They came down sick after our run this morning,' Matt was saying. 'They've been sleeping it off most of the day.'

Georgia released Charlie from his room. He looked like a ghost as he followed her into Isabel's bedroom. She was sitting up in bed, pale and with a massive bruise on her forehead. You said it wouldn't show here,' he said. 'But we're back! I've never been so happy to see these four walls in my life!'

'Oh, how are you feeling, you poor things?' said their mother, running up the stairs. 'Your friends told me all about it. Shall I heat you up some soup?'

'I feel absolutely fine now,' said Charlie, taking his mother by the waist and dancing her round the landing. 'Never better. Forget the soup – I could eat a horse!'

Chapter 21

The Gate of the Year

'I'm so sorry I wasn't here to look after you,' said Sarah Evans. 'I found your note about going running and just assumed you were OK. Why didn't you ring?'

'There was no need,' said Isabel. 'Georgia stayed to look after us.' Then she remembered she had to get their cover story straight. 'She wasn't feeling well herself.'

'Well, she looks fine now. And Charlie is obviously fighting fit. But you're very pale, Bel. And how on earth did you get that bruise?'

Isabel put her hand up to her forehead and nearly smacked it in exasperation. Of course! She hadn't been hit over the head in Talia but in England – even though it had been over four hundred years earlier.

'I think you must have had it worse than anyone,'

her mother continued. 'Of course Charlie has always been the stronger one.'

'No, Mum!' said Charlie fiercely. 'You're wrong. Bel is much stronger than I am.'

Sarah Evans looked amazed. But Isabel managed a weak smile. While their mother went down to cook up a feast, Charlie slipped the red pouch into her hand.

'Here,' he said. 'I never want to see it again.'

Isabel added the little lone tessera to its companions in the bag, then stuffed it under her pillow.

And that was the last thing she knew for fourteen hours. When she woke up next morning, the house was quiet. Charlie had evidently gone to school but no one had woken Isabel. She stretched luxuriously, all her tiredness gone. She checked that the talisman was still where she'd put it, then ran downstairs to the kitchen and smiled when she saw a note from her mother propped against the kettle.

We thought it best to let you sleep, it said. *Call me if you need me. Charlie much better. Love, Mum xxx*

She was ravenous now – she couldn't remember when she'd last eaten anything, either at home or in Talia. So she made a pot of coffee and a big pile of scrambled egg with a stack of toast. And then had a huge bowl of cereal and a banana.

She took her second cup of coffee out into the garden, which was full of spring sunshine. As she sat on the bench, feeling the warmth on her face, Isabel couldn't believe that she would soon be back in the 'other Italy' taking part in a sea battle of the kind that hadn't happened since the time of Elizabeth I in England. She hoped she'd still have enough strength to do whatever she needed to in Talia.

In Talia, though it was without phones or computers, a fast system of messages had brought news from the other world. Doctor Dethridge had managed to link one of Rodolfo's mirrors with the parallel world in the future; it showed the room in Islington that used to be Luciano's and was now Nick's.

Luciano did not often look at it; it could be painful for him. But in the early hours of the morning after Charlie's stravagation and the disturbance in the gateway, he and Arianna, Rodolfo and Silvia and William Dethridge were all sitting staring at the array of glasses and knobs and were rewarded with the sight of an excited Nick holding up a sheet of paper on which he had written backwards with black marker:

ISABEL AND CHARLIE SAFELY BACK. BEL NOT STRAVAGATING TONIGHT – KNACKERED.

'Whatte is k-nacker-ed?' asked Dethridge.

'It means exhausted,' said Luciano, grinning. 'But she did it.'

'We must let Flavia and the others know,' said Rodolfo, turning knobs and levers on his mirror array.

Luciano and Arianna went out into the courtyard of the palazzo.

'So that's all right then,' said Arianna. 'Do you think the gateway will go back to normal?'

'I don't know,' said Luciano. 'Remember how it leapt a year forward when Falco got "translated"? But I don't think it will do that this time. I can't believe

285

Isabel would have been brought to Talia in Classe's hour of danger if she wasn't going to be here for the battle.'

Arianna didn't answer straight away. They had had only the second row in their relationship when she found out that he was planning to take part in the sea battle. Since then she had been trying to forget about it.

Rodolfo wasn't pleased that Luciano was using his Easter break from university to join the Bellezzan navy either.

'Are you leaving with the fleet?' she said quietly at last.

'Yes,' said Luciano. 'I'll go when the Admiral does.'

Admiral Gambone was taking his ships down towards Classe in the next few days. Not all at once: just two or three ships at a time, in order not to attract too much attention. The Gate people still thought they would have the advantage of surprise, so he wanted them to continue in that belief.

'And nothing I can say will make you change your mind?'

He shook his head. 'I'm doing it for Bellezza,' he said. 'I'm going to be its Duke after we're married. You'll be the ruler still, but I want to do my best to help defend the city. We can't have this constant threat from the east. We must make sure the Gate people are thoroughly defeated.'

Arianna could have said that one inexperienced young sailor couldn't do much to help the battle-hardy Admirals of Bellezza and Classe win against the massed galleys and guns of the Gate people but she didn't. After all, Luciano was not just a Stravagante but a settler from another world; it hadn't been his choice to translate to Talia but nevertheless he had defeated death to do it and there was something remarkable about him. He seemed to lead a charmed life. Perhaps his presence would act as good luck mascot for the fleet?

But in her imagination she saw him brought to shore wrapped in a sail, his body shattered by cannonfire. Or, perhaps worse, she imagined being told that he had drowned at sea in the thick of the battle and saw him sinking through the green waves, his black hair floating around his pale dead face.

No, it must not be. If she couldn't stop him, she'd have to think of a different plan.

With the whole day to while away, Isabel looked up 'Earthquake +England +1580' on her computer.

It was true. An earthquake that would probably have registered nearly 6 on the Richter scale if they'd been able to measure it had shaken Elizabethan England at 6 p.m. on 6th March 1580. It probably had its epicentre in the English Channel but had caused bits of buildings to fall in London and in several places in France. A girl in London had even been killed by falling masonry.

Isabel shuddered. Her head was really hurting now. On an impulse she went out and walked towards school. There was St Edwards, with a just perceptible kink in the straightness of its tower. Feeling foolish, Isabel went and laid her hand on the bricks. There was a big jagged crack that had been filled up with mortar.

'You're looking at our claim to fame,' said a friendly voice behind her.

Isabel jumped.

'Sorry – I didn't mean to startle you.'

It was the vicar; she had seen him before. He was one of those modern vicars in jeans and a black polo neck, only in his thirties. Isabel knew he had a wife and four small children. But she and her family were not churchgoers.

'It's OK,' she said. 'I was just looking at the damage.'

'It happened a long time ago,' said the vicar.

Isabel remembered his name: Rhys Daniels.

'1580,' they said at the same time, and laughed.

'Are you OK?' asked Rhys, looking at her closely. 'Are you off sick from school or something? That's a very nasty bruise.'

Isabel wondered what he'd say if she told him she got it at the same time as his church tower was damaged!

'I'm fine,' she said. 'I was off sick yesterday and woke up too late to go in today. But it's the Easter holidays next week.'

'I know,' said Rhys ruefully. 'It's a busy time for vicars.'

Isabel smiled.

'You know about St Edward's?' he asked.

'Not really – only about the earthquake,' said Isabel. 'I was thinking about how the church would have been quite new then and here it is hundreds of years later, but still with a sort of scar from that time. I was thinking about how what we study as history was once just, you know, today, for the people living through it.'

'You're right,' said the vicar. 'Most people never think about that though. I suppose I do more than most because I spend my working life thinking and talking about something I believe happened two thousand years ago.'

Oh no, thought Isabel. *He's going to talk about God.*

But he wasn't. He was just interested in the past – as she was. Isabel wondered what he'd say if she told him she visited the sixteenth century every night.

Filippo hadn't been able to stay behind to wait for Isabel's flag-training. He left for Bellezza on the Friday, missing Isabel's next stravagation, but he knew that she and her brother had survived their adventure.

He met Luciano at the Arsenale, where he was running errands for Admiral Gambone.

'We are like ships that pass in the night,' said Luciano, but saw from Filippo's puzzled frown that this was not a Talian expression. 'I mean I must soon leave for Classe, just as you arrive.'

'I shall not stay long, Cavaliere,' said Filippo. 'Once I have conveyed all my messages to the Admiral, I too must go back to Classe.'

'Not long now,' said Luciano.

He was feeling nervous. He had been kidnapped, more than once, drugged, fought in a duel – had even died, for goodness sake – and yet he had never taken part in a battle on land or sea. He felt ridiculously unprepared. Although he didn't envy Filippo's limp and scar, remembering only too well how he had come by them, he did wish that he himself looked a bit harder and more experienced.

Then, seeing Filippo's expression, he realised that the young Nucci was feeling just as nervous as he was. Luciano put a hand on his shoulder.

'Come to visit us in the palazzo before you go back,' he said. 'Arianna would like to see you again and we have an old friend of yours staying with us.'

Luciano saw from Filippo's face that he knew who he meant. 'I'm sure she'd like to see you too,' he added.

They looked out together in silence at the Bellezzan fleet, moored in deep water. It wasn't as large as the fleet in Classe but there were still two ships being fitted out with sails and cannons. There would then be sixty-five fighting galleys; the Classe fleet had twenty more than that so they would deploy a hundred and fifty vessels altogether.

'Will it be enough, do you think?' asked Filippo, echoing Luciano's own thoughts.

'Andrea thinks there will be about two hundred on the Gate people's side,' said Luciano.

'So I've heard,' said Filippo. 'But mostly galleys. They won't have the big ships with guns that we have.'

'Then we must trust to our guns,' said Luciano.

*

There was a state of tension throughout Bellezza; rumour had rustled through the city that the lagoon would soon be under attack. Like most rumour, it was composed about equally of fact and guesswork. But

Bellezzans knew that their fleet was mustering and that was enough to create fear and excitement.

The news had reached Princess Beatrice, who was still sheltering in the Ducal Palace. She was not in Arianna's confidence about state matters but she was very popular with the servants, who gave her snippets of gossip as they dressed her hair or brought her hot chocolate.

'A battle at sea,' was the whisper. 'Here or further down the Talian coast. The Gate people. An enormous fleet of galleys. Bigger than Bellezza has ever faced. Terrible odds.'

So when Arianna came to tell her she had a visitor and she saw Filippo Nucci enter the room in naval uniform, Beatrice immediately feared the worst. She didn't know how he might be involved in the Bellezzan fleet but she felt straight away that he was going into danger and had come to say goodbye.

'Principessa,' said Filippo, bowing as well as his hurt leg would let him.

'Please don't be so formal, Filippo,' said Beatrice, coming forward to take his hand. 'We can use each other's names surely? Haven't we known each other since we were children? And we have been through a lot together.'

'Beatrice,' said Filippo, overcome.

It was true that he had come to say goodbye, not knowing if he would return alive from the battle, but now that he saw her, the goddess of his mosaic, smiling kindly at him, he resolved to do more.

Arianna caught his eye and said hastily that she was afraid she must leave them alone since she had remembered an urgent task she had to do.

They scarcely heard her. Beatrice was looking at Filippo's scar and he was gazing into her eyes.

'Your poor face,' Arianna heard the princess say softly, as she left the room.

Outside the door she ran into Luciano and surprised him by the fervour with which she hugged and kissed him.

'Do you know,' she said mischievously, 'I think the same thing will be going on in there very soon.'

'Between Beatrice and Filippo?' said Luciano. 'I hope so. But won't that make Fabrizio even more angry with Bellezza?'

Arianna shook her curls at him. 'What do I care about that?' she said. 'If his sister is happy with her choice, that's good enough for me.'

'Your mother would say you are thinking like an island girl and not like a duchessa,' said Luciano, smiling.

'Well, I *am* an island girl, really,' said Arianna. 'And sometimes I think I will make a better duchessa for it. Anyway, I have made my own choice, even though I am the ruler, so why should I begrudge her choice to another young woman with no responsibilities of state to hinder her?'

*

Classe was in an even worse state of jitters than Bellezza. Not only was their fleet mustering but the Duke was drilling his soldiers too. Classe did not have much of a standing army since no one could remember when last one had been needed, but Duke Germano had been recruiting for weeks. In this he had been helped by Enrico, who had revealed an unsuspected skill at enlisting men of Classe who would never have dreamed they had a calling as soldiers.

Other men were repairing the walls of the city which faced inland towards Giglia. They were not massive and the cannon mounted on them were not very modern. And the foundries down in the Classe Arsenale had been so busy making shot for the fleet that the weapons on the wall had a serious shortage of ammunition.

But the important thing was that the city was aware it was going to be attacked, by land and sea, and its people were ready. Now that it was not much more than a week away, they just wanted to get it over with.

They had stacked sandbags against the sides of those churches and temples nearest to the walls, to give some protection to the precious mosaics inside. Germano had even commissioned Fausto's workshop to take copies of the ones in the most vulnerable buildings.

Andrea made his regular report to the Duke. Germano greeted him in his small office, wearing full military uniform, decorated with silver braid and tassels. Vitale sat at his side, occasionally patting the plumes on the helmet that the Duke had set aside on his desk.

'They have been moving their fleet, ten ships at a time, for months,' said the pirate. 'Almost the full two hundred are at Ladera on the coast opposite Talia now.'

'You are putting yourself in a great deal of danger to come back and forth between them and us,' said the Duke.

'I shall not be able to do it much longer,' said

Andrea. 'I have to take the *Revenge* to join them in Ladera within a day or two. But I want to talk to Isabella again. She has not come today.'

Germano told him about Isabel's adventure with her brother and ending up in her world over four centuries too early.

'Do you think she will be able to come back to us?' asked Andrea, alarmed.

'These things are beyond me,' said the Duke. 'But your mother seems to think so.' He shook his head. 'There's another matter I wanted to talk to you about,' he said.

'Your Grace?'

'Flavia has been telling me about what happened with your father,' said Germano. 'I know it is painful for you to speak of it but I wanted to say that if we both come through this battle, I intend to issue you with a pardon, in recognition of the provocation and of the service you have done the State.'

'I can only thank you,' said Andrea, feeling as if a crippling burden might be lifted from him. Then his face fell; he could never forget that the monster he had killed shared his blood.

'You have done so much for us in Classe,' said the Duke. 'I owe you this. You shall not have to wear a disguise in my city much longer.'

When Charlie got in from school, he brought the rest of the Barnsbury Stravaganti with him. Isabel was so glad to see them all. She made sure that her brother knew who they all were and where they had travelled to in Talia. Even Nick.

But after a while, Charlie said, 'Sorry, guys. This is all just too weird for me. I mean, I know you aren't lying. I've been there. But I can't think about it. It creeps me out.'

'That's what Alice felt,' said Sky quietly.

'So I'm going to leave you to it,' Charlie said, making for the stairs. 'But if you ever need someone to give you cover or something, you can count on me. And I would say, look after Bel, except that I know she can look after herself.'

'Wow,' said Georgia softly when Charlie had gone. 'That's impressive. I bet he hasn't said that before.'

'I've never understood how someone could just walk away from Talia,' said Nick.

'I can,' said Sky. 'I think if you haven't been chosen – if you go there by accident or try to go when you aren't supposed to be there – then it just doesn't feel right.'

'Yesh has never wanted to go there,' said Matt. 'She's not scared of it the way Alice was but she just doesn't have room for it in her life. And she doesn't want to muscle in.'

'Well, that's all right then,' said Georgia. 'Sorted. Charlie will cover for Bel whenever she needs it but not try to interfere. Best of both worlds.'

'You're all forgetting something though,' said Isabel. 'I don't know if I *can* get back to Classe. Or if I do, whether I'll get back here OK.'

'You've done it once and that was the hardest,' said Nick. 'I bet you'll be all right.'

'There's only one way to find out,' said Sky. 'And I'm definitely coming with you this time.'

When Isabel materialised in the baptismal bath, she didn't have to wait long before Sky turned up beside her. They had both stravagated from their own homes but it felt curiously intimate to have travelled together. Sky, who was wearing Charlie's old Dracula's cloak over his pyjamas again, smiled at her.

'We seem to be in the bath together,' he said.

Isabel climbed out to hide her confusion. Sky was looking round the Baptistery with slow enjoyment.

'It's amazing, isn't it?' he said. 'Last time I was in such a hurry to get to Flavia's and find out what had happened to you that I didn't really have time to look at it.'

'I suppose I've got a bit used to it,' said Isabel, seeing it again from Sky's point of view. 'But yes, it really is amazing to think that all that beauty is made up of squares no bigger than the ones in my talisman.'

'I wonder if there'll be time for you to show me the other mosaics in the city?' said Sky.

'I hope so,' said Isabel. 'I'd love that.' But then they heard such a loud shout from outside the Baptistery that all thoughts of the great art of Classe went out of their heads.

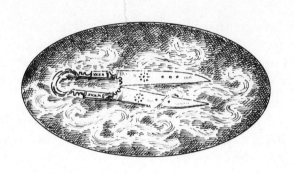

Chapter 22

Death on the Water

When Luciano came to say goodbye to Arianna, they both knew it might be for ever. They didn't exchange many words; it was too serious for that. Luciano was leaving on the Admiral's consort ship, the *Duchessa*, in the early hours of the morning. It would slip through the waters of the Lagoon and out into the Adriatic, with the Admiral's *Goddess* and a third ship, and head for Classe.

He was coming to love the life on the water. The complicated set of rules and systems by which the mariners took care of the vessel and the way they interacted with the armed men on board fascinated him. This wouldn't really be put to the test until the battle began but he had seen enough of it to enjoy the camaraderie and the skill.

'It's always harder for the one left behind,' said Arianna.

'I'm not leaving you behind,' said Luciano. 'You are always with me. But I have to do this. I hoped you would understand.'

'Oh, I understand,' said Arianna but then she bit her lip. She didn't want what might be their last memory to be of quarrelling.

'You come back to me, do you hear?' she said, trying to be playful. 'If you don't, I'll kill you.'

They both laughed but hysteria and tears were lurking under the laughter.

And then Luciano was gone and Arianna could let all her emotion out. But she was not the sort of person to cry for long. *Action*, she thought to herself. *That's what he wants and I want it too.*

She sent for Barbara.

*

Isabel and Sky hurried out into the street and found a crowd of people looking towards the city wall. They mingled and tried to overhear what was going on.

'It must have started,' someone was saying. 'That was cannonfire from the battlements.'

Isabel looked at Sky in dismay. If the land attack from Fabrizio really had started earlier than expected, then the Gate people might be coming too. And she wasn't ready. She dragged Sky off to the piazza and bumped into Enrico.

'Steady, Signorina,' he said, giving Sky a curious look. He remembered 'Brother Tino' from Giglia.

'Can you find out what's happening?' Isabel asked.

'On my way to,' said the spy.

He left them and they made their way down to the harbour. Isabel saw that Andrea's caravel was just about to cast off from the quay.

She ran over the cobbles, stumbling and tripping and leaving Sky to catch her up.

'Andrea, Andrea!' she called.

He saw her and leapt on to the quay, yelling at the sailor who was casting off to hold the rope awhile.

'Isabella,' he said, 'I'm so glad to see you. You got here without trouble?'

'Yes,' said Isabel, 'but never mind about that. Has something happened?'

'Many things,' said the pirate, maddeningly. 'But why do you ask?'

'There was a crowd in the square,' said Isabel, still out of breath. 'They were saying that the land battle has begun. They heard cannonfire.'

By then Sky had joined them. Andrea looked him up and down. 'Can this be your brother, Bella Isabella? He does not look like your twin.' He didn't seem the least bit bothered about the cannonfire.

Isabel concentrated on not blushing. 'Of course not. He's my . . . friend. From my world,' she added. 'You know, another one like me.'

'Call me Tino,' said Sky. 'That seems to be my name in Talia.'

Andrea gave Sky his hand. 'You come at a time of trouble for the city,' he said seriously. 'Perhaps you too can help us if you are ready for a fight.'

Then he turned to Isabel. 'I know nothing about a land battle. My concern is with the sea. But listen –

are you going to be on the flagship?'

'I . . . I think so,' said Isabel. All the business with Charlie and the gateway had caused her to lose sight of what her role was going to be in the battle. 'I need to talk to Filippo.'

'I heard he has gone to Bellezza,' said Andrea. 'I think you'd better get down to the *Tiger*.'

'Thanks,' said Isabel.

'So this is goodbye,' said Andrea. He embraced her warmly, with Sky looking on, unsure about this silver-toothed brigand. 'I feel we shall meet again, Isabella. Our story is not yet over.'

And then he broke away and jumped back on deck, nodding to the sailor to loose the rope from its mooring.

'Come on, Sky,' said Isabel. She didn't want to watch the caravel disappearing into the distance.

They hurried down to the fleet but Isabel was faster than Sky. She didn't need to stare about her at the boats, the quay-traders and the screeching gulls the way that he did; she was used to them now. Eventually they made their way out of the busy harbourfront area and away towards the navy's moorings. It had swelled in size with all the Bellezzan galleys that had been joining it in the last few days.

'There's the Admiral's ship,' she told Sky. 'The *Tiger*. The flagship of both fleets together. That's where I'm supposed to be for the battle.'

Sky gave a low whistle.

'That looks pretty real,' he said.

*

'Are you sure, milady?' asked Barbara. 'It seems such a shame.'

She was holding a mass of Arianna's heavy red-brown hair in one hand and a large pair of scissors in the other.

'It won't have long to grow back before your wedding,' she said.

'There won't *be* any wedding if Luciano gets himself killed in Classe,' said Arianna grimly.

'Never say that, milady,' said Barbara, waving the scissors wildly as she tried to make the hand of fortune gesture. 'It is bad luck.'

'It is bad luck to have my fiancé sign up for a battle he has no need to fight,' said Arianna. 'At least if I'm with him we can die together.'

Barbara was appalled.

'Cut it all off,' ordered her mistress. 'I can't hide it under a cap during a sea battle. It's not like a trip to Padavia. If we make it back, both of us, I'll call it a new fashion.'

The maid sighed but did as she was told. Tenderly, she gathered up the fallen curls and wrapped them in a muslin scarf. Then she helped Arianna into the clothes she wore as Adamo on her visits to Padavia.

'Now you must change into my dress,' Arianna told her. 'You are about to give the longest impersonation of your life.'

'Will you . . . ? Will you take Marco to protect you?' asked Barbara fearfully.

'No,' said the young Duchessa, tying her own mask on to the maid's face. 'Do you think I would put your husband's life at risk when I am going to try to save my own love?'

The first week of the Easter holiday went faster than any other in Isabel's life. At home she listened to her parents and Charlie talking about hot cross buns and Easter eggs but it was as if she heard them from somewhere far away and deep underwater.

Every night she travelled to Classe, sometimes with Sky and sometimes alone. The commotion in the street had been a false alarm. One of the more ancient cannon on the walls had blown up when the soldier in charge had tried a test firing. He and another man had been killed in the explosion and two others badly injured. It had really brought home to the people of Classe that this was no drill and that there would be many more casualties this spring.

The Admiral himself taught Isabel his flag system and during the day she muttered it to herself – 'Green means "Advance in formation", blue and white means "Peel off and re-form", red means "Retreat" . . .'

When she wasn't travelling to Talia, she was dreaming about ships and sails and flags and cannons. She hadn't seen Andrea again, nor expected to, but Filippo was back before the end of the week, looking happy and excited even though he was going to be on the flagship's consort and in the thick of the battle.

The other Barnsbury Stravaganti were supporting Isabel through this time and she was only glad that they weren't at school. She knew she was really only half in present-day London; so many of her thoughts were in Classe.

'Are you nervous?' Georgia asked her on Easter Saturday.

'What do you think?' Isabel replied. 'People are going to be killed and I shall see it. But it's not that I'm not afraid of dying myself. I figure that I wouldn't have been "chosen" in order to be killed off.'

'I'm sure you're right,' said Sky. 'We've all been in dangerous situations and survived.'

'Not Luciano,' said Nick quietly.

'But that was different,' said Georgia. 'He died here, not there.'

'It's still dying though, isn't it?' said Matt. He always felt uncomfortable when the talk turned to what had happened to Luciano. 'Being "chosen" didn't save him.'

'So the worst that can happen to me is that I might get stuck for ever in Talia,' said Isabel, trying to smile. 'That wouldn't be so bad.'

'I'd come and visit you,' said Sky.

But the joy of hearing him linking himself to her publicly in this way was offset by the thought of never seeing Charlie or their parents again. Isabel wondered, not for the first time, how Luciano could bear it. He must be very strong.

'So, when's the big day then?' asked Matt.

'Everyone seems to think it will be Monday,' said Isabel. 'That's Andrea's inside information.'

'So you'd better stuff yourself with chocolate tomorrow,' said Nick. He had got very used to the celebrations of his new world, especially ones involving tasty food. 'You'll need plenty of calories to keep you going.'

'Will it be over in a day though?' asked Georgia. 'I

mean, I don't know anything about old sea battles but can it all be decided before you need to get back?'

'Charlie will cover for me if I have to stay overnight,' said Isabel. 'It will be Tuesday here and the parents will be back at work, thank goodness, so it shouldn't be so hard.'

'Good thing they didn't plan to take you away for Easter,' said Sky, remembering the time he had been in Cornwall. But he had been with Alice then, so he pushed the memory away.

'The Spanish Armada battle took only one day,' said Matt helpfully. 'I looked it up. But most of the Spanish ships were sunk by English storms after that.'

'We'll have to hope the Talian weather is on our side,' said Isabel.

'And the Battle of Lepanto was over in five hours,' said Nick.

Isabel was grateful that her friends had taken such an interest in the coming fight but none of them had to be aboard ship in the midst of it. Even if Sky stravagated with her on Monday, he wouldn't be allowed in the fleet.

And when Monday came, she was just relieved. She asked Sky to stay behind and went to bed early, still feeling slightly sick after the amount of chocolate she had consumed in the last two days.

Charlie knocked on her door. 'Can I come in and say goodbye?' he asked.

'I'm planning to come back,' said Isabel.

'*Au revoir*, then' said Charlie. '*Auf Wiedersehen, arrivederci.*'

'*Arrivederci*,' said Isabel, letting him give her an awkward hug. 'That sounds the most Talian.'

'And good luck,' said Charlie seriously.

'You will let the others know if I don't wake up tomorrow morning, won't you?'

Charlie held up his mobile phone. 'They're all on speed-dial,' he said.

'Thanks,' said Isabel. 'Now go. I have to fight a battle.'

Arianna felt light-headed literally, with her shorn head under its metal-lined cap. She had bribed one of the arquebusiers on the *Duchessa* to let her take his place. He had been reluctant but she whispered that she was working as a spy for the real Duchessa and offered him so much silver that he couldn't say no.

She had picked him out from a distance as being the closest in size to her and there was an awkward moment when they changed clothes, which she was reluctant to do on the quay of the Arsenale. Fortunately, there was an empty shed nearby and she had paid him enough to insist on his turning his back.

'What is your name?' she asked.

'Mario Bailadora,' he replied. 'What's yours?'

'Adamo,' she said. 'Adamo da Bellezza. You must call yourself that until the battle is over.'

The young arquebusier shrugged. He had been quite looking forward to taking part in his first sea battle but 'Adamo from Bellezza' had given him enough silver to compensate him for the loss of that ambition; he would pass the battle drinking some of it away in the nearest tavern.

Arianna took his weapon and squared her shoulders

and then made her way aboard the *Duchessa*. It was Admiral Gambone's consort ship, the one that would stay beside him in the coming action. More importantly, it was the ship that Luciano would be on. And it pleased her that it bore her title, if not her name; it seemed like a good omen.

It felt less so after a day and a half at sea. She kept herself to herself, not sure that she could convince a bunch of Bellezzan fighting men of her masculinity. And she glimpsed Luciano only occasionally; as an aristocrat, he travelled in the Captain's cabin, while she was squashed on the gun deck with no shelter.

She had been very relieved to see the harbour of Classe with the majestic fleet riding at anchor. But once the three Bellezzan ships had found a place for themselves, Gambone, the three captains and Luciano had gone in a small boat to meet Classe's Admiral Borca and Filippo Nucci, while she and all the other fighting 'men' were left to cool their heels.

*

'This is the worst thing she has done yet,' fumed Silvia, as soon as Barbara's impersonation was discovered.

'I tend to agree,' said Rodolfo, white-faced. 'This is carrying devotion to Luciano too far.'

'What exactly did she tell you?' Silvia demanded of the maid.

'Very little, Signora,' said Barbara. 'Only that if he were going to die, she wanted to die alongside him.'

Silvia snorted. 'Ridiculously dramatic. And recklessly irresponsible as usual.'

'But there is nothing we can do about it,' said Rodolfo. 'I'm sure she didn't tell Barbara which ship she was going on, though I suspect it will be Luciano's.'

'The *Duchessa*,' said Silvia. 'Ironic, isn't it?'

'The *Duchessa* wouldn't take a woman on board,' said Rodolfo. 'I imagine she used her young man's clothes again, Barbara?'

'Yes, Signore,' admitted Barbara. 'And she made me cut her hair.'

'Well, that's it,' said Silvia. 'We can't get a message to the Captain of the *Duchessa* demanding he strip and search all the men on his ship. What possible reason could we give?'

'Arianna would evade him if we did,' said Rodolfo. 'No. I think we have to ask Barbara to go ahead with this impersonation – it shouldn't be for more than a week, if Andrea was right about when the battle will begin. And after that we must hope Arianna will come back to us.'

'I am happy to do it, if that is what the Signore wants,' said Barbara.

'Didn't Flavia tell us that the Princess of Fishes was between the King of Serpents and the Eight of Birds when she read the cards?' said Rodolfo to Silvia when Barbara had left them.

Silvia waved her hand wearily. 'I can't remember. I've never understood that cartomancy of yours. What does that mean?'

'The King of Serpents possibly means Flavia herself – a merchant. And the Eight of Birds is self-defence.'

'If you say so,' said Silvia. 'And then what?'

'That Arianna is quite capable of looking after herself in Classe,' said Rodolfo.

'I hope you are right,' said Silvia. 'And I hope your cards will help her when she's on the deck of a ship with a cannonball whistling through the air towards her.'

*

When Isabel arrived in Classe early on the morning of 17th April, it was like a ghost town. All the people must have been at the harbour or out by the walls. She hurried down to the quay, worrying that she might be too late for the battle. A small boat should be waiting to take her out to the Admiral's flagship. But when she got down to the seafront, the harbour was in confusion: wreckage from several ships was bobbing in the water, while a thick pall of smoke hung over everything, leaving an acrid smell in the air. Isabel saw to her horror a severed leg float up against the harbour wall, bumping into the stones and then falling back again, only to be thrown back against the wall by the next small wave.

'What happened?' she asked a grim-faced bystander, who was watching some small fishing boats trying to sift through the gruesome wreckage in the water. Isabel was trying hard not to be sick.

'Fireships,' said the man. 'Two of them.'

'What are they?' asked Isabel.

'Empty ships packed with gunpowder,' said the man. 'The Gate people sent them into our line of battle in the night.'

'So the battle has begun?' said Isabel. There was a

heavy lump in her chest that felt like a solid iron cannonball. She was too late.

'Not really,' said the man. 'When the fireships exploded in the night, they took down four of our ships from the middle of the line.'

'Four?' said Isabel, horrified. She had seen how many men could fit on a fighting galley. 'What happened to the men on board?'

Her informant looked at her as if she was mad and pointed silently to the leg she had been trying not to look at.

'What do you think? The Admiral ordered the fireships sunk but it was too late by then. That's why the Gate people sent them in the dark – so we wouldn't be able to see them coming.'

'The Admiral,' said Isabel. She realised that his flagship, the *Tiger*, would be commanding the centre of the line. If the Gate people's fireships had veered in a slightly different direction, that leg could have belonged to someone she knew.

'Signorina Isabella,' called a voice through the smoke.

She made out another small rowing boat amid the debris in the water; it was slowly making straight for her, the name *TIGER* just decipherable in white paint on its side.

This is it then, thought Isabel. *I'm about to join in the battle.*

And after what she had just seen and heard, she couldn't believe she would survive it.

Chapter 23

The Battle of Classe

Admiral Borca was pacing the deck, smarting from the loss of his ships and men. Not only was the combined fleet now down to a hundred and forty-six against the Gate people's two hundred, not only had he lost hundreds of fighting men and mariners, but his adversary had not played fair.

Borca had a distaste for fireships. He'd heard of the tactic but would not have deigned to use it himself; it seemed to him like cheating. But their use also meant that the Gate people knew the Talian fleet would be waiting. That put both sides back to square one: the Gate people had lost the element of surprise but the Talian fleet had lost the advantage of being prepared for the invasion.

The combined fleet of Classe and Bellezza had

pulled out of harbour overnight and got into their three-squadron formation with great discipline and skill. The Admiral commanded the centre from the flagship *Tiger*, with Filippo on the consort ship, *Sea Dragon*, and forty-eight more Talian ships. Forty-four since the fireships had headed for the centre of the fleet in the dark.

The bulk of the Bellezzan ships were on the left flank, commanded by Admiral Gambone from the *Goddess*. His consort ship was the *Duchessa*. The ships on the right flank were led by the *Santa Maddalena* and the *Silver Dolphin*. The three squadrons had been roughly equal in number before the fireship attack.

And as dawn broke and the wind from the east that had swept the wreckage of ships and men into harbour blew the thick shroud of smoke into shreds, the Talian fleet saw what they were up against.

The Gate fleet had adopted a three-part formation too. They were near enough that Borca could see how many ships there were in each squadron. Sixty in the centre against his forty-six. Their right flank against his left were pretty evenly matched. But their left flank had at least thirty galliots as well as over fifty galleys.

It was at this moment that Isabel was rowed up to the *Tiger* and climbed the ladder to board the ship. A ragged cheer went up. The men of the *Tiger* had come to see 'Isabella' as a kind of mascot. They had no more idea than she did what help she could be in the coming battle but they believed they'd be better off with her on deck.

She tried to smile and wave back at them but it was

hard to put aside what she had seen in the harbour. The air was clearer out here in the deep water and she could see oily patches on the surface, marking the spots where ships had sunk – Talian galleys and enemy decoy ships too.

And she could see the Gate people's fleet.

The ships seemed to stretch for miles, fanned out into battle formation. Isabel's only consolation was that the Talian fleet must look equally intimidating to the Gate people, even if with fewer ships. But of course the enemy had drawn first blood.

The two fleets were drawing closer to one another, each keeping as far as possible in line with their Admiral's flagship. To Isabel it seemed as if the Talian fleet was moving more slowly but she felt a surge of pride to see how straight their line was, the ships separated one from another by about a hundred yards. She wondered how the men felt on board the ships that had closed the gaps where their comrades had been blown out of the water.

'Don't worry,' said the man on the whipstaff, seeing her expression. 'Old Borca has something more up his sleeve yet.'

And then Isabel saw why their galleys had been moving more slowly. They were waiting for four other light oared vessels that were towing massive sailing ships out in front of the fleet. These were the four galleasses, great merchant galleys that had been modified to carry heavy guns and had big wooden defensive bulwarks grafted on to them.

Soon they were in place, apparently becalmed vessels abandoned by their galleys in front of the Talian navy: the *Hand of Fortune*, the *Swallow*, the

Mermaid and the *Falcon's Flight*. They were really no more than floating gun platforms, full of gunners and other fighting men, with hardly any mariners aboard. They weren't planning to go anywhere.

There was an eerie silence as the men aboard the Talian galleys stopped rowing. Nothing could be heard but the harsh breathing of the rowers who had halted, the creak of wood and the odd clink of sword against shield. It seemed as if both fleets held their breath.

*

The leader of the Gate people was Ay Adem, aboard the flagship *Samira*. He was commanding sixty galleys in the centre, with Andrea aboard the *Raider's Revenge* as his consort. But Adem was beginning to suspect that all was not as it seemed with his Talian spy. For a start the Talian fleet was much larger than he had expected. And they had already been drawn up in battle order.

But he had been sending ships up and round the coast to Ladera for weeks, so any efficient spy network could have discovered the Gate people's plans. Still, not many people had known the date that they planned to launch the attack.

The day before had not begun well: as soon as the Gate fleet had assembled in the deep water off Ladera, a flock of large black birds had blown from left to right across the path of the ships. The Gate people were if anything even more superstitious than the Talians and the men saw this as a bad omen. Among the galley-slaves chained to the rowing benches were many captured Talians, and Adem knew that they silently exulted to see their masters cowed by a few birds.

He had ordered an extra ration of bread and water to be distributed to the rowers on their journey to Classe, and now he strode about the deck of the *Samira*, waiting for the right moment to give the battle signal, conspicuous in his peacock-blue robes with vermilion sash. It was a point of honour with the Gate people not to disguise their leaders. It showed their fearlessness to stand out as such obvious targets.

His left squadron was commanded by Adem Dolmay, whose skill with his galley, the *Duha*, was legendary; people said he could manoeuvre it as easily as if he were riding a horse. On the right was Ay Quana, who had a reputation as a fierce fighter. Ay Adem was lucky in his officers; they were as ready for the fight as he was.

Now all the fighting men were ready to raise their banners and all the oarsmen ready to strain their muscles for the advance. The gunners stood by the touch-holes with their tinderboxes in hand, primed to set light to the fuses.

It was nearly noon.

*

Fabrizio di Chimici looked every inch the warrior in his shiny new armour and plumed helmet. He rode up and down the lines of the Giglian army, on his grey stallion, encouraging his men. But the experienced military men of the line saw him differently. To them he was like a boy with a box of toy soldiers. They knew that their hope of victory and personal safety lay not with this glittering figure but with the army's General, who was a grizzled man of fifty in armour that had been battered in many encounters and had no shine left on it.

The General knew that Classe's defences were not in a good state of repair but it did not make him careless. Every siege and battle was different and the difference between victory and defeat could turn on a tiny mistake or defect.

Once the Giglian force was in sight of Classe's walls, they spread out and set up camp with efficient discipline. Siege-engines were trundled forward, cooking fires were lit and tents set up so that it was only a matter of hours before the army was ready to attack whenever the General gave the signal.

Inside the city, Duke Germano was encouraging his men. He had a General too, but, unlike the Giglians, the army of Classe had a great deal of respect for their Duke. He was a much-loved ruler and they appreciated the fact that he was out there with them, instead of staying safely inside his palace.

Perhaps only he knew how much danger the city was in, threatened simultaneously by land and sea. There was nothing he could do now about the fleet; he had to trust in the two admirals and the bravery of their men. And in the strength of their ships.

*

On the decks of the Talian fleet the fighting men prepared to raise their banners. Admiral Borca was standing by his flagman, as conspicuous in his glittering armour and purple plumed helmet as the Gate Admiral was across the water.

They gave the signal almost simultaneously: the Gate people set light to the touch-holes and the Talian galleasses fired their heavy bronze cannon.

The devastation was immediate.

Isabel, on the gun deck of the *Tiger*, thought she had become deaf and blind. The noise of the cannon was like nothing she had ever heard, a hundred times louder than she had expected. And the smoke quickly enveloped both fleets.

How on earth am I going to see the flags in all this? she thought.

Then she remembered her training. She flung herself at the rigging and climbed to the crow's nest. At the beginning of the morning, there had been a lookout there, as there had on every Talian ship, but now there was no need and Isabel had it to herself.

The noise wasn't much less at that height but it did lift her a bit clear of the smoke and she could see the Admiral's flag. It was still green – 'Advance'. Isabel clung on to the mast and tried to stop trembling. She could see that the four great galleasses were making a quarter-turn and readying to fire again and it was obvious from her new vantage point that the Gate people had come off worse last time.

Up here, so far above the deck, she felt a bit safer but she knew that was an illusion. If a cannonball smashed into the mast, she would be hurled into the sea or into the mass of arquebusiers and bowmen. She tried to thrust the thought down.

The Talian cannon boomed again and now Isabel could hear the cries of wounded men and the splash of bodies falling into the sea as well as the noise of the great guns firing. And the appalling noise of galleys being split in half and breaking up.

From her high viewpoint, Isabel could see that the Gate people's galleys were getting closer; she could hear the incessant throb of the drums they used to help the oarsmen keep time. And now she could hear the shouting of their leaders urging the men on and the snapping of their oars as Talian cannonballs raked the length of the enemy's galleys along the side.

It was clear that the Gate people didn't have such heavy guns as the Talians. They were straining at their oars with all their might; clearly their strategy was to get close enough to board the Talian ships and let the armed men fight hand to hand.

Isabel swallowed hard. What would happen to her if – when – the *Tiger* was boarded?

And then she felt ashamed and wondered whether the men on board were thinking the same thing. Surely to be a fighter you had to forget about your own personal safety and just hurl yourself at the enemy?

The ships were close enough now for the arquebusiers and bowmen to start firing. Isabel could hear the whip of arrows and the rattling sound of small gunfire. How on earth did the fighting men manage not to kill the people on their own side? The air on the deck below must be full of flying arrows and shot.

Friendly fire. That's what it was called when a soldier got killed by someone on their own side.

The awful TV news phrase came back to Isabel as she swayed dangerously at the top of the mainmast.

She promised herself that if she ever got back safely to her comfortable twenty-first-century life, she would never use those words.

And then there came an almighty crash and the sound of splintering closer than any other; the *Tiger* had been rammed.

*

The Giglian army was firing on the walls of Classe, doing considerable damage. Under the cover of fire, soldiers were running forward with scaling-ladders. The Classe army was firing back valiantly but the shortage of men and ammunition was hampering them.

Duke Germano, up on the walls, raised his visor to wipe the sweat out of his eyes. He wondered how the fighting was going out at sea.

Better than here, I hope, he thought, and sent up a prayer to whatever divinity might be listening.

*

When the *Tiger* and the *Samira* collided, the noise was incredible. The two ships smashed together, then recoiled. It was the recoil that dislodged Isabel from the crow's nest. As she fell, she instinctively curled into a ball, having just time to be terrified of all the possible fates she could suffer – breaking her back by falling on a spar, being trampled underfoot in the hand-to-hand fighting, being hit by a cannonball, arrow or shot from an arquebus, cut down by a sword . . .

And then she hit the water.

Isabel hadn't learned to dive yet and the shock of the freezing water, together with the stinging where her back hit the surface, almost stopped her from turning round and cutting back up to the top of the water. It was so quiet and calm underneath the waves; she could hear nothing but a sort of gentle roaring in her ears. When she surfaced, shaking the wet hair out of her face, there was a scene of carnage all around her.

The sea was full of men, dead and dying, oars, casks, barrels and bits of broken spars and rigging.

And the water was red.

This was a hell such as she had never envisaged. All along the line, ships were ramming into each other with splintering crashes and the air was filled with the shouts of warriors and the screams of wounded men. She couldn't see anything clearly and the effort of staying above water and keeping herself away from some of the horrors floating around her was already exhausting.

It can't be going to end like this, she thought, spluttering and coughing as the unbearably polluted water went up her nose. Her wet skirts were dragging her down. And then, *But why not? What's so special about me when all these men are dying?*

And then the bulk of a ship loomed up in front of her through the smoke. It was a black galleon with a dolphin figurehead. It was the *Revenge*!

Isabel manoeuvred herself round to the side of the ship and yelled up to the deck. She couldn't see anyone and didn't know if there was anyone on board left alive. The *Revenge* didn't seem to be tangled up with any other vessel but it was hard to tell from the confusion in the water.

A head appeared over the side then disappeared, but she recognised it as belonging to one of Andrea's pirate crew. Could he possibly have recognised her too, all bedraggled as she was in the water?

A rope ladder was thrown down over the side to her; the most beautiful sight Isabel could remember seeing for ages. In minutes she had swung herself on to it and grappled her way up the side, her dress streaming with sea water and blood.

Andrea met her at the top and wrapped her in his cloak,

'Oh, Andrea,' she sobbed. 'I . . . I'm so glad to see you!'

'You're not safe, even here,' he said. But he put an arm round her and yelled to one of his men to fetch her some spirits. He held a leather bottle to her lips and poured into her some fiery nameless liquid that made her splutter almost as much as the foul seawater had. But it was warming and gave her heart.

'Better?' asked Andrea. 'Now I think the best thing would be for me to get you out of here.'

Privately Isabel agreed with him. She felt a coward for thinking it, but she was a hugely relieved that someone else was going to take matters out of her hands.

Andrea ordered his men to slip the *Revenge* between the Talian ships and head for shore; the entire combined Talian fleet knew not to fire on his vessel.

'Ay Adem knows I betrayed him,' he told Isabel. 'He saw that I didn't fire on the Talians. He'd be out to get me but I suppose he has more important things to think of right now.'

'So you are in danger too!' said Isabel. 'And I don't even know if the *Tiger* is still afloat. I was in the crow's nest when the Gate people rammed it.'

'That was the *Samira*, Ay Adem's ship,' said Andrea. 'The two flagships going head to head.'

Then there was a blinding flash as if a meteor had struck and fire broke out in three places on the *Revenge*'s deck. Crewmen were on it straight away with buckets of seawater. But the fires did not go out and carried on burning fiercely.

Andrea swore. 'Look away, Isabella,' he ordered, moving her to one side.

He shouted more orders to his men, which Isabel didn't catch. They all turned to face the fires. When she next looked, the fires were out.

'What is it?' she asked fearfully. She could see more fire eerily burning on the surface of the water.

'Liquid fire,' Andrea said, white-faced. 'The Gate people have the secret of it. It can't be put out by water.'

'Is it magic?' asked Isabel, feeling stupid for saying it.

'No, it is science, but science not known to many,' said Andrea.

'How can it be put out then?'

'Only three ways that I know,' said Andrea. 'Sand, which smothers it. Very strong vinegar. And urine.'

'So . . . Oh, I see,' said Isabel, embarrassed, then thought how stupid it was to care about a thing like that when they were in the middle of a battle and probably all going to die.

'Old urine is best but we have to work with what we have,' said Andrea.

'TMI,' said Isabel.

He was still looking puzzled about this remark when the cannon struck.

The first cannonball smashed into the middle of the ship, holing it below the waterline. The second, which was almost simultaneous, hit the mainmast, which fell on to the deck, crushing any crewman in its path.

All was chaos. Isabel couldn't see Andrea any more. There was shouting and swearing and screaming from men who had been injured. She couldn't believe that she was upright and unscathed. She wasn't even quite sure who had fired on the ship.

The uninjured pirates had gathered on the main deck and were organising themselves to lift the mast. Isabel just looked on, miserable and useless. There were two dead crewmen under it – and Andrea.

Isabel rushed to his side. He was very pale and there was blood on his face but he didn't seem to have any head injury. His left leg was crushed and Isabel quickly looked away from it. She covered him with his own cloak; she had no idea what to do next.

'Isabella,' he croaked.

'I'm here,' she said. 'I'm so sorry.' Tears were streaming down her face.

'Someone has to tell the fleet about the liquid fire,' he managed to say, grimacing with pain.

'I'll go,' she said. At last there was something she could do.

'Tell them what I told you,' said Andrea. 'Get the men to lower the little boat for you. Take two of them with you to row.'

One man for a spare, thought Isabel.

'I will,' she said. 'Hang in there, Andrea. I'm sure you can be fixed if we get through the battle.'

He smiled weakly. 'Goodbye, Bella Isabella. I'm glad you came to Talia.'

Isabel refused to let this be goodbye. 'I'll come back for you,' she promised.

But when she reached the little boat, the sailors shook their heads. It had been smashed to splinters by cannonfire. She looked back to where the first mate, Salvatore, had pulled Andrea to one side and propped him against the mizzenmast. The Black Raider was unconscious and no threat to anyone any more. And the whole ship had a dangerous list; it was taking in water fast.

Isabel looked at Andrea and then at the sea. There was only one thing to do.

*

Arianna had quickly regretted her decision. She was caught on a death trap and couldn't even see Luciano. The smoke was everywhere, a choking, stifling thickness that stung her eyes and throat. And the noise was unbelievable.

The *Goddess* and the *Duchessa* had both been rammed by their opposite numbers from the Gate side. The Gate ship had hit the *Duchessa* bow to bow, its beaked prow running over the first few benches of rowers, like the maw of a sea monster; all the men on the front benches died instantly. Then Gate people poured on to the *Duchessa* and Talians on to the Gate ship.

Arianna had time to notice the name painted on its side – the *Yildiz* – and to wonder what that meant. After the impact, time seemed to have slowed down and she could see things clearly: details like the scimitars and two-handed swords the Gate people were using to good effect at close quarters.

I could die here and Luciano would never know, she thought.

The arquebusiers had stayed on their own ships, along with the archers. It was only the sword-and-buckler men and the pikemen who had boarded each other's vessels. But it was really hard to take aim in any effective way, especially with so many Talians in the path of the shot and arrows.

Arianna had no idea whether she had killed anyone or not. Her entire attention was focused on staying alive. She rammed the metal-lined cap further down on her head and fired determinedly, unable to judge where her shots were going.

The press of fighting men had pushed her to the side of the ship and she thought that if the worst came to the worst she would hurl herself into the sea. She glanced over the side between shots, attracted by a woman's voice shouting. She had believed herself to be the only woman in the fleet.

She couldn't believe her eyes; it was Isabel!

The Stravagante was thrashing around in the water, clearly at the end of her strength.

'Isabella, Isabella!' cried Arianna.

'Arianna?' spluttered Isabel incredulously. 'Is it you? Can you help me?'

Arianna set her arquebus aside and lowered a ladder into the water. She clambered down it herself to help the bedraggled Isabel up on to the deck. It was hardly a safe place to be though.

'Is this the Admiral's ship?' Isabel asked, disorientated. She didn't know how she had managed to swim through the dreadful wreckage a second time.

'No,' said Arianna. 'It's his consort ship – the *Duchessa*.'

Isabella had floated further to the left than she meant; she wanted Admiral Borca but had veered into the left squadron. But that still didn't explain the presence of Arianna, dressed as an arquebusier.

'Why are you here?' asked Isabel.

'Luciano is on this ship,' said Arianna. 'He doesn't know I'm here though. Why are *you* here?'

'I have to get a message to the Admiral,' said Isabel.

'Let's go and find the Captain then,' said Arianna. 'I'll take you.' They made their way back along the deck to the poop. The boards were slippery with blood and worse. But both of them were beyond caring what they saw.

The Captain was on the poop deck, directing operations as well as he could. Arianna was thrilled to see that Luciano stood beside him, sword in hand. She couldn't help herself. She dragged Isabel forward as the two men looked at them in astonishment.

'Arianna?' said Luciano, as if in a dream. 'What happened to your hair?'

'Who are these women?' demanded the Captain. 'And what are they doing on my ship?'

'This is Isabella, who might just be our salvation,' said Luciano. 'And this is the Duchessa of Bellezza.'

Chapter 24

The Duke

Isabel had just enough strength to tell the Captain about the liquid fire and how to put it out. Then she collapsed, completely spent. Arianna knelt beside her and put her arms round her.

But the Captain and Luciano were deep in consultation; Isabel heard the word 'vinegar' a few times.

And then they came over to the women.

'Your Grace,' said the Captain, making his bow, even though all was carnage and chaos about them, 'I shall keep you as safe as I can – but you have seen what it is like on board my ship.'

Arianna waved an impatient hand. 'Don't worry about me. I issue you in advance a ducal pardon for anything that might happen to me. The Cavaliere and

Isabella can be my witnesses.'

'Then, with your leave, I should like to send the Cavaliere in a fast frigate behind the line here to warn all the ships about the liquid fire and how to combat it.'

'Please, Arianna,' asked Luciano, 'don't ask to come with me. I'll be perfectly safe behind the line of fire.'

'I cannot command you, Your Grace,' said the Captain, 'but I urge you to stay in my quarters with your friend for the time being. I must tell my own men about the devilish fire that could break out on my ship in a moment.'

'How will you put it out?' asked Arianna, who had not been listening very carefully to Isabel's message but filling her eyes with the sight of Luciano, alive and uninjured.

'Well, the Cavaliere has had an ingenious idea,' said the Captain. 'We have barrels of vinegar on board with onions and other vegetables pickled in them.'

Arianna pulled a face; she had eaten some of this gruesome fare, which the Talian fleet insisted on their men eating every day with their salt meat and dry biscuit to avoid scurvy. Then her face brightened.

'You could use the vinegar to put the liquid fire out?' she said. 'How clever!'

'I must get the barrels up on deck in readiness,' said the Captain.

'And I must go and tell all the others,' said Luciano.

He allowed himself one kiss with Arianna, then hugged Isabel and left them.

*

Filippo Nucci was unhurt on the *Tiger* and astonished to see Luciano in the bow of a small fast frigate, tearing about behind the battle-line and shouting up to the Talian sailors. It was none too soon; as the barrels of pickles were being brought on deck, the little clay grenades with their load of liquid fire were cast from the enemy ships. Immediately the oarsmen, who had been unchained for the purpose, tipped the acrid vinegar out on to the little fires and doused them. The deck was soon covered with tiny onions, cauliflower florets and other incongruous sights.

Filippo was glad to be directing this operation; he had felt useless during the fighting and he was worried about Isabel. She wasn't in the crow's nest and he hadn't seen her for ages. But it was hard to keep track of time during a battle. How long had it been since the signal to fire had been given? It was impossible to see the sun to gauge how far it had passed over the sky since noon.

But gradually, as the galleasses continued to fire on all the Gate ships that had not closed in for a melee, and the liquid fires were put out as soon as they started, the battle began to turn the Talians' way.

Ay Adem in his brilliant robes was fired on and killed. Admiral Gambone, raising his visor so that he could shout his orders more clearly, was shot through the eye by an arrow; he died before hitting the deck.

Adem Dolmay, commanding the left flank of the Gate people, led his squadron south of the Talian fleet, aiming to encircle them and attack from behind. But the Captains of the *Santa Maddalena* and the *Silver Dolphin* led the Talian right squadron chasing after him, thinking he was fleeing. And their heavier guns did such destruction to Dolmay's ships that the threat was averted.

*

Up on the battlements, things were not going so well for Classe. The Duke was everywhere, trying to encourage his men and helping his General by carrying orders from one part of the defences to another, as if he were a young ensign and not the city's elected ruler.

The Giglian army had made several breaches in the wall and it was only a matter of time – what with those and the men on the scaling-ladders – before they would be inside Classe's defences and hand-to-hand fighting would begin. There had been no battle of that kind in Classe within living memory.

It was to put such thoughts out of his mind that Duke Germano rode back and forth under the walls. He was on his way to the easternmost part of the city's defences, when he was deafened by the sound of cannon and a ball punched through the stones of the wall. His horse shied, terrified by the noise, and threw his master out of the saddle. The horse bolted back to the centre of the city where he knew his comfortable stable was; he had no experience of being a warhorse.

Germano lay in front of the breach, winded and concussed by the fall. And then a second cannon-shot, aimed at the same spot, found its target and massive stones from the rift bombarded his inert body.

*

The *Tiger* and the *Duchessa* limped back into port,

gradually followed by all that remained of the fleet. It would be many days before it was known how many ships and men had been lost. But their side had carried the day!

Isabel stumbled ashore, dazed and confused. How could this be victory? The harbour was still full of the sickening debris that was the aftermath of a sea battle. She was not inured to the horrible sight even after her two swims through the bloody water with its flotsam of human remains. The men who were still alive were worse than the corpses and body parts. Very few Talians could swim and they were begging, screaming to be rescued before they went under for the last time. There had been nothing she could do for them. Some had been pulled out of the water only to die on board of their injuries and be thrown back into the water to bob about among the living and the dead.

Arianna had found Luciano on the side of the harbour and they embraced, wet and filthy as they both were. They clung on to each other with all the relief of two people who had not expected ever to see one another again. Then they saw Isabel and called out to her.

'It was brilliant, what you did,' said Luciano. 'I think you really did save the day for Talia. If we hadn't known how to put those fires out, we'd have lost most of the fleet.'

Isabel could only nod; he might be right. But just now she felt too numb to react. She turned towards the sea. The remnant of the fleet was coming back in as organised a formation as it could manage. But there was no sign of the *Raider's Revenge*. Had it sunk? Was Andrea still alive?

As they walked back towards the trading part of the harbour, they found a crowd gathered round a messenger. Someone recognised Luciano and called out to him.

'Cavaliere! Cavaliere! The men on the walls need reinforcements. The Duke is dead!'

The three young people were stunned. While they tried to take this news in, they were joined by Filippo, who miraculously had acquired no further injuries in the battle. He was the one who galvanised the weary arquebusiers, pikemen and archers into action. Then he and Luciano rounded up the least injured as they came off the ships and, after a swift swig of spirits which Filippo ordered all round, he led this impromptu and very wet army up to the walls.

Luciano went with them but ordered Arianna and Isabel to stay behind.

'Keep her here, Isabella,' he said. 'Even if you have to rope her to a chair!'

But Arianna was not about to fight another battle today. The two women went to Flavia's house, where they were fussed over, given hot baths and a change of clothes. It was still only early evening; the sea battle had taken five hours.

*

Up on the walls the ragtag army of Classe couldn't believe their eyes when they saw the fighting men of the fleet coming to stand alongside them.

They were just in time. Giglian soldiers were pouring in through the breached walls and the cannonfire had paused so that the foot soldiers could do their work without danger from their own side.

Grand Duke Fabrizio, in his silver armour, sneered when he saw the men ranged against him: a makeshift army mingled with a disreputable collection of armed men smeared with blood and clad in sodden battle-kit.

And then he realised what that meant. These were the men who would have been fighting at sea with the Gate people. The battle must be over, but where were the conquering Gate people, who were to deliver the city to him?

'Get back, Your Grace,' said his General, not too politely. He had sized the situation up immediately and seen that the defending forces had been almost doubled by these reinforcements.

And there would be no help coming from the sea.

The land battle went on for another couple of hours. There had been nothing like it in Talian history. For fighting men to come straight from a sea battle into an encounter on land was unheard of. But these men were desperate; they had lost their ruler, although their enemy didn't know it, and now they hurled themselves at the Giglians, shouting 'Duke Germano!' as their battle-cry.

Filippo was everywhere, not allowing his limp to stop him from urging and encouraging his raggle-taggle army. And whenever he stopped, he was with the men firing on the enemy.

The arquebusiers and archers fired down on the Giglian forces from the walls, while the pikemen and sword-and-buckler men fought bravely at close quarters. It was too much for the invaders and, after losing many men, the Giglian General sounded the retreat.

He didn't consult Fabrizio or even care if he lost his rank as a result; he was not prepared to sacrifice more men to what was obviously a lost cause.

The Battles of Classe were over.

Charlie didn't have to cover for Isabel. She was down to breakfast at about the average time for a teenager in the school holidays and her parents were at work anyway. Charlie was in the kitchen making toast.

'Put some in for me, Charlie,' she said. 'I'm starving.'

'Bel!' he said. 'What happened? Are you OK?'

'I'm fine,' she said. 'Just hungry. But it was bloody awful. I mean, we won – I think – but it was literally bloody.'

'And you're not injured? I mean there as well as here?'

Isabel shook her head. She had been drenched and buffeted and had used every ounce of energy she possessed to do what she had to do in Talia but she was unhurt, at least in body.

Her mental state was different. If only the memories of sights and sounds and smells didn't travel with her from the other world to this!

Charlie came and put his arms round her.

'Toast,' she said, blinking back the tears, 'and butter, and marmalade.'

'It shall be yours, little sister,' he said.

'Duke Germano is dead,' said Isabel. 'And probably Andrea too.'

And then she really lost it.

Flavia hurried down to the harbour as soon as Isabel had stravagated back. She left Arianna sleeping in a comfortable bed, with strict instructions to a servant to get her anything she might need but not to let her leave the house. But the merchant couldn't stay at home herself, not while in doubt about what had happened to Andrea.

The smoke was slowly clearing from the harbour but that only made the gruesome sights in the water more visible. Ship after ship came back into port, even the *Santa Maddalena* and the *Silver Dolphin*, who had chased down the left flank of the Gate people's fleet.

Rumours were rife of the number of casualties on each side. And there was no sign of a black galleon. Flavia helped at the improvised dressing station that sprang up near the quay.

An innkeeper gave his downstairs room over to the enterprise, providing free food and drink to the wounded and the helpers. Numbers swelled as the survivors of the land battle joined them. But no man in black with silver teeth was among them.

While women tended to the injured, the men of Classe set themselves to the hideous task of dragging bodies and limbs from the harbour. They would continue to drift in for weeks but for now they were laid on trestles and washed and their jaws bound up. A trail of wooden boxes came from the coffin-makers to give the victims their last home.

But the most elaborate was saved for the battered body that was borne into the centre of town on an improvised stretcher by six soldiers. Citizens came out into the streets to pay their respects as Duke Germano was carried to his palazzo and to his Duchessa, widowed along with so many women of Classe that day.

Isabel went back to bed after her toast and slept through till mid-afternoon. After a shower, she felt almost human. Charlie told her that her friends had called but he had sent them away, telling them to come back at teatime. On cue, the doorbell rang and the Barnsbury Stravaganti were all there, together with Ayesha.

Perhaps her presence encouraged Charlie. Anyway, he stayed to hear Isabel's account of the battle.

'So that's it,' said Isabel. 'There's so much I don't know. But I think I must have done what I was supposed to in Talia.'

'Are you going back tonight?' asked Sky. He was massaging her hand, which he had taken during one of the most difficult parts of her story.

'I don't think I can help myself,' said Isabel, conscious of his touch. 'I need to know the rest of what happened. Particularly to Andrea.'

'I can't believe that the Duke died,' said Georgia. 'It seems so unfair.'

'I know. And that's what it's like in a real war,' said Isabel. 'It's not like a computer game where if you have the right skills you'll win. There might be other people I know who have died.' She put her head in her hands.

'And it doesn't matter if you *don't* know them,' said Nick unexpectedly. 'Somebody did. From what you say, there must have been hundreds – maybe thousands – killed.'

'And not just Talians,' said Ayesha. 'The Gate people who died are just as dead. And they had families just like the people on your side.'

Isabel was somehow glad that she hadn't said 'our side'. She was pleased to have two more neutral people present.

'You're right,' she said. 'People's nationality doesn't seem to matter any more when there's only bits of them left.'

'And you did all that?' asked Charlie. 'Swam through that – that horror scene – twice?'

'If I'd known what it was I'd have to do in Talia,' said Isabel, 'I think I'd have left that talisman where I found it.'

Sky squeezed her hand.

'But when I actually had to do it,' said Isabel, 'it wasn't too bad, because it was the only thing to do. And I was the only one who could do it.'

When Luciano got back from the walls, bloody and exhausted, he automatically went to Flavia's house. The merchant wasn't there but it wasn't her he was looking for.

Arianna was just waking up. Flavia had given her one of her sleeping draughts and she felt back to normal. But she gave a little gasp when she saw Luciano.

'It's OK,' he said, forgetting she didn't know that expression. 'It's not my blood – at least not much of it. I've got a few small cuts – that's all.'

'And the battle?' asked Arianna, hugging him, all filthy as he was.

'Grand Duke Fabrizio has a nice new reason to hate me,' said Luciano, smiling. 'And to hate Filippo. He was wonderful. He got a horse from somewhere and took Germano's place.'

'Is he "Oo-kai" too?' asked Arianna.

'He's fine,' said Luciano. 'Just tired, like me. Do you think Flavia would mind if I had a bath?'

Arianna immediately became all Duchessa and ordered Flavia's servants around, getting them to heat water and fetch towels and scented oils.

After half an hour's soak and a glass of Bellezzan red, Luciano was feeling much better.

'I suppose I should go down to the harbour and see what the news is,' he said, but even as he tried to get up all his limbs screamed at him to stay where he was.

'I absolutely forbid it,' said Arianna imperiously. 'You are my Cavaliere and I am your ruler and I say you must stay here. And let me remind you that you made me stay behind when you went off playing soldiers on the city walls.'

'I give in,' said Luciano. 'Your word is my command and I am your miserable slave. But can I at least tell Rodolfo about the battle?'

*

It was late evening before Flavia found her son. He had been brought in on a stretcher, pale as death. His left leg stopped at the knee and there was a terrible smell of blood and tar about him. But he was alive – just.

The *Raider's Revenge* was at the bottom of the sea, holed by the Gate people. But Andrea's remaining men had saved him, lashing him to a spar and two of them floating him back to land, hanging on to their own pieces of broken ship. One of them was Salvatore. They had been swept off course far to the south of Classe and got ashore there. They had found a smith to strike off the pirate captain's mangled lower leg and apply hot tar to the stump.

Then a cart had taken them all back to Classe. Andrea was delirious by then, muttering about unquenchable fire and Isabella – and Ay Adem coming to get him.

'The Gate people's leader is dead,' Flavia told him, soothing his brow. 'Our fleet won the battle. Isabella was very brave.'

She had him moved to her house and washed and laid in clean sheets and she nursed him herself, through the fever and out the other side when they both wept for the mutilation of his body.

'But you are alive,' she said. 'And so many are not. Duke Germano was killed.'

Andrea immediately cursed himself for being an ungrateful dog and tried to get up to see Germano's widow, to pay his respects. But it was too soon.

He fell back, raging at his own weakness.

'He was going to give me a pardon if we both survived,' he said.

'I have it here,' said Flavia, showing Andrea a piece of vellum with the ducal seal. 'Germano wasn't the sort of man to wait to fulfil a promise. And I'm sure he knew there was a strong likelihood he wouldn't return.'

'He was a good man,' said Andrea. 'May Classe find another even half as good.'

*

The Duke's funeral was attended by the rulers of all the city-states not governed by the di Chimici. Though they too were represented in a way by Princess Beatrice, who came from Bellezza with Arianna, Rodolfo, Luciano, Silvia and William Dethridge, who all wanted to say their farewells to a great ruler.

At the service in the cathedral, Rodolfo delivered a tribute, which he began by making an announcement.

'I know that Duke Germano would wish all those gathered here to know the final outcome of the sea battle of Classe,' he said. 'So I shall start by saying that, in spite of being outnumbered, the combined fleets of Classe and Bellezza, under the leadership of Admiral Borca, defeated and routed the Gate people's fleet.'

If they hadn't been at a funeral in a church, the congregation would have cheered.

'The Talian fleet lost four vessels to the Gate people's fireships,' continued Rodolfo. 'And a further ten of our ships were lost and twenty more seriously damaged. We sank twenty Gate ships and captured thirty more. But a further sixty of their vessels are damaged beyond any hope of immediate repair. And our brave captains captured thirty more of their ships as they fled. Only sixty of the Gate people's ships reached Ladera and only thirty of those ships rowed back to their own country.'

Isabel, sitting near the front of the congregation, thought it sounded like the football scores on TV. But without any mass communications, she supposed this was how news was disseminated in Talia.

'Many brave men died on both sides in the sea battle,' said Rodolfo, 'including Admiral Gambone of Bellezza. We lost two thousand men. The Gate people lost seventeen thousand.'

The terrible figures reverberated round the hollow cathedral.

'And then in the further battle for the walls,' said Rodolfo, 'two hundred more men. Among them the man we are here to mourn, Classe's beloved Duke and leader, Germano Mariano.'

Isabel scarcely heard the rest of the speech. She was still stunned by the thought of all those dead men. And they were all men; Arianna had been the only other woman who had fought in the Battle of Classe. It was hard to believe, looking at her now in a sombre purple robe and black velvet mask. Her shorn head was covered by a black lace veil.

One of those men might have been Andrea, thought Isabel. He was there in the cathedral, pale and thin, leaning on Flavia's arm and using two sticks. Isabel could hardly bear to look at him. He was so unlike his old piratical self.

And there was Filippo Nucci, injured in an earlier violent attack. *Why do people do that sort of thing to each other?* wondered Isabel. Filippo was a kind of hero now, for organising and leading the men from the ships to the walls, where they had turned the fortunes of Classe. Isabel wondered how many of the two hundred who had died in the land-fighting had been men who had survived the sea battle.

But in the end she had to stop thinking about things like that. And be grateful that people she knew and cared for, like Filippo and Andrea, were still alive.

In accordance with Talian tradition, there was a huge party in the square after Germano had been laid to rest. It would go on all night but Isabel could stay only till dusk. She had been so tired ever since the battle that she hadn't stravagated every night. But she had felt she must be here to say goodbye to the Duke.

'I wonder what will happen to Vitale?' she surprised herself by saying out loud.

'The old Duchessa doesn't think she can take him with her when she goes to live with her daughter,' said Filippo. 'The next Duke will be his new master.'

'But who will that be?' asked Isabel. She hadn't really thought about it but she knew the Dukes of Classe were elected, not heirs to the post.

'Well, the Senate has asked me if I would stand for election,' said Filippo modestly.

'Really?' said Isabel. 'That's brilliant! I mean, you'd be brilliant. You will do it, won't you?'

'There is one person I need to consult first,' said Filippo, but Isabel could see he was smiling.

'No danger of Classe not staying independent then,' she said, grinning back at him. 'But how do you think the Grand Duke will feel if his sister is your Duchessa?'

'I imagine he'll be spitting mad,' said Filippo calmly. 'But I can't worry about that. There's something about being in a battle, especially one you can remember in all its detail, that makes you sure about what you want.'

You're right, thought Isabel.

Next day, after the last lie-in of the holiday, Isabel went round to Sky's flat. He was surprised to see her; they usually met at Nick's or the coffee bar and rarely just the two of them.

'Come in,' he said, opening the door wide. There was a comfortable tabby cat sitting on the kitchen table, which Sky shooed off.

'Is your mum in?' asked Isabel.

'No, she's out to lunch with Paul,' said Sky. 'Was it her you wanted to see?'

'No,' said Isabel, her heart thumping. 'I just wanted to make sure we were on our own.'

'That sounds promising,' said Sky, smiling at her.

'I wondered if you'd like to go out,' said Isabel. 'You know, with me.'

'Sure,' said Sky. 'Where shall we go?'

'No, I mean . . .' Then she saw he was smiling even more broadly. She punched him. 'You swine . . .'

Much later, when they had been kissing for a long time, Isabel said, 'Your mum's boyfriend, Paul – he's Alice's dad, isn't he?'

Sky sighed. 'Yeah,' he said. 'Alice and I were never going to work, were we?'

'Because of that?'

'That and other things. Mainly because she hated it if I even talked about Talia, let alone went there. It'll be good to have a girlfriend who doesn't freak out about it.'

There was more silence and more kissing.

'But you know I'm going to the States after A levels?' asked Sky.

'Yes, you said.'

'I'll be away a year,' he said. 'What are you going to do?'

'I think I'll have a gap year,' said Isabel.

'Where?'

She looked at him, sitting with her on the sofa, with his arm round her, as naturally as if they'd been together for years. The old Isabel would never have dared ask him out.

'Well,' the new Isabel said, 'I've never been to America.'

Epilogue: *A Part of the Whole*

The new Duke of Classe was getting married. Duke Filippo had been elected unopposed and awarded the highest honour of the city, the silver Victory Medal. His bride, Beatrice, had been cast out of the di Chimici family by her brother as soon as he heard of her intention. She was no longer a princess but would soon be Duchessa Beatrice of Classe.

Beatrice had responded to the Grand Duke's ten-page tirade about her treachery with the simple note:

Dear Fabrizio,
I am sorry you no longer regard me as your sister. I shall always think of you as my brother. I promised I would marry no one but Filippo. I did not say which one.

Give Bino a kiss from his devoted aunt and your loving sister,
Beatrice

And Fabrizio had not been able to stop Gaetano and Francesca from attending the wedding. Arianna and Luciano were delighted to see them and took the opportunity to give them their own African cat, the gentle Amica. Vitale was very interested to meet his sister again but he was now definitely Filippo's cat.

Vitale had been taken to see Germano's grave, which was something that Talians did with dogs who had lost their master. He had whined for several minutes, then gone back to lean against Filippo's side. His transfer of loyalty was complete.

The Bellezzan court was in Classe for the second time in recent weeks; the citizens had not wanted to wait long for the election and Filippo hadn't wanted to wait any time at all for his wedding. Luciano and Arianna had taken Admiral Gambone's body back to Bellezza for a burial with full naval honours and were ready for a more cheerful ceremony.

But Rodolfo was still in sombre mood. He wanted Arianna to issue an invitation to all the independent city-states to join an official alliance. Fabrizio di Chimici had overstepped a line by invading a sovereign city-state without provocation. Even though the Grand Duke's alliance with the Gate people was in tatters, Rodolfo thought he should be made to realise how far he had transgressed.

He had suggested this plan to Arianna before they left Bellezza and she had readily agreed. But her father had more to say.

'I think it is time I gave up the Regency,' he told his daughter. 'You are old enough to rule in your own right. I don't think you need me any more.'

'I shall always need you,' said Arianna, putting her

hand on his arm. 'But I'll do what you advise about the rule of Bellezza. Why now though, I wonder?'

'Because if I wait till your marriage it might seem as if I were handing my authority over you to Luciano,' he said straight-faced.

He was rewarded by the expected contemptuous snort.

'You see?' he smiled. 'You are your own ruler and can be Bellezza's too.'

He had forgiven her for rushing off into battle after Luciano, though her mother was still seething about it.

Isabel was looking forward to a Talian wedding.

'Can I bring a plus one?' she had asked Filippo, who had not understood until she explained further.

So Sky was with her in Classe as her official partner. He had bought a pair of black shoes and went to bed wearing them and a pair of black trousers, a frilled white shirt he had bought in a charity shop and Charlie's Dracula cloak over the lot. Isabel thought he looked gorgeous, but he had been careful to lock his bedroom door in case his mother saw him going to bed in such an outlandish outfit.

Isabel herself had been offered a place of honour at the wedding. The story of her heroism at the Battle of Classe had spread round the city like the liquid fire she had helped overcome.

It was no good dipping her head and trying to hide behind her hair here; everyone knew who she was. And everyone seemed to want to be her friend. She had never been so popular.

Her status in Talia had been affecting her life in the other world too. And she had needed the strength it brought her. Alice had made up her differences with Georgia, though they would never again be as close as they used to. But she was still furious with Sky and looked daggers at Isabel whenever their paths crossed.

But Isabel was still friends with Laura and Yesh, even though Laura knew nothing about Talia. And now she had Georgia, Nick and Matt, as well as Sky. Five close friends and a gorgeous boyfriend. And that was without counting all the new people who had become part of her life in Talia.

Her relationship with Charlie had never been better. As soon as she had stopped being jealous of him, it had flourished. He now looked up to her as someone special and was always talking about how brave she was. He had even asked if she'd like to try out for the swimming team but she had refused. Isabel never wanted anyone to depend on her swimming again.

She looked round the great church, which was nearly full. Gaetano was going to give Beatrice away, so Francesca was sitting next to Isabel and Sky in the front row. Isabel was a bit in awe of her; she was so tall and beautiful. But she was friendly too, like her husband. They had left their African cat in Filippo's stables.

Filippo was standing waiting for his bride, looking as nervous as any young groom in spite of his new status as Duke of Classe. Although he still used a cane, he was in better shape than his groomsman. Andrea still needed two sticks to get about and would for some time, but Fausto was making him a beautifully carved wooden leg for when he was healed enough.

'Then you really will look like a proper pirate,'

Isabel had told him when she heard.

'I'm giving up piracy,' he said. 'For good.'

And he told her about the old Duke's pardon, which had been proclaimed throughout the city. His good name had been restored and he no longer needed to live as an outlaw. In fact, once Filippo had been elected and made known Andrea's work as a government spy, the ex-pirate, too, had become a local hero.

Isabel looked at him, still dressed in his characteristic black and silver. He had made a handsome pirate but would be an even better merchant, she thought. He was joining Flavia in her business. After all, he knew the value of merchandise better than most.

Andrea might have lost a limb in the fight but he had gained so much. The most important thing had been a secret that Flavia had told him while nursing him back to life: the man he had killed had not been his father. Flavia's husband had been violent to her almost as soon as they had been married and she had found consolation with someone else.

'Fausto!' Andrea had guessed straight away.

Flavia had never told the mosaicist that the boy was his, but now that Andrea was free to live in the city again, she thought it was time.

Isabel could see that there was a new calm about Andrea; he had lost his haunted look.

I bet he finds himself a girlfriend soon, she thought.

The little band at the back of the church struck up a fanfare. Looking towards the great oak doors, Isabel spotted Enrico in a brand-new blue suit. She smiled, remembering that Luciano had told her how he was going to order the spy to have one of Flavia's deep scented baths before he was allowed to put it on. She was glad that Beatrice would not be met by Enrico's usual oniony odour the minute she entered the church.

He had fought surprisingly valiantly on the walls of Classe and Filippo himself had given him the city's purple ribbon, which he wore now on his chest.

There were so many people that Isabel knew in the cathedral. Looking round at them, she realised just how much would have been lost if the Gate people and Fabrizio di Chimici had succeeded in their military alliance. Classe would have been overrun and looted and finally handed over to the di Chimici family. She wondered what puppet Fabrizio would have set up as Duke and whether the citizens would have been sold into slavery to the Gate people.

When the Talian fleet had chased the galleys of the Gate people back to Ladera, many slaves had leapt out of the enemy ships and been rescued by the pursuers; nearly a third of them had turned out to be Talians themselves.

And the alliance of the di Chimici and Gate people wouldn't have stopped at Classe; if they had succeeded, they would have made their way up to Bellezza and might have taken that city too. Isabel shivered. Sky put his arm round her and she leaned into the warmth of his body.

Isabel didn't want to think about battles and war and death any more.

She watched Beatrice walk up the main aisle of the cathedral, her glittering silver dress reflecting the light of a thousand candles. It was the first time for over a year that the princess had worn any colour other than black. The candles shimmered too in the mosaics that decorated the whole of the interior. Every picture on the walls glowed with colour and gleamed with silver. And these miracles of beauty and invention were made up of hundreds of tiny tesserae, each one playing a vital part in the whole.

Isabel felt she understood every insignificant one of them.

Historical Note

Classe is a combination of present-day Ravenna and the real Classe in Italy. I have placed the city on the coast, with its harbour, as modern Classe is, but with the mosaics of Ravenna. The ones in Classe are of course silver in background rather than gold. It is a lagoon city, as Ravenna used to be.

The Battles of Classe, at sea and on land, are entirely imaginary, but I have been influenced by Roger Crowley's description of the Battle of Lepanto (1571) in *Empires of the Sea* (Faber, 2008) and by John Francis Guilmartin Jnr in his *Gunpowder and Galleys* (Cambridge University Press, 1974).

Eagle-eyed readers will notice that Easter in Talia does not coincide with Easter in our world. I have used the date for Easter in Italy in 1580 but Easter fell later in our world in 2006.

The Sea Battle of Classe (17th April 1580)

THE TALIAN FLEET

(Combined fleets of Bellezza and Classe)

50 GALLEYS ON LEFT FLANK
led by *The Goddess*
(Admiral Gambone)
with *The Duchessa* as consort

The Hand of Fortune

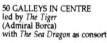

The Goddess

50 GALLEYS IN CENTRE
led by *The Tiger*
(Admiral Borca)
with *The Sea Dragon* as consort

The Swallow

The Tiger

50 GALLEYS ON RIGHT FLANK
led by *The Santa Maddalena*
with *The Silver Dolphin* as consort

The Mermaid

The Santa Maddalena

The Falcon's Flight

Talian Coast

THE GATE PEOPLE'S FLEET

55 GALLEYS ON RIGHT FLANK
led by *The Mehtap*
(Ay Quana)
with *The Yildiz* (Adem Deviz) as consort

The Mehtap

60 GALLEYS IN CENTRE
led by *The Samira*
(Ay Adem)
with *The Raider's Revenge* (Andrea) as consort

The Samira

55 GALLEYS ON LEFT FLANK
led by *The Duha*
(Adem Dolmay)
with *The Seher* (Ay Mushtaree) as consort

The Duha

N

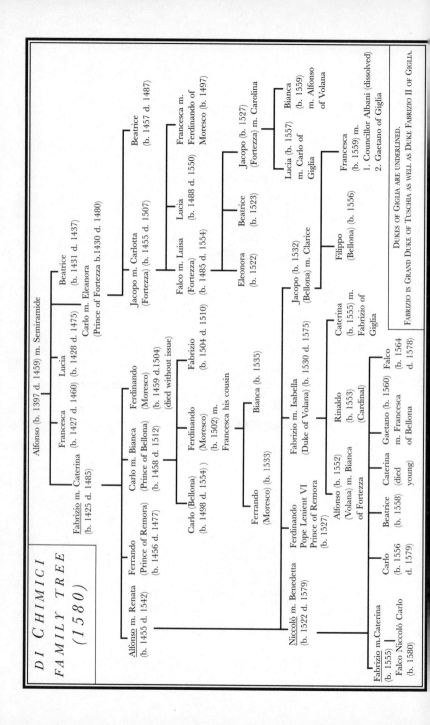

DI CHIMICI FAMILY TREE (1580)

Alfonso (b. 1397 d. 1459) m. Semiramide

Francesca (b. 1427 d. 1460)

Lucia (b. 1428 d. 1475)

Beatrice (b. 1431 d. 1437)

Carlo m. Eleanora (Prince of Fortezza b.1430 d. 1480)

Fabrizio m. Caterina (b. 1425 d. 1485)

Jacopo m. Carlotta (Fortezza) (b. 1455 d. 1507)

Beatrice (b. 1457 d. 1487)

Francesca m. Ferdinando of Moresco (b. 1497)

Falco m. Luisa (Fortezza) (b. 1485 d. 1554)

Lucia (b. 1488 d. 1550)

Jacopo (b. 1527) (Fortezza) m. Carolina

Eleonora (b. 1522)

Beatrice (b. 1523)

Lucia (b. 1557) m. Carlo of Giglia

Bianca (b. 1559) m. Alfonso of Volana

Alfonso m. Renata (b. 1455 d. 1542)

Ferrando (Prince of Remora) (b. 1456 d. 1477)

Carlo m. Bianca (Prince of Bellona) (b. 1458 d. 1512)

Ferdinando (Moresco) (b. 1459 d.1504) (died without issue)

Fabrizio (b. 1504 d. 1510)

Ferdinando (Moresco) (b. 1502) m. Francesca his cousin

Carlo (Bellona) (b. 1498 d. 1554)

Bianca (b. 1535)

Ferrando (Moresco) (b. 1533)

Niccolò m. Benedetta (b. 1522 d. 1579)

Ferdinando Pope Lenient VI Prince of Remora (b. 1527)

Fabrizio m. Isabella (Duke of Volana) (b. 1530 d. 1575)

Jacopo (b. 1532) (Bellona) m. Clarice

Filippo (Bellona) (b. 1556)

Francesca (b. 1559) m.
1. Councillor Albani (dissolved)
2. Gaetano of Giglia

Alfonso (b. 1552) (Volana) m. Bianca of Fortezza

Rinaldo (b. 1553) (Cardinal)

Caterina (b. 1555) m. Fabrizio of Giglia

Fabrizio m.Caterina (b. 1555)

Carlo (b. 1556 d. 1579)

Beatrice (b. 1558)

Caterina (died young)

Gaetano (b. 1560) m. Francesca of Bellona

Falco (b. 1564 d. 1578)

Falco Niccolò Carlo (b. 1580)

DUKES OF GIGLIA ARE UNDERLINED.

FABRIZIO IS GRAND DUKE OF TUSCHIA AS WELL AS DUKE FABRIZIO II OF GIGLIA.

Dramatis Personae

 **In Talia**

Flavia, a trader and Stravagante
Andrea, her son, a pirate
Salvatore, Andrea's first mate
Germano, Duke of Classe
Anna, Duchessa of Classe
Fausto Ventura, a mosaic-maker
William Dethridge, aka Guglielmo Crinamorte, a
  Stravagante, resident in Bellezza
Rodolfo Rossi, a Stravagante and Regent of Bellezza
Silvia Rossi, his wife and the former Duchessa of
  Bellezza
Luciano Crinamorte, aka Lucien Mulholland, a
  Stravagante resident in Bellezza
Arianna Rossi, the Duchessa of Bellezza, daughter of
  Rodolfo and Silvia
Giovanni Gambone, Admiral of the Bellezzan fleet
Michele Borca, Admiral of the Classe fleet

 **The di Chimici**

Fabrizio, Grand Duke of Tuschia
Caterina, his Grand Duchess
Gaetano, Fabrizio's younger brother
Francesca, Gaetano's wife
Beatrice, Fabrizio and Gaetano's sister
Rinaldo, Cardinal of the Reman Church

Ferdinando, Pope Lenient VI
Filippo, Prince of Bellona

 **The Nucci**

Matteo, the head of the family
Graziella, his wife
Filippo, their only surviving son

 **in 21st-century London**

Isabel Evans, a Stravagante
Charlie Evans, her twin brother
Sarah Evans, their mother
Tony Evans, their father
Laura, Isabel's friend
Georgia O'Grady, a Stravagante (see *City of Stars*)
Nick Duke, aka Falco di Chimici, a Stravagante
    (see *City of Stars*)
Sky Meadows, a Stravagante (see *City of Flowers*)
Alice Greaves, Sky's girlfriend
Matt Wood, a Stravagante (see *City of Secrets*)
Ayesha, Matt's girlfriend, Isabel's friend
Vicky Mulholland, Lucien's mother, Nick Duke's
    adoptive mother

Acknowledgements

So many people have helped me with *City of Ships*. Robert Field was my main source of information on mosaics and mosaic techniques. And the reason I now own so many.

Fellow writers Viv Richardson and Anne Rooney put me in touch with books and people who might help me with sixteenth-century naval warfare. Seb Goffe suggested the Greek fire.

And the indispensible London Library sent me lots of books on a wide range of recherché subjects from pirates to weaponry.